Little

Flower

Books by Christine Marshall
With illustrations by Steve Marshall

Becoming Cinder
White As Snow
Forever Sleeping
Promised Beauty
Final Lock
Little Flower

RISE OF THE GIANTS
BATTLE OF THE GIANTS
LAST OF THE GIANTS

The Last Mapmaker
A Series of Intentional Disasters
Volume 1, Volume 2, Volume 3

NOBLESTONE and the Lost Dwarves
NOBLESTONE and the Secret Forge

Illustrated Guides:
Dragons and Flying Creatures
Folk Creatures
Unexpected Creatures
Insects and Mechanical Things

Little Flower

A Retelling

Christine Marshall

To my sisters -
Cynthia and Colleen.

"Sisters are different flowers from the same garden"
~Maya Angelou

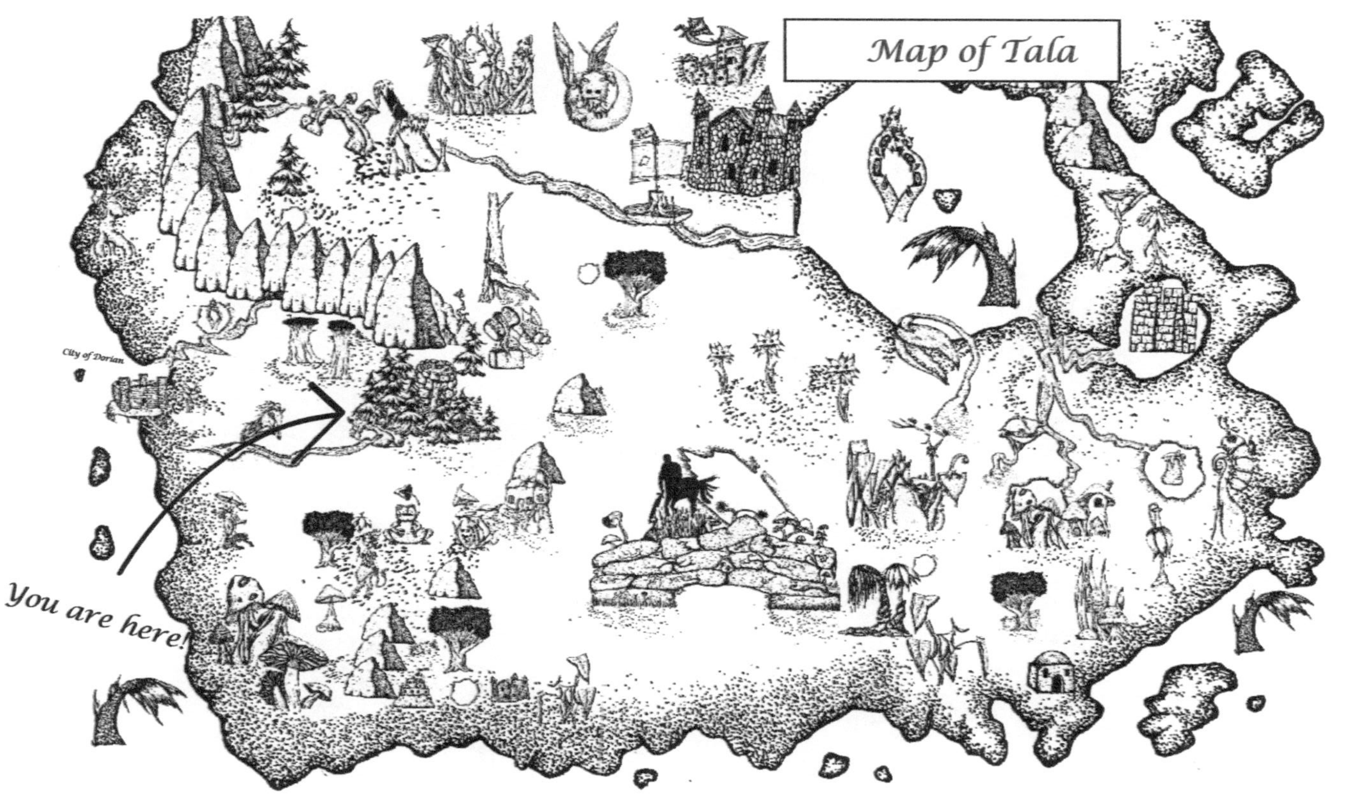
Map of Tala
City of Dorian
You are here!

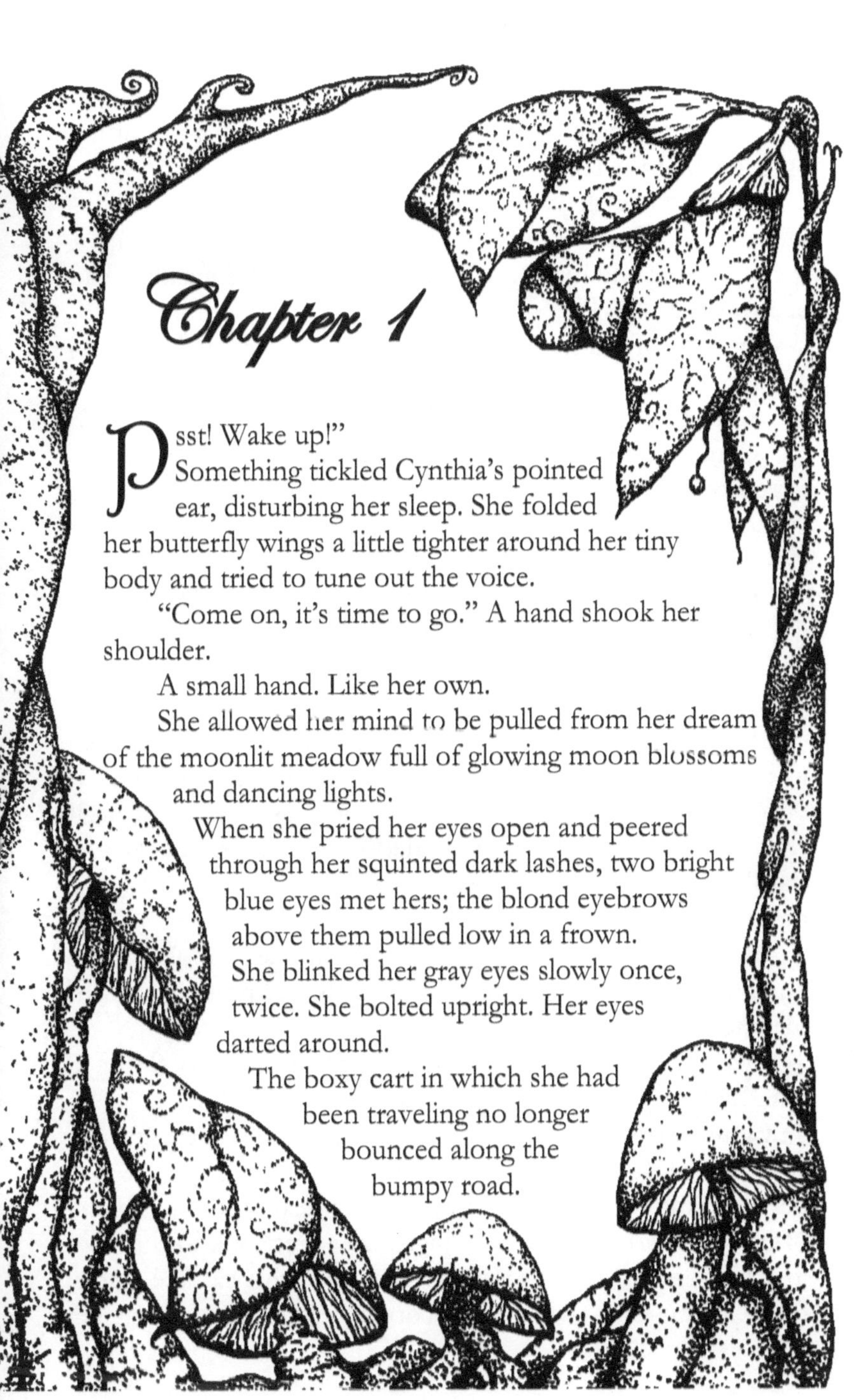

Chapter 1

"Psst! Wake up!"

Something tickled Cynthia's pointed ear, disturbing her sleep. She folded her butterfly wings a little tighter around her tiny body and tried to tune out the voice.

"Come on, it's time to go." A hand shook her shoulder.

A small hand. Like her own.

She allowed her mind to be pulled from her dream of the moonlit meadow full of glowing moon blossoms and dancing lights.

When she pried her eyes open and peered through her squinted dark lashes, two bright blue eyes met hers; the blond eyebrows above them pulled low in a frown.

She blinked her gray eyes slowly once, twice. She bolted upright. Her eyes darted around.

The boxy cart in which she had been traveling no longer bounced along the bumpy road.

The other animals that had been captured had already begun to make their escape by running, slithering, or flying out of the open back of the solid-roofed wagon.

How she had slept through the crash of the cart and chaos of dozens of animals rushing toward freedom at breakneck speed was beyond her. The dream of the peaceful meadow had been so real.

The lock of the small steel cage in which she had been held captive for two days had been busted and the door pried open. Her rescuer leaned half-in, half-out of the cage.

"Come *on!*" He nudged her again. The miniature person stretched one of his hands toward her for her to take. "You've got to get out of here!"

Cynthia's mind snapped back to the present.

She met the bright blue eyes again, trying to make sense of the situation. Her rescuer was about twice her own height. Not a human, or a Forest Person, then. His pointy ears beneath his pointy hat and his bare feet gave his identity away. A brownie.

"What are you doing?" She took his hand and allowed him to help her stumble out of the cage onto the slanted wooden floor of the wagon. Her crumpled blue dress untwisted itself and the hem swung to her knees. She tucked her wavy, shoulder-length silver hair behind her ears and waited for the brownie to answer.

"Setting all of you free, of course. What does it look like I'm doing?" The brownie turned on his heels and bounded out of the wagon.

Cynthia flapped her silvery butterfly wings and fluttered after him, staying close to the ground.

Clouds covered the moon and stars overhead, erasing the shadows of her surroundings. The still, cool night air had devolved into chaos. Animals called to one another in a variety of growls, hoots, and cries. Winged creatures took to the skies in a flurry of feathers and talons. An aggressive cat-like animal that Cynthia had seen in the corner of the cart during her captivity yowled on the other side of the cart, out of her line of vision.

To her relief, even in the low light, she caught a glimpse of a group of dust bunnies as they hopped toward the tree line.

"Good, they made it out," she whispered to herself.

Glowing wisps, disturbed by the sudden influx of visitors to the woods, scattered above the tops of the fir trees, mimicking the hidden stars. A large, red cat with long black tufts of fur at the end of each ear and a bushy tail slinked away, its mouth stretched into a toothy, mischievous grin.

A crash from nearby drew Cynthia's attention. She flew toward the sound. The brownie who had rescued her had just released more animals from another cage. She arrived just in time to catch a glimpse of the enormous eyes and wide ears of three or four koalabirds as they flapped their thickly feathered wings to lift themselves off the ground. The brownie stood with hands on his hips and a satisfied smile on his face as he watched them fly into the cover of the forest.

Once the koalabirds had disappeared, the noise died down and quiet settled over the scene.

Cynthia hovered near the brownie, mouth agape. "Did you do all of this?" She gestured at the mess around the little man.

He wore a proud expression. "You bet I did!"

Cynthia's eyes roved the scene of destruction. One of the wagon wheels lay broken in pieces on the ground, causing the wagon to rest askew. The pair of long-necked, tiny-winged, furry pack animals that had been pulling the wagon were nowhere to be found. The contents of the wagon had been scattered all around the area: sacks of dry goods, a lidded barrel of apples, packets of exotic spices, bolts of dyed wool, rope, animal traps, clothing, tools, even coins littered the ground.

A few of the other creatures- a masked racoon, beady eyed raven, and antlered thistle-hare- that had kept her company in the wagon over the past few days rummaged through the burlap sacks, crates, jars, and barrels with lids pried open. The animals probably looked for their own belongings. Or perhaps they searched for other valuables to collect as well.

Before Cynthia could ask about the man that owned the wagon, a flash of light a little down the road from the disaster caught her eye. A swarm of fireflies, bright spots against the dark nighttime, surrounded the bad-tempered human man that had captured Cynthia and the others. He batted the fireflies away from his scraggly beard and stringy, shoulder-length hair, but every time he managed to escape one or two, a dozen more lunged at him. Their flames scorched his threadbare clothes and seared his leathery skin. He shouted in rage and… pain.

Despite the pleasant nighttime temperature, a shiver ran down Cynthia's spine. Her breath hitched. "They're not hurting him, are they?"

The brownie that had rescued her turned to face her. "Eh, I doubt it. Besides, what's the worst that could happen?"

Cynthia turned her wide, gray eyes onto him. She nodded with a frown.

The brownie brushed away her concerns. "He'll be fine. Now, do you know which way you need to go? I suggest you take flight as soon as possible. And a word of advice: Stay away from people like him in the future." He motioned at the burly man being overrun by the tiny balls of flame.

Cynthia couldn't believe her ears. It's not like she had *asked* to be captured.

She lived in a garden owned by

a Forest Person called Magnolia near a village along a riverbank. The Forest People could talk to animals and communicate with plants, which made living near one an adventure all on its own! Magnolia's abilities allowed her to have a stunning garden full of every kind of plant life imaginable. And creatures of all kinds liked to visit to speak with Magnolia.

Cynthia's quiet life involved visiting the other animals in and around her garden home, while keeping Magnolia company.

It wasn't an exciting life, exactly, but Cynthia had no plans to change it any time soon.

That all changed against her wishes when Cynthia made a flight into town to visit some dust bunnies in the bookshop. While there, she, along with several of her friends, had been captured by this man. She didn't know who he was or what he planned to do with herself, her dust bunny friends, or any of the other creatures he had collected along the way. All she knew was he was on his way to a place called Dorian, where he hoped to "fetch a good price for the fancy fairy."

Now that her friends had fled into the forest, and the others had all been set free, too, the brownie was right. She should try to find her friends and together they could make their way home.

A shrill whistle came from the edge of the woods. "Brother, time to go!"

"That's my cue. Good luck!" The brownie tipped his hat at her and skittered into the darkness.

Cynthia hovered just above the rutted road, her wings holding her aloft and her pale blue dress fluttering from the breeze her wings created.

Something tugged at her heart. A feeling came over her that the scene of the disaster wasn't quite deserted yet. Before she could leave, she felt compelled to check to make sure everyone else had made it out safely. She couldn't leave anyone else stranded.

She studied her surroundings. The racoon, raven, and thistlehare had finished collecting items from the overturned bins and bags and had disappeared. The cages all lay empty where they had been pried open by the brownie. Nothing stirred among the debris scattered across the road.

Her mind settled. No one needed any help. Well, except maybe the man still being pummeled by fireflies. But it would be foolish to try to help him. She knew this. But she couldn't bring herself to fly away knowing he struggled.

The choice to assist was removed from her when the man ran further down the road away from the wagon, the fireflies following at a quick pace. She wouldn't be able to fly fast enough to keep up, so there was no longer any point in trying.

Cynthia sighed and floated toward the cloudy night sky. If only she could have done more for him.

Now she needed to get her bearings and fly back to her home. The dust bunnies would be well hidden in the understory of the forest by now. She would keep an eye out, but she doubted she'd be able to reunite with them before they found their way home, too. The wagon had taken her far from home, but she should be able to find her way back. It would just take some time.

A grunt, followed by a crash, came from the other side of the now-empty, driverless wagon.

Was there another of the previous captives nearby, like the racoon and raven, looting the wagon for valuables? Or had the brownies missed someone still held prisoner?

Her mind told her she should just leave.

But her heart disagreed. What if someone needed her help? What if someone was injured?

Without even fully making a choice, Cynthia floated toward where she had heard the sound, staying close to the side of the wagon. She didn't want to startle an injured creature and become injured herself!

She edged around a scattered set of dented cookware,

alongside a heap of crumpled books, over a dirty bedroll, and skimmed above a spilled canister of dried beans.

A clatter came from the same place she had heard the previous sounds. She moved slowly toward the noise, preparing herself for potential danger.

"Ugh!" A frustrated cry reached her ears.

Curiosity pulled her toward the sound faster. She released the tension from her shoulders and relaxed. The brownies must have stuck around after the owner of the cart and all of the freed captives had fled.

She rounded the front end of the wagon, fully expecting to see at least two miniature men poking around in the debris.

No sign of the brownies, or any creature for that matter, greeted her.

She hovered in place and examined the broken ceramic pots, splayed parchments, and overturned water jug for the source of the muted sounds. The low light made it difficult to sort through the details.

"Hello?" she called in a timid voice.

The shuffling stopped and the air stilled.

Cynthia flew closer to the strewn contents of a spilled crate of purple potatoes. She landed on light, bare feet on the bumpy dirt road and tiptoed around the edge of the half-empty burlap sack.

"Is someone there?" she said in a soft voice.

Nothing responded, but a shuffling sound reached her ears.

Her heart sped up. Bumps spread up and down her arms and the back of her neck. She wasn't alone, but was she in danger?

She kept her wide, silver wings extended, ready to fly at a moment's notice.

Careful steps around the banged-up potatoes carried her closer to the source of her investigation.

A quiet grunt muffled behind a large ceramic bowl drew Cynthia's attention to her left.

"I know you're there." She tried to keep her voice steady, but feared she wasn't very successful.

A heavy sigh came next, followed by the shifting of body weight and rustle of clothing.

Cynthia's own pointy ears helped her discern the sounds of light footsteps on the dirt road as the source rounded the empty bowl.

"Oh!" Cynthia jumped. Her wings held her off the ground momentarily, before she settled her tiny, bare feet in place again.

The miniature person, only slightly bigger than herself, scowled. "What?" he snapped.

Normally comfortable talking to people and creatures alike, Cynthia suddenly found herself at a loss for words.

Chapter 2

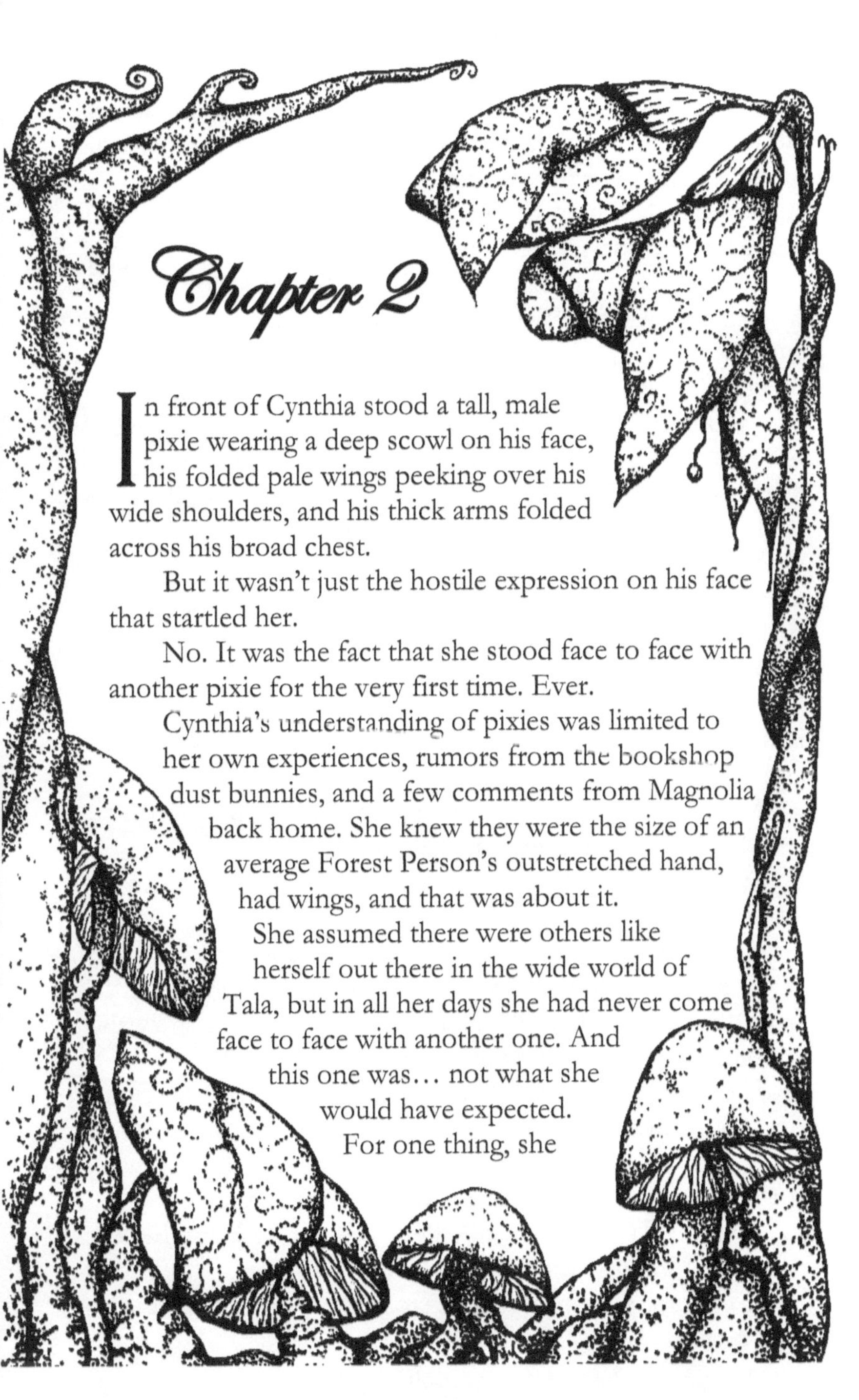

In front of Cynthia stood a tall, male pixie wearing a deep scowl on his face, his folded pale wings peeking over his wide shoulders, and his thick arms folded across his broad chest.

But it wasn't just the hostile expression on his face that startled her.

No. It was the fact that she stood face to face with another pixie for the very first time. Ever.

Cynthia's understanding of pixies was limited to her own experiences, rumors from the bookshop dust bunnies, and a few comments from Magnolia back home. She knew they were the size of an average Forest Person's outstretched hand, had wings, and that was about it.

She assumed there were others like herself out there in the wide world of Tala, but in all her days she had never come face to face with another one. And this one was… not what she would have expected.

For one thing, she

didn't recognize him from the wagon. She had spent several days locked up in there and had become acquainted with the other captives, at least by name, if not more.

But she definitely hadn't seen another pixie in there. Or heard anyone else say anything about another pixie.

Where had he come from? Was he here to scavenge items from the wreckage? Why would a pixie want any of this stuff anyway?

Her curiosity piqued as she studied him. He was at least head and shoulders taller than herself, had long legs covered by brown linen pants, and wore a pale green, short-sleeved tunic over his broad chest. A bulging satchel hung diagonally across his body; the bag part rested on his hip. Like her, he wore no shoes on his feet. His fists, now clenched at his sides, flexed the muscles in his thick arms beneath the tight sleeves of his shirt.

He narrowed his eyes at her. "What are you staring at?" His words dripped with contempt.

Her eyes wandered back to his face. His mouth turned down in a deep frown. When she glimpsed his icy glare, she gasped and took a step back.

What had she done to deserve such a hostile reaction?

"Well?" the man growled.

Cynthia stuttered. "N-nothing. I… I was just… Are you alright?"

He raised one eyebrow at her but didn't answer.

"It's just… I don't remember you from the wagon. Are you from around here, or…?" She held her breath while she waited for him to explain his presence here.

The other winged person narrowed his eyes even further. "I don't have to answer any of your questions." He turned on his heels to stomp away from her, exposing his back- and his wings- for the first time since she had stumbled upon him.

"Oh, my!" Cynthia's hands flew to her mouth and her eyes rounded. "Your wings!"

His wings, so very different from her own in their creamy

color, larger size, and leaf shape, looked crumpled and torn.

The man froze. His damaged wings trembled. He scowled at her over his shoulder. "I'm fine," he said through gritted teeth. "You can go now."

She reached a hand toward him. All concerns about his reasons for being there vanished. She wanted to offer some assistance, but what could she do for him?

When he saw her movement, he stiffened. His words came out in a low growl. "Don't. Come. Any. Closer."

She sucked in a sharp breath. "Are you in pain? What may I do to help you?" She twisted her hands together. Her throat tightened and her eyes stung.

She couldn't imagine how much that kind of injury would hurt. Had it been recent? Or had they been damaged like that for a long time? How did an injury like that even happen? Her own wings drooped and quivered at the thought.

"I said, I'm fine." He grumbled and took several heavy steps toward the opposite side of the road from where they stood.

Cynthia took a timid step after him. "But… can you fly? How will you make your way home?"

"You sure do ask a lot of questions," he grumbled just loud enough for her to hear.

Cynthia flinched. Magnolia and Cynthia's dust bunny friends said the same thing. She tried to stop, but she had a curious nature. Instead, she did her best to keep her questions to herself. It would seem she hadn't done a very good job just then.

"I'm only trying to help…"

She bit her tongue to force herself to stop talking. He hadn't asked her for help. She pulled her shoulders lower and tucked her hands around herself.

The squeak of bats overhead reminded Cynthia of the dangers for a pixie in the woods, especially at night. She needed to be careful. She didn't know this pixie or his purpose for being at the crash site. She would be better off leaving him and making her way home. Alone.

The thought left her feeling sick to her stomach. She couldn't just leave him if he needed help.

While she contemplated what to do or say next to try to offer whatever assistance she could, he turned and looked her up and down, then scoffed.

Compared to him, she imagined all he noticed was her slight stature, dainty hands, delicate wings, and 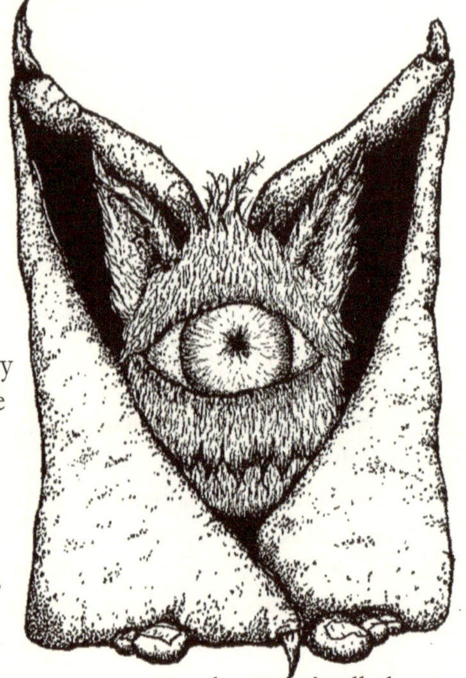 worried face. As far as appearances went, she wasn't all that impressive.

"As if you could even help me if you wanted to." He turned on his heels to leave.

It was the truth. But still, her heart tugged in his direction.

Before he could disappear into the woods, Cynthia's mind raced for something to say as she took two brave steps closer. "Wait! Please! I want to help. My name is Cynthia. I… I've never met anyone like you before."

The man folded his bulky arms over his chest. "And what is *that* supposed to mean? *Someone like me?* Broken? Alone? Angry?"

Cynthia dropped her outstretched hand. She shook her head, eyes still wide and unblinking. That was not the smartest thing to say. She had offended him. Again.

"No. Someone… with wings." She glanced at the little bit of cream-colored wing that she could see over his shoulder, wincing at the crumpled state of it.

His eyes narrowed and his head tilted slightly. "What do you mean, you've never seen someone with wings. You're a pixie, aren't you?"

Cynthia shrugged. "I guess?" This was not the conversation she had been expecting.

"What do you mean, you guess?" He stepped closer to her. He moved slowly around her as if to study her more carefully.

She followed him with her eyes and head but kept the rest of her body stationary. His gaze wasn't threatening, but still, no one had ever really *looked* at her before.

"You have wings," he stated in a matter-of-fact tone.

She nodded.

"You were born from a flower blossom?"

"Yes…"

As he circled her, she got a closer look at his features, as well. His cream-colored wings had dark spots like a leopard. They were heavily creased like clothing that had been left on the floor for a while, and she noticed several tears along the edges. She made an effort not to visibly wince at their appearance.

When she got a chance to look at his face up close, her heart skipped a beat. His buttery hair, strong jawline, and sharp nose complemented his piercing dark eyes. And under the muted moonlight, she could just make out some freckles across his cheeks and nose. A flutter in her stomach caught her by surprise.

He circled behind her, out of her line of vision. She remained still, though he could probably hear her heart pounding.

When he finished his inspection, he stood in front of her again. A bit closer than before, but still far enough away that she wouldn't be able to reach him if she stretched her arm as far as it would go.

"And you have abilities related to the blossom from which you were born?" he quizzed.

All her inner observations about his appearance and attitude disappeared in an instant. "*Abilities?*" she asked. Were pixies supposed to have some kind of… abilities? This was news to her! "Like what?"

The winged man raised his eyebrows. "Well, if you don't know then I certainly can't tell you." His tone sounded mocking.

"Why not?" She took a half step closer. If she had some kind of magical abilities, she needed to know!

He let out a short laugh and gave her a questioning look. "Wait," he stopped himself. "You *really* don't know?" His frown deepened.

She shook her head, heat rushing to her cheeks. Her wings drooped further, and her stomach squeezed. She placed her palm flat against her front and pressed against the pain.

"Wow. I just assumed you were being difficult." His features softened ever so slightly. "How do you not know… any of this?"

"Like I said, I've never met anyone like you… or like me… before." Her voice came out barely above a whisper and she focused her eyes on the ground.

The man heaved a deep sigh. "Look. I'm sorry." He sounded frustrated. "I wasn't trying to tease you or make you feel bad or anything. I just thought…" He dropped his hands to his sides and sighed. "Never mind. Wherever you're from, you should head back there now. The forest isn't safe. That awful man will be back for his cart eventually." The other pixie kept his voice calm, no longer angry or annoyed, but still unfriendly.

Cynthia glanced up at him. "But what about you? Your wings are damaged. Can you fly?"

He shook his head. "Don't worry about me. I can take care of myself." He squared his shoulders and folded his arms again. "Now, get out of here." This time his words weren't forceful. It sounded like he was actually concerned about her safety.

"I can't just leave you here…" Cynthia hesitated. Her fingers knotted together.

The man stiffened again. "And how will you be able to protect me if that man comes back? You don't even have any abilities. And you're the smallest pixie I think I've ever seen. Please, for your own good, just go."

Cynthia took a step away from him and hugged herself. Other than when the man had captured her, she had never been treated so unkindly before.

She desperately wanted to know more about pixies. A part of her wanted to know more about this *particular* pixie, which surprised her. She shoved those thoughts aside.

The truth was, he didn't want her there, for whatever reason. She could insist on staying, but what good would that do?

Disappointment squeezed her stomach even tighter. She met his eyes and gave him a slight nod, doing her best to keep her face neutral but probably failing miserably. "If you insist."

She glanced at the sky for any signs of the bats before rising into the air and allowing her silver wings to carry her higher. She made herself not look back.

A tug on her heart in his direction slowed her ascent. She had never left someone behind that needed help. Magnolia had ingrained in her to always do good no matter what. But it was more than that. She felt the physical strain to help, even if she felt hesitant.

Plus, he was a pixie! How could she just go back home now when she had the chance to learn about her kind?

She hovered for a moment. Hesitated. Should she turn back and insist that she stay with him? Maybe he really did need her help.

That was just wishful thinking. She gave him one last longing look and then fluttered her wings a bit faster to carry her away from him for good.

A deep sigh from below caught her attention and she pricked her ears in the other pixie's direction.

"Wait," he called.

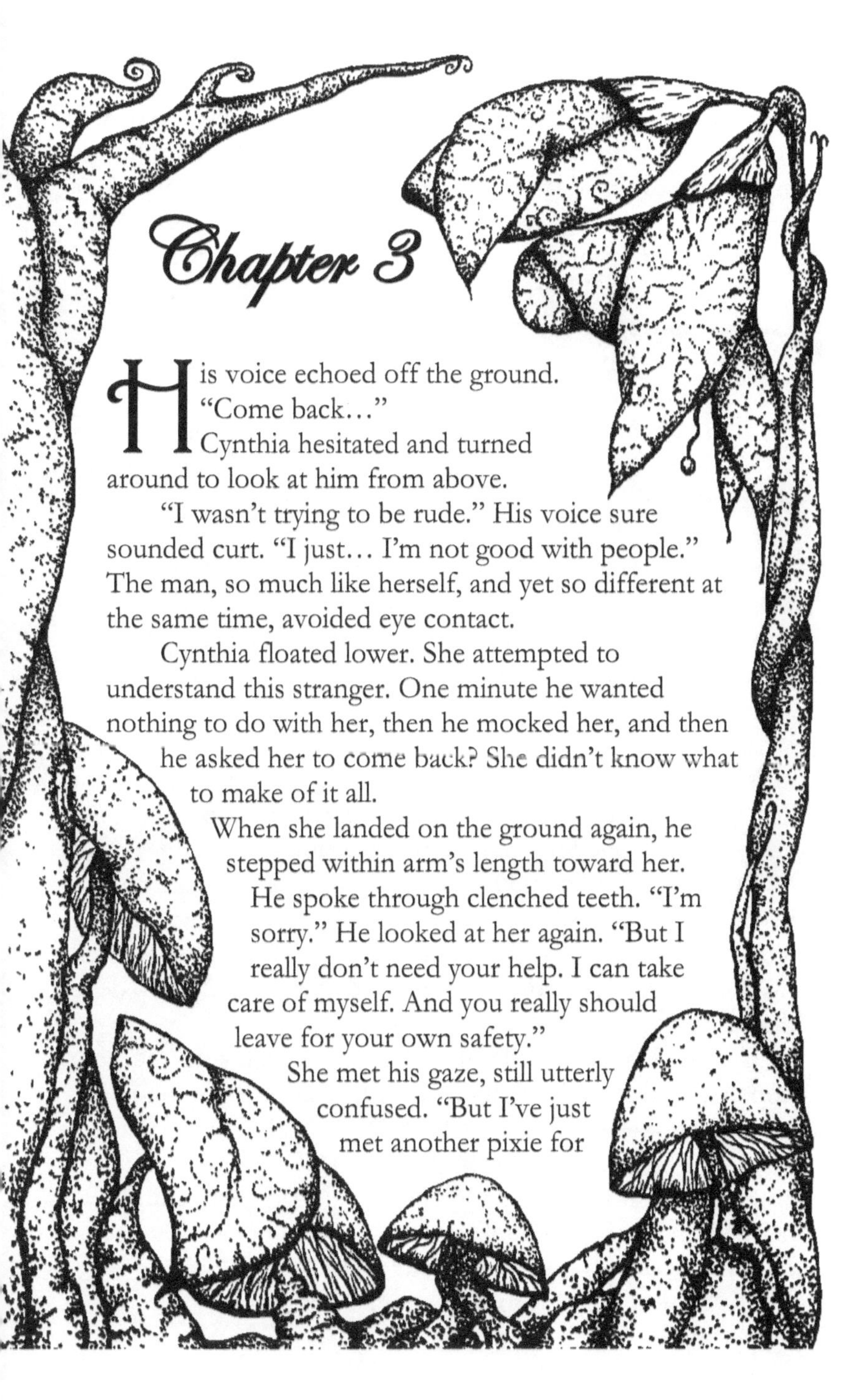

Chapter 3

His voice echoed off the ground. "Come back…"

Cynthia hesitated and turned around to look at him from above.

"I wasn't trying to be rude." His voice sure sounded curt. "I just… I'm not good with people." The man, so much like herself, and yet so different at the same time, avoided eye contact.

Cynthia floated lower. She attempted to understand this stranger. One minute he wanted nothing to do with her, then he mocked her, and then he asked her to come back? She didn't know what to make of it all.

When she landed on the ground again, he stepped within arm's length toward her.

He spoke through clenched teeth. "I'm sorry." He looked at her again. "But I really don't need your help. I can take care of myself. And you really should leave for your own safety."

She met his gaze, still utterly confused. "But I've just met another pixie for the very first time." She tried to keep the pleading out of her voice, but didn't think she was very successful. "I want to know more. I have no idea how to help you with your wings. But perhaps we can work together? You can help me learn about who I am, and I can help you figure out how to fix your wings?"

He frowned. "There is no way to fix my wings, I'm afraid. They are damaged beyond repair."

She looked away and nodded. He would know better than she.

But something inside of her couldn't just let it go.

She took a deep breath. "Do you live around here? Or are you lost, too?"

He hesitated.

She held her breath. If he didn't need her help getting home, then there really wasn't anything she could do for him. Her presence would be completely useless. She'd just end up leaving with all her questions unanswered.

He let out a deep sigh.

She was bothering him again by asking too many questions. "It's fine." She waved her hand as if to erase her words. "You don't have to tell me anything. I'll go. Thank you for telling me about pixies." She fluttered her wings again.

Before her toes could leave the ground, words rushed from his mouth. "I don't live around here." He gestured at the dark woods on either side of the rutted road. A pained look crossed his face, as if admitting anything to her caused him deep discomfort.

Cynthia landed on the ground again, clinging to the little hope she had left. "Well, then at least I can help you find your way home. It will be easier if I can fly up and get our bearings from time to time, won't it?"

He stared at her with an intensity that made her squirm. He nodded once. "Fine. I'll tell you what you want to know about our kind, you help me find my way home."

She allowed her lips to turn into a slight grin.

"But." He held his palm toward her to tell her to stop. "If there's any sign of danger, you fly away as fast as you can. Agreed?"

It was better than she could have hoped for. "Agreed." She grinned wide at him.

He pinched the bridge of his nose and closed his eyes as if he couldn't believe he had just agreed to this.

When he opened them, she gave him an expectant look.

"What?" he asked with a confused expression.

"I told you my name, but you didn't tell me yours." She tipped her head to one side. Her silvery-blue hair, the color of the underside of a silver birch leaf, or like Magnolia said, the color of frozen moonlight, fell away from her face and touched her shoulder. She waited for him to say something.

"Fox," he grumbled.

She raised her eyebrows. That was a unique name! She kept her thoughts to herself. He didn't seem like the kind of person who would appreciate a comment like that.

"Nice to meet you, Fox. Should we get going?" She pointed the direction that he had started to walk toward before.

He didn't move.

"Well?" she asked, expectantly.

He shook his head and sighed. "We need to gather supplies first. Walking for days through the forest won't be easy. We'll need to strategize."

She nodded. She should have thought of that. Normally she could just fly wherever she needed to go, and since she never went far away from home, it never took very long to get anywhere. She had never traveled long distances before, and especially not at a walking pace.

Her shoulders sagged.

He squinted at her. "It's fine. I'll get stuff. You just…" He waved his hand around as if he didn't know what to do with her. "Just wait here."

She only hesitated for a moment. "Actually, I can help. I'm not totally useless." She kept her voice light and wore a smile on her face. "What should I be looking for?"

After a cursory glance from Fox, he answered her question. "Food. Clothing. Blankets. Something to help carry it all in…"

"Right! On it!" She lifted herself from the ground and floated above the wreckage.

The distant cries from the wagon owner proved that he still battled the fireflies. They had at least a little time before he came back.

She saw lots of the things Fox had listed. The only problem was, they were all human sized. Each bean from the spilled container was the size of her torso. And they were hard as stone.

"Perhaps if we boil it into a soup?" she pondered as she turned one over in her hands.

She clutched the bean in her arms and continued her search.

When she couldn't find any of the other things they needed, she returned to where she had left Fox.

He wasn't there. Had he gone without her? Used the excuse of finding supplies as a distraction to get rid of her?

But he had agreed that she could help him. Again, maybe he was just toying with her to get her to leave him alone long enough so he could set off on his own.

Her shoulders slumped.

Something clattered to the floor of the inside of the wagon. She relaxed. He must be inside it to look for things. Why hadn't she thought of that?

She fluttered back into the overturned wagon. "So, what'd you find?"

"AAAH!" Something in the corner of the wagon screamed and tossed a handful of dried flower petals into the air. They fluttered to the ground like confetti at a party.

Cynthia froze. It wasn't Fox in the wagon. It was something… furry. A predator? She hugged the bean tighter and readied herself to take flight.

"You scared the moonlight out of me!" the furry thing said from underneath its arms covering its face.

"Likewise," Cynthia replied. If she had *scared* it, then she probably didn't need to be *afraid* of it.

"Don't mind me." The creature shuffled around in the dark corner of the wagon, hiding its face from Cynthia. "Just gathering my things and then I'll be outta' here like a firefly in a rainstorm."

Cynthia waited for the furry creature to emerge so she could get a good look at him.

He remained in the shadows of the corner. He made scraping sounds as he moved items around, and his feet shuffled on the lopsided floor. She couldn't exactly tell how large he was, or what kind of animal he might be.

"Excuse me? Is everything alright?" Cynthia asked when he still had not emerged after a few moments.

"Everything's fine. Just gathering my things!"

"Yes, you said that already... Do you need help with anything?" Cynthia took a step closer.

She caught a glimpse of the creature in the shadows. He was much larger than she had realized. Should she leave? Find Fox? Or stay and offer to help?

Before she could decide, Fox hoisted himself into the wagon. "Who are you talking to in here?" Fox glanced furtively around the enclosed space.

"Um…" Cynthia pointed in the corner where the shuffling had suddenly stopped. She looked at Fox and shrugged.

"Come on then, let's go. I made a pile of supplies." Fox turned to exit the wagon.

Something wrapped around Cynthia's ankles from behind. It pulled her backwards.

"Gotcha!" the gravelly voice said.

Cynthia shrieked. She flapped her wings to keep herself from falling forward onto her face, but the rope kept her tethered to the creature.

The more she tugged on the rope, the tighter it squeezed her ankles. But if she stopped fighting, then the thing would surely pull her toward it. Without knowing what its intentions were, she couldn't allow that to happen.

She fought against the rope, flying upward and side to side to try to get the creature to release her, but it was no use!

Movement below caught her attention as she struggled against the rope.

Fox darted forward toward a pile of thread spools and scissors on the floor. He quickly rummaged through until he found what he must have been looking for. With a human-sized needle for a sword gripped in his hands, he lunged for the creature hiding in the dark shadows.

He grunted with the effort of stabbing into the darkness.

Whatever lurked in the shadows shrieked. "I give up! Stop!"

Instantly the tension on the rope vanished. Cynthia hovered above Fox with the rope dangling from her ankles into a heap on the floor.

Fox backed away, still holding the needle out in front of him and taking deep breaths. Without taking his eyes off the shadows, he took hold of the rope and rubbed it against a man's shaving blade leaning against the side of the turned-over box of supplies.

"It's alright, Fox." Cynthia bent her knees to reach the rope around her ankles, and slipped her feet out from the looped end. It fell to the floor with a thud.

She flew to the floor to stand beside Fox.

"What do you think it is?" she whispered to him.

Fox dropped the end of the rope and motioned for her to get behind him. He still held his sword toward the threat.

Cynthia stayed put. If she needed to, she could fly away. She was safe enough where she stood.

"Come out where we can see you," Fox ordered the hiding creature.

The creature emerged from the darker corner of the wagon. Cynthia and Fox both recoiled at his appearance.

His bulbous nose, the texture of a warty toad, emerged first, followed by the hairy body, bare hands, and strange three-toed feet. The darkness and shadows made it impossible to get a good look at its coloring or distinct features.

"I didn't mean it," the thing said, holding his hands out in front of him. He didn't take his eyes off Fox's makeshift needle-sword.

From the height Cynthia had been hovering above them only moments earlier, she could have easily brushed her feet on the tips of its furry ears poking up from the sides of his head.

Cynthia took a step closer to Fox, just in case. It suddenly felt safer behind the sword than not.

Beside her, Fox glared at the creature.

It was at least two times taller than Fox, so why was it cowering in fear like that?

"I'm just a big scaredy cat," the creature whined.

"You are not," Fox growled in reply. "I've seen scaredy cats, and they look nothing like you."

The creature's mouth twitched beneath his large nose, like he was trying to hide a smirk.

Fox didn't hesitate. He sidled sideways, motioning for Cynthia to stay behind him.

"Now, get out of here before I stab you again," he threatened the creature.

The creature nodded, hoisted a bulging sack onto his back, and skittered past the pair.

Cynthia watched it hop from the wagon and scurry into the forest.

Cynthia heaved a sigh of relief and smiled at Fox. "That was close! I'm sure glad you showed up just then!"

"You shouldn't talk to things hiding in shadows." Fox lowered the sword and scolded her.

Any hint of friendliness that Cynthia had sensed when they had agreed to help one another had vanished. Her heart sank.

Fox tossed more words at her as he left the wagon. "Like I said, I made a pile of things. We need to divide it up so we can each carry some. Come on."

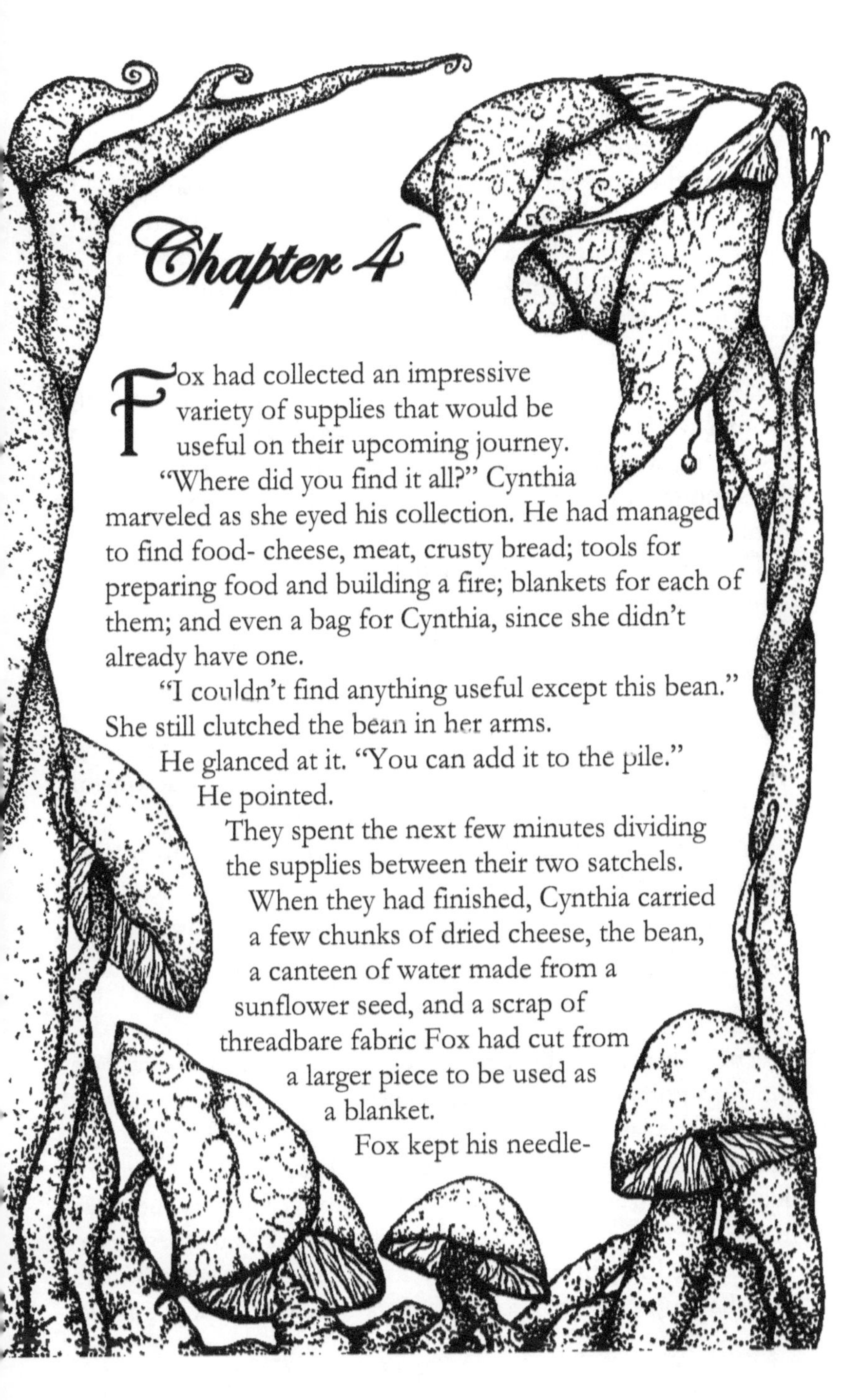

Chapter 4

Fox had collected an impressive variety of supplies that would be useful on their upcoming journey.

"Where did you find it all?" Cynthia marveled as she eyed his collection. He had managed to find food- cheese, meat, crusty bread; tools for preparing food and building a fire; blankets for each of them; and even a bag for Cynthia, since she didn't already have one.

"I couldn't find anything useful except this bean." She still clutched the bean in her arms.

He glanced at it. "You can add it to the pile." He pointed.

They spent the next few minutes dividing the supplies between their two satchels.

When they had finished, Cynthia carried a few chunks of dried cheese, the bean, a canteen of water made from a sunflower seed, and a scrap of threadbare fabric Fox had cut from a larger piece to be used as a blanket.

Fox kept his needle-sword by threading it through the canvas of his satchel. He also carried the thimble they could use for boiling water, a ball of wax-coated string, and a chunk of flint. "We'll be able to build fires if we need to." He explained the purpose of both the flint and the waxy string. "It will be much easier using these."

Cynthia nodded but had no idea what he meant. She had never had to build a fire out of nothing before. Magnolia always had a cookfire in her stove inside her house. If Cynthia ever needed anything warmed, Magnolia took care of it for her. But Cynthia rarely did. Living inside a preserved pumpkin house didn't lend well for having fire inside of it. The windows were large enough to let in daylight, and she liked the darkness at night.

Fox marched across the rutted dirt road toward the fir forest, opposite from the direction the strange big-nosed creature had gone. When Cynthia realized that Fox had already started off without her, she snapped herself out of daydreaming of home, her soft wool bed, and silky blanket.

"Wait up!" She fluttered her wings to catch up with him. "Do you know where we're going?" she asked, a little out of breath.

"Not yet. But I do know we need to get away from this wagon. Either some other scavenger will show up, or the owner will return. Either way, we need to get away from here and find a place to rest and make plans."

The pair walked through the woods, away from the wagon and any potential danger. The pale moonlight barely shone through the layer of clouds overhead, which made the forest darker than it would have been otherwise. The blend of deciduous and evergreen trees towered above Cynthia and filled the air with the scent of pine and fall leaves. The feathery ferns and pointed mushrooms on the forest floor grew tall enough that she didn't have to crouch to walk beneath them. It was like a forest within a forest compared to Cynthia and Fox.

Cynthia thought she saw eyes peeping at them beneath flowers or from behind mushrooms from time to time, but since Fox didn't seem concerned, she chose not to be, either. As long as they stuck together, they would be safe. Probably.

And, she reminded herself, she could always fly away if she needed to.

She kept up with Fox's quick pace using a combination of hurried steps alternating with fluttering just above the mossy forest floor.

After several minutes, Cynthia broke the silence. "Where is home for you, Fox? I mean, in which direction do you think we'll need to go?"

Fox didn't answer.

Cynthia hurried to add, "I'll get a lay of the land in the morning from above, but it will be helpful to know what I'm looking for."

"South." One word. That was it.

"South? Alright…" How was she supposed to help him get home if he kept all of his answers vague?

"The wagon was headed west. So, we need to go south." He kept scanning their surroundings, probably for threats, though Cynthia didn't think they really had anything to worry about.

"Well, tell me about home. Maybe that will help me figure out a more precise direction when I fly to get our bearings in the morning." This was like prying a big carrot from dry soil. She had to work it loose before she would get it to come out.

"There isn't much to tell." Fox didn't elaborate.

Yep. A big, stubborn carrot. Maybe if she started talking, it would loosen his tongue a little, too?

"I'll tell you about my home, then." She explained about Magnolia and Cynthia's home in the garden.

She could picture the hollowed-out pumpkin in which she lived, the rows of vegetables and fruit orchard, and the sunlight filtering through the variety of trees around the perimeter of the yard.

Magnolia's bronze skin, copper eyes, high cheekbones, and long black hair filled Cynthia's mind. She was a tall woman, even for a Forest Person, which gave her the air of an authority figure. But she had a kindness about her that allowed people to trust her immediately. The reminder of her warm smile and gentle manner gave Cynthia a feeling of homesickness.

Cynthia missed her simple garden home and her quiet afternoons with Magnolia. Magnolia didn't talk much about her own life, but Cynthia had learned bits and pieces about her tragic lost love, shattered family, and years of brokenhearted solitude. Though Magnolia had a lot of sadness in her past, the Forest Person remained pleasant and happy, in a quiet sort of way. Cynthia enjoyed her company.

Cynthia kept her thoughts about Magnolia to herself, and instead talked about her long-haired, tall-eared dust bunny friends at the bookshop and how she liked to visit them there and talk about the things they learned while hiding beneath furniture and behind books.

"I'm allergic to dust bunnies," Fox murmured beneath his breath.

Cynthia ignored the comment and continued. She soon found herself recalling the day she was captured.

"We were sharing a plate of butter cookies that I had mixed up earlier that day, when we heard one of their siblings crying for help.

"We followed the sound and found their brother caught in a trap in the alley behind the bookshop. Before we could figure out how to set him free, the man from the wagon showed up. He had heard that his trap had sprung, as well.

"As soon as he arrived, all but the two sister dust bunnies fled to hide around the alley. But the sisters refused to leave their brother. I knew I had to stay with them, too. I couldn't just abandon them!"

Cynthia's heart raced as she relived the terrifying experience of the oversized, smelly man looming over them, scooping them all up in his calloused, dirty hands, and dropping them into a chicken wire cage.

"Well, that wasn't very smart, was it?" Fox interrupted her thoughts.

"What do you mean?" His words stung. She knew what he meant, obviously. If she hadn't stayed with her friends, she wouldn't have been caught. But kindness and loyalty were always the right thing to do.

"I mean, your loyalty landed you in a cage alongside the others." Fox stated the obvious.

Cynthia didn't finish the story. The man had been gleeful at his bonus prize of a pixie, and Cynthia had resigned herself to being a prisoner, not willing to try to escape if she couldn't help her friends do the same. But she didn't want to hear Fox's thoughts about that decision, either. She could only imagine the hurtful, but honest, things he might say to her. Nothing she hadn't thought to herself plenty of times.

"Do you make a habit of putting yourself at risk, then?" he continued the conversation.

"No," Cynthia murmured.

"Well, from what I've seen, that's exactly what you do. And if you keep it up, it's only going to end badly for you eventually. It doesn't sound worth it, if you ask me."

She had never been scolded so much before in her life. She hadn't asked him for his opinion about her choices. Not once.

Even though she didn't exactly enjoy his harsh words, it appeared she had been right about one thing. Talking to him loosened his tongue. Just, not in the way she had hoped.

"So," Fox continued talking, "you've really never met another pixie before?" He sounded doubtful, like he couldn't believe that it could be true.

Was he *trying* to be hurtful? His judgement of her left her feeling even smaller than her apparently, according to Fox, small-for-a-pixie size.

"No." She shook her head. "I've spent a little time with Forest People, near the human village, and with a variety of animals, but I've never met another pixie before."

"And no one ever told you anything? Or asked about your abilities? Or anything?" Disbelief edged his words.

She let out a small laugh to mask her hurt feelings. "No. I mean, should they have?"

"I don't know. It seems like at least this Magnolia person should have done something to teach you about our kind, where we came from, that sort of thing."

A pain pricked her heart. He was right. Magnolia should have told her something about pixies, shouldn't she have?

Fox, unaware of the thoughts circling in Cynthia's head, continued his speech. "Although I suppose it's just like *them* to leave you to fend for yourself." His voice hardened.

This startled Cynthia from thinking about herself and turned her attention back to the other pixie. "Fox? Are you alright?" She rested her hand on his arm.

He glanced sideways at her and stared at where her hand touched him. He looked at her face, his eyes clouded, and the muscles on the sides of his face bulged from the pressure of his jaw clenching and unclenching. "It's nothing." He pulled his arm from her touch and faced forward again. "What would you like to know about pixies?" He changed the subject.

Dropping her hand back to her side, and setting aside her own hurt feelings, she said, "Everything! Start from the beginning!"

He sighed. "Well, pixies are born from flower blossoms."

Cynthia rolled her eyes. "I know that, obviously."

"And since your name is Cynthia, you were born from a forsythia plant, right?" He kept his eyes forward while he questioned her.

She kept his pace, taking two steps and a couple of wing flaps for every one of his long strides.

"Nope." She answered his question. "Moonlight Lily."

He paused his steps and leveled her with a surprised look. "Really? Moonlight Lily? Those are incredibly rare flowers!"

His words felt like praise and her silvery wings lifted her slightly off the ground at the feeling that blossomed in her stomach.

He turned away again and continued at his quick pace. "Then why aren't you called Lily? Or Moony or something?" he asked matter-of-factly.

He probably didn't mean for his words to sound harsh, but their flatness brought Cynthia to the ground again.

She shrugged. She had never shrugged as much as she had since meeting Fox. She told herself to stop and just answer his questions with words.

"Lily is such a common name. And 'Moony'? Really?" She glared at him, but with his eyes focused on their surroundings, he didn't catch her expression.

"So, why Cynthia?" he asked.

She didn't answer his question about her name, which was kind of rude, if she thought about it. She chose not to think about it. Instead, she asked him the same question.

"So, why Fox?" She hovered beside him again to keep up. "Were you born from a *fox* flower?" She tried to make her words sound lighthearted.

She must not have succeeded, because Fox didn't answer. He ground his teeth and paused.

He marched toward a weeping willow tree and parted the drooping branches covered in pale green leaves. He peered beneath the canopy.

With a quick glance over his shoulder, he said, "We can rest here tonight." He disappeared through the curtain of branches.

Cynthia paused, then followed.

Beneath the canopy of the weeping willow branches, she spotted a patch of perfectly domed white button mushrooms that grew in an exact circle.

This would be the perfect opportunity to lighten the mood again after offending him about his name. "Did you know humans think these are pixie circles? There are all kinds of rumors about what they are for, but they protect them fiercely!" She smiled at him and waited for his reaction.

Fox ignored her comments as he approached the circle of mushrooms and pointed at them. "Well, then we should be safe here." He entered the circle ahead of her and dropped his satchel to the ground.

Cynthia landed beside him and did the same. Her mind raced as she tried to think of something else to say, but she came up with nothing.

Fox unrolled his thin blanket and spread it on the ground. He glanced around their surroundings and pulled a patch of moss from the ground outside the circle of mushrooms and placed it by his blanket.

Cynthia did the same. She peeked at him from the side. There was so much she didn't know about him and why he agreed to allow her to travel with him. She wanted to trust him, but she didn't know if she should. Without even planning to, some of her more serious questions escaped her lips.

"Why didn't I see you inside the cart? And how did your wings become damaged?"

She hoped she didn't sound suspicious. But she needed to know. She had agreed to help him. To travel with him on foot through the woods. But could she trust him?

He had been judgmental and rude. But he had also protected her from that creature inside the wagon and insisted that she leave him more than once for her own safety.

He leveled a stare in her direction and clenched his jaw, but he didn't answer her questions.

He lowered himself to the ground, wincing from his damaged wings, and rolled onto his side away from her. "Use moss as an extra blanket if you get cold." His voice was muffled, but she managed to hear his next words. "I live near a narrow lake surrounded by dwarf golden willow trees."

It wasn't nearly the quantity or quality of answers she had been looking for, but at least he had told her *something*. Hopefully she'd be able to use that tiny morsel of information to help them figure out where they needed to go.

As for whether she could trust him or not? Well, she'd just have to wait and see.

The scrap of fabric she had acquired wasn't much of a blanket, so she did as he suggested and gathered an extra sheet of moss to tuck around herself for the night. She made sure she didn't settle too close to Fox, but also stayed close enough that she could feel safe.

As her body sunk closer to sleep, her mind raced. *Was* it her fault she had ended up in this situation? Should she have hidden from the man instead of sticking it out with her friends? How was she going to survive days traveling through the woods with Fox? She had never done this before. Was Magnolia worried about her? Or would she have assumed that Cynthia had moved on, like she had said pixies were prone to do from time to time?

She ended up falling asleep with more questions than answers.

"HELP ME! HEEEEELLLLPPPP MEEEEE!!" The sharp cry from above their hiding place ripped Cynthia from her sleep for the second time in a row.

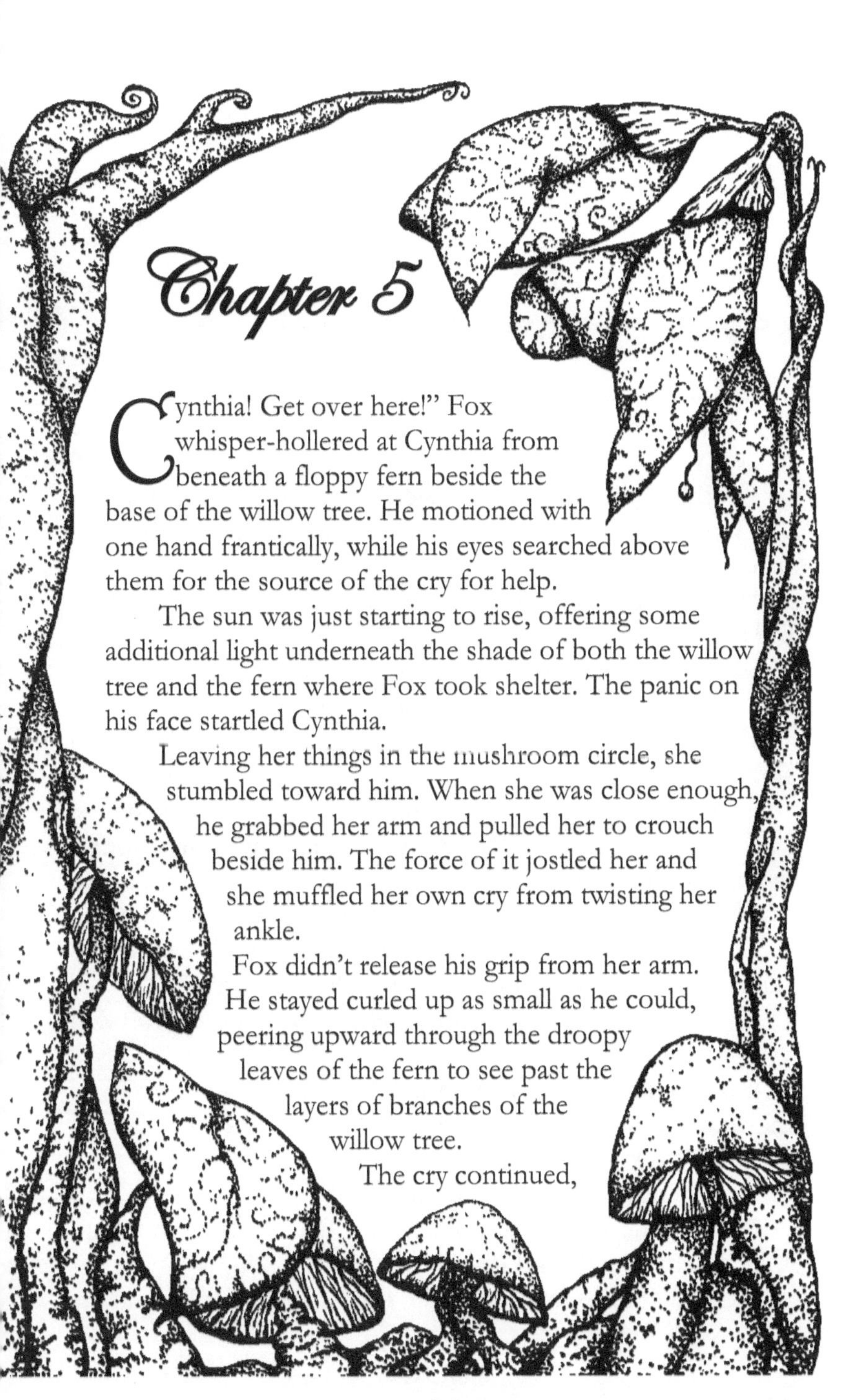

Chapter 5

Cynthia! Get over here!" Fox whisper-hollered at Cynthia from beneath a floppy fern beside the base of the willow tree. He motioned with one hand frantically, while his eyes searched above them for the source of the cry for help.

The sun was just starting to rise, offering some additional light underneath the shade of both the willow tree and the fern where Fox took shelter. The panic on his face startled Cynthia.

Leaving her things in the mushroom circle, she stumbled toward him. When she was close enough, he grabbed her arm and pulled her to crouch beside him. The force of it jostled her and she muffled her own cry from twisting her ankle.

Fox didn't release his grip from her arm. He stayed curled up as small as he could, peering upward through the droopy leaves of the fern to see past the layers of branches of the willow tree.

The cry continued,

circling above them. "Help me!"

"I wonder what's wrong?" Cynthia tipped her head back, too, to try to spot the source of the sound.

"What do you mean?" Fox asked without taking his eyes off the sky.

"What do you mean, *what do you mean*?" Cynthia turned her eyes to his face. Deep concern wrinkled his forehead.

"I mean, what do you mean, *what's wrong*?" Fox pulled the two of them further beneath the fern. "It's a hawk. Hunting. It's calling out that it's found something good to eat. I just hope its next meal isn't us!"

Cynthia shook her head. "It's calling for help. Can't you hear it?" The call for help was clear. Why did he think it was hunting them?

"Of course, I can hear it." His tone became more frustrated, like he was dealing with a difficult child. "I hear the hawk calling out. From experience, it means it's found its prey!"

"No, it's calling for help," Cynthia countered.

Fox grumbled. "Think what you want. I'd rather be safe than sorry."

Cynthia pulled her arm from his loose grip and rubbed it.

Fox glanced down. His eyes widened. "Did I hurt you? I wasn't trying to…"

"No, I'm fine." Cynthia dropped her arm to show she had received no harm. "But I don't understand, Fox. The hawk is calling for help. It's saying, 'help me.' Don't you hear it?"

Fox furrowed his eyebrows. "Are you saying… you can *understand* the *hawk*?"

Cynthia nodded and frowned. "Of course, I can understand the hawk. Are you saying you *can't* understand the hawk?" Wasn't it a pixie thing?

Fox leaned away from Cynthia. "No, of course I can't understand the hawk. I'm not a Forest Person that can talk to animals, you know. And it's not one of my abilities."

Cynthia's stomach turned over. Fox couldn't understand the

hawk. Because he's not a Forest Person. But Cynthia wasn't a Forest Person, either. So why could *she* understand the hawk? If only Magnolia had told her more about pixies. If only she had asked!

"Wait, are you able to understand *all* animals?" Fox's eyes widened.

Cynthia didn't respond. She sat stunned into silence. She had always assumed that it was normal for her kind to be able to talk to animals. The Forest People she had encountered all understood animals to some degree, even if they were more into plants than creatures. And no one had ever been surprised by this ability of hers before.

Wait. Ability. Was this one of her "abilities" that Fox had mentioned before?

"Cynthia?" Fox said her name. "Are you alright?" He sounded more frustrated than concerned.

She looked at him. "I think so. I think… maybe talking to animals is one of my abilities?"

Fox returned his eyes to the sky, still concerned by the "hunting" hawk. "Your guess is as good as mine."

"Help me!!" The cry came again.

"Well, ability or not, I can understand the hawk, and it needs help." Cynthia stood to leave the protective cover of the fern.

"Are you senseless?" Fox grabbed her arm again and tugged her back to the ground. "You can't go out there. You'll get eaten alive!"

Cynthia gently pulled her arm free again. She stood and rested a hand on Fox's shoulder. "No, I won't. It's clearly asking for help. I must see what I can do."

Fox stood and blocked her path. "But what if it's a trick? What if it *wants* you to think it needs help, and then it plans to just eat you anyway?" Fox's face reflected his genuine concern.

Cynthia shook her head. "I don't think it would do that. Besides, if I know someone or something needs help and I refuse to help, then I'm just as bad as a hawk hunting pixies, aren't I? I can't assume the worst out of everyone I come across. I'm not going to hide behind a mushroom like a scared little fungus troll. It's just not in my nature." She stepped around him.

He stood with his mouth open.

She glanced over her shoulder before she allowed her wings to carry her above the clearing. Maybe she was too trusting, but she couldn't just ignore the begging for help.

"What if it's a trick?" he shouted at her from below.

"And what if it isn't?" she shouted back.

Cynthia flew in the gentle morning breeze toward the circling hawk. It certainly did appear to be in a hunting pattern as it searched the forest below. But hawks usually hunted in meadows or clearings. While Fox and Cynthia had stayed in a "clearing" proportional to themselves, it wasn't more than a slightly less dense part of the woods underneath a willow tree. She didn't think the hawk would waste its time trying to hunt through the foliage and undergrowth.

The breeze tossed Cynthia's silvery-blue wavy hair around her face as she hovered high above the trees. She cupped her hands around her mouth and called loudly

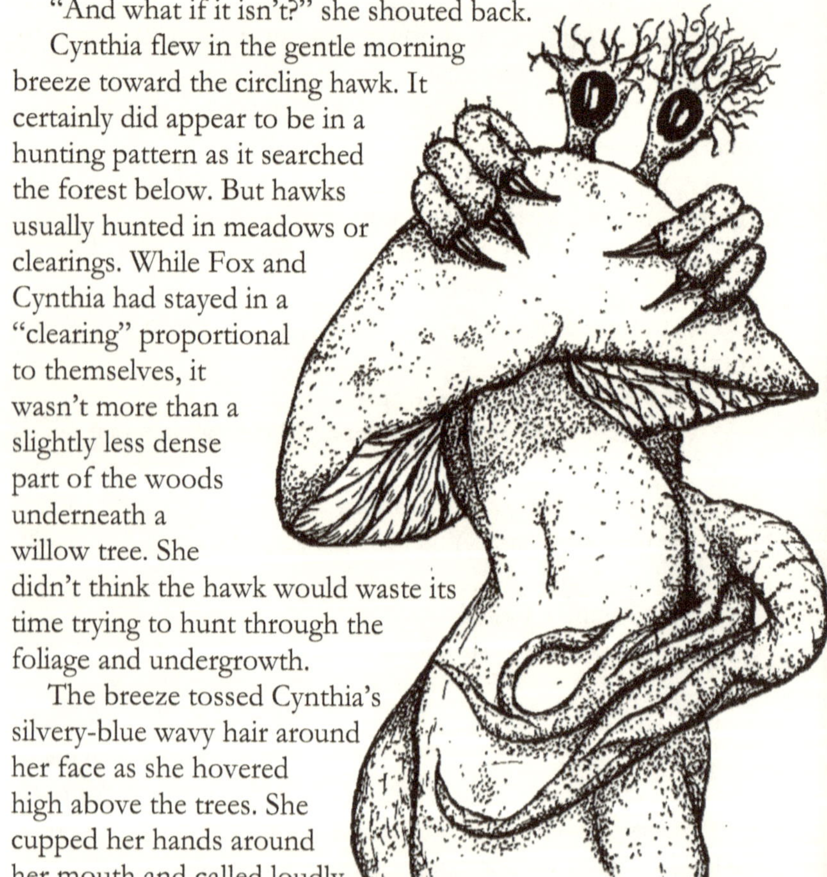

to the hawk. "Hello, friend! What is your trouble?"

Fox's words about it being a trick tickled the back of her mind. Though she trusted her instincts, she couldn't push his concerns away. She prepared to dart away from the hawk if it seemed threatening at all.

The hawk caught sight of her. It circled on the wind without flapping its wings, soaring closer to her with each turn but saying nothing.

The horizon brightened in pinks and purples behind the hawk. The light cast the hawk in shadow in front of Cynthia. She squinted against the rising sun to try to see the bird clearly.

Cynthia's heart raced. She had never second-guessed her instincts for helping before. But Fox's doubt wouldn't leave her mind. She braced herself for an attack, while hoping with all her heart that the hawk wouldn't try to eat her.

"May I help you?" Cynthia yelled again, waiting on edge for the hawk to make its move.

What would she do if it decided to attack? Dive super-fast? Try to dodge?

Once it flew close enough, the hawk continued to circle around Cynthia, keeping her nerves on edge.

This was it. It was going to snatch her right out of the air and take her home to feed its young!

Cynthia's heart sank. Fox was right. She was too trusting and now she was going to pay for it.

"I have lost my BABY!" the hawk cried. "She fell right out of the sky into the trees! I cannot see her anywhere! Please, help me!"

Cynthia's heart lifted. It wasn't a trick after all! This mother hawk really was in distress. Her instincts had been right all along.

"I can help you. What happened, exactly?" Cynthia pivoted in the air to keep her eyes on the hawk so the bird could hear her words as she circled.

"We were having a flying lesson. She got tired. Before I could tell her what to do, her wing cramped, and she dropped! I tried to catch her, but I was too late. I don't know where she went! She's not making any noise. What if… what if she's…?" The hawk's cries grew more distressed and her flying more erratic.

"It's going to be alright, Mama. I'll help you find her! Where did she fall?" Cynthia scanned the foliage below.

"Just over there." The hawk flew back toward where she had been circling before, nearer where Fox and Cynthia had slept.

"I will help you find her," Cynthia assured the mother again.

She descended closer to the treetops. The mother had keen eyesight, but probably didn't have the same acute hearing that Cynthia had.

She held her breath and listened intently to the sounds of the forest. She strained her hearing past the rustling of dry fall leaves in the breeze, bird chirps and squirrel chitters, and the sound of a distant woodpecker banging against a tree trunk in its search for breakfast.

"There!" She darted toward the squeaks that sounded out of place for that time of day.

Cynthia descended through the foliage until she came upon a frazzled young hawk tangled in some winding emerald vines attached to the trunk of a tulip leaf maple tree. The baby still had some of her downy feathers layered underneath a scattering of new, sleek feathers that matched her mother.

The baby cried out when she saw Cynthia, frantic for her mother.

"Shh, shh, it's alright, I'm here to help you!" Cynthia soothed the hawk with her voice.

She kept her own wings' motion slow and smooth, and made no sudden movements.

The baby calmed down. Cynthia helped detangle her from the vines. When she had been freed, the baby perched on the branch just below where she had been stuck, clearly exhausted from the ordeal.

Cynthia called for the mother hawk. She flew up out of the canopy to get her attention, then helped reunite her with her baby.

The mother shouted her relief to see her baby safe and sound. She sang nothing but praises for Cynthia's help. "I wish I could repay you! If only there was anything I could do!"

"I am trying to find my way back to a narrow lake? South of here." Would that description be enough to get helpful directions? If only Fox had been more specific. But that was the only information she had. "Do you know the way? Could you possibly offer us a ride?" Cynthia asked.

Why hadn't she thought of that before? If they could get a ride, it would speed up their journey from days- or longer- to only hours, maybe. Depending on how far away this lake was.

"I must take care of my baby. I am afraid I cannot carry you in the direction you need to travel. I'm sorry." The baby hawk snuggled into her mother's side as the conversation continued. "I can tell you how to get to the home of the Forest People. They will know where to go. To find them find the river that runs west."

The mother hawk remained perched in the tree branch beside her exhausted baby, preening the baby's feathers and checking her over for injuries.

Even though Cynthia hadn't been able to secure a ride or even get very clear directions on how to help Fox find his way home, Cynthia was glad she had helped the hawk. And even though the Forest People weren't what they were looking for, maybe they'd be able to help Fox figure out how to fix his wings in addition to helping both of them find their way home.

Cynthia descended through the feathery branches of the grand fir trees and kept an eye out for the willow tree. A thought occurred to her. Did Fox pick that as a place to sleep because it reminded him of home?

Once she spotted the weeping branches of the willow tree, she flapped her wings to carry herself forward. She parted the branches and glanced around the area to search for Fox. A shaft of sunlight illuminated the mushroom circle where they had slept and where their belongings still lay.

Cynthia landed just outside the mushrooms and stepped toward the fern. She lifted the fern branch and peered inside.

Fox paced beneath the fern. The ray of sunshine illuminated his face. A shadow of Cynthia danced beyond him against the tree trunk.

Fox froze when he realized she had returned. He stared at her with wide burgundy eyes as if seeing her for the first time.

Heat flooded Cynthia's cheeks. He was even more handsome in the daytime than she had thought the night before. The color of his eyes matched the small burgundy freckles sprinkled across his face. His creamy wings with burgundy spots, though damaged, stood out against the shadows and almost glowed where the sunlight shone upon them.

And the way he looked at her made her feel suddenly self-conscious and nervous at the same time. Her stomach did a flip, and she swallowed her nerves.

Why was he looking at her like that? Was he impressed because she had done something kind and returned safely? Or was he about to lecture her again for taking risks? Or maybe her hair and dress looked terrible from her recent ordeal! She ran her hands over her pale blue dress to check for something that might make him look so surprised.

She found nothing out of place. "I told you everything would be alright," she said in a breathy voice, nervous from his intense gaze.

He shook his head. "It's not that," he said in awe. "It's… your wings!"

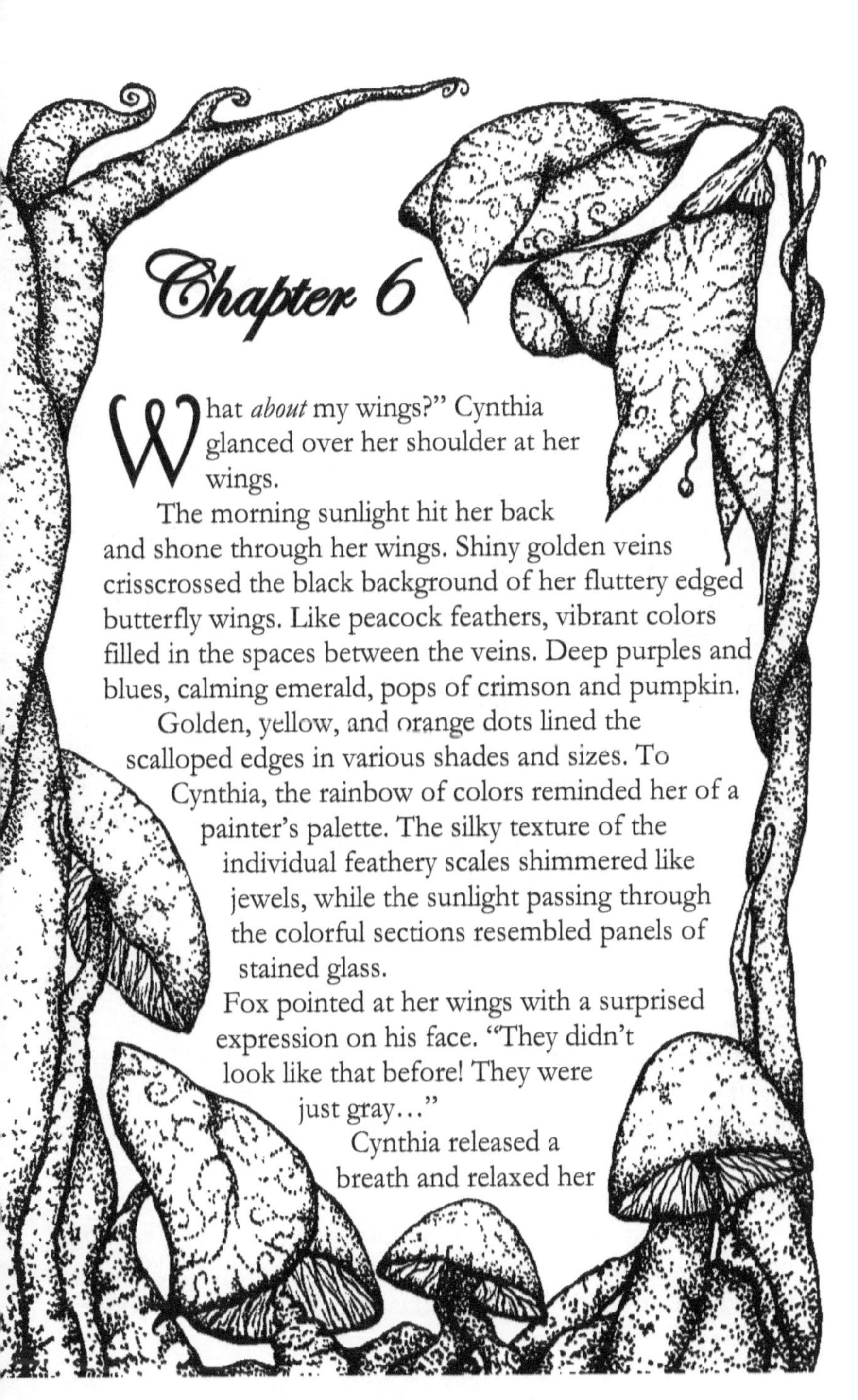

Chapter 6

hat *about* my wings?" Cynthia glanced over her shoulder at her wings.

The morning sunlight hit her back and shone through her wings. Shiny golden veins crisscrossed the black background of her fluttery edged butterfly wings. Like peacock feathers, vibrant colors filled in the spaces between the veins. Deep purples and blues, calming emerald, pops of crimson and pumpkin. Golden, yellow, and orange dots lined the scalloped edges in various shades and sizes. To Cynthia, the rainbow of colors reminded her of a painter's palette. The silky texture of the individual feathery scales shimmered like jewels, while the sunlight passing through the colorful sections resembled panels of stained glass.

Fox pointed at her wings with a surprised expression on his face. "They didn't look like that before! They were just gray..."

Cynthia released a breath and relaxed her

shoulders. She waved away his concerns. "Oh, yeah. They are silver at night, and then they look like this during the day." She turned sideways and slowly flapped her wings so Fox could get a good look.

Her stomach flipped again while he stared at her.

"But... how... What??" He stumbled over his words as his eyes stayed locked onto her wings.

Cynthia furrowed her brow. "Why? What color do your wings change into?" She studied his wings over his shoulder. As far as she could tell, they looked the same.

"Um... they don't change..." he started to say. Then a strange look, almost of recognition, came over his face. His eyebrows shot up. His mouth formed a circle. His hand jumped into his pocket and pulled out something small and round. He glanced at it in his open palm, then shoved it back into his pocket again.

"Let me guess. Not normal, right?" Cynthia sighed.

Maybe nothing about herself was normal. It was already hard enough being a pixie in a human-sized world. Then she found out she's small even for a pixie, she can talk to animals- unlike other pixies, and the fact that her wings change based on the time of day was unusual as well. She wouldn't let all of this get her down, though. Being unique was better than being the same as everyone else. Even if it did make her feel even more "other" than before.

"Definitely not normal." Fox continued to stare at her wings.

Cynthia flinched at his unfeeling words and folded her wings together to make them less conspicuous. He wasn't admiring her wings after all. He just thought she was strange. She had a feeling she would need to continue to remind herself that different was good.

Fox moved his eyes from her wings to her face. When he noticed her troubled expression, his own eyes widened. "That's not what I meant!" He covered his face with one of his hands.

"This is why I don't talk to people," he murmured to himself. He ran his hand down his face and sighed. "It is definitely unique to have wings that change, Cynthia, but that's not a *bad* thing. Your wings are… stunning." His eyes flicked to her wings again, then back to her face. "Trust me," he gulped.

She blushed and ducked her face. Alright, maybe different really *was* good. Or maybe he was just saying that to make her feel better.

Either way, receiving compliments from a good-looking guy like Fox was not something Cynthia was used to. She willed her cheeks not to turn too red and tried to keep a calm expression on her face.

He poked at the ground with one of his bare feet. "So, what was the deal with the hawk?"

"Oh!" Cynthia perked up again. "It was a mother hawk whose baby had fallen into the trees. She needed help finding her baby. I was able to find the baby for her and help them get back on their way. In fact, the mother said…"

"That was really dangerous, you know." Fox folded his arms and frowned at her.

His harsh comment crushed her enthusiasm in an instant.

She blushed, again, but for different reasons. One minute he was making her feel all weak in the knees with his compliments, and the next he made her feel bad for her actions.

"But it wasn't dangerous," she argued in a soft voice. "It worked out fine. Like I was saying, the mother hawk…"

"It won't always work out that way, you know." He lowered his eyebrows into a scowl and looked down his nose at her, his mouth turned down into a frown. "You're too trusting. Some day you will put yourself in more danger than you can get yourself out of. And then what?"

His attitude and facial expression wiped away any sense of belonging she had started to feel at his compliment about her wings. She shrunk again.

Why was she letting his words affect her so much? She had never let anyone else's opinions of her concern her before. What was it about Fox that had changed that?

It must be because he was the only other pixie she had met. A part of her must want to impress him or make him connect with her on some level.

"Like I said earlier," she managed to squeak out. "I can't live my life always thinking the worst about others. What kind of life would that be?"

He stepped past her toward the mushroom circle. As he passed, he mumbled in such a bitter, quiet voice she almost missed it. "At least that way no one will let you down."

Wait. Had he been hurt by someone? Was that why he was being so hard on her? Maybe he didn't *want* to like Cynthia because he was afraid of getting hurt again.

If that was the case, she was sure she could change his opinion about kindness and trust. It might take some time, but their imminent on-foot journey would give her the time she needed to at least try to make a difference for him.

For now, she'd have to push aside his abrupt behavior and rude comments and just try to get to know him. And hopefully help him get to know her. Maybe that would help him let his guard down. Then she could learn more about pixies and possibly emerge from this whole unfortunate situation with a new friend.

Without even thinking, she blurted, "Cynthia is the name of the painted lady butterfly."

He looked over his shoulder at her while he lifted his satchel from the ground. "What?" He regarded her with a confused look.

"My wings?" She turned so he could get a good look at her now stretched-out wings again. "You asked last night what kind of name Cynthia was. Well, that's what kind of name it is. I think it suits me."

She gave him a hopeful smile. Would her efforts to ease his

distrust work? Or would she just get hurt by him in the end? It didn't matter. She had to try or else this whole thing would be a huge mistake.

He shook his head as if trying to clear a fog of misunderstanding and then nodded. "Alright," he said, like he didn't know why he should care.

Cynthia brushed aside her brief disappointment. She would keep trying. She had to. And she shouldn't expect anything drastic on her first attempt. Just like helping an injured animal or tending to a seedling in the garden, she needed to exhibit patience, kindness, and put in the work in order to see any results.

"So, should we head out?" She lifted her own bag from the ground and motioned for them to begin the day's journey on foot in the direction the hawk had suggested. She didn't tell him how she knew which way to go. She didn't want to start *that* whole conversation again. And he didn't question her, either.

For now, she would give him some space, show him that kindness pays off, and help him see the beauty in the world around him. And hopefully they would find a way to fix his wings, too.

The clear sky allowed the sunlight to warm the trees, shrubs, and forest floor, releasing all kinds of sweet smells from the previous moist days the area had experienced. Even though they were well into fall, the air felt warm for which Cynthia was glad. Her lightweight dress had short sleeves and only came to her knees. If the temperature became cold, she'd probably freeze without warmer clothing. Although pixies could withstand more extreme temperatures than their human counterparts, she still wasn't used to frigid weather and didn't want to find out what her cold tolerance might be the hard way.

Wait. Could all pixies withstand temperature changes? Or

was that yet another thing that set Cynthia apart from her kind?

She eyed Fox. With the moderate temperature there was no way to know if he would be bothered by cold or not. She added it to the list of things she wanted to know about pixies.

Cynthia tried to make small talk with Fox about their surroundings, the weather, and his favorite season, but he didn't answer any of her questions with more than one word at a time. He didn't care about their surroundings, he had no opinion about the weather, and he didn't have a favorite season.

She resigned herself to flying above him in silence. At least she could enjoy her surroundings, even if he chose not to.

Before long, the pair stumbled upon a highway, of sorts, through the woods for small creatures like themselves. The mossy ground cover had been worn away into a winding path around obstacles and beneath shady plants.

Cynthia landed beside Fox to inspect their discovery. "What good luck! We can follow it south and it will be so much easier than trying to climb over and under the foliage, mushrooms, rocks, and debris on the forest floor."

She glanced sideways at Fox. Even with his grumpy face, he still looked kind of cute as he decided what to do. She looked away.

He mumbled something about not believing in luck. His ill-tempered expression didn't change.

That was fine. If he wanted to see the worst in everything, he could. She would just try all the harder to point out the good.

He stepped onto the trail and Cynthia chose to walk beside him for a little while. Maybe that would improve his mood.

"See that plant over there?" Cynthia leaned across Fox and pointed off the trail to their right.

A feathery, rose-colored plant grew from a low clump of fuzzy blue-green leaves.

Fox gave the plant a cursory glance and returned his eyes to their path. He didn't acknowledge it otherwise.

"It's called old man's whiskers. You know, because it kind

of looks like a beard? It grows near Magnolia's house, too. It has really pretty bell-shaped flowers in the spring and summer, and then when fall comes, the leaves go from that pale greenish color to deep crimson. It's one of the most beautiful plants you'll find."

She smiled at Fox and waited for him to say something. He didn't say anything. He didn't even nod to show he had been listening.

She let out a silent sigh. Getting him to relax and enjoy himself would be harder than she had expected.

Maybe he didn't want to hear her spout off details about all the plants that she saw, but she smiled and enjoyed the sights for herself, anyway.

Monarch butterflies danced over the tops of the flowering milkweed plants. Based on the time of year, the seed pods would mature soon and burst open. She loved it when the fibers that protruded from the seeds caught the wind and blew away. It was like a dance.

Forget-me-not flowers dotted the sides of the roadway in enormous patches. Cynthia fluttered over them to take in their periwinkle, lavender, and sky-blue blossoms. She loved the way they blanketed the forest floor. One of her favorite things to do back home was spread out a blanket and have a picnic in a huge patch of forget-me-nots. She sighed at the sweet memories.

Fox gave her a funny look, but didn't say anything about her flitting from here to there to admire the nature around them. Eventually though, she returned to the road and walked along beside him.

A chipmunk bounded along the road as they made their way in silence.

"The way they move is so fluid!" Cynthia commented after the chipmunk had passed them.

"If you insist," Fox answered.

They marched past a slow-moving snail.

"I like your shell!" Cynthia complimented the snail on its swirly blue and brown design.

The snail blinked its eyes on the ends of tentacles and nodded its appreciation.

"The colors were so vibrant, wouldn't you agree?" Cynthia said to Fox after they had passed.

"Sure," Fox replied. Then under his breath he said, "It's not like I've never seen a snail before."

"I haven't really traveled much, you know." Cynthia folded her hands in front of her and took long strides to keep up with Fox. "I've mostly stayed in my village and in the woods and meadow around Magnolia's house. I live in the garden."

"You've said," Fox murmured.

She inwardly rolled her eyes at him. Of course, she knew she had told him some of this before, but she couldn't stand just walking along without talking about anything.

"Do you have any neighbors or family where you live?" she asked him.

"No," he snipped.

"Do you live alone, away from *everyone*?" She encouraged him to talk at least a little.

He didn't respond.

She let the silence hang heavy for as long as possible but then couldn't take it anymore. "Well, anyway, I've never seen such a variety of creatures before as I have since I

left home!"

"You mean since you were *captured* and *taken* from your home." Fox frowned at her.

She nodded. "Yes, that's what I mean. I'm just trying to focus on the positive side of my situation."

Why did he have to turn everything into such a negative? Was it so wrong for her to look at the bright side of things, even experiences like being captured? At least her friends had been released. She was sure there were other animals that would help them make their way back. Or else they'd be able to find a safe place to stay until they could.

A new creature approached, heading toward them from the other direction. Cynthia's eyes widened and she squeaked with surprise.

She grabbed Fox's arm, stood on tiptoes, and whispered into his ear. "Does that flower have… *legs?*"

The creature Cynthia referred to looked like a walking flower. Four long, narrow leaves extended from the daisy-like blossom; two longer, two shorter, like arms and legs. It sauntered down the trail, swinging its arms, tall enough that Cynthia tipped her head back when it walked past.

"It's a flowerfolk," Fox answered with no emotion. He didn't even take the time to admire the creature.

She didn't take her eyes off it until it was far down the path behind them. She whipped back around and flew backwards in front of Fox.

He kept his mouth in a straight line, not sharing her enthusiasm for the very first flowerfolk she had ever seen. But at least he wasn't scowling.

"If there are flowerfolk, does that mean there are other kinds of 'folk,' too? Like rocks and trees? How many different flowerfolk varieties are there?"

"So many questions," Fox mumbled. He didn't actually answer any of them.

While she faced the wrong way, she spied another creature approaching from behind. This creature stared at Cynthia the way that Cynthia had stared at the flowerfolk.

Or, more precisely, it stared at Cynthia's wings.

52

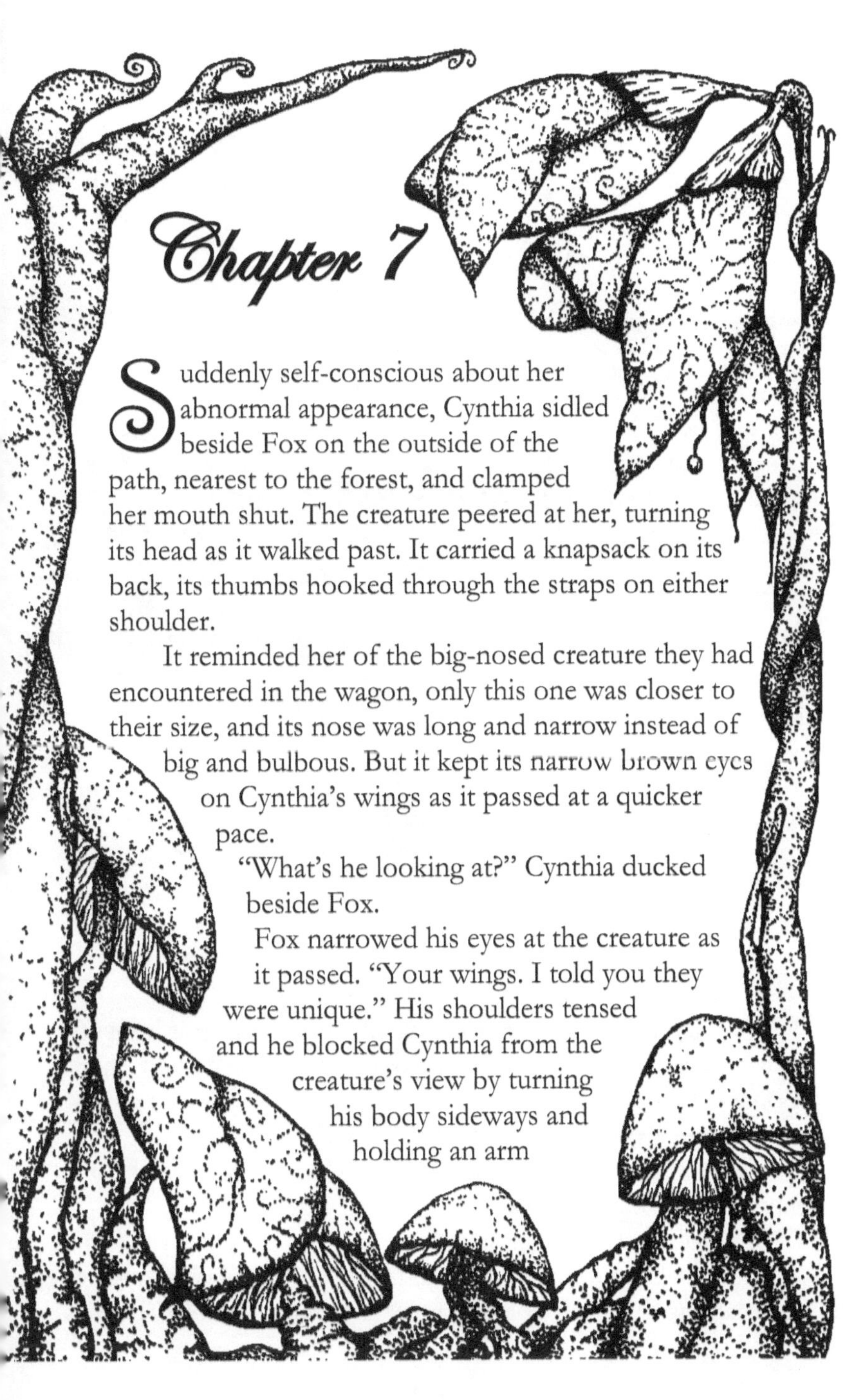

Chapter 7

Suddenly self-conscious about her abnormal appearance, Cynthia sidled beside Fox on the outside of the path, nearest to the forest, and clamped her mouth shut. The creature peered at her, turning its head as it walked past. It carried a knapsack on its back, its thumbs hooked through the straps on either shoulder.

It reminded her of the big-nosed creature they had encountered in the wagon, only this one was closer to their size, and its nose was long and narrow instead of big and bulbous. But it kept its narrow brown eyes on Cynthia's wings as it passed at a quicker pace.

"What's he looking at?" Cynthia ducked beside Fox.

Fox narrowed his eyes at the creature as it passed. "Your wings. I told you they were unique." His shoulders tensed and he blocked Cynthia from the creature's view by turning his body sideways and holding an arm extended until the creature was far ahead of them.

"Why did he make you so uncomfortable?" Cynthia asked, relieved that it was just her unusual wings that caught the creature's attention.

He glanced at her sideways and clenched his jaw.

"I just… didn't like the way he stared. Like you were a prize to be won or something," Fox complained.

Surprised by his protective reaction, Cynthia's heart skipped a beat.

She brushed aside the feeling and shook her head. "You are entirely too *un*trusting."

"Better safe than sorry," he answered curtly.

A bit later, Cynthia greeted a family of jerboas that hopped past them, their long fluff-tipped tails waving behind their mousey bodies.

"The little ones are so cute!" she gushed to Fox.

He didn't respond, although she thought she heard him mutter, "You think anything small is 'so cute.'"

She ignored him. Again.

A pair of chipmunks chattered in the trees above, talking again about Cynthia's colorful butterfly wings. Fox, of course, couldn't understand them, and she didn't want to raise his suspicions about their motives, so she didn't say anything.

But it was curious why so many creatures seemed in awe of her wings. Part of her felt embarrassed. But she pushed those thoughts aside. Her wings were different, which made her different. Made her special, she convinced herself. It lifted her mood to think this way and allowed her to ignore Fox's complaints and murmurings for the entire remainder of the morning.

After a brief lunch and rest on the side of the road underneath a cluster of tall, narrow mushrooms, Fox and Cynthia continued their journey through the afternoon.

As the sun moved across the sky it warmed the air. Less travelers passed by. Cynthia flew just above the road, the breeze keeping her cool under the sunshine.

The season was changing though. There would be more cool days than warm pretty soon. She tipped her head back and basked in the sun. She'd enjoy it as much as she could now before the weather changed.

The road led them to the edge of a body of water. Sunlight glistened off the water, making it sparkle. White water lilies dotted the surface, and where they shadowed the water, Cynthia could see bass swimming just below.

To a Forest Person or human, the water would be considered a pond. But to those closer to pixie-sized, it was a small lake.

"Should we go around?" Cynthia peered at the shore that lined the water. The edges as far as she could see grew thick with sedges and reeds. It would be difficult to travel.

Fox huffed. "Of course, there's a lake in the way."

"Oh, look!" Cynthia pointed to the other side of the body of water. "There's a ferry!"

A flat raft of thick, hollow reed stems, lashed together with the thinner, flexible blades of grass, traveled slowly across the water toward them. A ferryman stood atop, pushing the raft with a long pole that he dipped into the water to nudge the craft along.

Cynthia squinted to see if she could tell what kind of creature he might be, but the sun kept his front in shadow.

"Great. A ferry. This is a massive waste of time. We can just go around." Fox left the packed dirt of the road and began picking his way through the reed grass. It grew as tall as a forest compared to their own size.

Cynthia didn't budge. "Come on, Fox. This will be fun! Besides, you don't know how big the stream is that feeds this pond. We might end up having to cross anyway. At least this way it will be safe!" Would he listen to her and come back?

He turned to face her. "Safe? We don't even know who the ferryman is! We don't know if it's safe. What's 'safe' is keeping control of our journey in our own hands and not putting our safety in the hands of someone else."

She thought about his words for a second. Really, she could just fly over the water. She could just fly all the way to wherever their journey would take them. But Fox couldn't. That was probably frustrating for him. How could she help him see that it made more sense to cross now than to wait until later?

The ferryman moved closer to the shore. Cynthia could see him more clearly now.

"It's... a lizard!" Cynthia gave Fox an incredulous look and motioned him to come back. "Come see!"

He groaned and clenched his fists. "This is ridiculous." He stomped back to stand beside Cynthia.

"Look!" She pointed at the raft that wasn't too far from shore now.

A green, scaly lizard stood on two feet on the raft. It wore a scarf around its neck with loose ends that shivered in the slow breeze. The lizard's tail hung over the back of the raft and trailed in the water. It held the long pole with sharp-clawed hands, while the toes and claws on its feet were thicker and longer.

"Ahoy!" it called to them, waving one of its arms back and forth over its head. "Need a ride?"

Cynthia waved back. "He asked if we need a ride," Cynthia translated for Fox.

"Yes!" she called at the same time that Fox tugged on her am and yelled, "No!" while he pulled her off the road.

"What?" She stopped and stared at him. "Come on, Fox, where's your sense of adventure?"

"I'm afraid I don't *sense* adventure. And besides, I'm not in this for an adventure. I just want to get home."

Cynthia tugged on his arm this time. "Come on. It will be fun, I promise."

"You can't promise that," he countered.

"I can if you choose to let it be fun," she argued back.

He rolled his eyes and muttered. "I shouldn't let you talk me into things like this." But then he stomped back toward the road and the shore of the pond.

Cynthia clapped her hands and skipped to catch up.

Though she could have flown, Cynthia rode the raft beside Fox. Whereas he sat stiffly on the surface of the raft, she kneeled on the edge in order to better peer into the water.

"I see a fish!" she hollered and turned to smile at Fox.

"Imagine that," he mumbled.

The lizard kept his eyes on the pair. It looked like he grinned at them, but it could have just been the way his mouth was positioned on his face. Cynthia paid him little attention and kept her focus on her surroundings instead.

Her eyes and mind wandered as she soaked in everything. The lily pads, the dragonflies skirting just above the water in pairs, those bugs that dance along the surface without sinking, and some sparkly fish below.

"Magnolia should build a pond near our garden," she mentioned absentmindedly, tucking away that idea for when she returned home.

"Those certainly are some unique wings you have there." The lizard's sudden comment jarred Cynthia back to her present situation.

Cynthia turned around to respond to the lizard, when she noticed Fox's reaction.

Even though he couldn't understand the lizard's words, Fox stiffened and narrowed his eyes at the ferryman. "What did he say?" Fox growled at Cynthia.

"Nothing. Just commented on…" Should she tell him? Why did he react this way when he didn't even know what the lizard had said? But she wasn't one for dishonesty. "He just made a comment about my wings."

Fox ground his teeth. "That's what I was afraid of. Stay close. If anything unusual takes place, lift off and fly away. And do not return."

Cynthia crawled to sit beside Fox. Her heart skipped a beat at his nearness.

She ignored her heart's betrayal, and she smiled at the lizard instead. "Thank you," she told the lizard in a kind voice, then turned to Fox.

"What are you talking about? Why are you acting so strange?" she whispered to him. "You are being entirely too judgmental. This man is being nothing but hospitable. There is no reason why anything should happen that would require me to fly away." She frowned at him and shook her head.

Fox didn't take his eyes off the lizard. "Just do as I say. Please." It wasn't so much of a question as it was a command.

Should she argue with him? She didn't like contention, and his unease in the situation made her feel uncomfortable.

"Fine." She pulled her knees to her chest and wrapped her

arms around them.

"Thank you," Fox said.

No one spoke for the remainder of the trip across the pond. When the raft bumped into the shore, it jostled Cynthia out of her confused thoughts and back into the moment.

"Thank you for the ride," Cynthia said as she stood. Her balance wobbled a little on the wiggling raft.

Fox gently held her upper arm to keep her steady, and probably to help himself balance, too. Her arm tingled beneath his touch.

Fox didn't thank the ferryman and dismounted the raft in a hurry.

Cynthia gave him a scolding expression, then turned to the lizard. "What do we owe you for the ride?"

Fox groaned beside her.

She couldn't *not* offer something. Except, they didn't really have anything of value, did they?

Before she could figure out what they could use for payment, the lizard answered his question.

His forked tongue slid out of his mouth as he said, "Oh, you don't have to pay me anything." His squinty eyes gave him a sly look. He muttered, "Knowledge is payment enough."

Fox glared at the lizard while he tugged Cynthia away. "Time to go," he growled under his own breath. He kept his eyes locked on the lizard.

The ferryman blinked his black eyes and gave Cynthia a small nod. "Watch out for the pitcher plants along the shore."

"Um, thanks." Cynthia returned his nod with a weak smile.

This whole situation had been so awkward.

"What did he say?" Fox hissed in her ear as he tugged Cynthia away from the lizard, raft, and pond.

"He said to watch out for the pitcher plants?" Cynthia gave Fox a puzzled look. "What does that mean?"

Fox glared behind them at the lizard, who still watched them as they continued down the road. "It doesn't matter. Let's just keep moving."

They made it a short distance from the pond, but could still see the raft and the lizard, when Cynthia heard a strange frantic crying.

"Do you hear that?" she asked Fox, turning her head side to side to discover the source of the distress.

"Just keep moving," he answered.

She stopped. "Wait. I think its coming from over there." Cynthia moved off the well-traveled road toward a grove of strange looking plants. They grew to triple Cynthia's height and had long, tubular stems that opened wide at the top. They ranged in color from violet to green to burgundy.

One of the strange flowers vibrated, and a disturbing cry came from inside.

"Cynthia, wait!" Fox followed her between the stems toward the sound.

"Someone's in trouble." She ducked beneath a slim green leaf and approached the shaking plant.

As she lifted from the ground to get a better look inside, Fox held her wrist. "Don't get too close. These are pitcher plants. They are a pitfall trap."

"A what trap?" She looked down at him but still hovered with her feet off the ground.

"A pitfall trap. They lure bugs inside and then digest them. They're carnivorous." Fox looked warily at the plant in front of them.

It jiggled. The strange cry came from within.

"Oh!" Cynthia tugged her arm out of Fox's grip. "There must be someone stuck inside!"

She flew quickly to the wide opening at the top of the plant and peered inside.

"No, Cynthia. You don't understand!" Fox sounded frantic below. But with his damaged wings, he couldn't fly up to join her.

She glanced between the flower and Fox and back again. He wanted her to return to the ground. But how would she rescue the poor creature stuck inside the plant if she remained way down on the ground with Fox?

The compulsion to help urged her closer to the plant. She leaned over the opening at the top to try to see what could have gotten stuck inside.

"Stop!" Fox yelled firmly at her. "*This is the trap.* Come back down and let's get out of here!"

His forceful words startled her. She had never heard of a plant tricking people before. But Fox knew more about the world than she did.

After a long look at the plant trying to decide if she should follow her desire to help or listen to Fox anxiously begging for her to return to the ground, she shook her head.

She floated down until she stood beside him again.

He breathed a sigh of relief, took her hand firmly in his own, and dragged her away from the plant.

The pitcher plant no longer shook, and the noise suddenly stopped.

"What does it mean?" She frowned as she watched it over her shoulder.

"It was tricking you to try to help the 'victim' trapped inside of it. But *you* were the victim," Fox explained.

They hurried between the stems and out of the grove of pitcher plants, returning to the road again. Fox immediately released her hand and urged her to hurry down the road and away from the threat.

Strangely, her hand felt empty without his wrapped around it.

Now was not the time for such thoughts though. She analyzed the situation and asked. "So, the lizard was right to warn us?"

"I suppose so," he begrudgingly agreed. He still sounded like he didn't trust the lizard, though.

She couldn't figure out the reason no matter how hard she tried to understand.

A heavy silence hung in the air the remainder of the afternoon as they hurried down the road.

Cynthia's thoughts kept her busy as her wings carried her beside Fox.

Why had Fox been so concerned about traveling on the ferry? And why had he been so suspicious of the lizard the whole time?

The lizard had warned them about the pitcher plants. He had helped them, hadn't he?

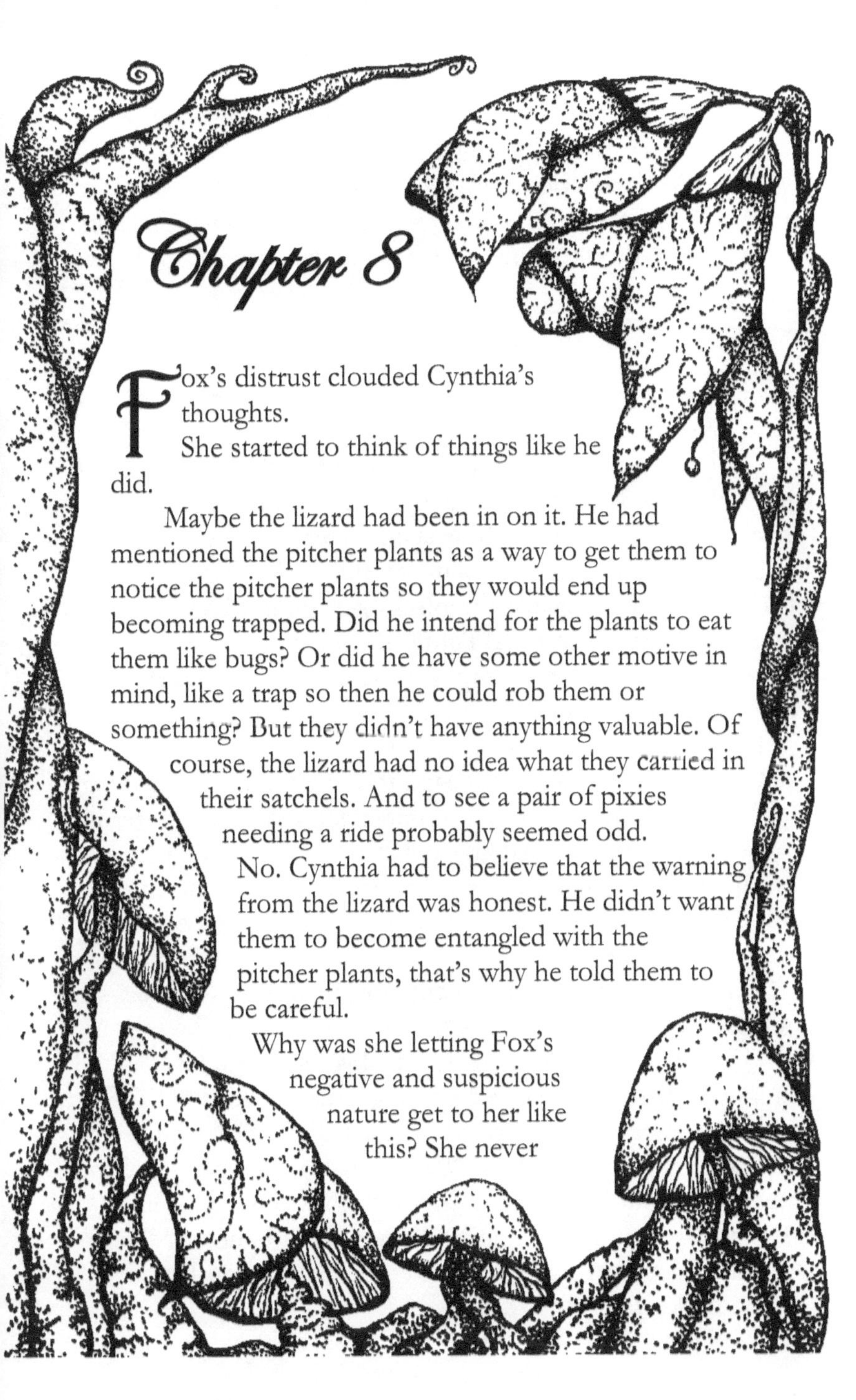

Chapter 8

Fox's distrust clouded Cynthia's thoughts.

She started to think of things like he did.

Maybe the lizard had been in on it. He had mentioned the pitcher plants as a way to get them to notice the pitcher plants so they would end up becoming trapped. Did he intend for the plants to eat them like bugs? Or did he have some other motive in mind, like a trap so then he could rob them or something? But they didn't have anything valuable. Of course, the lizard had no idea what they carried in their satchels. And to see a pair of pixies needing a ride probably seemed odd.

No. Cynthia had to believe that the warning from the lizard was honest. He didn't want them to become entangled with the pitcher plants, that's why he told them to be careful.

Why was she letting Fox's negative and suspicious nature get to her like this? She never thought ill of others. Always saw the best in everyone. Only wanted to help where she could.

But this new view of the world made things more convoluted. How was she to know who to trust? Like Fox said, maybe she *was* too trusting, and it would end up bad for her at some point.

Finally, when the sun began to sink toward the horizon, Fox broke the silence.

"Your wings really do change color based on the time of day." His words came out quietly, like he didn't mean to say them out loud, even though he spoke directly to Cynthia.

She pulled her wings forward so she could glance at them. The bright colors against the black background had begun to fade. The dark background lightened to a pale gray color. The pattern from the colorful shapes remained, but every part of her wings faded until they were both a single silvery gray.

Fox stared at the transformation.

Cynthia blushed under his gaze, too nervous to say anything.

When the transition was completed, Cynthia's butterfly-shaped wings were a solid gray color.

"Incredible," Fox murmured. He made eye contact with her, gulped, and glanced away. "We need to find a secure place to camp for the night."

Cynthia nodded her agreement, not sure if Fox saw it or not, but it didn't seem to matter.

When he turned from her, Cynthia saw that his spotted wings stretched, as if they ached to be useful instead of broken.

He led Cynthia between several clusters of tall, bright yellow mushrooms with small caps. "Be careful not to touch them too much with your hands. They are poisonous when consumed."

"Is that why we're camping in between a bunch of them?" Cynthia folded her hands to avoid touching the mushrooms.

He nodded.

It made sense, she supposed. For safety. But what did they really need to be protected from? No one would pay any attention to a pair of pixies sleeping on the ground!

Fox lit a small fire, filled the thimble with water from his canteen and set it over the hot stones to boil. While the water heated, he used a sharp stone to hack chunks off the single dry bean that Cynthia had brought along. He dropped the chunks into the pot of boiling water and cooked them until they were soft.

"Mash it into a paste or eat it like soup," he said as he scooped some into the bottom of an empty acorn for Cynthia.

He quickly gulped down his own bean soup and discarded the acorn, rinsed out the thimble, and returned it to his satchel.

Very efficient. He didn't even enjoy the meal! Cynthia took her time eating it, but in the end, she understood why Fox had eaten it the way he had. Without any herbs or seasonings, the soup was very bland. She ate the last few bites quickly.

"I have a question for you." Fox waited until Cynthia had discarded her own acorn bowl before he spoke.

She gulped. Was it good or bad that he started the conversation in this way? Normally people just talk. When they tell you they have a question, it's usually something uncomfortable or accusatory. She braced herself for whatever he might say next.

"How do you know where we are going?" Fox pinned her with his stare.

She relaxed. "Oh! That's easy. The hawk told me!" As soon as she said the words, she regretted them.

His eyes darkened and his ever-present scowl deepened. "I should have known," he complained. "You take directions from a predator."

"She wasn't a predator. She was a mother who lost her baby. I helped her. In return she told me how to find the Forest People."

"Find the…" Fox interrupted himself with a deep groan. He ran his hand down his face. "We are supposed to be heading south toward my home. Not trying to find Forest People!" He spoke through gritted teeth.

"If you had given me more clear information about where your home is, I may have been able to ask her for better directions. She said she didn't know where a 'narrow lake near willow trees' is."

"*Dwarf golden* willow trees," Fox corrected her.

Cynthia hadn't felt annoyed like this in a very, very long time. She took a deep breath to calm herself. Was he trying to aggravate her? Perhaps as payback for her constant good mood so far on their journey? She wouldn't give him the satisfaction.

"Right," she agreed. "*Dwarf golden* willow trees. But she said she knew where the Forest People lived. And if we find them, they'd be able to help both of us find our way home. And maybe they'll be able to fix your wings, too." She did her best to keep her words civil, but she was afraid she might not be doing a very good job anymore.

"This is not what we agreed to. Finding the Forest People was never part of the plan." He glared at Cynthia.

What was his problem with the Forest People? Did he not trust them, too?

Cynthia maintained eye contact. "Listen. I don't even know where home is compared to where we were, or even where we are now. The Forest People will help us. They might even be able to get word to Magnolia! And they'll be able to help you with your wings, too. Why is that such a bad thing?"

In her head, she pleaded with him to explain. But she was out of luck. As soon as she said it, he pinched his mouth closed, turned away from her, and pulled his blanket out of his satchel.

"You're too trusting." He snapped at her as he curled onto his side and covered himself with his blanket.

She sighed. How could she help him if he didn't want to be helped? It would be impossible.

She just wanted to go home. And to learn about other pixies in the process. She could find her way home faster without him, but who would be better equipped to tell her what she wanted to know about pixies?

Well, probably a different, less grumpy pixie would, even if he was handsome. And maybe the Forest People would know where one or two were.

But Fox was right here. And as much as he didn't want to admit it, he did need her help. She couldn't just abandon him when they didn't even know where they were.

Her wings and feet were tired after a long day of traveling. But she didn't think she could go to sleep with Fox upset at her. She had to find a way to smooth things over.

"Could you tell me something else about pixies?" she asked in a sorrowful, timid voice.

Would he talk to her?

Silence hung between them. Maybe he was already asleep.

Just when she was about to give up and lay down to rest, too, he rolled over to face her. He stared at her for several long minutes. She remained still, not wanting to do or say anything to jeopardize the potential that he just might talk to her again.

He sighed. Sat up. Leaned against a mossy stone behind him. She found a fallen branch to lean against and tucked her own scrap of a blanket around her shoulders, crossed her ankles, and smiled sweetly at him.

He rolled his eyes and did not return her smile. "What do you want to know?"

"I don't know. Tell me about the different kinds of pixies."

"There are as many different kinds of pixies as there are different kinds of flowers, you know."

She nodded, but didn't say anything.

"Alright. If that's what you really want."

"It is."

He spent the next little while instructing her on the pixies.

His voice came out smooth and calm, so different than his usual harsh, doubting tone. She watched his body relax as he talked. His face softened and she could see that he had subtle smile lines around his eyes. He probably had a dazzling smile when he wanted to.

She admonished herself for becoming distracted by his good looks, and forced herself to listen. She really did want to know about the pixies, after all!

He asked her some questions. "Think about the flowers you know about. Think about Magnolia's garden. What kinds of properties do the flowers have?"

"Healing, soothing." Cynthia listed the uses of flowers. "Some are bright and happy. Some seem gentle and soft."

He nodded. "Right. Those traits are passed on to the pixies born from their blossoms."

He talked about lily pixies and apple blossom pixies. Some of the pixies had scary traits, like poisonous bites, or memory altering songs. Others had kind personalities and healed or soothed.

For someone who doesn't want to talk about it, he sure is telling me a lot. Cynthia's eyes sunk closed as she listened to his soothing voice tell her what seemed like everything about pixies he could think of. *What else would he want to talk about?*

Her mind became vaguely aware of her blanket slipping from her shoulders and her head listing to one side. She slid down the branch and curled up with her back against it on the ground.

Fox's voice continued to hum in her ears. A sudden warmness enveloped her. He had tucked her blanket back around her shoulders.

She drifted to sleep with a smile playing at the corners of her lips.

The following morning, Fox didn't speak much at all. He

must have used up all of his words the previous night. He also avoided eye contact with Cynthia.

It stung to be rejected by him when he had been almost nice to her the night before.

She attempted smiling at him and chatting with him, but it only seemed to bother him more. His frown deepened and his grumbling became more incoherent the more she tried.

Cynthia set aside her hurt feelings, and promised herself that in spite of him, she would have a good day.

She continued to greet passersby on the road. More and more she heard the travelers whisper about her striking wings. A hooved troll wearing a flower on its head stared at her as it walked by. A pair of dragonflies zigzagged past overhead. They too mentioned her wings. A half dozen bees buzzing from daisy to daisy alongside the road paused their work to admire her wings as she walked by.

She didn't say anything to Fox, but his wary eye and glaring looks told her that even though he couldn't understand their words, he knew what was happening.

A family of bright green tree frogs hopped past, going in the opposite direction. The child whispered to her parents, "There she is! I knew it was true!"

Cynthia turned her head to stare at

them the same way they stared at her as they passed.

What did it mean? How did the family coming from the opposite direction know about her like she was famous or something?

Was this why Magnolia had never encouraged her to travel, or taken her anywhere? Was there something *wrong* with her besides just her unusual wings? Why did her wings make her so special?

"Thanks for talking to me last night. It helped me relax and fall asleep." Cynthia walked beside Fox in order to better speak with him.

He grunted a, "You're welcome," but still didn't look her in the eye.

"I was wondering, could you tell me what other pixies *look* like?"

That got his attention. He met her gaze. Her stomach did a little flip at the intensity in his eyes. She ignored the sensation and waited for him to say something.

"That's kind of a broad topic, you know. Every pixie looks entirely different from every other pixie. You might as well ask me to describe every rock at the bottom of a river or every leaf on an autumn tree."

She shook her head. "I know. I don't mean every pixie. But..." She was nervous to say what she was thinking. She didn't want him to think she was being arrogant or proud. But she needed to understand why her wings were so unique. "It's just... my wings. You know? Everyone's talking about them..."

"I noticed." He said in a dark voice.

She shrunk in on herself a little. So, he had known that's what they were all saying. Is that why he avoided her? Did he not want to be associated with her for some reason?

"Please," she said. "What makes my wings so different?"

He stopped on the road and turned to face her. She did the same. He looked her square in the eye. "Different is not always bad. Do you understand this? Your wings are unique. But that doesn't necessarily *mean* anything."

"But *what* makes them unique?" She pleaded with her eyes for him to explain.

He turned and continued walking. "Pixies wings look like part of the flower they are born from. They look like leaves or petals. Some are nearly transparent, but still veiny like leaves. Pepper pixies catch on fire, but they still have a leafy or petal look to them."

"They catch on fire?!" Was he teasing her?

He nodded. "Not relevant to this story." He waved away her disbelief.

If what he said was true, she might be the only pixie with butterfly wings. But why did that *matter*? Why did it make people stare? How did it make her special?

She slowed her steps and lifted herself off the ground to fly instead of walking. She could think better without having to worry about what her bare feet might step on.

Before she could ask Fox any further questions, or bounce any of her ideas off him, he motioned for her to return to his side. "Don't look back, but I think we're being followed."

Chapter 9

Cynthia instantly turned around, of course.

"I said *not* to turn around," Fox hissed at her.

She ducked her head, "Sorry. Instinct, you know?" She grinned at him.

He rolled his eyes at her sappy smile and hid one of his own behind his scowl.

"What makes you think we're being followed?" asked him.

"I can tell," was his only explanation.

"Who's following us?" She tried peeking over her shoulder in a sneakier way this time.

"Seriously, stop," Fox begged.

"Alright, alright." She tried to keep her eyes ahead of them, but it was so hard not to look back!

"A may bug," Fox stated.

"A may bug?" Cynthia looked up at him.

"That's who's following us. A may bug."

"But why would a

may bug be following us?" Cynthia doubted Fox's suspicions. It didn't make sense for anyone to be following them, let alone a may bug. Unless he just wanted a look at her wings, too.

"I can just… tell." Fox glanced sideways at her.

"Fine, don't tell me why you think a may bug is following us…" She stepped slightly ahead of him.

He easily caught up, of course.

"I don't know *why* it's following us, but I assure you, it is."

Cynthia shook her head. "Maybe it's just going the same way we are." She continued to resist the urge to turn around again.

Fox sighed.

"What?" She paused and waited for him to explain.

"Like I said, you're too trusting. It's following us. We need to find a way to lose it, or for it to lose us." Fox began scanning their surroundings almost frantically.

"Come on. We don't need to hide. If anything, we should just turn around and ask it…"

Before Cynthia could finish her sentence, or Fox could argue with her, a sudden jarring rumble shook the air behind them.

Cynthia ducked and clapped her hands over her ears. She turned to see the source.

The may bug had lifted off the ground. Its hard outer wings connected with its body in a "V," and its larger, thinner wings flapped with a repetitive pulse that made the hairs on the back of Cynthia's neck stand on end. Its catlike eyes had locked onto Cynthia.

Fox took one look at the bug that darted toward them. He threw his arm over her shoulders and pulled her from the road.

The loud hum followed.

They darted past a rock nearly as tall as Cynthia and crunched through a blanket of brown leaves.

The bug zig zagged in the air. It dove close, then burst upward again.

"I told you it was following us!" Fox shouted over the racket into her ear.

Cynthia glanced over her shoulder. She screeched at its nearness.

"Cynthia! This way!" Fox pulled her past a dewberry plant and away from the may bug.

She tripped on her own feet as she tried to dodge the may bug that now hovered directly overhead.

She stumbled onto her knees.

Fox lost contact with her.

The may bug wrapped its pointy legs around her torso and plucked her from the ground. A sense of triumph flashed in her mind before it vanished.

Fox darted toward the bug with a large stick in both hands, holding it like a club. He smacked the may bug with it over and over to try to get it to release Cynthia, but the club bounced off the shell-like exoskeleton that protected the may bug like a shield.

"Cynthia!" Fox yelled as the bug carried Cynthia higher away from him.

From the look of pain on Fox's face and the twitchy movement of his broken wings Cynthia could tell that he was trying to fly. But it was no use. His wings were broken, and they would not carry him off the ground.

He shouted and shook his fists into the air, desperate to do something to save her, but she remained helpless in the may bug's steely grip as it carried her away until Fox was only a speck below.

"Caught you," the may bug's scratchy voice said right above her.

Cynthia gripped the may bug's hard, black legs with both hands, afraid that her own wings had been damaged. If the bug let go, would she plummet to the ground far below?

"Why did you capture me?" she pled in a frantic voice.

The may bug shifted his legs around her.

She screeched in panic and clung on even tighter. If he

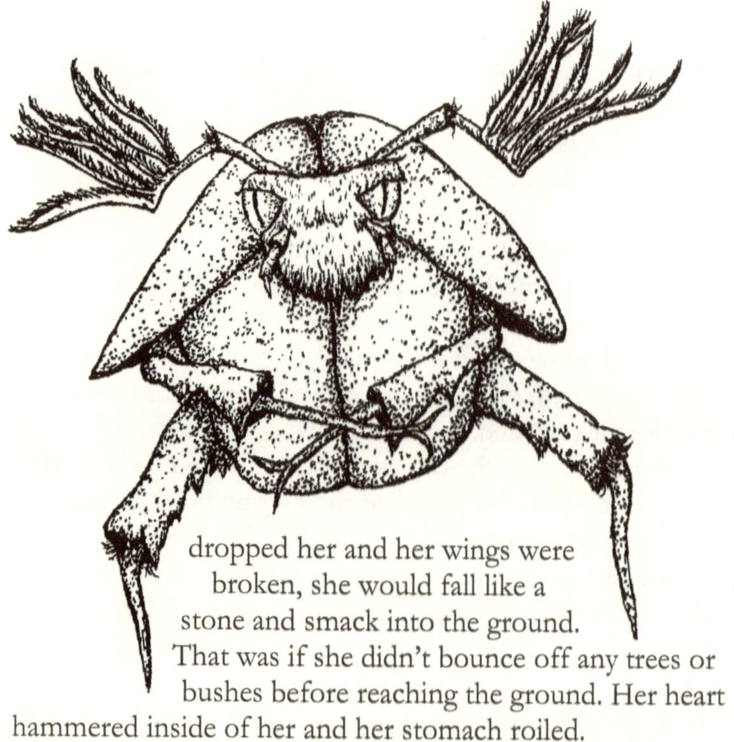

dropped her and her wings were
broken, she would fall like a
stone and smack into the ground.
That was if she didn't bounce off any trees or
bushes before reaching the ground. Her heart
hammered inside of her and her stomach roiled.

The may bug dipped as he flew, clearly struggling with her added weight. He bobbed up and down in the air, giving Cynthia terrible visions of falling to her death each time.

"There's a bounty on the pixie with butterfly wings," the may bug said between strained grunts from holding on to her and flying at the same time.

What? A bounty? Why? What did he mean by that? Someone wanted her captured? For what purpose? Was it for her wings, because they were rare?

When she had organized her frenzied thoughts, she said, "But why? I am not anything special."

The may bug paused in the air, dipping dangerously fast, as if her words had shocked him. "What do you mean?" he rasped. "You're supposed to be powerful. The price for your safe delivery is high."

Strangely, that gave Cynthia a small sense of relief. At least whoever mistakenly wanted her didn't want her dead. All she had to do was stay calm. Not panic. And come up with some way to get herself out of this. She could do it.

Fox would probably scoff at her positive thinking in this situation. She inwardly smirked, but then the thought wilted. Another glance down confirmed that she couldn't see him anywhere.

"So, what are your magical powers?" the bug asked her in a conversational way, as if he hadn't just snatched her from the ground and hauled her away against her will.

Should she tell him that she didn't have any? What would he do when he found out the truth? Would he just let her go? And if her wings *were* damaged, would she be able to stop herself from falling to her death?

But she wouldn't mislead this creature either. Maybe if she was nice enough to him, he would take her back to Fox and let her go. She just had to figure out the right words.

"The truth is…" She started to explain. What would he do if he didn't like what she had to say? She braced herself for the worst.

Before she could say anything else, an arrow sung as it whizzed past the pair and higher into the air.

The bug just managed to dodge it, almost losing his grip on Cynthia in the process.

She screamed and pushed herself back into the safety of the bug's arms.

Another arrow shot past. It nicked the bug's hard wings but bounced off harmlessly.

"Your friend is quite persistent," the bug complained.

What? She strained to catch a glimpse, but didn't see anything but forest. But if what the may bug said was true, then that meant *Fox* was shooting the arrows? Where did he even get them? Why was he trying to save her? Did he really think he'd be able to from way down there?

"Listen!" Cynthia decided that telling the truth as quickly as possible would be the best way to save the bug's life, and possibly her own, too. "I don't have any powers! I am just a regular pixie, plain and simple!"

The may bug didn't respond. He dodged another arrow and shifted her weight in his legs again. "That doesn't sound right. All pixies have powers."

Cynthia could almost feel the may bug's confusion and alarm inside herself.

"It's true!" Cynthia yelled. "You can take me if you really want to, but in the end, I doubt you'll receive whatever prize you seek when they realize you've captured the wrong pixie. What do you think will happen to you if you bring back the wrong pixie? How much do you value your own well-being? Enough to risk returning empty handed? Anyone that would want to capture pixies surely wouldn't think the life of a may bug is worth anything, either, right? Please! You must reconsider!"

The bug listened to Cynthia's cries as he dodged arrow after arrow, but he didn't respond. Several bounced off his hard outer wings; one whooshed between his feathery antennae. His legs momentarily slackened around her torso.

She let out a scream and tightened her grip. This was not going well!

"Please! Just release me! What if one of the arrows hurts you? What will you do then? Even if I was the right pixie-which I'm not!- you wouldn't be able to fly! Then where will you be? You'd be better off letting me go. Maybe you'll find another butterfly-winged pixie. Or better yet, don't collect bounties at all! Find honest work. I'm sure the Forest People would have something for you to do…"

The bug hummed as he thought through everything Cynthia had just thrown at him while he dodged the dangerously more accurate arrows from below. "I heard that the woman who seeks you is ruthless. A sorcerer of sorts. There's no telling what she'll do to me if I show up with the wrong quarry…"

"See? It's really not worth it! Just lower me to the ground and fly away. My friend won't harm you if you let me go. I promise!" She had no business making that kind of promise, but she could probably convince Fox to just let the bug fly away without trying to shoot it anymore.

The bug started to sink lower, but then he must have changed his mind. "Actually, I think I'll give it a try. You've got to be worth something!"

He dodged another arrow, but then the last one hit him squarely on one of his legs.

He dropped from the sky, just managing to keep himself from crashing to the ground at the last second.

Cynthia screamed and squeezed her eyes shut. "I'm telling you! I'm not worth it!" she cried.

The may bug stopped just above a tall white daisy. Another arrow shot past his head. He flinched.

Cynthia flinched, too.

Before she could beg any longer, the may bug opened his legs and released her. "You're right, you're not worth it."

Cynthia dropped onto the top of the daisy before she could test her wings. She collapsed onto her hands and knees. Her wings drooped on either side of her body.

"Thank you, Mr. May Bug." She breathed out in relief. "Your kindness will surely not go unrewarded. These things always have a way of evening themselves out. Good fortune will find you, no doubt, if you continue to try to do what's right."

"Yeah, we'll see." The may bug beat his wings with a loud hum and flew away faster than Cynthia thought possible.

She collapsed onto her stomach and buried her face in her hands.

What had just happened? Why did some lady want her captured? What would she have done if the may bug hadn't decided to let her go? Was it Fox that had shot the arrows? It had to be. No one else would have. And she didn't even want to think about the potential damage to her wings from the whole ordeal. Maybe she *would* be walking alongside Fox for the remainder of the journey, instead of hovering most of the time above the ground.

Calm down, Cynthia. You're getting ahead of yourself. No need to panic.

She controlled her breathing until she had calmed herself down. She braced herself for the potential pain, and rested her wings, too scared to think about what she would do if they had been ruined.

She stretched them to their full width without any pain. So far, so good.

She started to lift herself off the daisy, when a voice called from below. "Cynthia! You're alright! Thank goodness!"

"Fox?" Cynthia hovered above the flower and flew over the top of it until she could see the ground.

The range of emotions that flickered across Fox's face surprised her as she lowered herself to the ground to stand in front of him. When had he decided to care so much about her well-being? Certainly, he could actually find his way home safely without her help.

He startled her when he dropped his bow to the ground, gripped her shoulders with both hands, and scanned her with his eyes to make sure she was in one piece.

He had been the one to shoot arrows at the may bug!

She resisted the urge to ask him where he got the bow and arrows and instead rested a hand on each of his arms. She met his eyes as he returned his gaze to her face.

"I'm safe, Fox," she breathed, convincing herself just as much as him.

He closed his eyes and sighed with relief. When he opened them, his eyes met hers again. "I thought you were... I was afraid..."

"I know," she said quietly. "Me, too."

Silence hung between them for several beats.

Cynthia's mind tried to make sense of everything that had just happened, both with the may bug and with Fox's reaction to the whole thing.

Before she could come to any conclusions, Fox's eyes glanced at his hands on her shoulders and her hands on his arms. He cleared his throat, dropped his hands, and stepped away from her.

Was he about to say something to her? Express relief for her safe return? Or maybe lecture her again for being too trusting. But she hadn't done anything wrong this time.

"What did the may bug want?" he asked with concern. "Did he think you were a butterfly? I didn't think may bugs hunted butterflies…"

"He was a bounty hunter," she interrupted him. "Apparently, there's a reward for the pixie with butterfly wings."

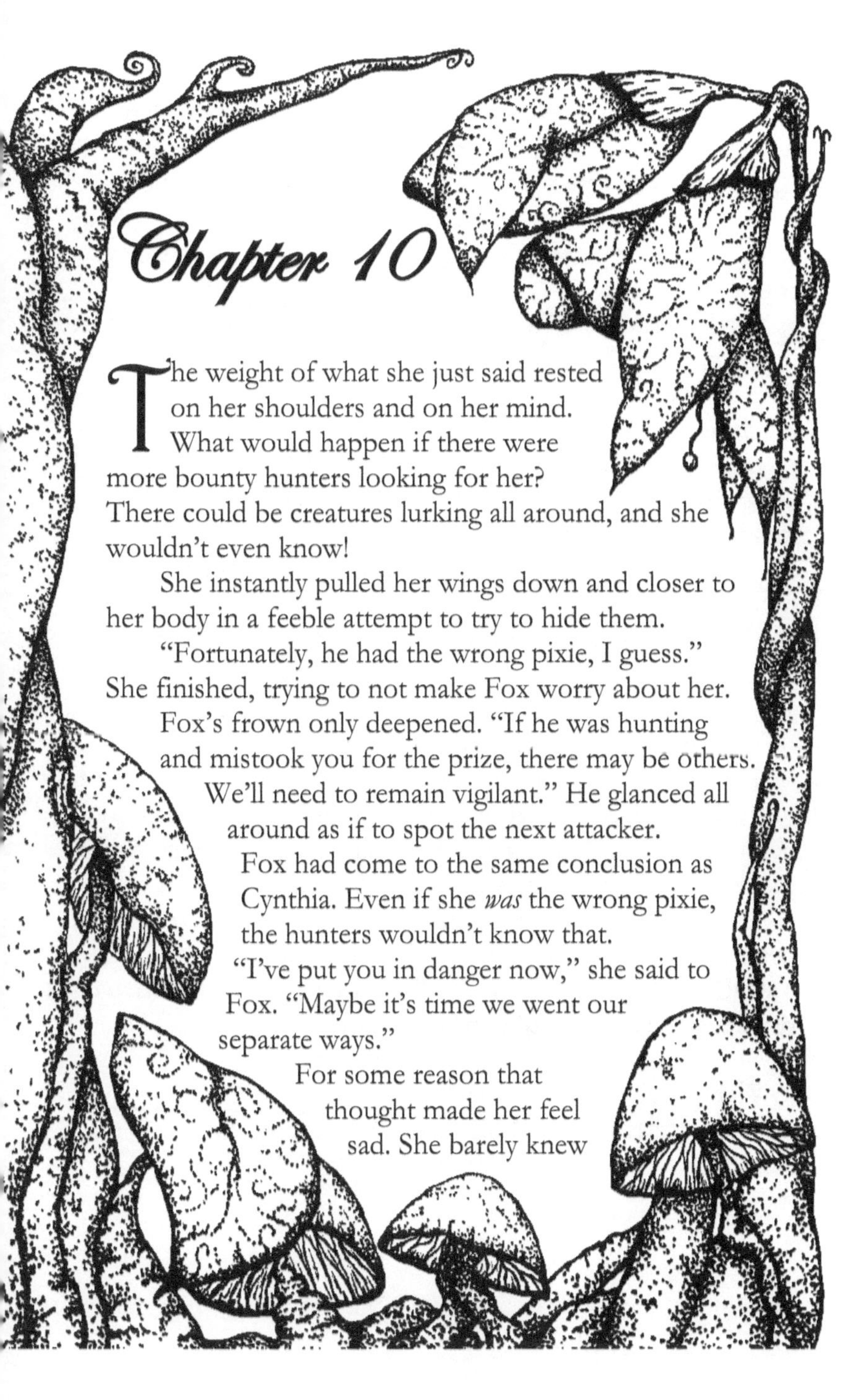

Chapter 10

The weight of what she just said rested on her shoulders and on her mind. What would happen if there were more bounty hunters looking for her? There could be creatures lurking all around, and she wouldn't even know!

She instantly pulled her wings down and closer to her body in a feeble attempt to try to hide them.

"Fortunately, he had the wrong pixie, I guess." She finished, trying to not make Fox worry about her.

Fox's frown only deepened. "If he was hunting and mistook you for the prize, there may be others. We'll need to remain vigilant." He glanced all around as if to spot the next attacker.

Fox had come to the same conclusion as Cynthia. Even if she *was* the wrong pixie, the hunters wouldn't know that.

"I've put you in danger now," she said to Fox. "Maybe it's time we went our separate ways."

For some reason that thought made her feel sad. She barely knew

Fox, but she wasn't ready to leave him yet, either. If she left him now, she knew she'd never see him again. Perhaps it was because he was the only other pixie she knew. What if she never met another one? How would she get her questions answered? And she couldn't deny the fact that it would be nice to have a friend like herself.

But he had wanted her to leave him from the beginning. Her heart sank and her throat squeezed as she prepared herself to take flight and find her way back home to Magnolia's garden.

"No." Fox's voice was firm.

She shot her eyes to his face. "What?" she breathed.

"Absolutely not. They'll be hunting the skies for a pixie, not looking for one beneath the canopy. We just need to stay off the roads, travel through the woods, and keep pressing forward."

Cynthia didn't even stop to think about her next action before she took it. She lunged toward him and wrapped her arms around his torso, careful not to touch his damaged wings on his back. "Thank you, Fox!" she murmured against his chest.

He smelled like sunshine and rain and pine needles. Her heart fluttered, but she dismissed the sensation as a reaction to her abduction and his attempt at rescuing her. Or, just maybe, the fact that he might consider her a friend.

He stood stiff as a board until she released him. A part of her was sad he hadn't wrapped his arms around her. Maybe he only thought of her as a smaller-than-usual pixie that needed his protection. But she could hope for more.

She stepped away. "Truly, thank you, Fox."

Fox gave her a confused look that she couldn't quite understand, then cleared his throat. He glanced skyward at the gray clouds. "The weather is changing. We need to keep moving."

Cynthia stayed close to Fox on the ground as they hurried

away from the patch of daisies where the may fly had deposited Cynthia. Fox stayed quiet and alert as they hurried through the forest of fuzzy daisy stems.

Fox constantly surveyed their surroundings, made sure Cynthia stayed right beside him, and several times made them stop and listen before they continued.

To break the tension, she poked Fox on the arm. "Where'd you get the bow and arrows?"

He gave her a surprised look. "Out of all the questions you could ask, that's the one you go with?" He sounded confused.

She shrugged and gave him a small smile. "It seemed like the least loaded question, you know? I want to know about the bounty hunter and why I'm being hunted. Or what my abilities might actually be. But it's not like you'd be able to answer any of those questions. So, I'm sticking with one that you can answer.

"I repeat: Where'd you get the bow and arrows? Did you make them yourself? Have you had them with you the whole time?"

Fox stared at her but didn't say anything at first. He sighed. Kept his eyes scanning their surroundings.

Finally, he answered. "I've had it for a long time. I did make them myself. They've been in my bag since we met."

"I figured as much." Cynthia smiled a little bigger at him. "You're a pretty good shot. I was worried you'd hit me though…"

He frowned. "I knew what I was doing."

She glanced at the bow loaded with an arrow that he held with one hand. "Still. Weapons make me nervous. Is it necessary to carry it?"

He nodded. "Yes." He didn't offer an explanation.

He was really that worried about her that he had to carry a weapon to defend them?

"I really don't want anyone getting hurt…" She pushed for

him to put it away.

"No one will get hurt. Unless they deserve it," he growled.

She relented. If he felt like he had to carry it, she wouldn't say anything else. And although the idea of being hunted made her nervous, she didn't know if it was serious enough to warrant a weapon. Or the defensive manner in which they traveled.

But Fox seemed like he knew what he was doing, so she'd let him take the lead.

The sooner they found the Forest People, she concluded, the better.

Fox poked at the campfire he had built inside a hollow log that night. "I've known you for less than a week and already you've gotten into more trouble than I have in years."

"I haven't gotten into that much trouble..." Cynthia disagreed as she ate her half dozen roasted pine nuts. The warm nuts felt so good in her belly. Her feet were sore from walking so much, even though she did fly alongside Fox for a good portion of the day to give her feet a break.

He scoffed. "You were captured by that miserable human man. That creature in the wagon had a rope tied around your feet. You nearly got eaten by a hawk. And you were kidnapped by a may bug. Not to mention the way the other creatures looked at you as we walked, and the fact that for some inexplicable reason, there's a bounty out for you! Seriously, it's like you attract trouble wherever you go." He licked his fingers as he finished eating his own pine nuts, too.

It's not like she had asked for any of those things to happen. And although some of the situations were of her own making, others were completely out of her control. But one thing stood out that he hadn't mentioned.

"If that's so, then *you* would be the biggest trouble I have attracted so far!" she teased.

His eyes darted to hers. "What do you mean?" He frowned.

She blushed at her words. She had messed up. Again. One thing she seemed to be really good at was saying something to make Fox's mood worse.

"I mean, helping *you*." She tried to recover from her mistake. "If I hadn't decided to help you, then half of those things wouldn't have even happened to me!" She kept her voice light to try to lighten the mood and distract him from the fact that she had implied that he was *attracted* to her in any way.

Wait, what? Where had that thought come from! That's not what she had meant *at all!* Was it possible that's what he had thought, though? Her blush deepened. Hopefully he wouldn't notice.

His shoulders relaxed a little and he looked at the fire again. "Right. Because *I'm* so much trouble. I did tell you I didn't need any help." He poked the fire with a stick.

That was true. But then he had suggested she stay... It wasn't worth bringing up, though.

Cynthia watched the sparks dance in the darkness as they floated upwards. It made her want to join them. To stretch her now-pale wings and really fly. She gazed at the cloudy night and let her mind wander from their current situation and reminisce about soaring high in the air.

"You could go now, you know," he said in a quiet voice.

"Hmm?" she asked, keeping her eyes on the sky and imagining floating above the trees.

"I see your wings stretching. You want to fly. It's dark, and your wings look... different now. No one would recognize you..." He continued to prod at the fire, sending more sparks upward.

She returned her gaze to him. *Did* he want her to leave? Why was he saying this? Was it just that obvious that she wanted to fly? But she didn't want to fly *away!*

What should she say? Should she tell him that she wanted to stay... with *him*? She finally had a connection with someone like herself. A friend that could really relate to her, at least to some degree.

He cleared his throat. "Now would be the best time, you know…"

Her heart skipped a beat. Could she do it? Could she leave?

She inwardly recoiled at the thought. She wouldn't leave him. She wasn't ready to give up on the potential friendship he had to offer. And the chance to help him heal his wings. And his heart.

She stretched her arms and wings and let out a yawn. "I'm actually really tired. It's been a long couple of days you know." She winked at him and gave him a mischievous grin.

He rolled his eyes and sighed but did not return her smile.

"I'm going to try to get some sleep." She settled herself beside the fire and allowed the heat to warm her from the outside, while, all on their own, thoughts of wrapping her arms around Fox warmed her heart from the inside.

Just as she drifted to sleep, she heard him whisper in a tender voice so different than his usual gruff and skeptic tone, "Goodnight, Cynthia."

Fox grumped through the woods in the morning, grumbling about the damp ground, the acorns and nuts that littered the forest floor that he had to step over, and the inability to maneuver easily through the underbrush.

They had made it well beyond the daisy field and found a gully in the woods. Fox did his best not to slip on the damp-with-dew fall leaves that blanketed the floor. Without the use of his wings, traveling through the terrain had become difficult.

"I wish we had a map," he complained. "Then we could really know if we were heading in the right direction."

"No need," Cynthia chirped. She flew skyward to assess their surroundings.

"Cynthia! Don't! It's too dangerous." Fox called after her,

frustration lacing his words.

She ignored his pleas and hovered in the air to get their bearings.

Thick clouds rolled across the horizon from far to the east, but the place they traveled still had clear skies and good weather. It didn't look like it would last, though.

The hawk had said to follow the river, and she could just make out the tell-tale break in the forest not more than a day's journey ahead of them. They were still headed in the right direction.

Once they found the Forest People, Fox could get his wings fixed and then he'd be able to continue on home.

And then she would go back home, too. Except, there were no other pixies back home. What she wouldn't give to live around other pixies. And not just a *certain* other pixie, she told herself, no matter how much she liked his broad shoulders and buttery hair.

She returned moments later to a deep scowl from Fox.

"How am I supposed to protect you from way down here if something were to happen while you were up there?" he grumbled.

"You seemed to do just fine the last time, shooting arrows like an archer," she answered in a cheerful voice.

He grumbled something under his breath in reply, and Cynthia hid a smile from him.

"Just promise me you won't put yourself in too much danger, alright?" he finally said out loud.

"I promise I won't put myself in too much danger," she grinned. "But I won't promise to stay stuck to your side either." She giggled at his scowl. "Here," she offered him a giant huckleberry. "You need more food in your belly to help with your mood."

"My mood is just fine," he complained.

She smirked at him.

He scowled at her and rolled his eyes.

"I'm sorry!" She giggled with a hand covering her mouth. "You're just so cute in the morning when you're like this!"

Her smile froze. Her face warmed. She had just told him he was cute!

Apparently, he hadn't noticed the meaning of her words. Which meant it was time to change the subject. "I'll give you time to wake up before I start teasing you for real, how's that?"

"Fine." His brow stayed lowered over his eyes and his mouth continued to frown.

They continued in silence for another hour before Cynthia couldn't take it anymore.

"Are you ready to be social?" she asked him in a sweet, teasing voice.

He rolled his eyes in response but didn't frown like he had been earlier.

"Good. So. I told you about my name. Now, you get to tell me about yours. Why are you called Fox?"

He heaved a deep sigh that seemed more forced than before, as if he was putting on a show of not wanting to talk about it, but really, he didn't mind. Good. She was getting him to let his guard down.

"I'm a Foxglove Pixie. Hence the name Fox."

She waited for more.

He didn't continue.

"And…?" she prodded.

"And… what?" he asked.

"And if pixies have magical powers, then what are yours?" she questioned.

"We don't have 'magical powers.' We adopt the essence of the flower we are born from which manifests as abilities. Each pixie is different, even if they're born from the same kind of flower."

"Right. Like I said, magical powers. So… what are yours?" She wiggled her eyebrows at him.

He suppressed a smile by pinching his lips together. A cute dimple appeared on one side of his face.

Her stomach did a little flip. She pushed it back into place with her thoughts and focused on the conversation instead of his dreamy dark eyes and tiny burgundy freckles.

What was coming over her? He was a friend. A *cute* friend who had become overly protective of her, sure, but still. Just a friend. She forced herself to focus on his words and not the fluttering of her heart.

"Well, foxglove flowers are considered a symbol of insincerity or deceit. The flowers can be toxic to larger animals and humans if consumed in large quantities. But the bell-shaped flowers can represent purity and grace. So, the flower symbolizes both healing and toxicity."

Cynthia hadn't been expecting such a detailed answer and forced herself to pay attention.

"Some foxglove pixies can heal; others have toxic saliva. Some can only tell the truth while others are prone to deceitfulness. There's a wide range of possibilities."

Cynthia's heart stilled. Was Fox a deceitful pixie? Was *he* the one trying to trick her by making her not trust everyone else?

"So… what are your not-magical-powers?" She tried to keep the mood light.

He stopped in his tracks and turned to face her.

This was it. She was about to find out the truth. Either he was toxic and deceitful, or helpful and healing. Which was it going to be?

She held her breath while she waited for his reply.

Please let him be a good guy! Her heart couldn't take it if he wasn't, not when she was just starting to have feelings for him…

"Everyone lies, Cynthia. *Everyone.*" His eyes darkened and he stepped closer to her.

Chapter 11

Was he threatening her? Or trying to tell her something? About himself, or everyone else? Did he think *she* was a liar?

"I don't believe that," she whispered and maintained eye contact.

His dreamy eyes had turned dark. The dimple in his cheek had disappeared.

She waited for him to do or say something else. To explain his strange behavior. But he didn't. He broke eye contact and stepped away from her.

Maybe a part of him had been trying to convince her to leave this whole time because *he* was untrustworthy, but he didn't want to hurt her in the process. Or maybe he really was a good guy, and he truly wanted to protect her.

She searched her feelings. For some reason, she truly did trust him. Her head told her it was foolish, especially because of his odd behavior at times, the way he looked at her sometimes like she was important, and other times like she was a bother. But her heart firmly believed he was trustworthy, even if she didn't understand why.

If only she could have asked him these questions. But his body language as he adjusted his bag on his shoulder remained closed off. He was done talking to her.

"We need to keep going." He turned to look at her again and frowned.

Great. He was about to try to send her off again.

"We should probably cover your wings, though. So you are less conspicuous. Especially if there are others looking for you."

"Oh!" she exclaimed. That wasn't what she had expected! "Yeah, that's probably a good idea."

She turned in a circle and pinched her lips. How could she cover her wings? Maybe that fabric he had found for her to use as a blanket?

"You can use these leaves." He handed her two large maple leaves, still green and soft with just a ribbon of orange at the tips. "You saw how people travel, wearing flowers and leaves for adornments and protection. It won't be out of the ordinary if we do happen to come across anyone."

She gave him a big smile.

He didn't acknowledge it.

"It's perfect!" She attached the leaves like a cape to her back. Then her smile fell. "That means no more flying. At all." She could already feel her feet throb from the excessive walking she would be doing from now on.

"We'll rest as needed," Fox said quietly. "Ready?"

She nodded and followed him through the underbrush, around patches of forget-me-not flowers, and over decaying logs and fallen tree branches. The going was slow. Her feet weren't used to all the walking. But if Fox could do it without complaining, so could she.

Her mind focused on Fox. On the way he had told her that everyone lies. He really believed it. But it wasn't true, was it?

Magnolia didn't lie. She was pretty quiet in general, and didn't say much to anyone, but she was never dishonest.

Why did Fox believe so strongly that everyone lies? And did that *everyone* include him?

She spent the next couple of hours watching him as they walked through the woods in silence. Would anything about his behavior give Cynthia a clue into whether she could trust him? She believed he was a good guy. But then, she believed the best in everything and everyone she came across, lately getting herself hurt or disappointed in the process.

If Fox turned out to not be trustworthy, then she would end up more than disappointed. She could end up in real danger.

But if his intent was to put her in danger, why had he protected her on several occasions? Why had he both insisted she leave to protect herself, and invited her to stay?

A thought occurred to her just then. She still didn't know how his wings had become damaged. Had he been a prisoner like herself, and the brownies had released him? She would have known he was a prisoner, though. Or had something else happened to him? Who *was* he?

And what about his secret pixie ability? She watched him carefully to see if he could magically grow plants, change his appearance, or control any elements. He definitely didn't have a magical voice or extra strength or anything. Not knowing much about pixies and what other abilities might be, it was too hard to guess.

Eventually the extreme ache in her feet drove all other thoughts from her mind other than wanting to give her feet a break by flying.

"Maybe I don't need the leaves." She squirmed beneath the leaves, wishing she could stretch her wings and fly even for just a few minutes.

"You do need the leaves," he stated.

Doubt seeped into her thoughts. Was he deceitful? Maybe he was trying to slow her down and wear her out on purpose. To make her easier to subdue.

She brushed those thoughts aside. She wouldn't let those doubts remain. She believed Fox to be good underneath his rough exterior. The brief moments of tenderness she had seen and heard over the past two days showed at least some kindness inside of him.

"Would it really hurt to fly for just a little bit?" she said, instead of voicing all of her other thoughts like she really wanted to. "I mean, there can't be too much harm."

"Shh!" He cut her off with a swipe of his hand. His eyes fixated to the bushes up ahead. "I heard something."

Cynthia listened carefully to hear whatever it was that caused Fox so much alarm.

She shook her head. "I don't hear anyth…"

He gestured with his hand for her to be quiet.

She pressed her lips together and stepped closer to Fox's side. If there were more bounty hunters, she would get her wish, lose the leaves, and fly again. Only she'd be leaving Fox behind. That was the last thing she wanted.

They took careful steps forward as they approached the place where Fox's eyes were directed. He held the bow loaded with an arrow in front of him, pointing to where he had heard the sound.

Cynthia's palms sweated and her heart pounded. She kept her eyes and ears open to anything out of the ordinary, ready to spring skyward at a moment's notice.

A twig snapped. The leaves of the bush trembled.

Cynthia released the leaves from her back and stretched her colorful wings. If it was a bounty hunter, there would be no denying who she was anymore.

Fox put his arm out in front of Cynthia, putting himself between her and the bush, then pulled back on the arrow, ready to release it into the bushes.

Cynthia finally heard the sound that Fox must have heard before. A mewing sound.

"Fox," she whispered. "That sounds like a cat or something. It sounds like it might be injured?"

He glared at her over his shoulder and widened his eyes, telling her with his expression to be quiet.

Sorry, she mouthed.

But she nodded toward the bush and shook her head. She really didn't think there was a threat.

The mew turned into a soft cry.

Cynthia sucked in a breath. "It's in pain, Fox. I bet we can help." She brushed past him and ducked beneath the branch of the bush.

Fox lowered his bow so that an arrow wouldn't be loaded and ready to shoot into her back as she passed.

She paused and looked back at him. "Are you coming?"

With a deep sigh and grumbling under his breath, Fox followed Cynthia into the underbelly of the prickly bush.

Fox muttered things about Cynthia being too trusting, putting herself in danger, making unwise decisions.

Cynthia ignored him. She was sure about this. Her stomach squeezed. At least, she had been. Fox's doubt started to seep into her own head.

"That's... not a cat." Fox froze when the pair came face to face with the creature that was, indeed, in need of help.

Cynthia smiled. Relief washed over her. She *had* been right. "No, it's not."

She tipped her head back to get a good look at the catlike-but-not-a-cat creature huddled and whimpering in front of them. A tangle of thorns snared the bushy, striped tail. It's big, sapphire eyes half hid beneath the tuft of light-colored hair on its head, which contrasted with the rest of the soft, dark fur. The nose of the animal reminded Cynthia of a pig's nose, which didn't match the catlike ears and paws.

Cynthia had never seen one up close before and hadn't expected it to be so… big. Her medium sized pumpkin that she called home would be dwarfed beside this creature.

"What is it, exactly?" Fox kept a wary eye on the creature.

"It's a trufflefox. You should know that of all people, *Fox*." She bumped his arm with her shoulder and grinned up at him. She raised her eyebrows at her own joke.

He didn't smile back but rolled his eyes and sighed heavily again.

"Oh, come on." Cynthia approached the furry animal. "It's not going to hurt us…"

"You don't know that." Fox still held his loaded bow with both hands, ready to use it at a moment's notice.

"I do know, actually. I can understand animals, remember?"

She turned away from Fox and focused her attention on the animal cowering in front of her.

"What's wrong, little guy?" she asked the animal as she tentatively reached out to touch his face.

The creature sunk further beneath his mop of hair half-hiding his face and Cynthia sensed its fear.

"Little guy, she says," Fox murmured behind her.

She ignored him.

The trufflefox whimpered his reply. "My tail is stuck, and there's a thorn in my paw."

He sounded rather pathetic in an adorable sort of way. Cynthia's heart melted. "I'm Cynthia. I can help you with that. We both can." She gestured at Fox behind her.

"Help it with what?" Fox wanted to know.

"His tail is stuck, and he has a thorn in his paw," she said to Fox. Then to the trufflefox, "Let's get the thorn out first, it's probably causing you the most amount of pain, then we'll figure out the tail situation. How does that sound?" She rubbed the animal's soft cheek with one of her dainty hands.

The trufflefox purred at her touch and slowly nodded his head. "Alright."

"What's your name?" she started a conversation with the trufflefox.

"Sam," he squeaked.

"Nice to meet you, Sam. Show me where it hurts." Cynthia waited for Sam to extend his injured paw so she could take a look.

He stuck one of his front paws out from its hiding place beneath his body and turned it sideways so Cynthia could get a good look. "It's this one."

"How'd you get caught up in here, anyway?" Distracting him would ease the tension and fear. For Sam, and for Fox, too, she hoped.

"I thought I smelled something delicious back here somewhere, and I followed my nose." He ducked his head. More of his floppy hair covered his face. "Then I got stuck trying to find it."

While Sam talked to Cynthia, she examined his paw. A long,

narrow, needlelike thorn poked out from the larger pad on the bottom. The pad had swollen and clearly become tender. Sam flinched when she gently touched the pad to see how deep it might be.

She looked right into his big, blue eyes. "It's going to hurt when I remove the thorn, but then it will feel better, I promise."

Sam squeezed his eyes shut and braced himself for the pain.

"Fox, can you give me a hand?" Cynthia said softly to Fox.

He stared, mouth agape. "You can't be serious."

She locked her eyes onto his. "I am serious. And I can do it by myself, but it will go a lot faster and easier if you help me."

She held her breath. This was another chance for her to see how he would react. What any of his potential abilities might be. If he was trustworthy.

Chapter 12

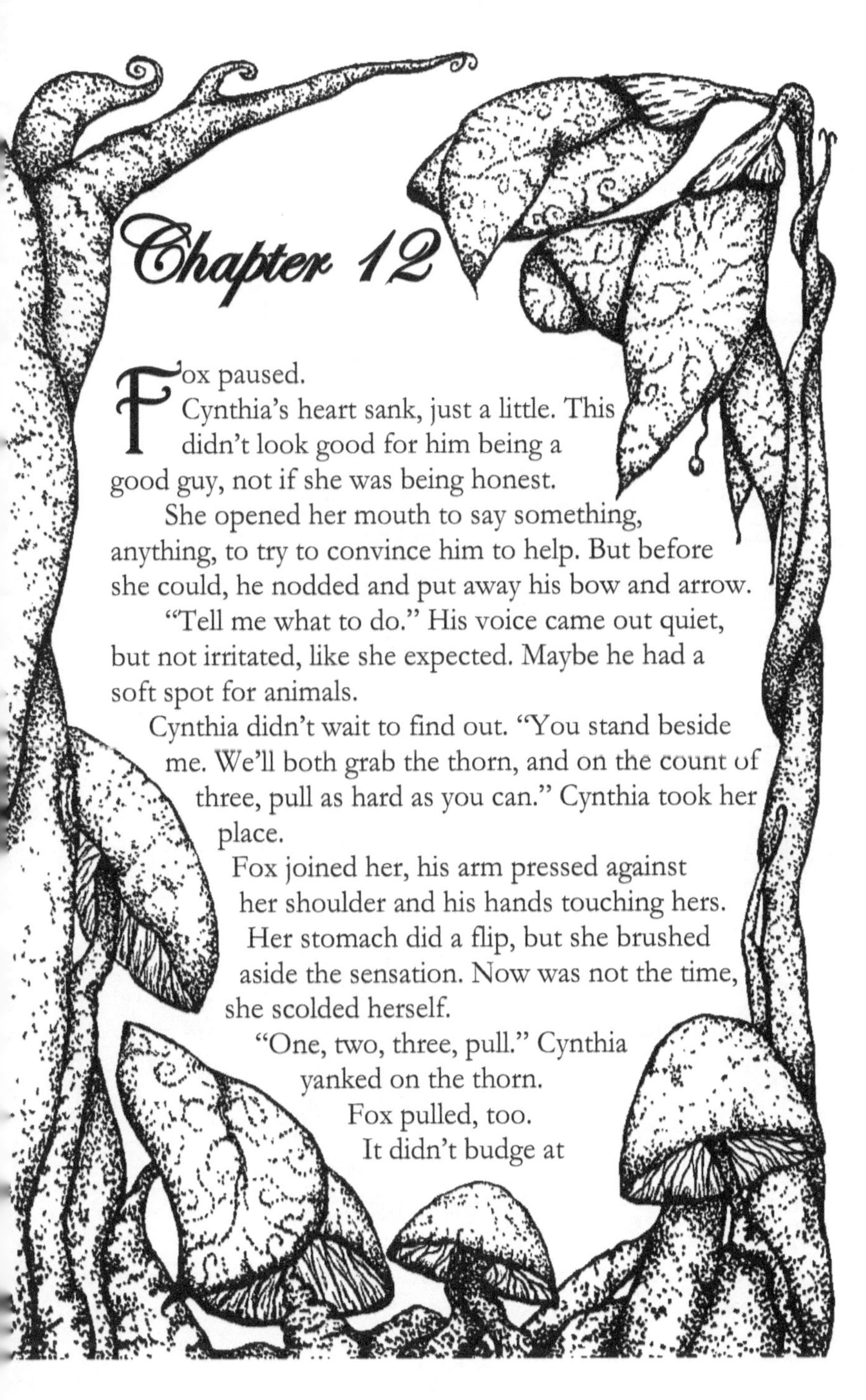

Fox paused.

Cynthia's heart sank, just a little. This didn't look good for him being a good guy, not if she was being honest.

She opened her mouth to say something, anything, to try to convince him to help. But before she could, he nodded and put away his bow and arrow.

"Tell me what to do." His voice came out quiet, but not irritated, like she expected. Maybe he had a soft spot for animals.

Cynthia didn't wait to find out. "You stand beside me. We'll both grab the thorn, and on the count of three, pull as hard as you can." Cynthia took her place.

Fox joined her, his arm pressed against her shoulder and his hands touching hers.

Her stomach did a flip, but she brushed aside the sensation. Now was not the time, she scolded herself.

"One, two, three, pull." Cynthia yanked on the thorn.

Fox pulled, too.

It didn't budge at

first. When it slid out of the trufflefox's paw, he whimpered.

Cynthia stumbled backwards.

Fox wrapped an arm around her back to catch her from falling.

The thorn dropped to the ground. From where it had embedded itself in the animal's paw to the tip was as long as Cynthia's arm.

She quickly rejoined Sam, pressed a wad of leaves and moss into the wound, and told him to place pressure on it to stop the bleeding.

"Once it's feeling better, we'll work on your tail." She stroked his other paw and waited for him to relax again.

Sam's breathing slowly relaxed and his ears perked up.

Finally, Cynthia was ready to help detangle his tail.

Fox helped where he could, and in no time Sam was free from his entanglement. With a limp, he followed Cynthia and Fox from underneath the bush.

Sam gave Cynthia a shy smile. "Thank you for your help." If he could blush, he absolutely would have been blushing.

Cynthia stroked his paw. "You'll feel better in no time."

"It already feels a lot better." He showed her his paw. The bleeding had stopped, and the swelling had gone down. "I'm a fast healer!"

"You sure are!" She let out a delighted laugh.

Fox rolled his eyes at the pair. He couldn't understand half of the conversation, which left him standing awkwardly observing, instead.

Sam laid his head on his paws to talk to Cynthia better. "I would offer you a ride, but you have wings, I see, so it would seem to be unnecessary."

"Actually…" Cynthia glanced at Fox.

As if Fox could read Cynthia's mind, his eyes widened, and he shook his head.

"We could use a ride," Cynthia said to the trufflefox while still making eye contact with Fox. "You see, my friend here has damaged wings. And we would get where we're going a lot faster with your help."

Sam's eyes lit up. "Certainly! Where are you headed?"

"We need to go to the river just south of here, do you think you could take us?" Cynthia pointed in the direction of the river.

"I would be delighted! Climb on!" Sam lay flat on the ground so the pixies could climb on easier.

"Wait, your wings." Fox handed Cynthia the leaves to cover her wings again.

Her wings drooped and she frowned. She gave him a pleading look.

He shook his head. "I know it's not ideal, but it's for the best."

She sighed and nodded. Before she wrapped the leaf-cape around her neck again, she used her wings to lift herself onto Sam's back.

Once again, the desire to stretch her wings and fly overwhelmed her. It's not like she had to do what Fox told her. He wasn't being bossy. She could just leave during the night, when her wings looked different, and fly far away from here back to her home in Magnolia's garden where she'd be safe.

But the thought of abandoning Fox just didn't feel right. Her gut told her she could trust him. And she wanted to see if she was right.

She fastened the leaves around her shoulders and allowed them to drape over her wings.

As Sam bounded through the woods, Cynthia held the hair in front of her with white knuckles.

Before long, Fox slid further down Sam's back on the soft, sleek fur, edging ever closer toward Cynthia.

Cynthia, on the other hand, slid further down the back, closer to the tail. If she wasn't careful, she'd be holding onto the tail and flapping in the wind! The thought made her laugh out loud.

"This is so fun!" she hollered to Fox. "I might have to fly after all, though, and meet you at the river…" It would defeat the purpose of covering her wings, but she didn't know how much longer she'd be able to stay on Sam's back.

Fox shouted against the wind at her. "Just hold on to me. It will help secure both of us in place better."

She nodded. Fox couldn't see from in front of her, of course. She gripped his shirt with her fists.

"It's not helping!" she said right into his ear from her close position.

He took one of her hands with his and pulled her arm, resting her hand on his stomach, then did the same with her other hand and arm, so that she hugged him from behind. "Lock your hands together," he instructed.

She did as she was told, her heart racing from the thrill of the ride, and, if she was perfectly honest, from her close proximity to Fox.

Heat rushed up her neck and into her face and she let out an embarrassed groan.

"What is it? Are you becoming motion sick?" Fox sounded concerned.

"No, no," she insisted. "Nothing like that." Her stomach may feel strange, but it definitely wasn't from motion sickness.

She focused her attention on holding on tight and tried to put thoughts of him out of her mind as they made good time through the forest and toward the river.

How come she suddenly felt so… strange at his closeness? She had been excited to make a pixie friend. And he wasn't the easiest person to get along with, even with her overwhelmingly positive attitude. But something about the way he tried to protect her, even when it was totally unnecessary, made her feel weak at the knees. No one had ever tried so hard to keep her safe before. Granted, she had never needed anyone to try so hard to keep her safe before, either, but still.

And then the situation with Sam. For once Fox had seemed

genuinely interested in helping another creature. He let his guard down, as well as his weapons, and trusted Cynthia that the situation would be safe.

How much longer would it take them to get Fox help? What would happen once he was healed and ready to go home? Was that the real reason she didn't want to leave him? Not just because she wanted to make sure he was safe, but also because, more and more, she knew she would deeply miss him once they parted ways.

In what felt like minutes but was more like over an hour, humidity thickened the air. Pine and alder trees gave way to willows and birch. The river would be close.

"I wish I could carry you further down river, but I really should be going home soon," Sam said as he slowed his pace to a walk.

Cynthia immediately released Fox's torso and scooted away from him. The instant chill from lack of contact was definitely noticeable.

Stop it, she scolded herself.

She slid off the animal's back and stood beside his face so they could talk easier. Fox stood close beside her, looking back and forth between them as they communicated, Cynthia with words, Sam with snuffles and mews.

"When you get close to the river, watch out for nixies," Sam warned. "They are quite dangerous if you aren't careful. Innocent passersby dipping their toes in the water have been known to disappear without a trace."

Cynthia had heard about nixies. They were like river mermaids with camouflaged skin and scales and hair that resembled water thyme. She also knew they liked to lure unsuspecting creatures into the water with their words and riddles.

Cynthia nodded. "Avoid Nixies. Got it."

Fox gave her a confused look.

"I'll explain later," she murmured.

"And make sure you don't fly close to the surface, or the lurking tiger fish might pounce. You never know if there's one in the water."

Cynthia translated the conversation for Fox when he started to look lost just standing there.

When she had finished telling him the warnings Sam had given them, he said, "I don't think the tiger fish will be a problem since I can't fly." He sounded really discouraged.

"Besides," Cynthia changed the subject. "We're used to being mistaken for a snack, aren't we?" She grinned at Fox.

Fox rolled his eyes, but she saw his lips twitch while he suppressed a smirk.

They walked together toward the riverbank, but not too close because of Sam's warnings.

Sam lay with his belly on his feet and peeked at the pair through his floppy fur on his head. His sapphire eyes moved back and forth between them. "Y'all are cute together. I'm glad I got to meet you."

Cynthia nearly choked at the words. "Oh, no… we're not…

it's not like that…"

Fox gave her a confused look. "What is it? What did he say?"

Cynthia was sure her face was as red as an apple but couldn't bring herself to repeat what Sam had said about them.

"It's… it's nothing." She waved away his question. She resumed talking to Sam instead. "Thank you, sweet friend, for the ride."

Sam blinked at her a few times, then stood again. "Good luck with your journey!" he called to them as he trotted back into the woods.

"What was that all about?" Fox asked Cynthia again, still obviously confused.

"Really, it was nothing…" Cynthia said, continuing to blush.

Fox gave her a questioning look. Could he tell she wasn't telling him everything? He didn't press her for more information.

Guilt stung Cynthia's chest. She didn't like being dishonest, even if it was to protect herself from embarrassment. And something he had said before about how everyone lies made her want to prove him wrong.

She sighed and opened her mouth to confess the truth.

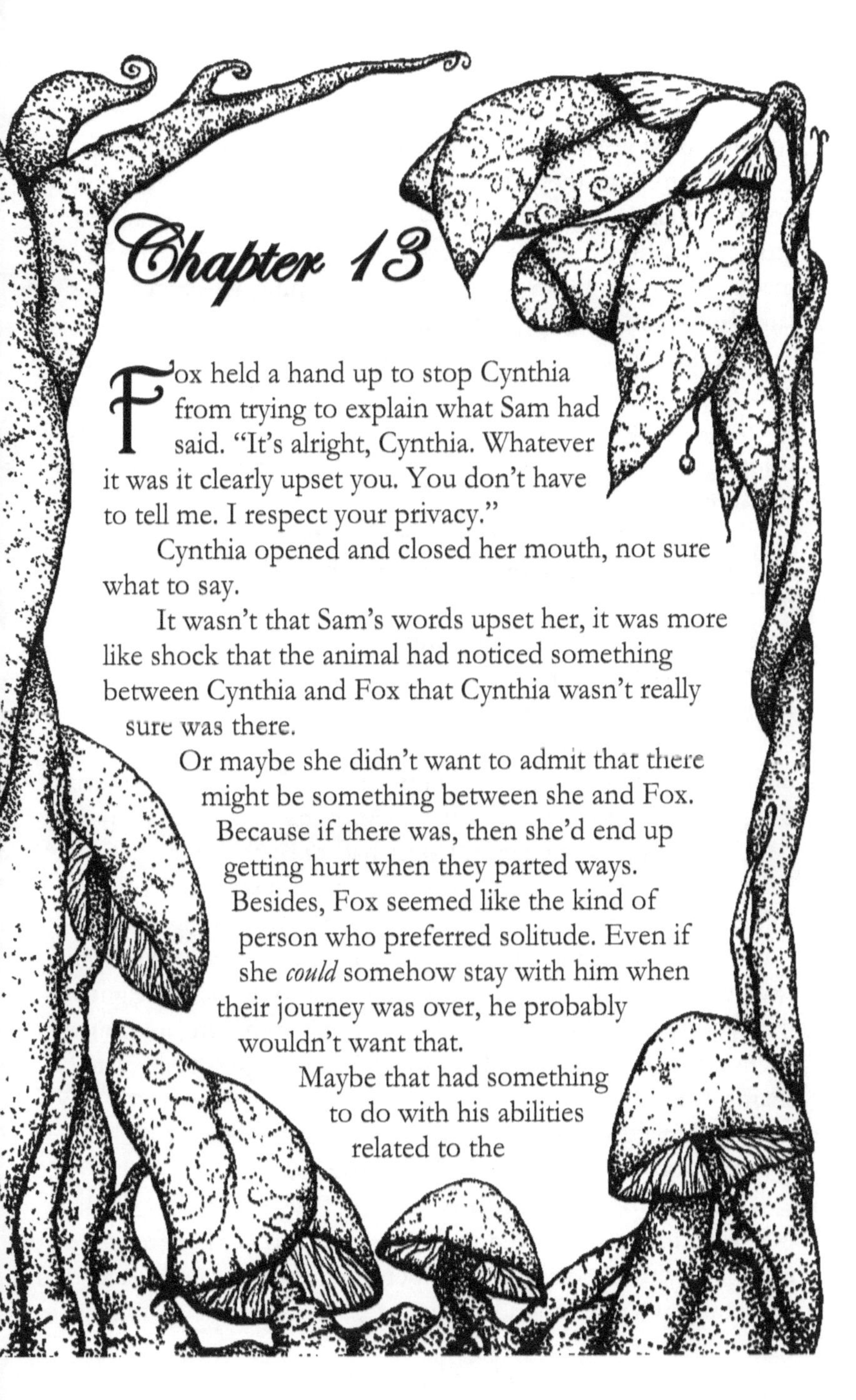

Chapter 13

Fox held a hand up to stop Cynthia from trying to explain what Sam had said. "It's alright, Cynthia. Whatever it was it clearly upset you. You don't have to tell me. I respect your privacy."

Cynthia opened and closed her mouth, not sure what to say.

It wasn't that Sam's words upset her, it was more like shock that the animal had noticed something between Cynthia and Fox that Cynthia wasn't really sure was there.

Or maybe she didn't want to admit that there might be something between she and Fox. Because if there was, then she'd end up getting hurt when they parted ways. Besides, Fox seemed like the kind of person who preferred solitude. Even if she *could* somehow stay with him when their journey was over, he probably wouldn't want that.

Maybe that had something to do with his abilities related to the foxglove blossom. Either he liked being alone because he couldn't trust anyone, or because he wasn't trustworthy.

And, anyway, there *wasn't* anything there. They had only known each other for a few days. She was just becoming attached to him because he was the first pixie friend she had made. It was to be expected. It had nothing to do with his handsome looks and protectiveness over her.

Fox gave her a rare smile. "Really, it's fine." He reassured her.

She nodded and avoided eye contact. The last thing she wanted to do was tell him what Sam said and have him outright reject her.

"It's getting late," Fox said before she could even decide how to change the subject. "Where should we set up camp tonight?"

Cynthia swallowed her embarrassment and turned her attention to the task at hand. She'd have to figure out her feelings for Fox another time.

The pair remained quiet as they prepared to camp for the night. They didn't have a cozy fairy circle of button mushrooms beneath a willow tree this time. And the temperature here beside the river was chillier than it had been the night before. They found a mossy outcropping of stones that offered protection from any surprise visitors through the night, and a way to retain heat from the fire. It gave a clear view of the night sky overhead. The stars twinkled and the moon shone bright.

Cynthia gathered twigs for Fox to use for the fire, and once he had it lit, they both settled on the mossy ground to warm themselves.

"We'll need to use moss and leaves for blankets tonight in order to stay warm enough," Fox instructed.

Cynthia nodded. She had thought the same thing. The meager fabric scrap wouldn't do much to protect her from the elements with the dropping temperatures. But she had decided she could wrap it around her waist over her dress to make a longer skirt. That would help keep her legs warm. And with the leaves still covering her back, she should be fine even if the temperature became too cold. It wouldn't be the prettiest outfit, but it was better than freezing!

After a meal of more roasted nuts and some water thyme tea, they both lingered beside the fire.

Perhaps Fox was reluctant to go to sleep because he was worried about their safety. Cynthia just wanted to understand him better. Maybe even find out for sure what his abilities might be, and whether his intentions for helping her were for the right reasons.

As she tried to figure out how to start the conversation, Fox decided to ask his own question. "Why are you so trusting?"

His abruptness startled her. She had been planning to ease into a conversation, lead it to where she wanted it to go in order to find out what she wanted to know.

But he just blurted his question right out.

She kind of just stared at him for a second, not sure how to answer.

He avoided eye contact and poked the fire with a stick. "You instantly see the best in everyone. It's like you don't even think about risks or anything. It's dangerous. You put yourself in harm's way unnecessarily."

He was right, in a way. She did see the best in those around her. She believed that everyone was basically good, just trying to make their own way in the world. Especially the people and creatures they had met so far together. It was a big world, and she, as well as the others she had met and helped, were trying to survive.

Sure, the may bug had nefarious intentions, but he was probably just doing what he thought he had to do to survive. Isn't that what everyone did?

But how could she explain that to Fox without him thinking she was being naïve?

After a few minutes of pondering, she was ready to try.

"When I first emerged from my blossom, I was in a field full of blossoming moonlight lilies being tended to by a group of Forest People. The blossoms glowed in the darkness, and I hovered above, looking around in every direction. None of the Forest People were around. I was utterly alone. I wasn't sure where I should go or what I should do, so, I waited. Surely one of them would return eventually.

"By morning, the blossoms had vanished, the Forest People didn't come back, and the meadow returned to normal. I decided I should probably go… but I didn't know where. I just picked a direction and started flying. When I reached the edge of the meadow of lilies, I saw a broken snapdragon egg with the baby still inside."

Fox groaned. "You didn't actually approach a snapdragon egg, did you?" He looked at her with wide eyes.

She gave him a sideways grin and nodded.

He rolled his eyes. "Of course you did."

She chuckled. "I landed just outside the egg and peeked in the hole. There was the baby, hiding in there."

"Yeah, hiding for some unsuspecting bug- or pixie- to fly too close!" Fox cried.

Cynthia nodded again. "Only, this baby snapdragon had underdeveloped wings. It couldn't fly. The area had suffered a minor drought, and his plant didn't get enough water."

Fox gave her a surprised look. "Oh!"

"I didn't know anything about how dangerous baby snap-dragons could be. All I saw was someone that needed help. So, I helped. I coaxed the baby out of the egg. We walked along the edge of the meadow for some time until we found a spider web that had bugs already captured on it."

"Let me guess, you asked the spider if you could have some for the dragon?" Fox sighed.

Cynthia brightened. "Yes, I did! And do you know what she did? She said yes."

"I can't figure out if you're brave or just inexperienced," Fox murmured in a quiet voice.

She ignored his comment. She supposed she was a bit of both at that point. "Let me finish. So, the baby got some food, and the spider told us where we could find someone to help him. That's how I found Magnolia. She contacted another Forest Person who came and took the baby dragon so she could heal it. And I decided to stay with Magnolia.

"Being trusting led me to my home and my family-of sorts." She thought of the dust bunnies and her other friends back home.

"But you've certainly been hurt, too, haven't you?" Fox said in a skeptical voice.

Cynthia lowered her eyebrows. "I suppose I have, yes. But any pain I have suffered has taught me empathy. Has grown me into a better version of myself. And those who I have trusted who haven't hurt me far outnumber those who have.

"Maybe it has something to do with the flower I was born from, or maybe it's just who I am. But I don't think I can stop giving others the benefit of the doubt until they prove to me that they can't be trusted."

This would be the perfect opportunity to segue into asking Fox about himself. Where was he from? How had he ended up at the site of the wagon disaster that night? What about his past, why was he so distrustful? And for her to determine whether she should really trust him, or not.

But he frowned and stood. Something she had said had upset him.

Her shoulders sagged. She thought by telling him her story, it would help him understand her better, and in turn give her the chance to understand him better, too. But, somehow, she had managed to offend him. Again.

He barely said good night to her before he wrapped himself in his makeshift bed of moss and leaves and turned away from her.

She reluctantly did the same.

By morning, Cynthia shivered beneath her blanket of moss and leaves, curling into a tighter ball to try to stay warm. The fire had long gone out, and the air temperature had dropped significantly overnight. A fresh, clean, cold scent filled the air that gave Cynthia dreams of snow and ice. It reminded Cynthia of the stories of the Mountain Guardian that Magnolia had told. The only reason she didn't feel the need to wonder if a part-man, part-eagle, part-moose would appear from between the trees was the time of year. This was no magical winter weather; it was the result of the change of seasons.

When she awoke, she was not surprised to see fluffy snowflakes the size of her face floating gently in the air. They melted when they touched the ground, but the message they brought was clear.

"Winter is coming." Fox's breath turned into fog between them as he said exactly what Cynthia had been thinking. "We need to move southward, or we'll get caught in the snow. And without my wings…" His wings trembled on his back as he attempted to use them again. "… we definitely don't want to get caught in the snow."

"So, what do we do?" Cynthia furrowed her brow and tried to come up with something. Her shoulders shivered. If only she was bigger or stronger. If the roles were reversed, and her wings were damaged, she had no doubts that Fox could just pick her up and carry her to their destination. But under the circumstances, that was definitely out of the question.

"Maybe we could ask an animal for help?" she suggested.

Fox shook his head. "We don't know who to trust." He glanced at her, then looked away as if he was embarrassed that he couldn't be as trusting as Cynthia always was.

But Fox was right. They didn't know who might be looking for her, and they didn't want to make it any easier for those who hunted her to find her.

"We'll just have to keep going." Fox rubbed his chin and looked around. His eyes squinted and his mouth turned down in a frown. "If only we had a way to travel on the river. A boat or something like it."

"Could we make one?" Cynthia perked up.

He shook his head. "I don't know how to make a boat. Do you?"

Her shoulders sagged. "I've never needed to make a boat before…"

Of course. Pixies had no need for boats.

"So… what do we do?" Cynthia hated repeating herself, but

short of walking through the woods again, she didn't know how they were going to survive the wintery weather brewing overhead.

"I hear you be lookin' for a way to travel down the river?" A soft voice came from the tree above where the pair had slept.

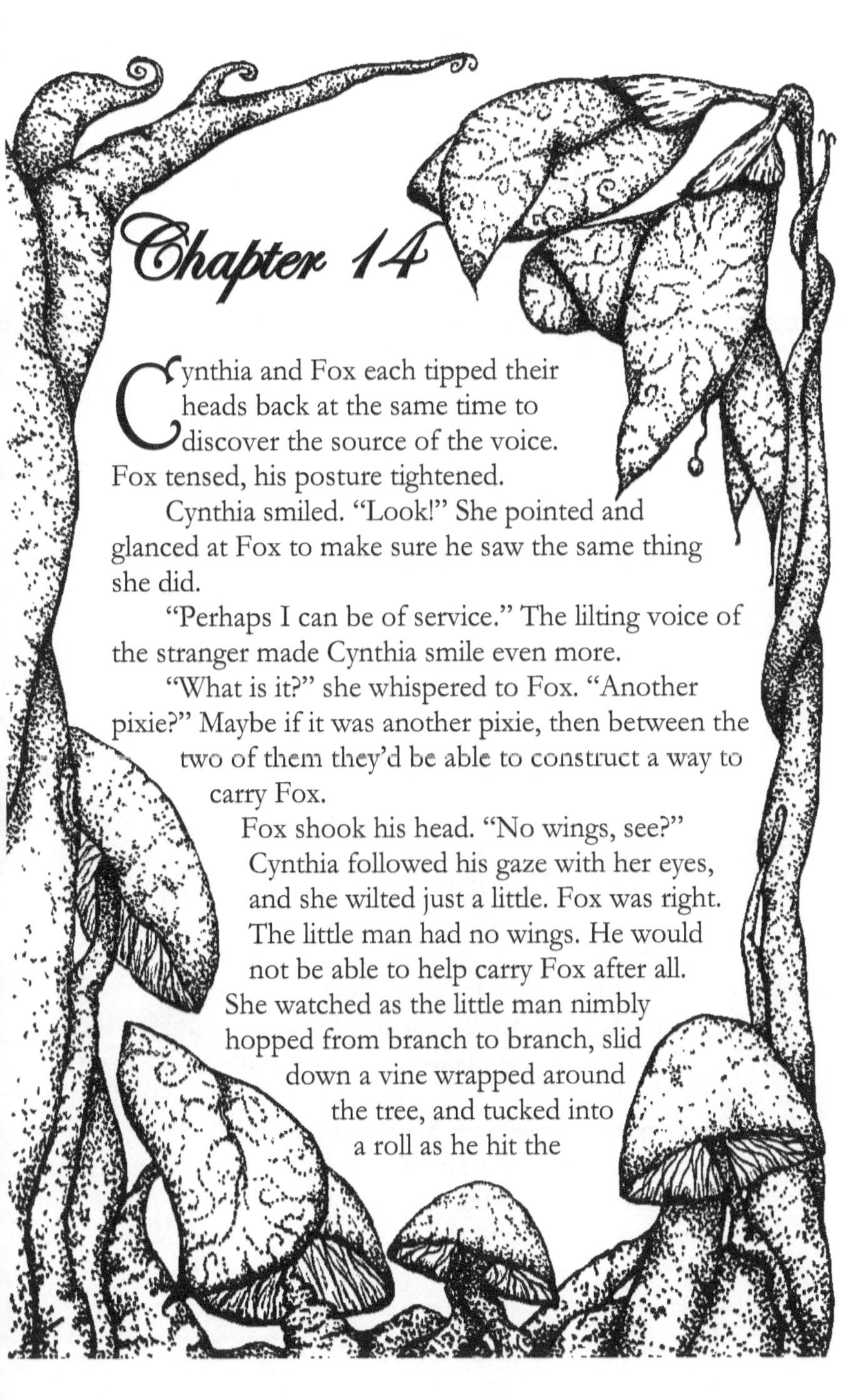

Chapter 14

Cynthia and Fox each tipped their heads back at the same time to discover the source of the voice. Fox tensed, his posture tightened.

Cynthia smiled. "Look!" She pointed and glanced at Fox to make sure he saw the same thing she did.

"Perhaps I can be of service." The lilting voice of the stranger made Cynthia smile even more.

"What is it?" she whispered to Fox. "Another pixie?" Maybe if it was another pixie, then between the two of them they'd be able to construct a way to carry Fox.

Fox shook his head. "No wings, see?" Cynthia followed his gaze with her eyes, and she wilted just a little. Fox was right. The little man had no wings. He would not be able to help carry Fox after all. She watched as the little man nimbly hopped from branch to branch, slid down a vine wrapped around the tree, and tucked into a roll as he hit the ground. He sprung to his feet and planted his fists on both hips.

The man, barely taller than Fox, which put him a head taller than Cynthia, had different features than either she or Fox, as well as the brownie that had rescued her a few days ago.

His nose filled up his face, his soft white beard matched his bushy eyebrows, and his ears looked almost like fins or flippers instead of pointed, like her own. He wore a long, floppy red woolen hat that came to a point with a fuzzball attached to the end, short pants over his skinny legs, and shoes that extended well past his toes and curled back in on themselves into a point. His oversized hands compared to the rest of his body made impressive fists at his hips, and his small eyes danced with delight.

"We don't need any help." Fox rested a hand on Cynthia's lower back and nudged her away from the little man.

"Fox, we do need help," she whispered before they could take a single step away. "And he might actually be able to help us."

Fox folded his arms across his chest. "Fine. But keep your wings covered," he murmured into her ear.

She rolled her eyes at him, but also made sure her wings were still hidden before she approached their visitor. "I'm Cynthia. This is Fox. And we do need to find a way to travel down the river."

Fox remained stoic beside her, but she ignored his mood and waited eagerly to hear what the man's solution would be.

"I'm Elfred. It's nice to meet such a beautiful couple as the two of ya'." Elfred rubbed his hands together and a glint lit up his eyes.

Cynthia's heart jumped into her throat.

Fox shuffled his feet beneath him.

Neither looked at the other or said anything.

Elfred waved for them to follow him. "I know just what to do. Follow me."

Elfred led them toward the water's edge. "We just need to

find a slow part of the water and find…" He peered over the riverbank, searching the surface for something.

If Cynthia knew what he looked for, she would have helped him, but she had no clue, so she just tagged along behind him.

"Aha! There it be!" He pointed at a flat green leaf floating on the surface.

"A lily pad?" Fox sounded doubtful. "It's not exactly a boat. It has roots in the bottom of the river."

"Aye. However, we'll cut the stem, and she'll float like a fall leaf on holiday. She'll carry the two of you, and keep yer feet dry at the same time." Elfred looked proud of his plan.

Cynthia placed a hand on his arm. "Thank you, friend! Do you think… can you help me figure out how to detach the pad from the stem?"

"Certainly, but it'll cost ya'." Elfred gave her an expectant look.

Cynthia's heart sank. "I don't have anything of value."

Elfred winked at Cynthia. "It's not about what ya' *have*, it's about what ya' can *do*. I know your kind have certain… abilities." He rubbed his palms together again. "I'd like to see!"

Cynthia blushed while Fox made a scoffing sound beside her.

Elfred looked back and forth between them. He raised his bushy white eyebrows. "Well?" He waved his hands to tell them to hurry up and show him their tricks.

Fox dropped his hands to his sides. He turned to Cynthia. "This is ridiculous. We'll figure this out on our own. We don't need his help." He pushed his way through the tall reed grass that grew along the riverbank. He poked around, rustling the blades with his movements.

Cynthia had no idea what he was looking for, and she wasn't surprised that he resisted sharing his abilities with Elfred. He hadn't even told her what his gifts were yet.

She sighed and looked at Elfred. "I'm sorry. You won't be

getting what you really want here. Fox… won't be showing anything. And I… don't have any abilities." She raised her hands at her sides and shrugged.

Elfred shook his head. "Come now. The pretty pixie with the butterfly wings doesn't know how to do anything special? I find that hard to believe."

How did he know? She glanced over her shoulder. Her wings poked out from one of the leaves that had slipped from its place.

"I've never seen wings quite like them before. They are something special, aren't they?" he added.

Cynthia blushed again at his complement but also embarrassed by the fact that she really didn't know what she could do. Other than talk to animals.

Maybe *that* would be enough to satisfy the little man.

Timidly, she said, "I *can* do *one* thing."

She looked around to see if she could spot any creatures nearby that she could try talking to. Other than a few white fluffballs floating across the surface of the slow-moving stretch of river, there weren't any signs of movement.

Her eyes darted back to the fluff balls. They weren't snowflakes or cotton puff or dandelion seeds. They were insects.

She climbed atop a smooth stone embedded in the ground so she could get a better look at the bugs. "Hello!" she called with her hands cupped around her mouth. "Hello, friends!"

Fox poked his head up from his search among the riverbank to see what she was up to. She ignored his scowl and continued with her plan.

Two of the flying fluffballs floated closer to the shore. Cynthia smiled and waved them closer.

They hesitated for a moment but then joined Cynthia on the shore.

Elfred's jaw fell open. "How did ya' do it?" he wondered out loud. He gave her a curious look. "Yer certainly not a Forest

Person…?" It was both a question and a statement.

The flying fluffballs beat their nearly invisible wings and their fluffy bodies floated up and down, side to side. Beady eyes nestled inside the fluff.

"Nope, I'm not a Forest Person."

"Amazin! And worth the wait! Let's get you and your husband? Boyfriend?… on that lily pad!"

Cynthia's cheeks flushed with heat. Before she could dispute his assumptions, Elfred pulled a large pair of shiny silver scissors from the pack on his back. He hopped from the riverbank to the lily pad, laid on his belly, and reached below the water. He snipped the stem beneath the pad and then paddled with his hands to bring the lily pad to shore.

Fox poked his head out of the reeds. "*Now* he decides to help." Mud smudged his nose and cheek, and he looked disheveled from his search for… whatever it was he had been searching for.

Cynthia ignored his comment and said, "Come on, let's get on!"

She shimmied onto the lily pad beside Elfred and waved Fox toward them.

Fox stared at the little man. "You're… not coming with us, are you?"

Cynthia gave him a look, begging him with her eyes for him to be polite.

"Wouldn't dream of it," Elfred said. "My home's here and all. But I do have one more suggestion. You'd move down river a lot faster if you had… help. Maybe ask your new fuzzy friends if they would be of assistance?" Elfred pointed at the two cotton-ball-flies that had followed Cynthia and hovered over the lily pad.

"Really?" she asked with a confused look on her face.

Elfred nodded.

"Would you mind… helping?" Cynthia asked the two bugs.

They bobbed up and down to show their approval.

"What do you have in mind?" Cynthia asked Elfred.

He pulled a long length of rope from his bag and tied the end into a lasso.

"Oh, brother," Fox mumbled and plopped himself into a seated position on the lily pad.

"I don't know…" Cynthia looked at the little flies. Would they get hurt? Would they really want to?

They both whispered their excitement at the idea, and Cynthia gave Elfred the go-ahead.

Elfred twirled the rope over his head and tossed it toward the fluffy flies. It circled one of them and he pulled it taught.

"Hold on tight." He handed the rope to Cynthia, "and tell them not to go too fast. But all in all, this should speed things along!"

He hopped from the makeshift river raft and waved from the shore as the cotton-ball-fly beat its wings and pulled the lily pad away from the edge of the water.

"Goodbye, Elfred! Thank you for your help!" She waved at the little man standing on the shore.

"Fare thee well, love birds. Have a happy life together!"

Elfred waved his arm in wide motions as they moved away from him.

"I hope he doesn't spread the word about you," Fox grumbled, seemingly unbothered by his comments about Fox and Cynthia as a couple.

"He helped us, Fox." Cynthia shook her head. "How can you still not trust him?"

"I didn't say I didn't trust *him*. I just said I hope he doesn't open his big mouth and tell everyone that he saw you. That's all."

Before Cynthia could respond, her feet lifted from the lily pad. She tugged on the rope. "Not too fast, or you'll pull me right of the raft!"

Fox smirked at her predicament. He patted the lily pad beside him, inviting her to join him in a seated position.

He held the rope along with her to weigh it down a little more. "There, now we can take on some speed."

His hand rested close enough to hers that she could feel the heat from him. It made her stomach flutter, as if the cotton-ball-flies danced in her stomach instead of along the surface of the river.

The sensation of moving fast along the surface of the water was not what Cynthia expected. She could fly pretty fast. She was used to the wind in her face and the joy of freedom of movement. But the ride on the surface of the water was bumpy, not smooth like flying. The lily pad swayed and bobbed as it skimmed along. The cotton-ball-fly tugged faster and faster as they went.

Each bump jarred Cynthia's jaw, rattled her head, and made her stomach roil.

"You don't have to do this, you know," Fox said.

Was her discomfort really that obvious?

"You can fly alongside…"

She shook her head. "We're sticking together…" Her words

came out garbled as the lily pad leapt off a swell in the river and landed again with a thud.

Fox smiled at her. "You don't look like you're enjoying yourself though…"

She gave him a sorry look and shook her head. "No, not really."

He wrapped his arm around her shoulders and tugged her against him. "If you insist on staying put, I can brace you, so you don't jostle quite so much."

Now Cynthia's heart raced for an entirely different reason. But Fox was right. Her side pressed against his did steady them both. The bumps weren't as bad, and the swaying made her feel less sick. Or maybe it was just the closeness of Fox that helped her feel better.

They continued on without talking for some time as she leaned her head against his shoulder and did her best to keep her breakfast inside her stomach. Boat riding was not something she ever wanted to do again after today. But for now, she would do her best to enjoy the ride… and the company.

"It's about to get bumpy!" The whisper of the cotton-ball-fly barely reached Cynthia's ears from above.

Cynthia's eyes widened as she leaned back to make eye contact with Fox and told him what the cotton-ball-fly had said.

They both snapped their heads to peer ahead of them. The water churned up ahead. White caps turned it frothy.

"Rapids!" Fox shouted. "Tell the fly to stop! We won't make it!"

Chapter 15

Cynthia tried to kneel. The raft hit a swell. She tumbled to one side. Fox caught her arm with his hand before she could be thrown overboard.

"Friend! Stop! Please!" she called over the slapping waves and rushing wind.

The little cotton-ball-fly couldn't hear her over the tumult.

"Let go of the rope!" Fox commanded, having already done the same thing.

She released the rope. The fly zipped ahead without them.

But the movement of the water continued to carry them too fast over the rapids.

Cynthia gripped Fox's arm with both of her hands. She braced herself for another jolt. The lily pad flew through the air, spinning Fox and Cynthia around like whirligig seeds.

Cynthia squeezed her eyes shut. The momentum of their spinning pulled Fox's arm through her hands. She couldn't hold on tight enough.

Her eyes flew open at the exact moment that she lost contact with Fox.

Her wings flapped beneath the leaf covers, but it was like trying to fly through a windstorm. She couldn't control her movement or her descent. The river raced toward her as she dropped out of the sky. Her wings whipped around her like leaves in the wind.

She braced herself for impact.

Another fact entered her mind about pixies at the last second.

Pixies didn't swim.

"Cynthia!" Fox's voice sounded garbled and strangely muffled.

Cynthia's body felt oddly heavy and her movements difficult.

"Cynthia!" his voice came again.

Another strange sound came from beside her, like something passing her at great speed. But it sounded strange. Like she was underwater.

The reality of her situation hit her then.

The boat had crashed. Her wings had failed her. She had hit the water at full falling speed. It must have knocked her out.

She jolted and forced herself to hold her breath. Her lungs screamed for air, and she forced her eyes open in the murky darkness.

Light glinted off something shiny as it swished past her again. Whatever it was, it was big. And it circled her.

Was it one of those tiger fish that Sam had warned her about? Or a nixie?

She kicked her legs and flailed her arms as she tried to figure out which way was up. Brightness shone above her head.

The surface. She propelled herself upwards and broke the surface of the water.

She gasped for air as water weighed her wings down, threatening to drag her under again.

"Cynthia!" Fox's voice was clear. And panicked.

She whipped herself around, struggling to stay above the surface, to find Fox. The ice-cold water numbed her hands and feet. Her teeth chattered and her breath fogged the air in front of her face.

"Over here!" Fox's shouting came from behind her.

With sluggish movements she turned in the water, barely keeping her chin above the surface. The slower current tugged her downstream. Her eyes locked onto Fox jogging along the riverbank, tracking her movements.

He held a long cattail in both hands and thrust it toward her.

She tried to grab it, but her numb hands and frozen limbs missed the offering.

He hurried further downstream to give her more time to plan her next attempt.

It worked. She wrapped her hands, then her arms around the fuzzy end of the cattail.

Fox heaved with all his strength and pulled her toward himself and the shoreline. She kicked her legs to try to aid in the rescue attempt.

With one final, hard yank, she burst from the water and flew toward Fox. The two collided in a heap of water, wings, and limbs.

"Watch out!" Fox wrapped his arms around her and tucked his body around her to protect her.

She peeked over his shoulder. A gigantic striped fish leapt out of the water, its whisker-lined mouth opened wide, showing off sharp needle-like teeth. It splashed onto the shore and flailed on the ground. But it's thrashing only slid it closer to the water, and away from Fox and Cynthia. A moment later, it slipped back beneath the surface.

Cynthia heaved a deep sigh. Her body shook uncontrollably

from the cold and her teeth continued to clatter against themselves.

"I-it's g-gone, F-fox," she managed to say even as her arms still clung to him for warmth.

"Cynthia!" Fox jumped and tried to pull himself away. "I'm so sorry, I…"

"D-don't l-let g-go," she whispered.

"We need to get you warm." His face wrinkled with concern. He turned his head back and forth like he was looking for something.

Lime colored river moss coated the ground with silver-leaved white willows poking out at random places. Beneath the willows, the reeds grew thick, and the agrimony with mauve stems and flowers dotted their surroundings.

A cluster of lamb's fluff plants stared at Fox and Cynthia with their wary eyes. They closed their leaves tighter around their fluff, as if afraid that Fox might steal it to warm Cynthia.

Other than the thin layer of river moss, there wasn't really anything they could use to warm Cynthia.

Cynthia couldn't take her eyes off Fox's face. How was he so dry? How had he saved her? How come she felt so safe wrapped in his arms?

"Stay here." He squeezed her shoulders and released her to stand.

It's not like she had the energy to do anything besides curl into a tighter ball and shiver even harder.

He limped away from her to gather some of the green moss from the ground. He was injured but hardly seemed to notice.

When he returned, he wrapped the thin blanket of soft moss around her shoulders. "I'll start a fire. We should be safe among the reeds for now. It's too cold for birds or other animals to be out and about now anyway."

By the time the fire had been built, and Fox had returned to huddle close beside her, leaning against a moss-covered smooth river rock, Cynthia's teeth had stopped chattering, and her body had stopped shaking. Her fingers and toes still felt numb, but she no longer worried that she was going to freeze to death.

"How come you're not soaked to the skin, too?" she wanted to know.

"I landed on the shore," he explained his dry state, "and I twisted my ankle when I landed."

"How will you walk?" she worried.

"It's not that bad. It will feel better soon, I'm sure." He brushed aside her fears. "And as for what to do now, I suggest we eat and rest. It's only going to get colder as night approaches."

He sat beside her and handed her a roasted nut, cooled enough for her to handle without burning herself.

"This is what you get for helping, you know." He murmured as he chewed his own nut.

Cynthia froze. Here she thought he was beginning to care for her, maybe in a special way. The way he had been frantic about her safety after she fell in the water. But now he was scolding her again? Besides, what did he even mean? "This wasn't Sam's fault," she pointed out, maybe a bit too defensively.

Her stomach twisted and her heart squeezed. She had a funny feeling in her throat, like disappointment mingled with betrayal.

"No," Fox agreed, "it wasn't Sam's fault. But if you hadn't

stopped to help him, then he wouldn't have given us a ride to the river. Elfred wouldn't have helped us with the raft, and you wouldn't have fallen in." The way he said it like he was just stating facts and not accusing her of being reckless hurt her feelings even more.

She didn't even know how to answer that. She chewed her nut and didn't speak. Her posture sunk. What if he was right? What if this all was because she was too trusting.

"Are you alright?" Fox asked her, checking to make sure she wasn't shivering too much or had hit her head too hard or something.

Cynthia yawned and nodded. "Yeah, just tired, I guess." Her mind continued to volley between self-doubt and hurt feelings.

"Let's try to get some sleep. But," Fox sounded nervous and rubbed his hands together in front of the fire. "I am worried that you'll get too cold. It would be best if we remained close." He avoided eye contact.

Cynthia silently gulped. But he was right. She was still cold. If she slept, it could make things worse. But her body was exhausted, and Fox's ankle needed more rest before he could walk on it without doing further damage.

She nodded. "Alright."

He wrapped his own moss-blanket around the two of them, and his arm around Cynthia's shoulders. "You can lean on me." His voice was low and quiet in her ear.

She did as he suggested and leaned against his shoulder. The added layer of moss combined with his body heat, and the chill gradually left her body, though her nose, fingers, and toes remained numb longer than the rest. Cynthia's eyes sunk closed before she had time to register much besides how safe she felt beside Fox.

The sky had darkened by the time Cynthia woke up, still snuggled up against Fox. His steady breathing told Cynthia that he hadn't woken yet. Her breath still came out in tufts of foggy clouds, but she no longer felt like she might freeze to death. The fire no longer burned bright but glowed with dying embers.

Moments later, Fox breathed deep, and his body stirred beside her. She shifted away from him, and he removed his arm from her shoulders. His own moss-blanket fell from around her, but with her own still wrapped around her shoulders, the change in temperature wasn't too drastic. Her clothes felt warm at last, and she could feel her fingers and toes again.

She had lost the extended blanket-skirt in the river, but with the blanket wrapped around her the cold wasn't too bad. She would need to figure out a way to cover her legs and arms if they were to be traveling through wintery weather.

"Thank you for saving me, Fox," she said in a quiet voice in the still night. The only sound came from the slow-moving stretch of river they had landed beside.

Internally, she still berated herself for having put them in such a terrible situation to begin with. She shouldn't have put them at risk like that.

He yawned and rubbed his eyes. He shook his head. "You should have left a long time ago. Then you wouldn't have been in any danger."

A twinge of pain stung her heart. He still didn't want her there? Even after everything they'd talked about and been through? She looked away.

What had she expected though? A softer response? Pity? Him telling her it wasn't her fault, that they were in this together, and that he wouldn't want things any other way?

She folded in on herself, holding her wings close to her body in a protective position. Tears stung her eyes. She looked at the ground and nodded.

"I know," she whispered. "I'm sorry."

"No, I didn't mean it like that." He sounded regretful, but he hesitated, as if he wasn't sure what he *should* say.

She didn't blame him. She was a total disaster. He would have been better off without her, for sure.

"I just mean, it scared me when you were in the water, and you were so cold afterwards, I was truly afraid that you… that it might end up…" He sighed and ran his fingers through his hair. "I would be so angry at myself if something happened to you because of me. That's all." He wrapped his arms and moss blanket around his bent knees.

What? He was blaming himself? That's not how it had sounded before.

But the emotion in his voice right then surprised Cynthia. She hadn't expected him to be so worried about her.

She squeezed her own blanket around herself tighter. She chose her words carefully, not sure what was happening between them anymore. "I know. But I can't just leave and never know what becomes of you. I promised I would help find a way to fix your wings, and I intend to keep that promise."

Silence hung between them for several beats as they stared at each other. Cynthia's heart sped up and her stomach fluttered. She could easily get lost in his gaze if it lasted long enough. She hadn't meant to start feeling… more for him, but somehow, it had started happening.

As if snapping himself out of a trance, Fox shook his head and stood. "We should gather something to eat and then figure out our next move." He reached for her with his outstretched hand.

Just his nearness warmed her more than the blanket anymore, and she allowed it to slip off her shoulders. She took his hand. He pulled her to stand in front of him.

"Whoa!" he whispered, his eyes locked onto her wings behind her.

She turned her head to one side to see for herself what he was looking at.

Her silvery nighttime wings… glowed. A brilliant ivory light illuminated their surroundings.

"That's… never happened before." Cynthia returned her gaze to Fox, still clutching his hand with one of her own.

He continued to stare at her wings, not releasing her hand, either. When his eyes returned to Cynthia's face, the light reflected in them, casting him in their warm glow.

"Maybe you *do* have special abilities, like the may fly said." His voice was a whisper as he searched her face, as if he could discover what her special abilities were by studying her closer.

Cynthia stiffened. "There's no way." She shook her head. "I'm telling you, I'm just a plain pixie. Always have been, always will be."

"There's nothing 'just' about you, Cynthia." Fox's eyes darted from her eyes to her lips and back again.

She found herself leaning closer to him, perfectly aware of their still clasped hands and his perfect face so close to her own.

Fox swallowed. He opened his mouth to say something to her. Was he going to ask if he could kiss her?

Chapter 16

Before Cynthia could find out if Fox wanted to kiss her, a cold, white blob of snow landed directly on top of the pair of them.

Cynthia shrieked. She wiped the cold wetness from her face and shook it from her head.

Fox used both of his hands to brush it from himself, and then from the moss blanket still wrapped around Cynthia's shoulders.

Another clump of snow landed just beside them. A third thumped to the ground nearby. The remains of the fire sizzled when a blob of cold whiteness covered it completely.

"We need to find shelter before it really starts to come down!" Fox grabbed Cynthia's hand while she reached for the extra discarded blanket on the ground. Fox pulled her through the reeds, away from the river, and toward the nearby trees.

They dodged the heaps of snow that fell heavy and wet out of the sky.

A quick search

revealed a hollow inside of an enormous broad leaf maple tree.

"It's not very big…" Fox frowned as he peered inside the trunk at the rotted-out cavity.

Another clump of snow landed just behind them. Cynthia jumped.

"It'll have to do!" Cynthia tugged Fox into the hollow. "The last thing we need is to get covered with more snow!"

Fox stooped to enter, though Cynthia walked upright. They stood facing each other in the tiny space, neither saying anything. Fox glanced at Cynthia, then away, then back again.

Cynthia rubbed her hands together, then folded her arms and tucked her hands beneath them.

Fox glanced at her thin mossy blanket and shivering body, cleared his throat and opened his mouth, but then changed his mind and closed it again.

After a long, awkward pause, Cynthia laughed out loud.

"What?" Fox lowered his eyebrows and studied her face.

"All of this." She gestured at the hollow tree, the snow falling in wet globs, and then between herself and Fox. "It's just too ridiculous. I never imagined my quiet life in Magnolia's garden would ever turn into something like this." She shook her head but kept a warm smile on her face.

Fox shrugged. He lowered himself to the floor of the hollow and settled on the decaying leaves and rotted wood. A sweet aroma filled the air.

Cynthia sat beside him. She kept her eyes on the opening to watch the snow fall outside. Before long, the ground had a blanket of white on it.

The cold humid air seeped through the thin moss blanket and Cynthia shivered a few times.

Fox fidgeted and shifted as if to find a comfortable position. He glanced at her sideways, then swallowed. "Sit closer. It will help." Fox motioned for Cynthia to scoot closer to him.

It would warm her to snuggle up beside him. Less of her body heat would escape, but also his nearness would keep her heart beating a bit faster than normal, which wouldn't hurt in keeping her warm, either.

She did as he suggested, and scooted toward him until their shoulders, arms, and legs touched.

The silence stretched between them again.

Fox finally broke the silence. "So, do you want to talk about how your wings were glowing before?" Fox asked Cynthia in a tight voice after they had settled in.

She glanced over her shoulder, beneath the mossy blanket. He was right, they weren't glowing anymore. What did that mean?

She shrugged. "I don't know what to tell you. Like I said, it's never happened before."

He leaned forward to peer upward at the cloudy, snowy sky. "Maybe it has something to do with the moon? Or the time of night?"

"Maybe…"

It was *possible*, but it didn't seem likely. She had lived her whole life and been awake at all times of the night at all cycles of the moon and she had never seen her wings glow before.

Could she just not have noticed? That seemed strange. They had glowed pretty bright earlier.

She glanced at Fox.

He gave her a warm, shy smile. Could it have something to do with… him?

Her face flushed, and she quickly looked away.

He cleared his throat and returned his gaze outside. "Well, I suppose for now we wait out the storm. I hope you don't mind?"

She chuckled. "Of course not." She wasn't going to say it out loud, but being stuck in a small space tucked up close beside him and watching the snow in the nighttime was quite magical. She didn't mind at all.

A part of her still worried about how little she actually knew about him, where he came from, or how he had come to be in the wreckage of the wagon that night.

She wanted to ask him about it. Really, she did. But if she tried to bring it up now, it would ruin everything. It might even make him angry. He could storm off right into the snowstorm! That would be dangerous.

Besides, she didn't want to spoil his better-than-usual mood. Or the fact that he kept glancing at her. She would much rather think about how close he sat and how handsome his face was.

Her hopes for a potentially romantic time with Fox were dashed only moments later when a field mouse scurried to join them in the hole. It shivered and flung gobs of snow all around, including all over Fox and Cynthia.

"Hey, watch it!" Fox complained as he swiped snow from his face. Again.

The mouse squeaked and brushed more snow off its fur with its tiny little clawed hands. She locked her beady black eyes onto Cynthia and let out a stream of squeaks.

Did the mouse know that Cynthia could understand her? But how? She was probably reading too much into the strange situation and allowing her disappointment over the mouse's interruption of her time with Fox to bother her a little too much.

She shoved those feelings aside and answered the mouse's questions. "I'm sorry, I don't have anything to eat, we just arrived moments ago ourselves," she told the mouse.

"Oh, that's a shame." The mouse's whiskers drooped. "I am so hungry and still a long way from home. I was gathering dandelion seeds for my family- they make an excellent soup topping you know- when the snowstorm hit." She gestured outside the tree with her little paw. "I saw this hollow and flew in a flash to find shelter."

With the added presence of the round mouse, Cynthia

pressed up against Fox's shoulder with her own. He scooted over as much as he could, then put his arm around her shoulders to give her a little more space.

The mouse looked back and forth between them. "I see I have interrupted something?"

"Just trying to stay warm and dry, like you." Cynthia hurried to correct the mouse. There was definitely nothing to have "interrupted." At least, there hadn't been yet.

Her heart sank a little. But, she reminded herself, Fox had broken wings, they were stranded in a snowstorm that they were definitely not prepared for, and they had a companion, for now.

"You are welcome to wait out the storm with us." Cynthia invited the mouse to stay.

Fox grumbled beside her. She could feel the rumblings from his rib cage pressed against her shoulders.

"Shh," she scolded. "She's hungry and cold, just like we are."

Fox sighed. "Well, in that case." He pulled his bag from where it hung on his side into his lap and used his free hand to fish around inside of it. "You can offer her this. You should have some, too."

He held out a leaf-wrapped parcel. Cynthia took it from him and opened it to find a chunk of a crispy butter cookie inside.

Her eyes flew to his face. "Fox! Have you been carrying this the whole time? Why haven't you eaten it yet?"

"I was saving it for an emergency. And I'm pretty sure this qualifies as an emergency."

His warm gaze sent heat rushing to Cynthia's cheeks. To distract herself, she accepted the cookie from Fox. After breaking it into three

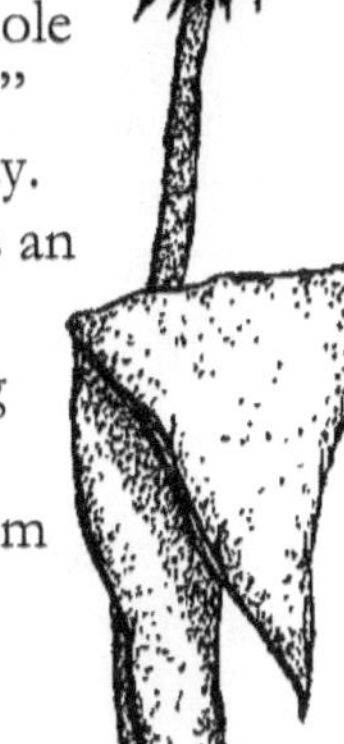

smaller pieces, she handed one each to
Fox and the mouse and kept the last one for herself.

Cythia ate her bit in a few satisfying bites. "This is delicious!" She licked the crumbs off her fingers.

Fox watched her with a satisfied half grin.

The mouse, on the other hand, nibbled her chunk in a frantic way, which left more crumbs on her felt coat. When the main piece had been consumed, she picked the smaller crumbs off herself one at a time. "Thank you, thank you." She released a heavy sigh and patted her stomach.

Cynthia passed along the mouse's thanks to Fox, though he clearly understood the sentiment even if he didn't understand the words themselves.

He shook his head. "It was nothing." He dismissed the gratitude.

But Cynthia knew how distrustful he was toward pretty much everyone, so for him to share like that was a big deal. She leaned against him a little closer and felt his arm squeeze her a little tighter.

She basked in his warmth while they waited out the storm and while the mouse cleaned her face and whiskers with her paws and fluffed her funny tail with her fingers.

When the mouse was finished, she curled into a ball. "Wake me when the snow stops, if you don't mind." She turned around three times where she stood, rolled herself into a fuzzy ball, and tucked her head beneath her arms. Her breathing slowed in no time.

Cynthia relaxed against Fox, now that the mouse was asleep. Even though she had already slept earlier, the coziness of her situation and the events of the last few days caught up with her, and before she knew it, she was drifting off, too.

In the morning, a quick glance outside proved the snow had stopped, but it had left a layer on the ground nearly as tall as

Cynthia herself. She shivered and Fox rubbed her arm.

"Are you cold?" He worried over her.

"Not particularly. I'm more concerned with how we are going to navigate this." She gestured at the snow outside.

"I can help there," the mouse said. "I'll show you how I get around in snow like this, and I can lead you to my home. You'll be safe and warm there, I can offer you some food, and then you can use our tunnels to be on your way."

The mouse spoke in such a matter of fact, nonchalant way, that Cynthia didn't even think to protest or disagree.

But when she told Fox, he frowned. "I'm not sure that's such a good idea…" He kept his voice low.

Cynthia doubted the mouse could understand his words, but she wanted to be careful just the same. She chose her words carefully. "We should accept her hospitality, don't you think? And it would make our journey all the easier…"

Fox leaned close and murmured in her ear. "I don't think we can trust her."

Chapter 17

Really? He was already distrusting of a simple little forest mouse in a snowstorm? What could he possibly be worried about?

"It's not like she's a bounty hunter, you know," she whispered back to Fox.

"No, but she's hiding something." Fox glanced over at the mouse.

"What makes you say that?" Cynthia gave him a confused look.

Fox wore a grim expression. "I can just… tell."

Cynthia studied him for a moment. She looked at the mouse who combed her fur with her fingers, ignoring the pair completely.

She turned back toward Fox and tugged him close so she could speak into his ear. "I don't see how she could be hiding anything. And she knows more about traveling through the forest in the winter than either of us, doesn't she? It would be foolish not to take her assistance."

He pinched his lips.

"Fine." He pulled away from her and prepared himself to crawl out of the hollow.

She had upset him. And just like that their connection evaporated. She sighed. Maybe she had been reading everything wrong the whole night. Maybe he really had just been trying to keep her warm and safe because he felt obligated to, since she refused to leave him behind.

She turned back toward the mouse. "Lead the way."

The mouse stood on her back feet and rubbed her face with her balled up paws. The look on her face was one Cynthia couldn't quite place, but she followed her outside anyway.

Fox trudged along behind them, clearly not happy about the turn of events. But that was only because he had trust issues, not because he was sad their cozy night together had come to an abrupt end.

Apparently, she was the only one left disappointed.

Fox remained quiet as they followed the mouse through the woods and away from the river. Hopefully they had made enough progress downriver toward the Forest People. Without flying above the trees to take a look, Cynthia couldn't be sure. But under the circumstances, it would be unwise to try.

The once brown and green forest dotted with color from the beginnings of fall foliage and autumn blossoming azaleas and rhododendrons had changed to shades of blue, gray, and white.

Cynthia had always thought of winter as just white. But the shadows from the plants and trees left streaks of blue, while the clouds covered the entire scene with a layer of gray.

The blanket of snow muffled the sounds of the forest. No bird chirps or rustling leaves reached Cynthia's ears. The only sounds came from the crunch of snow beneath the feet of herself and her companions. And the occasional deep sigh from Fox.

The cold air stung her cheeks and the inside of her nose

when she breathed. The trail of footprints they left behind them wound around clumps where the snow covered plants or bushes.

It didn't snow often back home. She wasn't used to the chilly temperature, but it wasn't too bad. The moss blanket, still wrapped around her shoulders, insulated her enough that she didn't feel the cold too harshly on her arms and legs. If they weren't lost and Cynthia didn't have to hide her wings, she would have flown around to bask in the sparkling beauty of it all. But under the circumstances, she thought it best to keep her feet on the ground. Even if the coldness tickled her toes.

The mouse darted over rocks and branches, around heaps of snow that had slid off the trees above, and underneath umbrellas of ferns growing around the tree trunks.

Her sporadic movements and twitchy whiskers put Cynthia slightly on edge, especially after Fox's concerns about the mouse's motives. *Was* she being suspicious, the way she glanced around every few steps to peer through the foliage at their surroundings? Or was that just the cautious way mice moved through a potentially hazardous environment?

Cynthia kept her senses tuned to their surroundings, the way Fox always checked over his shoulder, scanned their surroundings, and glanced at the trees and sky from time to time. It didn't seem like they were being followed. Nothing felt strange or out of place around them.

"Tell me about your family," Cynthia invited the mouse to share. Maybe if Fox could hear her story, then he wouldn't be so quick to judge.

"I have thirty-seven children." The mouse's words came out between puffs of cloudy breath and scurries back and forth.

Cynthia choked on her next breath. Thirty-seven! She didn't want to offend the mouse by commenting on the enormous size of her family. "You must have a large burrow then?" There'd have to be plenty of room for Cynthia and Fox in a burrow that size. Unless it was really crowded. The thought of being underground and surrounded by dozens of mouse pups overwhelmed her. Maybe Fox was right. Maybe this wasn't the best idea.

The mouse paused and glanced at Cynthia. Her whiskers twitched and her eyes darted toward the treetops. "Oh. Yes. It is big enough for us all." She abruptly turned around and continued her sporadic movements through the snow.

Cynthia turned around to look at Fox. *Thirty-seven*, she mouthed.

He let out a puff and rolled his eyes.

"What does your family like to do for fun?" She couldn't imagine trying to entertain that many children!

"Oh, this and that. Gather berries. Draw. You know." The mouse gave vague answers.

Maybe she was just distracted by traveling?

Cynthia was about to give Fox a concerned look. Maybe they couldn't trust the mouse after all. She was kind of distant.

But then the mouse started talking again. "Actually, one of my pups is quite a talented artist. She can paint like no other. She has decorated our burrow with numerous paintings of flowers and her siblings."

Once the mouse started talking about one of her pups, the words kept coming. Before long Cynthia felt as if she knew the family well herself.

She gave Fox a satisfied smile. There was nothing to be worried about after all.

As the sun rose the temperature rose as well. The snow on the branches and leaves above them dripped fat, heavy drops onto the ground, and threatened to soak them in an instant.

"How much further?" Cynthia asked the mouse while dodging water drops from above. If she wasn't careful, she'd end up soaking wet again!

The mouse peered over her shoulder. "Not too much farther, dear." She plucked an orange underdeveloped maple leaf from a sapling near the ground and used it as an umbrella to protect herself from the threat of instant saturation.

"Brilliant!" Cynthia beamed at Fox as she did the same. She wore a smile across her face that Fox did not return. "Aren't you going to take one, too?" She pointed at another leaf perfect for an umbrella.

"I'm good." Fox shook his head.

Cynthia shrugged. She wouldn't let his bad mood and distrust of others keep her from enjoying herself as they marched through the sloppy, quickly melting snow.

Fox kept his lips pressed shut and a wrinkle drew a line between his eyebrows from his frown.

"We're almost there, no need to worry!" the mouse called from up ahead.

The further they walked the

colder Cynthia's feet became. How much further would they have to travel before she could warm her feet in the mouse's home?

Except, mice didn't generally have fires in their homes, did they? How would they warm up once they were inside? Perhaps just being underground would offer the warmth they would need to undo the chill from the crisp air.

"Here we are!" The mouse stood on her hind legs and held out one arm to show off the entrance to her home. "Safe at last." Her whiskers twitched on the sides of her face.

Snow lightly dusted the pile of dirt on the ground beneath a tall, leafy bush. A perfectly round hole formed a dark circle at the center of the dirt pile. Cynthia never would have seen it if the mouse hadn't pointed it out to them. The way the snow drew lines away from it marked the pathways the residents used to go in and out of the round hole.

Cynthia hesitated. She looked at the mouse.

The mouse returned her gaze with an expectant stare. She blinked her large black eyes, but didn't say anything else to Cynthia.

Cynthia leaned forward to peer into the hole again. She hadn't ever gone underground before. Quite the opposite. She preferred treetops and open skies to being under the canopy of the forest, let alone below ground.

Her heart sped up and a new chill ran down her spine. *Was this some sort of trick? Or was Fox's skepticism rubbing off on her? What would the mouse gain from trapping them below ground? It just didn't make sense.*

"Quickly," the mouse glanced up. "Before any predators spot the entrance to my home…"

Of course. That's why the mouse was on edge. She didn't want to give away their secret.

Cynthia relaxed her shoulders and pressed her hand against her stomach to stop the fluttering of her nerves.

She took a step toward the hole.

Fox stepped close to her side and gripped her arm with one hand. "Wait." His voice barely made a sound into her ear. "Don't go any closer. Something is wrong here." His eyes darted around the small clearing. He glanced up into the tree branches and narrowed his eyes as if to see better.

"What is it?" Cynthia whispered back. A strange feeling tingled the back of her throat, and her palms grew moist.

"I don't know. Just… something is off." Fox's posture stiffened and his grip remained firm, like he was afraid to let go of Cynthia.

"Please don't delay." The mouse twisted her tiny, clawed fingers together and glanced to her left. "You'll be warm in no time…"

Cynthia heard the hesitation in the mouse's voice and saw the way her eyes darted to one place over and over.

The shrubs in the direction that the mouse had just glanced quivered. Something was definitely hiding in there. The hairs on the back of Cynthia's neck stood on end.

Even though Fox didn't know what the mouse was saying, her behavior must have triggered something for him. His grip on her arm tightened just the tiniest bit, ready to tug her away from the mouse and the hole at a moment's notice.

"We have to get out of here," he said through gritted teeth.

She gave him the slightest nod and locked eyes with him. Dread kept her eyes open wide, waiting for Fox to tell her what to do next.

He had a look of determination on his face. His eyes hard. His jaw set.

She shivered. But not from the cold anymore.

The mouse glanced at the bushes again. "Please, do as I say." Her voice came out as a high-pitched squeak. Fear laced her words.

What was Cynthia to do? Fox was right. Something was very wrong. And it seemed like the mouse was in trouble, too.

Cynthia opened her mouth to ask the mouse what was going on.

Before she could get a word past her lips, the threat revealed itself from the bush. Or rather, revealed *themselves*: a pair of sharp nosed, long clawed, heavily armed moles.

The mouse curled herself into a smaller fluffy ball and lowered her ears. She took a slight step away from the oncoming threat that towered above her, and Fox and Cynthia, too.

"I tried, I really did," she squeaked.

Cynthia looked back and forth from the mouse to the intimidating moles and back again. "She was working with them?" she whispered to herself.

"More likely *for* them." Fox's low voice in her ear startled her. "She's afraid. Which means, we probably should be, too."

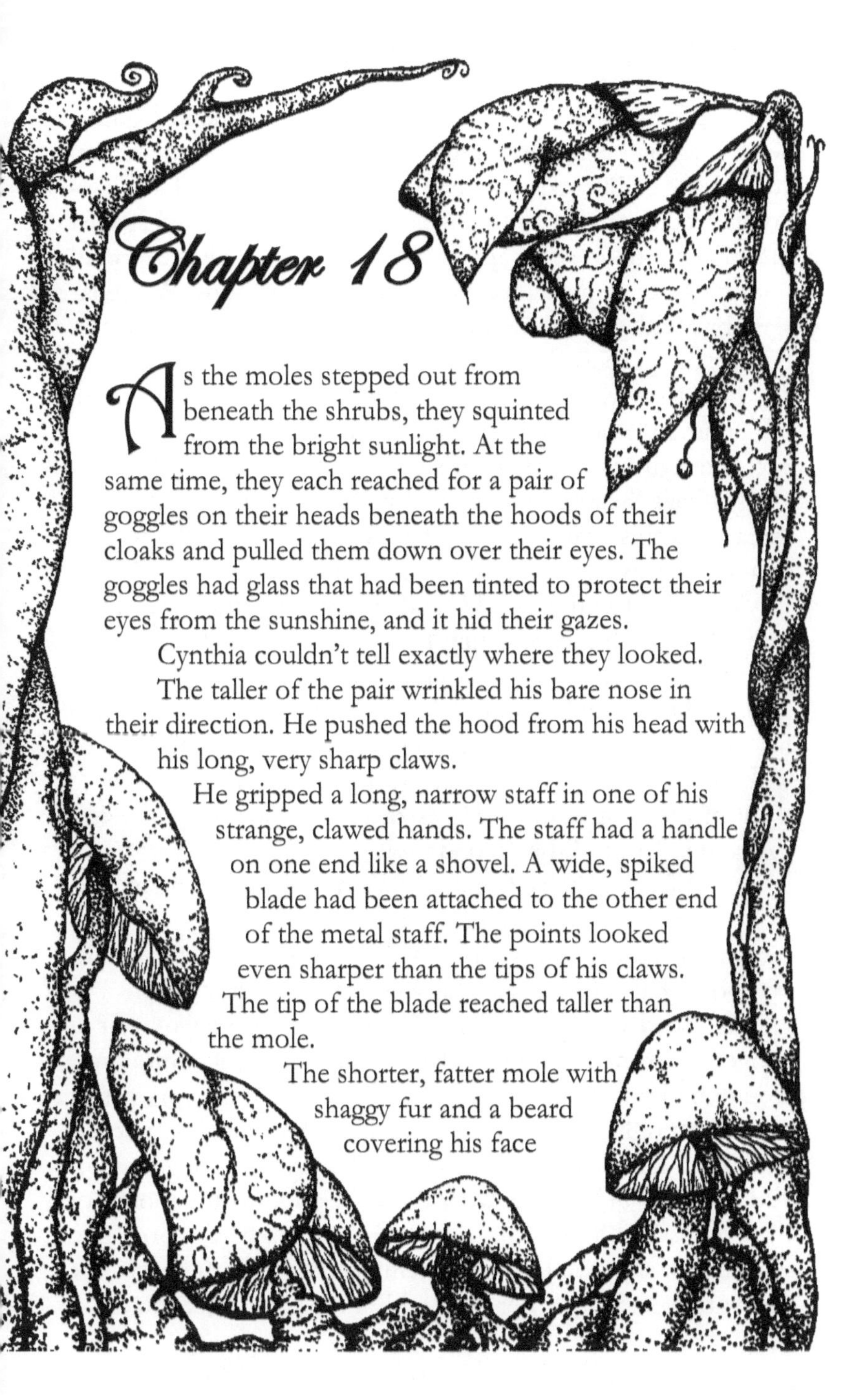

Chapter 18

As the moles stepped out from beneath the shrubs, they squinted from the bright sunlight. At the same time, they each reached for a pair of goggles on their heads beneath the hoods of their cloaks and pulled them down over their eyes. The goggles had glass that had been tinted to protect their eyes from the sunshine, and it hid their gazes.

Cynthia couldn't tell exactly where they looked. The taller of the pair wrinkled his bare nose in their direction. He pushed the hood from his head with his long, very sharp claws.

He gripped a long, narrow staff in one of his strange, clawed hands. The staff had a handle on one end like a shovel. A wide, spiked blade had been attached to the other end of the metal staff. The points looked even sharper than the tips of his claws. The tip of the blade reached taller than the mole.

The shorter, fatter mole with shaggy fur and a beard covering his face waddled forward on his short legs. His hood remained on his head, shading his features. He fiddled with a gear-shaped clasp at the base of his neck that held the cloak in place. The claws on his feet, shorter than the ones on his hands, scraped against the snowy ground as he approached. He carried his weapon in both paws at an angle across the front of his body. A similar staff but with a pickaxe attached to one end. Equally sharp. Equally dangerous.

"I'm so sorry," the field mouse whispered. "They threatened my family. Please, do as they say." The mouse whimpered to Fox and Cynthia between her shivers.

Cynthia's heart felt like it would crack. The moles had threatened this sweet mouse's family? No wonder she was so afraid! She was just trying to protect her loved ones.

"We will." Cynthia nodded and whispered to the mouse. She wanted to reach a comforting hand out to touch her, but she was afraid of making any movement at all.

The shorter mole motioned for the mouse to join him and his companion, away from the pixies. The mouse obeyed without hesitation. She scurried over to them only to cower in front of the shorter mole. He escorted her roughly by the arm to stand in front of the second mole.

Fox stiffened beside Cynthia. "We need to fight and get out of here," he insisted underneath his breath.

Cynthia met his hard stare. "We need to protect her family. We'll do what they want so that her family will stay safe."

His scowl deepened. "There's no need to put yourself at danger for some random mouse that lied to us the entire time. You don't know who those moles are or who they work for. If we do this right, we can escape unharmed, Cynthia. Especially you. You can fly. They won't stand a chance capturing you."

Cynthia couldn't hear what the moles said to the mouse or to one another, not with Fox whispering his hard words into her ear. But she saw the mouse tremble in front of them, gesture to Cynthia, and shake her head without making eye contact.

These moles were dangerous. Cynthia shook her head at Fox. "I can't just leave you behind. Who knows what will happen to you? Or to the mouse. Or her family. No, it's not worth it."

He growled his reply. "You're saying *you're* not worth it. That's ridiculous."

She leaned closer to his ear and watched her breath leave goose bumps on his neck. "*You* don't have to stay. You can slip away while they're talking to the mouse. I'll make a distraction if I have to. They're clearly after me. Run away. Protect yourself. I'll be fine."

"That's a lie. You don't know if you'll be fine."

She blushed as he called her out. Was it a lie when she said something like that to protect someone she cared about? Was it a lie if she said it to make herself feel better? To trick herself into believing it was true?

Maybe not a lie in the sense of intentionally deceiving someone for her own gain, but it wasn't the truth, either.

"I know." She lowered her eyes. "But it's not necessarily *not* true, either. If I do what they say, they probably won't harm me. You can escape. Please."

Fox set his jaw and shook his head. "I'm not leaving you behind. We can escape together."

Cynthia gave him a pleading look. "I won't fight them. I won't leave the mouse's family in danger. I'll do whatever they want to keep the mice safe." There was no denying the truth of that statement, even though it left her stomach in knots.

Fox gave her a begrudging nod. "Fine. Then I'll go along, too. But if at any point they try to hurt you…"

Cynthia rested her hand on his arm. "I don't think they will…"

He covered her hand with his own. "But if they do…" He kept his gaze locked onto her face.

She nodded. Then they would fight. The words did not need

to be spoken.

Although, the thought of trying to escape these oversized, bulky creatures that carried frightening weapons only fueled Cynthia's hope that it wouldn't come to a fight. She didn't think they stood a chance of winning.

By the time they had made their decision, the moles had finished their conversation with the mouse and turned to face the pixies.

One of the moles jabbed his bladed weapon in their direction to emphasize each word as he gave his command. "No funny business. Keep your wings where we can see them. Hand over your satchels. Follow."

Cynthia did her best not to flinch with each movement of the sharp blade as she removed her satchel and gave it to the mole. The items inside weren't hers anyway, so it didn't matter much to her. But the stubborn look on Fox's face indicated that he wouldn't give over his belongings so easily.

"Please, Fox." Cynthia pleaded with him.

He ground his teeth but did as she asked and forcefully shoved his bag into the outstretched claws of one of the mole guards.

He frowned at Fox, but didn't retaliate.

Cynthia breathed a sigh of relief.

The shorter mole lowered himself into the hole first. The mouse scurried after it.

Cynthia gasped. They were entering the mouse's hole? Was her family in immediate danger? Then a thought occurred to her. "Is this even the mouse's home?" Cynthia whispered to Fox.

He had released her hand and arm by now but stood protectively beside her with his hand hovering close to her back.

Fox didn't respond to her question.

The obvious answer was "no." She moaned inwardly. How gullible was she? No wonder the mouse had been uncomfortable when they had arrived. And no other mice had come out to greet her.

"Where do you think it goes?" Cynthia murmured.

"Only time will tell," Fox answered in a grim voice.

Cynthia dropped her moss blanket that covered her wings, squatted beside the hole, and pressed her hands against the cold, wet, snowy ground to avoid getting her dress too wet. She dangled her feet into the hole and allowed herself to drop into the darkness.

With Fox and the other mole blocking the entrance above her, the darkness hit her like a wall. She shuffled out of the way so Fox wouldn't land right on top of her.

Musty air filled her lungs, making it difficult to breathe. The closed space pressed in from all sides. The knowledge that the world existed entirely above them loomed over her. The feeling that it could collapse onto them at any time drove her heart to beat faster. Her hands shook. Her breathing sped up. Her mind raced. If she had been able to see anything, her vision would have blurred.

Only a moment later, Fox pressed a hand against her lower back. "It's alright. I won't leave your side," he whispered into her ear. She felt the weight and truth of his words.

"Thank you," she breathed back. She allowed herself to lean into his touch and forced her breathing to slow. She wouldn't panic. She would do what the moles wanted. She would be safe.

"This way." The gruff voice of the mole in front of her sunk into the dirt walls of the tunnel.

Cynthia gulped and hesitated.

"Do as he says," the mole in the rear demanded.

The mole's weapon thumped against Fox's body in the darkness. He sucked in a sharp breath.

Cynthia didn't want anyone getting hurt! She hurried after the mouse and the first mole down the tunnel. Away from the shaft of daylight. Further into the darkness.

Seeing while underground turned out to be a very different thing than being able to see well on a starry night. The moon and stars, clouds and colors made it easy to distinguish things above ground, even on a dark night. But here, below ground, everything just looked black.

The moles immediately returned their tinted goggles to rest on top of their heads. Apparently, they had perfect vision in the pitch dark.

Cynthia's eyesight tried to adjust to the darkness, but the others- Fox, the moles, and the mouse- looked like shadowy versions of themselves. Even her own hands and feet were barely visible. She stumbled along behind the first mole guard and the mouse and could feel Fox's presence close behind her.

Just knowing he was there gave her a small sense of comfort as they journeyed through the near-blackness.

Other than a few turns, the tunnels felt exactly the same. Dark. That's it. Without anything to look at, they could have been traveling for minutes or hours. It was impossible to tell.

"Please," the mouse begged after scurrying on all fours for some time. "When will I be released to go to my family?"

The pleading of the mouse tugged on Cynthia's heartstrings. Any sense of doubt about her decision to not flee or fight earlier vanished. She had done the right thing. Even if Fox disagreed. Even if it meant something bad was about to happen. She couldn't let innocent creatures suffer because she was, somehow, a wanted pixie.

She edged her way past the mouse to get closer to the mole.

Fox hissed his distress at her actions, but she ignored him.

"Mr. Mole, please let the mouse go. She's done what you asked," Cynthia pleaded on the mouse's behalf.

"It's not up to me, girly. It's up to the boss." The mole continued his march through the dark tunnels.

"And, who's your boss?" Fox demanded from behind Cynthia. He had edged past the mouse, too, to stay close behind Cynthia.

"Wouldn't you like to know." The mole at the back of the group laughed at Fox's question.

"They're bounty hunters," the mouse whispered. She let out a squeak of pain.

Cynthia turned on her heels and hurried to the mouse's side. "Leave her alone!" she shouted at the mole that had hit the mouse with the broad side of his weapon.

Fox groaned at Cynthia's outburst, but the mole did not react.

Cynthia helped the mouse regain her feet and wrapped an arm around her back. A strange sense of guilt and fear overwhelmed her, but she brushed it aside.

"Thank you," the mouse whispered. "And I really am sorry."

"Shh. I know," Cynthia answered.

Her thoughts raced. The moles were bounty hunters, like the may bug? It didn't seem like they'd be so easily persuaded to let her go, like the maybug had been. They carried weapons and worked in a group. There would be at least three, including the "boss," but more likely there'd be more. How was she going to get herself and the mouse and Fox out of this mess? Even though she didn't think it would work to talk them out of it, she had to try.

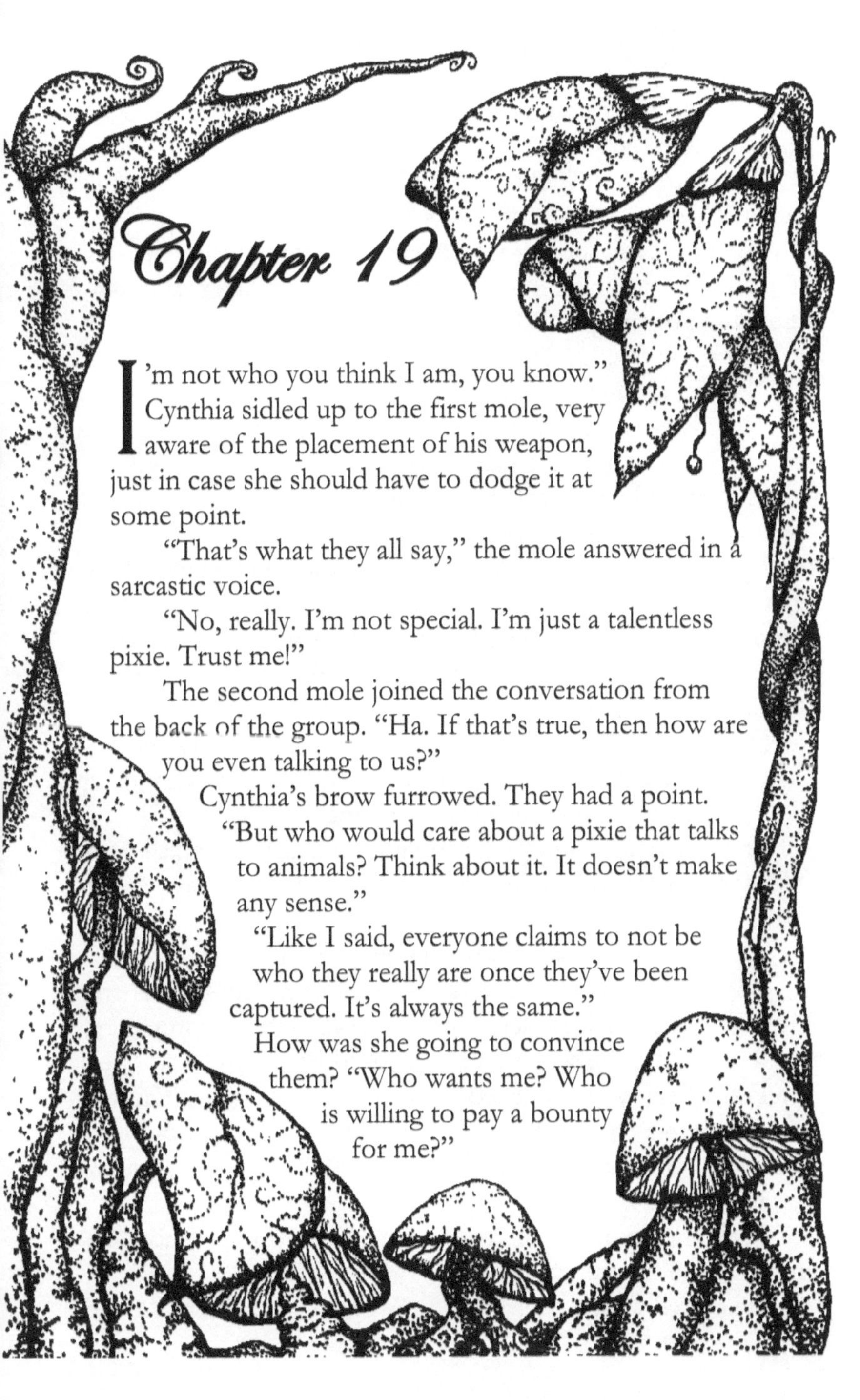

Chapter 19

I'm not who you think I am, you know." Cynthia sidled up to the first mole, very aware of the placement of his weapon, just in case she should have to dodge it at some point.

"That's what they all say," the mole answered in a sarcastic voice.

"No, really. I'm not special. I'm just a talentless pixie. Trust me!"

The second mole joined the conversation from the back of the group. "Ha. If that's true, then how are you even talking to us?"

Cynthia's brow furrowed. They had a point.

"But who would care about a pixie that talks to animals? Think about it. It doesn't make any sense."

"Like I said, everyone claims to not be who they really are once they've been captured. It's always the same."

How was she going to convince them? "Who wants me? Who is willing to pay a bounty for me?"

"It's doesn't matter. All that matters is the payment is high," the second mole started to say.

"That's enough." The first mole silenced his partner. "She doesn't need to know any of this."

"What are my special powers even supposed to be?" Maybe if she could find out, she could prove to them she wasn't who they thought she was.

"Don't know. Don't care," the first mole stated.

"Please, if you would only listen…"

The mole abruptly turned around. He shoved Cynthia against the wall with the handle of his staff.

She gasped, her back pinned in place and the metal rod pressed against her neck.

Fox lurched forward, but the second mole pulled him to the ground and stood with one foot on his chest and the sharp point of the pickaxe pointed at his neck. Even in the darkness Cynthia could imagine the glare on Fox's face and the clench of his jaw.

She hoped he wouldn't do anything rash. The darkness and tight space would make a fight deadly. And there was no telling if any of them would walk away unharmed.

"No. More. Talking," the mole growled in Cynthia's face. "Or your mate over there won't live to see the outcome of this little venture."

Cynthia nodded with wide eyes and a racing heart.

The mole stepped away from her and continued his trek through the tunnel. "Release him," he called to his companion.

Reluctantly, the second mole released Fox.

Fox's fists were clenched at his sides and his jaw muscles worked in his cheeks. He wanted to do something about what had just happened, but he must know that there wasn't anything to do.

She joined him and placed a hand on his arm. She shook her head. "Don't," she whispered.

He glared at the moles but murmured his agreement with

Cynthia.

She wanted to talk to Fox about their situation, but she couldn't risk the moles doing more harm to the mouse or Fox in order to keep her quiet.

Instead, she focused on the turns they took through the maze of tunnels. It helped keep her mind busy and her thoughts to herself. Before long she lost track of their location. The darkness pressed in on her. It would feel like a miracle if she ever saw daylight again.

The tunnel came to an abrupt end. The moles and their captors stood in front of a metal door crisscrossed with rivets. Enormous hinges lined one side, and a strange, twisted metal handle protruded from the other.

The first mole knocked in a specific pattern, then stood back.

Cynthia swallowed her fear. What would greet her on the other side?

The hinges groaned and squealed as the door swung open at an excruciating slow pace. New smells assaulted Cynthia's nose: mildew, damp stone, wet fur. She did her best to breathe through her mouth.

Flat stones of all shapes paved the floor. Roots hung from the ceiling like fringe. Water dripped from their ends at random intervals so that it sounded like slow rain. A few mushrooms grew in scattered clumps in the far corners. Strange antennae-like appendages extended from their tops, and the tips glowed a faint green color. It gave the room an eerie glow, but did not offer much in the way of improving Cynthia's ability to see much more than the shapes of the moles and their weapons. The details remained obscure.

The moles pushed Fox, the mouse, and Cynthia through the door and told them to stop when they reached the center of the room on the other side. Fox instantly put a protective arm around Cynthia's shoulders.

Another dozen moles with similar staffs as her original captors, each with a different weapon attached to one end, stood around the perimeter of the room.

Near the back of the room stood a wide, short glowing blue toadstool with orange spots sprinkled on the cap.

A bulky mole wearing a velvety cloak sat on top. A grub wriggled between his fingers. He stared at Cynthia in the dim lighting, then put the head of the grub into his mouth and ripped it in half with his teeth. The squelch it made and the drips of grub guts down the mole's chin made Cynthia's stomach churn.

The menacing mole scanned her up and down with his tiny black eyes as he chewed on the grub. He popped the second half of the grub into his mouth and licked his fingers one at a time before he hoisted himself off the toadstool.

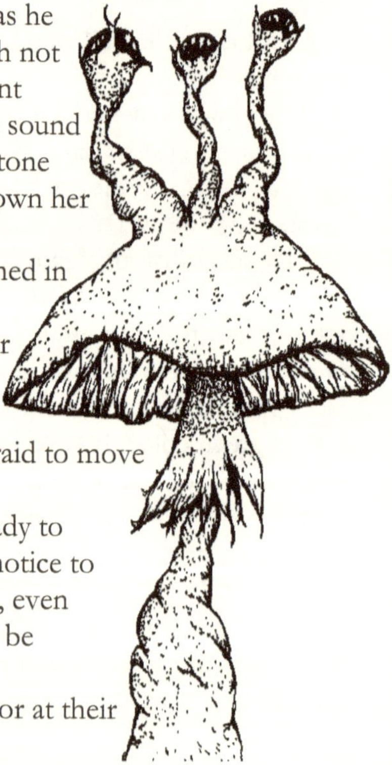

He waddled from side to side as he stepped closer to Cynthia, his girth not allowing him the ease of movement that the other moles enjoyed. The sound of his claws scraping against the stone floor with every step sent chills down her spine.

Cynthia flinched when he loomed in front of her. Her legs trembled.

Fox's arm tightened around her shoulders, and he pulled her closer against him.

She remained perfectly still, afraid to move even a single muscle.

Fox stood tense beside her, ready to spring into action at a moment's notice to protect her and make their escape, even though escape at this point would be impossible.

The mouse cowered on the floor at their

feet.

The mole circled Cynthia, Fox, and the mouse. He looked down his nose at Cynthia, specifically. "This is the one?" His voice rumbled across the stones and the earthen walls absorbed the noise. "She's awfully small. Are you sure she's the right one?"

One of the moles that had roughly escorted them through the tunnels answered their boss. "She's the one the scouts spotted in the woods. It's hard to tell down here, but she fits the description."

"I can see that for myself!" The boss mole spat the words at his minion.

The guard mole shrunk in on himself and backed flatter against the wall. Even the other moles were scared of this big one. What did that mean for Cynthia and Fox?

The boss mole hobbled back to his toadstool chair and huffed a deep breath as he hoisted himself on top again. "Put them in the prison. Then send word that we found her."

"But sir, what if she's not the one?" another mole guard dared to ask.

With a wave of his hand, the mole was silenced by a spear blade in his side from another of the guards. He crumpled to the floor in a heap and remained still.

This did not bode well for Cynthia and Fox. She exchanged worried looks with Fox, easier to see with the light of the mushrooms and their close proximity to one another.

He looked just as desperate and afraid as she felt.

The two guards that had captured them before roughly separated them.

"Wait," the boss mole grumbled. He rubbed his chin with his claws, then pointed at Cynthia. "Clip a sample from her wings to send to the buyer for confirmation."

Fox rushed to put himself between Cynthia and the boss mole. "What? No! That's barbaric!"

"Do it!" the boss shouted at his guards.

Three moles stepped forward from the wall. Two of them held Fox while he flailed to try to protect Cynthia. They pinned his arms behind him and pushed him onto his knees on the ground. He screamed at them and fought against their restraints.

The third told her to hold still while pointing his sharp blade menacingly toward her face.

Afraid of what they would do to Fox or the mouse if she didn't comply, she stood still, folded her arms, and squeezed her eyes shut. She had never cut her wings before. Would it hurt? Would it ruin them?

She hissed from the sting as the mole sliced off one of the lower scallops from her right wing. The pain didn't last, though her wing did flinch and throb even after the mole delivered the section to the boss.

"Now take them away," the boss commanded.

"It's alright, Fox," Cynthia breathed at Fox. He still grumbled harsh threats that Cynthia wasn't sure the moles could even understand. If they did, they didn't show it.

The guards dragged them down another side passage away from the room. One of them squeezed Cynthia's arm with his claws. She winced, which only made his grip tighten. A sharp pain raced from her arm where the mole's claws squeezed her, toward her heart.

"I won't try to escape," she whimpered, trying to keep up with his quick steps.

He snorted through his nose but said nothing.

The pain of his claws digging into her arm urged her to keep up, but without much light she tripped her way down the tunnel.

She cried when she stumbled, and he yanked her upright again.

"You're hurting her!" Fox roared. Then he grunted. The mole that dragged him along must have hit him in the stomach again.

"I'm fine," Cynthia tried to reassure Fox. But she didn't feel fine.

The dirt walls and floors changed suddenly to precisely placed stones. Walls like Cynthia would imagine inside a castle dungeon. They weren't kidding when they used the word prison. Any hopes of being able to dig their way out of an earthen burrow vanished.

Iron barred prison cells lined either side of the tunnel. Glowing mushrooms hung at regular intervals from the ceiling, giving everything an orangish hue.

A winged man of some kind, not much bigger than Cynthia herself, huddled in the corner of one cell, his hard-shelled, spotted wings folded on his back like a shield. He eyed Fox with a strange look and a grimace as they passed. Another cell stood empty of prisoners, but a tattered tunic with dark stains lay in a crumpled heap in the middle of the room.

The guards tossed the mouse into the next cell. She scurried to the far wall and curled herself into a ball without making a sound.

Before Cynthia had time to react, the guard shoved her into the cell opposite the mouse. He slammed the iron-barred door closed behind her.

Cynthia tripped and landed on her hands and knees with a thud. Without any time to register her surroundings, the mole slammed the lock into place. The clang echoed off the stone walls, ceiling, and floor. Cynthia flinched.

From the scuffle in the hall, Cynthia could tell that they had to use force to get Fox into the cell next to her own. They shouted at him, but he couldn't understand them, of course. His moan of pain indicated that he had been struck. Again.

Cynthia wilted. She didn't even try to stand. Her cooperativeness hadn't earned the mouse freedom for herself or her family like she had expected. All it had done was put them all into a dark prison deep underground.

A sob escaped her lips and her shoulders trembled.

"Are you alright?" Fox's frantic voice came from the cell beside her.

Cynthia crawled to the bars and lowered herself to the ground. She leaned against the bars in the corner closest to Fox's voice. She nodded, though Fox couldn't see, of course.

Her arm ached from the mole's claws squeezing it so tight. Her palms and knees stung from where she had landed on the floor of her cell. Her eyes and head ached from trying to see in the darkness. She wrapped her arms around herself.

She didn't even bother to brush away the tears that silently fell down her cheeks. Her dirty hands would only make a bigger mess if she tried.

"Cynthia?" Fox's voice sounded even more alarmed.

"I'm fine." Cynthia strained to make her voice loud enough for Fox to hear.

She heard him slide down the stone wall inside his cell, and his voice sounded close as he spoke. "I'm sorry…" he started to say.

"Fox, stop. Please. This is all my fault." She choked on her words and couldn't bring herself to say anything else.

Fox sighed. She could imagine him running his hands down his face, although she didn't know if he would, since his hands were probably covered in dirt and mud, too. The image of his dirt-stained cheeks and his worried expression made her lips want to smile, but her heavy heart prevented that from happening.

"We'll figure a way out of this. I promise." He sounded determined.

She was sure he was determined, but she didn't know how they'd possibly get themselves out of the prison of a colony of greedy moles that cared little for each other's safety, let alone the well-being of their prisoners.

A shuffling sound followed by a pained moan came from

the far, dark corner of Cynthia's cell.

Cynthia pulled herself to her feet to investigate the source.

Fox must have heard her movements. "What is it? Are you alright?" She heard him stand, too.

"Yes. It's just…" Her voice came out hoarse from her tight throat and thick emotions, but she forced herself to remain calm. Panicking would not help them escape. And as of now, that's all she wanted to do.

She edged closer to the rustling.

"What's going on?" Fox wanted to know.

"There's someone else in my cell with me."

Chapter 20

e careful!" Fox insisted.

Cynthia nodded.

Then she remembered that he couldn't see her. "I will. I'll tell you if anything's wrong." Even though it's not like he could do anything about it. Still, she appreciated his concern.

Whatever lay in the corner of her cell didn't move much even as she spoke in a hushed voice to Fox and took careful steps closer.

The only light in the prison came from a few glowy plants outside the cells. Cynthia squinted to try to make out the source of the sound.

Her cellmate adjusted their position on the ground.

Cynthia gasped. She rushed forward and kneeled beside the animal. She examined the squeezed-shut eyes and furrowed brow on a smudged, sunken face that resembled her own. Another moan escaped from its lungs.

"What is it?" Fox sounded distraught

that he couldn't be there to protect her.

"A faun."

The upper half of the creature looked like Cynthia: arms, torso, face, hair. But the legs resembled matted furry goat legs, with dark hooves instead of feet. A surprisingly long, feather-tipped tail lay limp on the ground alongside the creature.

"A what?" Fox sounded confused. It also sounded like he was pacing on the other side of the wall. How long would it take before he tried to break through the stone barrier that separated them?

"A *faun*. I think. She's injured. And starving." Cynthia spoke just as much to herself as to Fox. "How long has she been in here?"

"Be careful. It could be a..." Fox started to say.

"A trap. I know." For some reason, she had already thought it. "But I don't think it is. This faun is clearly hungry and in pain. She can barely lift her head from the ground."

"How large is it? Describe it to me." The wall between them muffled Fox's frustrated voice.

"Just a second." All worries for her own safety flew from her mind as she examined the injured creature. "She's about your length, maybe a bit taller. She has feathers on her head and tail."

"Feathers? Tail?" Fox's voice rose. "You're not making any sense."

Cynthia didn't understand it either, but she didn't know much about the world she lived in. As far as she knew, fauns came in as many different varieties as pixies. Or dust bunnies.

"Her feathers and fur are dirty. She's so malnourished, her tunic is hanging off her body like rags." Cynthia choked on her words.

Fox remained silent.

Cynthia didn't blame him.

"How can I help you?" Cynthia spoke softly near the faun's head. She stroked her feathers with a gentle hand, careful not to aggravate any unseen injuries. Compassion for the creatures injured and destitute state spread from her heart to overwhelm her senses.

The faun moaned again, but Cynthia couldn't make out what she tried to say.

Cynthia marched to the door of her cell and banged against the bars. "Hey! I need water over here." She held the bars with her hand and pressed her face against them, trying to peer down the aisle of cells.

Fox groaned from his own cell. "What are you doing?"

"The faun needs water. And probably food. But we'll start with water," she said to Fox. Then to the moles that had to be patrolling somewhere nearby, "Hello?! I need water!"

"You're going to get yourself hurt. Or worse!" Fox scolded from somewhere beside her on the other side of the wall.

"I don't think so. I think they want me unharmed." She bit her lip.

That was true, but the thought remained that they didn't need *Fox* unharmed. The one mole had called Fox her "mate." The moles thought of Fox as her friend, or of them as a couple. Either way, they could tell that Fox was important to her. Hopefully they wouldn't use him to get her to comply with whatever it was they were going to do to her!

She pushed those thoughts aside. The best thing to do in a bad situation was serve someone else. And there was someone right there in her cell that needed help. She would press her luck until it couldn't be pressed anymore. And that started with demanding water from her captors.

"You can't always put others before yourself. When will you learn that?" Fox sounded really annoyed this time. Almost angry.

"Probably never." She tried to see if anyone had heard her yelling and was coming with water yet. "Listen. I've learned that kindness always has a way of being returned, one way or another. I can either sit here and wait for whatever disastrous fate awaits me, or I can try to help this faun. Either way, my fate will be the same. But perhaps the kindness will be returned when I least expect it. And if not for me, then for someone else out there who needs it." She paused, then shouted through the bars again. "I. NEED. WATER!"

"Stop your shouting!" A mole appeared in the aisle between the cells. He had his hands covering the sides of his head. "I heard you the first time. Here." He pulled a metal flask from his belt and thrust it between the bars. Then he hurried away before she could even try to thank him for the water.

Cynthia rushed to the faun's side and carefully poured water into her mouth. She had no idea how clean this water was, but something had to be better than nothing.

Some of the water dribbled down the faun's face, but most of it made it down her throat. When the flask had been emptied, Cynthia placed it outside the bars for the guard to retrieve the next time he came along.

In the meantime, Cynthia would await her fate beside the faun. She leaned up against the stone wall, wondering what someone could possibly want with a pixie like herself.

Sunbeams shone through the bright summer leaves of the pumpkin vines in Magnolia's garden. Cynthia strolled beneath them, enjoying the smell of the freshly tilled soil and the sweetness of the giant orange pumpkin blossoms. She inhaled deeply and lifted her face to bask in the ray of sunlight.

Something blocked the sun from her face. Her eyes opened to discover what made the shadow. The wrinkly, grimy face of the man who had captured her grinned down at her. One of his enormous, calloused hands reached for her, ready to scoop her up and carry her away.

She screamed and dodged the man's grab. She raced along the garden, between rows of feathery carrot tops and strawberry plants creating a ground cover.

The man released a menacing laugh. He tromped through the garden after her. The sounds of plants being squished beneath his oversized boots made Cynthia flinch.

Where was Magnolia? How had the man found Cynthia? Why did he want her in the first place?

"Gotcha!" the man's brusque voice barked.

A basket woven from dried reeds plopped over her on the ground, trapping her in place. She pressed against the stiff walls, frantic for a way out.

This was it! She had been captured, again!

"Help!" she cried while she banged against the walls of her prison.

The basket walls changed from dried grass into iron bars. The ground beneath her morphed into stone tiles instead of loose garden soil. The daylight turned into near-blackness.

Cynthia gasped and her eyes flew open. Her breath came hard and fast. Sweat dotted her forehead and moistened the back of her neck.

Her eyes darted around at her surroundings. She forced herself to control her breathing.

She was in the mole's prison. She had fallen asleep. Her heart sank. If only she could have woken in her home. If only *this* was the dream.

An image of Fox's face trying to hide a smile flashed in her mind. If she had never left home, she would never have met Fox. It's not like she was glad she had been captured, freed, and captured again. But she was glad she had met Fox and had the opportunity to learn more about pixies. And more about herself.

Cynthia rubbed the sleep out of her eyes. She stretched her sore back, her arms and legs. She slowly flapped her wings a few times to give them a little exercise. Who knew how long it would be before she'd be able to really fly again, or how long she would stay trapped down here underground.

Her movements must have caught Fox's attention. "I'm glad you got some sleep," he said from the other side of the stone wall.

"How long did I sleep for?" Cynthia asked in a tired voice.

"Several hours. I would guess it's morning by now," Fox answered.

Had he slept at all? Or had he stayed awake to somehow protect her from within his own prison cell?

"I didn't think I'd be able to fall asleep so soundly in a place like this." Her eyes wandered over the dark stones and drippy ceiling.

"It's been a long couple of days," Fox pointed out.

She couldn't agree more. And it had been more than a couple of days. An entire week in the man's wagon. And then six days traveling by foot with Fox.

"How are you doing? Did you sleep?" Cynthia scooted across the floor to lean against the wall adjacent to Fox's cell.

"Sore." He didn't answer the question about sleep.

Flashes of Fox being prodded, struck, and kicked entered Cynthia's mind. "Are you injured? From the moles?" Her voice came out filled with concern. And desperation. How were they going to get out of here?

"Nothing I can't recover from." Fox's own voice sounded tight. He was hiding the magnitude of his injuries from her, she was sure.

"Fox, be honest. Are you alright?" Cynthia wished she could see him for herself. Tend to his injuries. Hold his hand.

He didn't respond right away. Finally, he said, "I'll be fine, I promise."

Cynthia released a deep, troubled sigh. "I can't believe this." She didn't think she had to explain that by "this" she meant being trapped in an underground prison with no way to escape. "What are we going to do?"

Before Fox could respond, a grunt came from the hallway between the prison cells.

A grumpy mole dropped a bowl of food into Cynthia's cell, and then into Fox's. Both bowls landed on the ground with a clatter. Next, he tossed in a metal flask. It skidded across the floor and bumped against the wall opposite from where she sat.

When he had delivered meals to the other cells, the mole shuffled out of the hall without speaking a word to any of them.

"At least they don't plan to let us starve," Fox grumbled from the other side of the wall.

Cynthia's stomach rumbled. The last thing she had eaten was the butter cookie they had shared with the mouse inside the tree.

She hurried to the bowl. One look inside made her gag. Half a dozen live grubs as long as her forearm and twice as big around wriggled inside the bowl. Their exoskeletons and clawed feet clattered on the sides of the metal bowl. A terrible stench wafted off of them.

Fox's voice came from the other side of the wall. "I know it's not appetizing, but you'll need your strength if we're going to get out of here." She heard him crunching one of the grubs and swallowing forcefully to get it down.

"Do you have a plan?" The bowl scraped against the floor as Cynthia shoved it away from herself.

One of the grubs almost managed to climb its way out of the

bowl when another trampled on top of it and pulled it back inside. If she didn't eat them, they would soon be her cellmates, too

Maybe she'd just drink the water for now. She pried the dented, rusty lid off the top of the metal canister and took a sip. She immediately spat it out. It was the dirtiest water she had ever tasted.

"Please at least try to drink?" Fox begged. "And no, I don't have a plan. Not yet. But we'll think of something."

Cynthia forced herself to take two swallows of water. The grime in the water left grit between her teeth. A metallic taste filled her mouth. She set the water container beside the bowl of grubs.

Movement from the corner of her cell reminded her about her injured cellmate. She glanced at the unappetizing meal before her.

Maybe the faun would eat it. Except, if Cynthia didn't want to, it wasn't likely the faun would want to, either. But if the faun was hungry enough… then maybe she would.

She picked up the bowl and cup and padded across the cell.

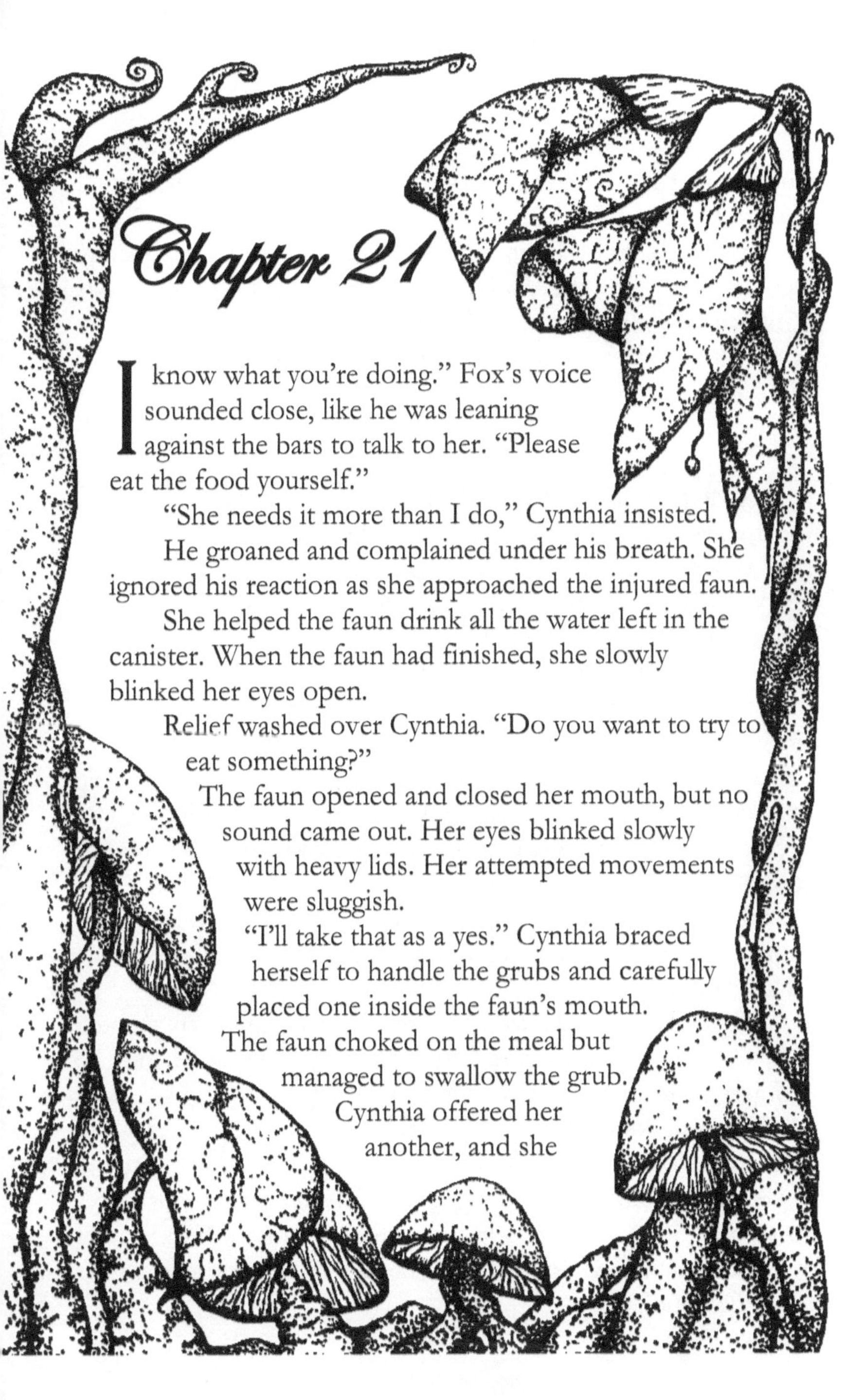

Chapter 21

I know what you're doing." Fox's voice sounded close, like he was leaning against the bars to talk to her. "Please eat the food yourself."

"She needs it more than I do," Cynthia insisted.

He groaned and complained under his breath. She ignored his reaction as she approached the injured faun.

She helped the faun drink all the water left in the canister. When the faun had finished, she slowly blinked her eyes open.

Relief washed over Cynthia. "Do you want to try to eat something?"

The faun opened and closed her mouth, but no sound came out. Her eyes blinked slowly with heavy lids. Her attempted movements were sluggish.

"I'll take that as a yes." Cynthia braced herself to handle the grubs and carefully placed one inside the faun's mouth. The faun choked on the meal but managed to swallow the grub. Cynthia offered her another, and she nodded with a grimace.

Once all six grubs were gone, the faun rested her head on the floor again. "Thank you," she whispered as her eyes slipped closed and she fell asleep.

Cynthia sighed. The thought of eating live grubs completely repulsed her, but she couldn't deny the empty feeling in her stomach. How long would it be until she was offered something even slightly more palatable to eat? Or would she have to reduce herself to eating grubs, too?

Cynthia settled herself in the corner of her cell near the bars, where she could better talk to Fox. She'd have to figure out how to stomach eating live grubs the next time they brought food.

With nothing else to do but talk, Cynthia told Fox more about Magnolia and home. It helped keep her mind off the dank dungeon and the hopelessness of their situation.

"Magnolia has an enormous garden behind her little two-room house. She grows everything you can imagine! Pumpkins, potatoes, cabbage, leeks, sugar snap peas, beans. There's a big strawberry patch, too, which I love walking through. The berries smell so sweet when they're ripe, and when they're not, the plants still have a scent that makes your mouth water. She has these trellises for growing grapes that allow them to dangle where she can easily reach them. It's a magical tunnel for slowly flying beneath."

"What does she do with that much produce?" Fox wanted to know. He sounded tired. Hopefully by talking to him he could rest, even if he didn't actually fall asleep.

She kept going. "She sells them at the marketplace in town. Everyone loves her purple sugar snap peas. They say they're the sweetest around. They're longer than me and each pea is larger than my head! And her golden cherry tomatoes and silver unicorn fruit are so popular that she has a hard time keeping up with demand!"

Fox yawned. "That sounds nice."

Cynthia sighed. It was nice. Her heart twinged. Would she ever see it all again?

"What do you like to do while Magnolia gardens and sells the fruit? Besides visiting your dust bunny friends in the bookshop." Fox urged her to continue talking.

He had remembered about the dust bunnies in the bookshop? She hadn't even known if he had been listening when she had rambled on about her home when they first met. He seemed so annoyed by her very presence that she assumed he had tuned it all out.

His attentiveness eased her homesickness just the tiniest bit.

"In the evenings Magnolia likes to sit in her comfy chair by the fire and read out loud. She reads all the classic works, as well as journal entries from Forest People about animals and plants they have discovered or tended to. Sometimes she finds misinformation in the animal guides and she'll write little notes to correct the facts. I've learned a lot about Tala that way, but it seems there's still so much more that I don't know."

It was strange that in all that time Magnolia had never talked about pixies before. Questions nagged at her in her mind. Why hadn't Magnolia ever talked to her about pixies? Was she trying to keep something from Cynthia? Or did it just not seem like a big deal to her, since apparently they were quite common in Tala. But if Fox was right, Cynthia was unique. Or at least her wings were.

"What else?" Fox's words came out slow and tired. Good. Maybe he'd be able to relax and get some rest, too.

She kept talking. "We have visitors from time to time. Other Forest People who come with messages from family or friends, or to carry important news. She rarely tells me what the messages say, and I don't pry. If it was important for me to know, she'd tell me. Everyone's entitled to their privacy."

Cynthia stopped. Her mind wandered back to home. To her

dust bunny friends. Had they made it back? To the other creatures from the cart that had been captured and then released by the brownies.

Her mind circled back to Fox and all of the unanswered questions she still had about him. Had he been there in the cart? Why hadn't she seen him or heard about him if he had been? What was his purpose for being there that night?

His words about everyone being dishonest snuck into the back of her mind. The fact that he knew that she was being followed. Hunted. Did he know something more about it than what he told her? Her heart skipped a beat. Was he in on it, too? Maybe his intent wasn't finding his way home but taking her somewhere for a reward. Maybe that's why he had been so frustrated that she wanted to find the Forest People instead of finding his home.

Dread filled her stomach. Had she placed her trust in the wrong person entirely?

His timid voice barely reached through the thick stone walls. She leaned closer in order to hear him better. "I don't really have a home. Not like what you have with Magnolia."

Cynthia froze. This is what she had told herself she wanted. To know who he was, where he came from. But was she ready to hear the truth? What if she didn't like what she heard?

But she couldn't bring herself to stop him. She braced herself for the worst. Her chest tightened and she held her breath while she waited for him to say more.

"I have a landing place, near the lake that I mentioned, that I go back to from time to time." Fox's voice remained quiet, like he wasn't sure he wanted to tell her anything, either. "But it's secluded," he continued. "No one lives around me. I am always on the move. I don't like staying in one place for too long. It makes it easier to not make friends, or form attachments to people or places. It makes it easier to cut ties when I need to." He sounded so sad.

Cynthia shook her head. Why would someone want to live

like that? Alone. Friendless. What could his reasons be?

Maybe if she could get him talking about it, she could find out more.

She kept her voice calm as she eased the conversation toward where she desperately needed, but wasn't sure wanted, it to go. "What is your home like? Or, the place that you 'go back to from time to time'?"

"It's nothing special. Just a hollow in an oak tree with the bare minimum of furnishings, a stove for cooking, and a bed. Even the animals leave the tree when I'm around." He let out a nervous chuckle. "I guess they don't like my company, either."

"That sounds… lonely." She said it so quietly, she didn't know if he'd be able to hear.

He shifted his position on the other side of the wall. She was making him uncomfortable. But she hadn't asked him to talk about this. He had started on his own.

She pinched her lips. What should she say? "Have you always lived there?"

He paused. "No."

Would he say more?

Silence hung between them.

Finally, he said, "I once lived with a dozen other pixies in a huge hollow tree. But I couldn't take the constant noise. Or the way they were always worried about each other's business. It seemed like all they wanted to do was talk about each other behind one another's backs. Or offer unsolicited advice. It felt like one or another of them was always watching me, all the time. I could never get a moment's peace. They were all so… two-sided."

He stayed quiet for a minute.

"So, I left." He said it suddenly. Then he didn't say anything else.

How desolate would it be to always be alone? Was it really better than being with a lot of other pixies in one place? Who would want that kind of solitary life?

Or maybe it wasn't the other pixies that were the problem. Maybe *he* was the problem. Maybe he didn't like them being concerned with his business because his "business" was something that might upset the others. Especially if that business was morally questionable.

She warred with herself. She wanted to trust him. She trusted *everyone*. And look where that had gotten her. But she just couldn't imagine him being, well, a bad guy, either.

"What do you… do? While you're traveling around." She edged closer to being able to ask him the harder questions. How had his wings gotten hurt? Why did he not trust anybody? Why had he agreed to let her travel with him? Who was he, really?

Silence hung between them, thicker than the stone wall.

The longer the silence stretched, the more her nerves wreaked havoc on her stomach. Nausea climbed its way up her throat.

He let out a deep sigh. "You won't believe me if I tell you." His voice sounded pained.

She swallowed her anxiety about learning the truth. She *had* to know, even if it changed everything.

"You can tell me anything, Fox. But only if you want to." She held her breath and kept her body perfectly still.

His clothes scuffed against the floor as he changed position again. He let out a long, slow breath, then inhaled, ready to tell her.

Chapter 22

I'm a bounty hunter." His voice sounded rough, like his throat tried to keep him from telling Cynthia the truth.

And for good reason.

Cynthia's heart immediately tripled its beats. Her spine stiffened and her palms started to sweat. Pain stabbed her in the chest. His words felt like sharp thorns against her soft heart.

"*What?*" She leaned away from the wall. Away from Fox.

The walls of her cell spun. The floor tilted. She squeezed her eyes shut to block out the sudden dizziness and pressed her hands against the sides of her head. She did her best to control her breathing so she wouldn't pass out.

He had betrayed her. She had trusted him and he had betrayed her!

She bent forward to put her head between her knees. Her breaths came faster, shallower.

Fox's next words sounded too far away. Muffled, like when Cynthia had nearly drowned in the river. "Cynthia? Are you alright?"

Cynthia wanted to ask him why he had done it. Why he had lied to her. And why he told her the truth now. But she couldn't get her throat to loosen enough to be able to speak. While her head spun circles around this new, alarming information, Fox kept talking.

"I wanted to tell you. As soon as I met you, I knew there was something different about you. Special. But it wasn't until I saw your wings the following morning that I knew who you were. The pixie with the butterfly wings. I had the mark for you right in my pocket."

"Stop." The word came out like the croak of a frog. Cynthia swallowed and said it again, more clearly, before Fox could keep talking. "Stop, Fox. Please."

Fox did as he was told.

If there had been a time for having a lot of questions, that would have been the right time. But for the first time ever, Cynthia's mind drew a blank.

The uneven stone wall pressed against Cynthia's back. The hard floor pushed against her legs. The darkness thickened around her. The rushing of her blood in her ears overwhelmed her.

"I'm sorry."

Fox's apology breached the chaos in Cynthia's head, cut through the raging doubt and fear that gripped her chest, and settled in her heart like a seed in freshly tilled soil.

"I never meant to hurt you. I never meant to... care." Fox paused, then continued. "And I promise you Cynthia, I never meant to turn you in. I knew it the moment I realized who you were."

A calm washed over Cynthia like fresh rain on a spring day. Somehow, she knew he told the truth. She trusted him. Even though by all accounts she knew he was the last person she should trust.

"I believe you," she whispered, and she meant it.

Fox let out a cry as if he had been holding his breath, waiting for those very words. His rough hands against his stubbled cheeks told Cynthia that he might even be wiping away tears.

She was surprised to find tears trickling down her own face, too, probably leaving tracks down her dirt-stained cheeks.

"Tell me," she whispered.

Somehow, he heard her request.

"It's a long story…" Fox sounded reluctant now that the truth had been exposed.

Cynthia let out a single chuckle. "I've got nothing else to do."

Fox sighed. Heavily. "Here goes."

Cynthia prepared herself to hear more. But then a thought occurred to her. Could there even be more that would be more upsetting than the few words he had already spoken? And yet, she didn't hate him. She wasn't afraid of him. She knew that he truly did want to protect her. She *knew* he could be trusted.

"I had been traveling along the road for some time, when I came across that wagon."

Cynthia wanted to be upset that he was still being vague, but something told her to be patient. So she tried.

Fox shifted his position on the other side of the wall. "I knew the guy driving the wagon was up to no good. And I knew that he carried… valuable cargo… inside the wagon." Fox hesitated. His low voice trembled. "This is going to make me sound like a terrible person, Cynthia. I hope you will wait and hear the whole thing before you decide to hate me forever."

"Keep going." Cynthia didn't reassure him, but made sure she didn't sound bitter, either.

"Alright." He sounded sad, but he kept talking. "If I had known the true nature of his cargo, though, I would have done more than just follow the wagon and wait for the opportune moment to investigate potential prizes for myself inside."

Cynthia made mental notes of what she heard. Like a tally

list of the good things he did compared with the bad. Wanting to help versus collecting bounties.

"I followed him until nightfall, so I'd be able to sneak in without being caught myself. You can imagine my surprise when the wagon abruptly stopped before I could make my move! I don't know exactly how the brownies knew that there were creatures inside that needed help."

He sounded frustrated, like he should have known better himself.

Cynthia gave him a minute to continue. When he didn't, she prodded for answers. "So, what happened?"

Fox rushed through the next part, like it wasn't an important part of the story. "The brownies stretched some sort of line across the road. When the pack animals walked into it, they tripped and stumbled. While the man dismounted the wagon seat to see what the problem was, the brownies darted out from the woods, released a jar full of angry fireflies, and unhitched the animals from the wagon."

Cynthia had vaguely been aware of the abrupt stop in her sleep. The sounds of a scuffle outside. And the cries of pain from the man who had captured her and her friends. Then the brownie had awoken her and helped her out of the cage.

"Those two little men sure made a mess of things," Fox complained.

"The mess ended up worth it, though, right?" Cynthia asked in a quiet voice.

She didn't understand Fox's contradictory statements. He found people that didn't want to be found so he could be paid, but he felt bad about the prisoners inside the wagon. He didn't trust anyone but wanted to help people. He was suspicious of the man but seemed frustrated that the brownies had taken action. The creatures had been freed, but a "mess" had been made.

Before she could ask him any of the questions starting to form in her mind, he kept talking.

"I offered to help the brownies. They refused at first, but when I insisted, they asked me to help free some of the creatures. A bunch of the cages had fallen out of the wagon when it toppled sideways, so I started with the cages already outside."

"Fox, wait." Cynthia couldn't let the story continue until she understood him better. "I don't understand. This is very confusing…"

"I know," he sighed. "But it will make sense in the end. I promise." He sounded defeated.

She paused. Should she insist on answers now, or let him keep talking?

Before she could decide, he kept talking. "That's how I managed to damage my wings, actually." She heard his rough hand rub the stubble on his jaw line and could imagine the strained look and deep frown he wore.

"One of the cages held this furry dragon-cat-thing. I don't know what it was. But it was jammed in a cage too small for its size. It had wicked teeth and claws and was clearly enraged at being stuck. I tried to calm it down by telling it I was going to set it free, but when I pried the door of the cage open, it attacked me. My wings took the brunt of it."

"I know the creature." Cynthia set aside

her own pain at learning the truth about Fox. He had been hurt. No one deserves to be hurt like that. "It's cage hung from the roof of the inside of the wagon, not far from my own." She shuddered at the memory of being locked in a cage. "That animal was dangerous. You're lucky to be alive!"

"I'm not so sure about that," Fox murmured.

"What do you mean?" Cynthia's breath hitched.

"What good is a pixie with broken wings?" Fox hadn't sounded this dejected since Cynthia had met him. "I'm completely useless now, more than ever."

They remained silent for several long moments.

"You showed up right after the animal ran away. I couldn't believe my eyes. Again." His voice softened. "I really am lucky you showed up when you did. I was ready to give up on the world at that point, Cynthia. To do something stupid or reckless. But something about your kindness made me stick around to see what you were all about. And then when I realized you were the one with a bounty, but you weren't a terrible person like all the other bounties I've captured? I haven't ever met anyone like you before. I've only been hurt and let down by others. I've only ever hurt those around me. I didn't want to allow you to change my mind about the miserable world in which we live. But… you have." He ended with his voice an affectionate whisper.

Cynthia's heart fluttered and swelled. "I don't know what to say," she whispered back. If only she could see his face.

But the wall that separated them was as thick and solid as ever.

"Thank you for telling me…" she said quietly.

He didn't say anything else.

She closed her eyes and leaned against the rough stone wall. Her stomach grumbled. She placed a hand over it and pressed on it. She'd have to end up eating the grubs sooner or later.

Before she even realized it, Cynthia felt tears begin to leak from her eyes again. "I'm so sorry, Fox. This is all my fault. I should have listened to you. I…"

"Stop, Cynthia. This isn't your fault." He heaved a deep sigh. "It's mine. I should never have let you stay with me. Once I realized who you were, I should have done more to protect you. I'm the bounty hunter. You are innocent."

Cynthia shook her head and swiped at the tears again. "You tried to tell me to leave you. Multiple times. You tried to tell me not to follow that mouse. I should have listened. I shouldn't have been so selfish."

"How can helping someone be considered selfish?" Fox prodded.

"The mouse definitely didn't need my help. *You* don't really need my help. I just wanted…" She hesitated but decided to spit it out. "I wanted a friend."

Cynthia heard a thud, like Fox punched the wall or floor or something. He growled his next words. "I *knew* something was wrong when the mouse showed up. I never imagined this being the outcome, though." Fox sounded angry, but at himself.

"What do you mean?" She quieted her sniffles so she could hear him better.

"Remember how I said the mouse was hiding something?" he asked in a low voice.

"Yes," Cynthia answered.

"It's more than just a gut instinct. I *knew*." Fox emphasized the last word.

Cynthia waited for him to say more.

He didn't.

She recalled his words about how everyone lies. The time he could tell the may bug was following them. His reactions to some of the travelers and the ferryman. His knowing the man in the wagon was up to no good. And even his wariness of the innocent little mouse mother.

It clicked.

"That's your ability, isn't it?" she gasped. "You can *tell* when someone is lying, can't you?"

He took a deep breath and released it. "I became a bounty hunter to get rid of the scum of Tala. With my ability to sense lies, it was the perfect job. I would receive an assignment, find the wanted person, and I could always tell right away that they were bad people. It made it easy to collect the bounties on them.

"It is probably the worst ability I can think of. Believe me when I tell you that *no one* is trustworthy. And yet, here you are, giving your trust freely to everyone around you all the time.

"That's why when I met you and sensed your complete goodness, and then figured out who you were, I knew I couldn't turn you in. I knew there would be others looking for you, though. I had to make sure you stayed safe. I had to do everything in my power to protect you, at all costs.

"You are the most honest, kind, giving… *true* person I've ever met." His voice caught in his throat. "What I wouldn't give to have *that* ability."

Suddenly the stone wall between them felt too thick. She was too far away from him. She wanted to be closer.

Cynthia reached her hand forward through the bars and bent her elbow. If only she could reach him.

His hand connected with hers and gripped it tight.

He cleared his throat, as if trying to suppress his emotions. "I've never told anyone before," he whispered. "I don't think I've ever talked to anyone this much in my life." He let out a nervous chuckle.

"Thank you for telling me. I hope I haven't done or said anything to let you down…"

She recalled how she had refused to listen when he warned her about the mouse. How she had promised him everything would be alright if they just did the right thing.

Guilt stung her chest. "From now on, I'll listen when you say something is wrong."

He squeezed her hand. "None of this is your fault. You couldn't have known about my ability. The thing is, I gave you no reason to trust *me*, and time and again you stayed by my side. Even when I wasn't the easiest to get along with."

She chuckled through her drying tears.

"No one has been able to see past my… unlikability… before. I don't know if it's somehow *your* ability to see the best in everyone, or if it's just who you are. But either way, thank you. For saving me."

"I haven't done anything to save you! I've gotten you captured!" Cynthia shook her head.

Fox released her hand. "About that… I have an idea."

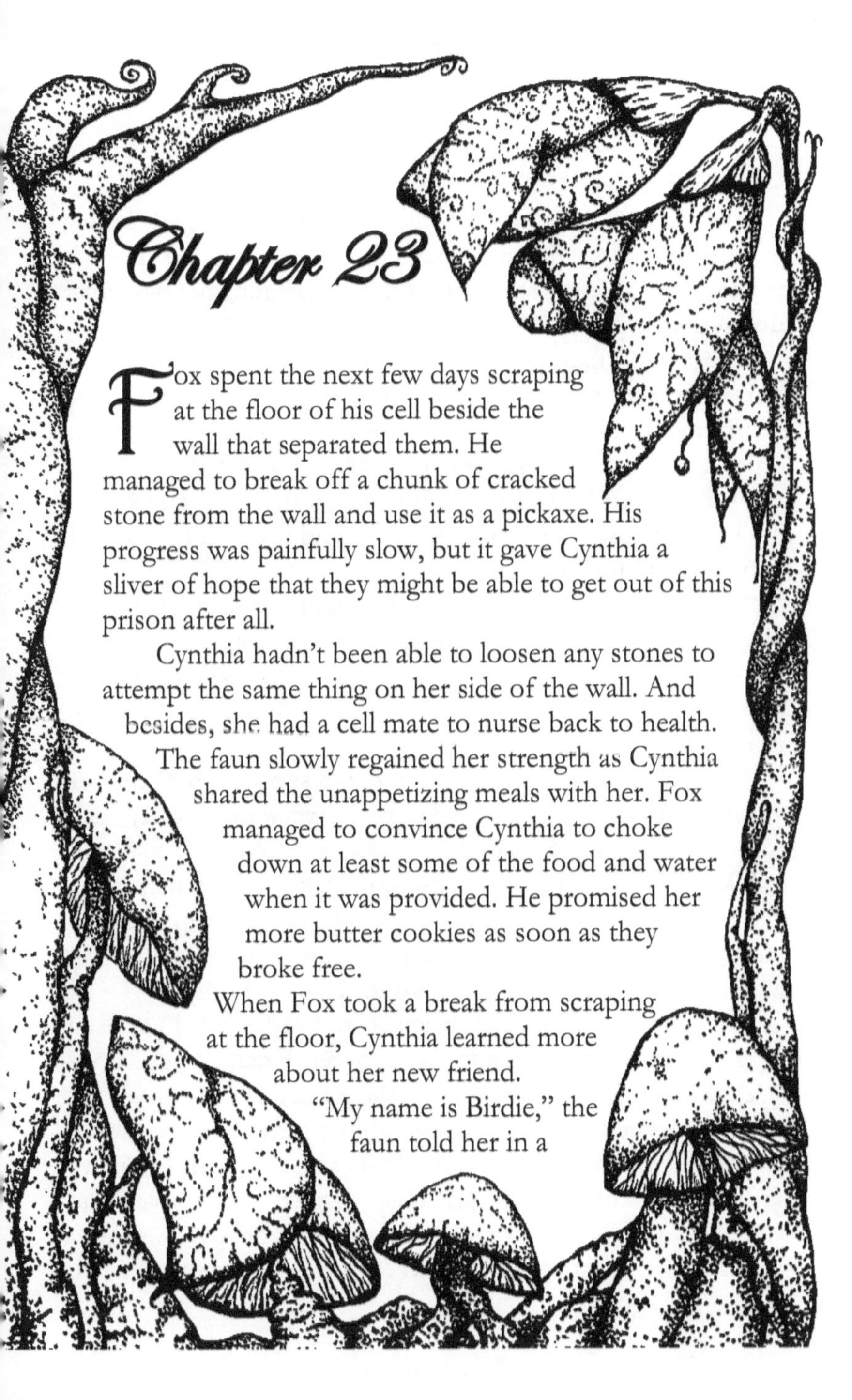

Chapter 23

Fox spent the next few days scraping at the floor of his cell beside the wall that separated them. He managed to break off a chunk of cracked stone from the wall and use it as a pickaxe. His progress was painfully slow, but it gave Cynthia a sliver of hope that they might be able to get out of this prison after all.

Cynthia hadn't been able to loosen any stones to attempt the same thing on her side of the wall. And besides, she had a cell mate to nurse back to health. The faun slowly regained her strength as Cynthia shared the unappetizing meals with her. Fox managed to convince Cynthia to choke down at least some of the food and water when it was provided. He promised her more butter cookies as soon as they broke free.

When Fox took a break from scraping at the floor, Cynthia learned more about her new friend.

"My name is Birdie," the faun told her in a

honeyed drawl between bites of food.

Cynthia smiled. "What a wonderful name."

"It's because of my feathery hair." She motioned at the broken, matted feathers on her head. Her shoulders fell. "I promise they are much prettier, usually." She hung her head and turned away.

"I can see that they are beautiful." Cynthia assured her friend. And it was true. Even in the low light and dirty environment, they still had a sheen to them that caught Cynthia's eye with Birdie's movements.

Birdie leaned against the wall between their cell and Fox's. She told Cynthia, and Fox, when he could listen, how she had come to be in this place.

"The moles wanted me to show them the location of my village. We have a way of finding our way through the woods that other creatures just don't have. The moles wanted to bribe my people to be guides or something. I still don't quite understand it.

"But our kind are private. We don't socialize outside our species very often, other than to assist a wayward traveler back onto the right path if needed.

"When I refused to help the moles, they threatened me. I still refused to show them to my village, so they captured me and dragged me down here. I've been here at least a full moon cycle, I believe. Although, it's hard to tell.

"My legs were injured when I resisted, and I've been struggling in the cold darkness to recover. Finally, I gave up. I accepted my fate and curled up in the corner to die.

"That's when you came along." Birdie's eyes glistened when she looked at Cynthia. "Your kindness saved my life. I hope to be able to return the favor." She wiggled her hooves and winced. "I just have a bit more healing to do first."

"I couldn't just let you starve to death," Cynthia said to Birdie.

"Yes, you could have." Fox's muffled voice joined the conversation.

Cynthia rolled her eyes and shook her head. No matter what Fox said, he was wrong. She couldn't have lived with herself if she hadn't tried to help.

If only she could do something for the mouse in the cell across the aisle. The poor thing had been curled in a ball in the corner of her cell since the first day. She had declined food and water, and Cynthia was afraid she would end up wasting away like Birdie had done. But no matter what she said to try to convince the mouse that things would be alright, the mouse didn't respond. The mouse was either too ashamed of her actions that had landed them all in a prison, or too distraught at the fact that she had failed in protecting her family.

"Mice hibernate," Fox suggested when Cynthia shared her concern with him. "Maybe she's gone into a hibernation state until she gets released."

"Maybe." Cynthia hoped that Fox was right.

After listening to Fox dig at the wall for what must have been nearly a week, Cynthia didn't know how much more of it she could take. Even so, she was grateful for Fox's effort to try to get to her. And then they would be able to dig their way out together.

What would it be like to be with him face to face again? Especially after he had been so vulnerable with her? Would his mood change? Or would he still be distrustful of everyone they encountered as they continued their journey? Would they discuss his being a bounty hunter, or would they just pretend they never talked about it?

Maybe he would pretend like nothing had happened between them. They would just continue their journey in the light of day as if everything below ground wasn't real.

No, she had to believe he would still want to be with her the way she wanted to be with him. But what about after they found the Forest People and fixed his wings? Then what? Would he return to living alone, trying to rid the world of evil all by himself?

These were all things she'd have to figure out if they managed to escape.

No, *when* they escaped. Optimism would be necessary if they were going to pull this off.

"I feel awful that you have to do all the work," Cynthia spoke with Fox through the wall.

They didn't have to worry about getting caught. The moles only came by once a day to give them food and water.

And although they didn't have daylight to mark the time, the daily appearance of the guard helped Cynthia feel some sense of how long they had been down there.

A week. They had been trapped underground for an entire week. Her wings ached to stretch and soar. Her back longed for a soft bed, even if it was just moss on the ground in a hollow tree. Her belly still tried to reject the disgusting grubs provided once a day for their meal, but she forced herself to hold it down. She needed the nourishment.

"If we don't get out of here soon, I might just turn into an underground mushroom troll." Cynthia rolled her neck and leaned against the wall. "Is there anything I can do to help it go faster?" She knew the answer, but she felt like she would burst with her inability to aid Fox in digging them out.

Fox huffed and puffed as he worked to dig underneath the wall. "Trust me, if you could help, I'd let you." He sounded exhausted. How was he supposed to fully heal from his injuries from the moles if he had to work so hard?

"Soon enough," she promised. "Once you make it through, I can take over to dig out underneath the bars and then we'll get out of here. Except..."

She hesitated to tell him what she had been thinking about their escape plan. And *who* their escape plan involved.

Fox's digging stopped for a moment. "Why do I get the feeling you're about to say something about Birdie or that mouse and us needing to rescue them, too?"

Cynthia bit her lip. How did he know that's exactly what she was thinking? "It won't take that much longer..."

He scraped at the floor again. "Yes, it will. The hole to get out will have to be much bigger if we take Birdie with us. And how would she even come? Would we carry her? And then we'd have to dig *another* hole across the aisle for the mouse, who we don't even know wants to be rescued! And what about the other prisoner? We can't just leave him behind if we're planning on bringing everyone else with us. Which means another hole. By then we would be caught for sure. And I don't want to think about what might happen to us if we get caught."

Cynthia heard his shudder after he finished talking.

He had a point. But she still felt really guilty thinking about leaving Birdie behind, especially.

Fox continued his lecture between scrapes and huffing breaths. "And I don't need to remind you that digging our way out of our cells is as far as our plan goes. We don't even know where we're going to go after we dig our way out of your cell! Nope. It's not happening. We'll get you to safety, then we'll figure out what to do about the mouse and Birdie."

"That's not acceptable!" Cynthia argued. She hated disagreeing with Fox after he had been so open with her, but she didn't think she had it in her to leave any of the other prisoners behind.

"Maybe we can steal the keys and set everyone free?" she suggested.

Fox groaned and his digging stopped for a moment. "We don't have weapons. And those moles are way too big for us to take on without a way to defend ourselves. It won't do anyone any good if we go and get ourselves killed. We'll be able to find help on the surface."

"He's right," Birdie interrupted. "You must leave me behind. If and when I get out, I'll find a way to take the mouse with me. Or send someone back to rescue her."

"Are you sure?" Cynthia wrung her hands together. How could she just leave them behind? The mouse was there because of her. And she couldn't leave Birdie here, not knowing if she ever made it home or not!

Before she could come up with an argument, the dirt beside the wall trembled.

"I made it!" Fox hollered. He dug a little bit longer until the stone pushed all the way through the hole and into Cynthia's cell.

Just the sight of his hand right there in front of her made tears sting her eyes. She grabbed his hand and squeezed it tight. Then the tears fell for real.

One landed on his dirty hand. "Are you alright?" he worried.

"Yes." She swiped away the tears, no longer bothered about her face staying clean. "I'm just so happy to see you, finally!"

He laughed. "But you can't see me! Only my hand!"

"It's good enough!" She composed herself.

When she studied his hand more carefully she gasped. Besides being caked in dirt, his skin cracked at the creases, had broken blisters and angry red areas from rubbing against the stone and dirt.

How had he managed to dig with his hand so raw?

She slid the stone out of his hand. "I'll finish the hole while you rest."

His hand disappeared to the other side of the wall again. "I won't turn down that offer." She heard Fox collapse onto the floor and breathe deeply. He must be so exhausted. She would help as much as she could to get them both out of there as soon as possible.

She had just started her work to expand the hole, when the sounds of many feet coming down the aisle reached her ears.

She shoved the stone into the hole then sat on top of it to hide it. She waited for the guards to pass.

A crew of four mole guards approached their cells.

"It's your lucky day!" one of the guards said as he noisily removed the lock from the bars of her cell. "You're being transferred."

Chapter 24

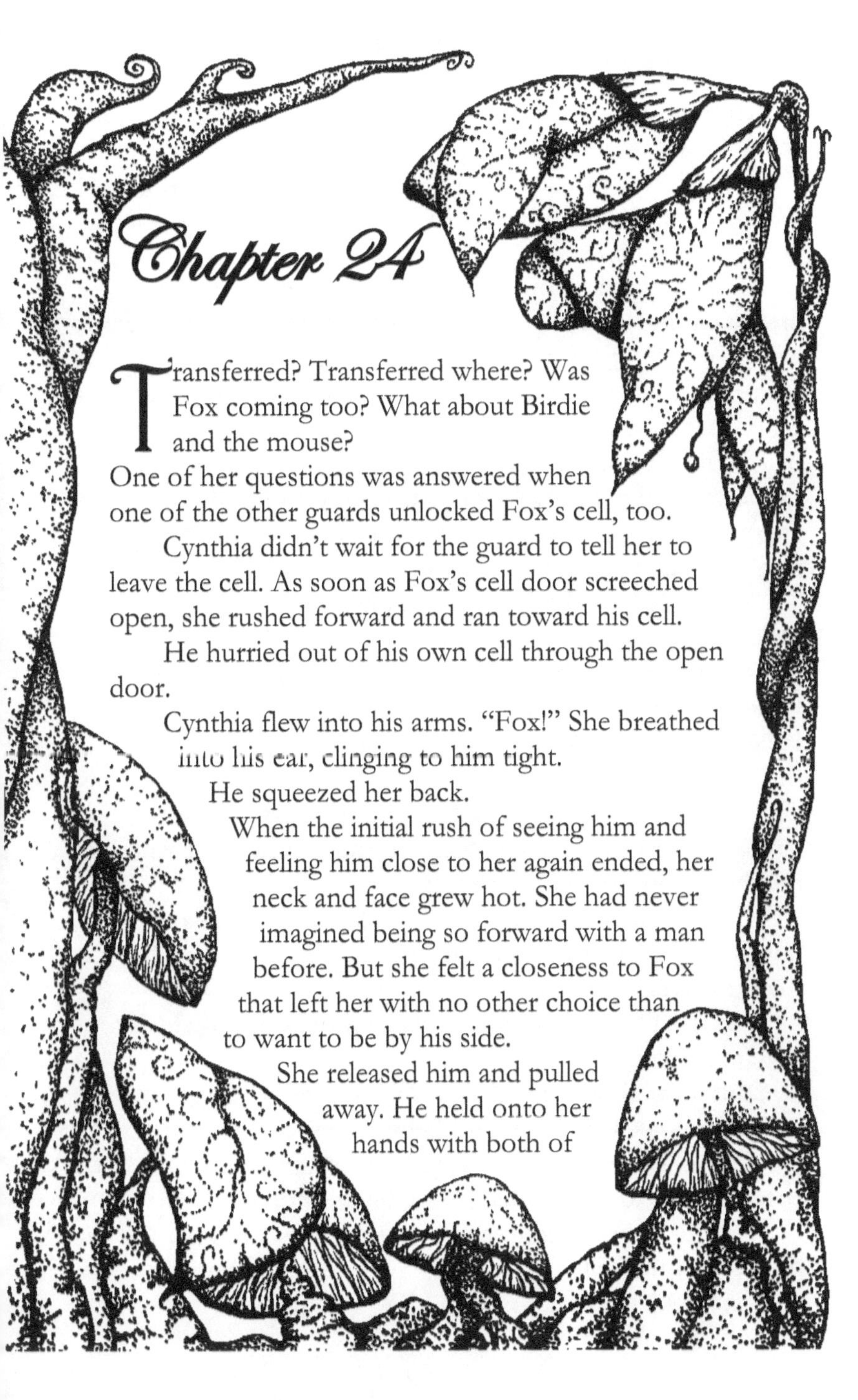

Transferred? Transferred where? Was Fox coming too? What about Birdie and the mouse?

One of her questions was answered when one of the other guards unlocked Fox's cell, too.

Cynthia didn't wait for the guard to tell her to leave the cell. As soon as Fox's cell door screeched open, she rushed forward and ran toward his cell.

He hurried out of his own cell through the open door.

Cynthia flew into his arms. "Fox!" She breathed into his ear, clinging to him tight.

He squeezed her back.

When the initial rush of seeing him and feeling him close to her again ended, her neck and face grew hot. She had never imagined being so forward with a man before. But she felt a closeness to Fox that left her with no other choice than to want to be by his side.

She released him and pulled away. He held onto her hands with both of his while his eyes roved over her as if making sure that she really was safe and unharmed like she said.

Her hair was probably a mess, her hands and face smudged with dirt, and her clothes dingy and wrinkled, but she didn't even care.

All she cared about was Fox. His wings looked more crumpled and ruined than they had before, he had a yellow bruise on one of his cheeks, and his pants had been torn open revealing healing cuts on both of his knees. The still raw cuts on his hands looked extremely painful, and his bloodshot eyes proved how poorly he had been sleeping the past week.

Tears filled her eyes. Her heart ached for him. But a look of angry determination hardened his features as he pulled her close to his side and glared at the mole guards.

"Where do you think they're taking us?" she whispered into his ear, worry lacing her words.

He squeezed his hand around her waist and shook his head. "I don't know. But we need to stick together no matter what." He gave her a look as if to confirm that she would listen to him this time.

"Of course," she answered. After everything that had happened and that she had learned, she would listen when he told her his impression of people.

"Come on. Get a move on!" the guard complained. He poked his blade-tipped staff in their direction, about to prod them forward.

"No need!" Fox held his hand out to tell the guard to stop. "We're coming."

"But what about Birdie? And the mouse?" Cynthia wheeled around to look at the two cells behind her.

"Please, do as the guard says." Fox begged Cynthia to not tempt the guard into actually using his weapon on them.

"But..." Tears filled Cynthia's eyes as she gazed at Birdie at the back of the cell.

Fox tucked a lock of Cynthia's stringy silvery blue hair

behind her ears and wiped her cheek with his thumb. "I know. But we can't risk it. Not right now. Please." His voice sounded so caring and sincere that for once Cynthia didn't feel like she should disagree with him. Even though every part of her wanted to demand the guard release the other two prisoners with them.

Fox was right. It would do no good. And the moles were ruthless. They couldn't be reasoned with. She had nothing of value to offer to make a bargain. The situation was out of her control.

She said a quick, tearful goodbye through the bars to Birdie.

Birdie nodded in her direction and gave her a weak smile. "Everything will work out, you'll see," she said with a raspy voice.

The mouse, as usual, stayed in her ball and didn't respond to Cynthia's emotional farewell.

Fox took her hand, and the pair followed the mole guards through the tunnels in a different direction than where they had come the first time.

The moles marched at a quick pace, and Cynthia's lack of movement over the past week made it difficult for her to keep up. She stumbled over her feet but kept all her complaints to herself.

The moles guided them through the dark tunnels, glowing mushrooms only lighting them at long intervals. In between the glow from the mushrooms, Cynthia couldn't see much at all.

Any hope of keeping track of their turns down different tunnels in order to somehow find their way back quickly evaporated. Cynthia was well and truly disoriented in the maze of tunnels. Even if she managed to escape, she'd never be able to find the prison, or Birdie, again.

Before long, the only thing she could keep track of was the heavy footsteps of the guards in front of and behind her, and the awareness of Fox's presence at her side.

Eventually, the guards stopped in front of a small cave with a few extra mushroom lights dotting the dirt walls. Racks of supplies, weapons, tools, and other items lined the alcove. Another mole manned the station, asking the guards what they needed.

A sixth mole, smaller and skinnier than the others, and not carrying a weapon of any kind, spread a parchment on the counter in front of him. "Here's the rendezvous point. Watch out for the angler trolls. They're out in full force this moon cycle." He pointed at a passageway on the map that Cynthia couldn't make out.

The higher-ranking guard pointed at the parchment and followed a trail with one of his long, pointed claws.

Cynthia tried to see where the tunnels would take them, but the lighting was too dim, and the moles blocked her view of the map.

The supply mole shoved items in two small satchels and plopped them on the counter on top of the map.

"Here are the sacks of supplies for the prisoners," the supply mole announced to the guards. "Make them carry their own. And here are the nets to bind their wings and hands. Boss's orders." He dropped a pile of woven string beside the bags.

Fox looked at Cynthia for an explanation, since he couldn't

understand the moles' words.

"They're going to bind our wings!" Cynthia gave Fox a worried look.

One of the guards took a poorly constructed net in his paws and approached Cynthia and Fox.

Fox stepped between the guard and herself. "You will not lay a grimy claw on her," he growled.

Another guard pointed his hook-ended spear in Fox's direction. "You'll do as he says, or you'll pay the price."

Fox didn't need to understand the words in order to understand the threat. He growled at the guard with the weapon. "Leave her alone!"

The guard followed through on his threat and smashed the curved end of the hook into Fox's stomach.

Fox doubled over in pain.

"NO!" Cynthia screamed.

"Don't move!" The mole holding the net threatened Cynthia.

She stayed perfectly still, but didn't take her eyes off Fox.

He groaned in his curled-up position on the floor of the tunnel with his eyes squeezed shut. He panted, as if the wind had been knocked from his lungs.

"Fox," she whimpered. She scanned him with her eyes for any signs of blood. Had the hook pierced him?

"I'm fine." He managed to squeeze out the words between puffs of air and groans of pain.

He pulled himself to his knees and growled at the mole with the net again. "I said…" he staggered to one knee. "… leave her alone."

The guard that had struck him raised his weapon to do it again. Only this time the barbed hook pointed right at Fox's face.

"No! Please, stop. I'll submit." Cynthia begged the mole guards. "Please don't hurt him again."

The moles looked at each other. The one holding the weapon aloft waited to see what Fox would do.

"Please, Fox," she pleaded. "Don't do anything to stop them. I'll be fine." She couldn't stand the thought of him being hurt again. Or worse.

His face betrayed his anger at the moles, but he nodded to agree with Cynthia.

The mole holding the net roughly turned Cynthia around. "Arms up, wings down." He wrapped the net snuggly around Cynthia's torso and tied it off in the back, over her wings.

Once it was in place, it was impossible for her to open her wings. Flying would be out of the question. "It's not like I can fly in these tunnels, anyway." She murmured under her breath.

Then her breath hitched. Did that mean they were taking her above ground? Their chance of escape above ground would be much higher. Even with her wings bound.

"Now your hands." He motioned for her to lower her hands and put them together in front of her. She did as she was told, and he bound them together with ropes.

"Your turn, tough guy." The guard holding the weapon roughly prodded Fox forward.

Fox flinched at the contact with the weapon, but didn't resist or argue.

They did the same with Fox that they had done with Cynthia, even though with his broken wings it was completely unnecessary. But there was no way for them to know that, and Cynthia figured if Fox didn't say anything then she shouldn't either.

Fox and Cynthia stood side by side, her shoulder pressed against his arm. The moles shoved satchels toward each of them. "This has your food and canteen inside. Lose it, and you'll starve."

Cynthia nodded. Fox took the two bags while glaring at the guards. Cynthia could feel his anger seething beneath the surface.

"Please don't do anything," she begged him in a whispered voice.

He helped her wear the satchel over her bound hands and wings.

"As long as they don't hurt you..." he growled between his clenched teeth.

Carrying the satchel with her hands bound proved to be difficult as they trudged through the dark tunnel. One of the moles led the entourage while two mole guards marched behind. Fox and Cynthia were outnumbered, in a weakened state from being locked up for so long with little in the way of nourishment, and exhausted.

How long would it take for them to get wherever they were going? Who were the moles rendezvousing with? Would their situation be worse after the "transfer?"

The questions plagued Cynthia's mind as she trudged through the tunnel between Fox and the lead guard. The only thing keeping her going was knowing that Fox was there right behind her. And if he could help them escape, at any point along the way, he absolutely would.

They made camp inside the tunnel after walking in silence for hours. By the time they stopped, Cynthia's feet throbbed, and she did her best to rub them with her bound hands. Fox helped her get something to eat from her pack when she struggled to open it, and she quietly thanked him for his help.

The moles huddled together to scarf down their meal of dried grubs. They crunched and slurped and wiped their faces with the backs of their furry hands.

Cynthia's stomach churned, but she forced herself to eat her food, too.

"Are you doing alright?" Fox whispered to Cynthia, keeping an eye on the mole guards as he spoke right into her ear.

She nodded. She wanted to cry, but she wouldn't let the tears fall this time. She had to stay strong.

Fox checked her wrists where the ropes rubbed. He clenched his jaw when he saw the skin starting to rub raw beneath the ropes. She flinched and sucked in a sharp breath as he tenderly ran his fingers over them.

"I'm fine, I promise," she whispered. "I just want to get out of here." Her chin trembled.

The look on Fox's face reminded her that he would do anything to protect her, even at the risk of his own safety.

"Whatever you do, Fox, please don't get yourself hurt." She stared into his eyes.

His features softened and he nodded.

"Hey, you two. Separate!" one of the mole guards ordered. He jumped to his feet and stomped toward them.

His sudden outburst startled Cynthia and the angry look returned to Fox's face.

"He wants us to separate." Cynthia clung to Fox's hands. The last thing she wanted was to be away from him.

But it couldn't be helped. It was either do as the guards said or run the risk of Fox getting hurt again.

She slipped her hands from him and stood. She allowed the guard to lead her several paces away from Fox. He roughly shoved her back to the ground. The palms of her hands scraped against the dirt, but she managed to resist the urge to cry out. She didn't need to egg Fox's anger on any further.

Cynthia lay curled in a ball with her hands and wings bound tight. She could just make out Fox's form through the darkness as he glared at their captors. She wanted to talk to him so badly. To ask him a million questions. To find out if he could think of any way for them to escape.

She tossed and turned on the hard dirt floor of the tunnel for the several hours that the moles insist they rest. One of the moles stood guard while the others curled into balls and slept soundly.

Her mind kept racing with her worries. Where were the

moles taking her? What would happen to Fox when they got…
wherever they were going? What would happen to *her*?

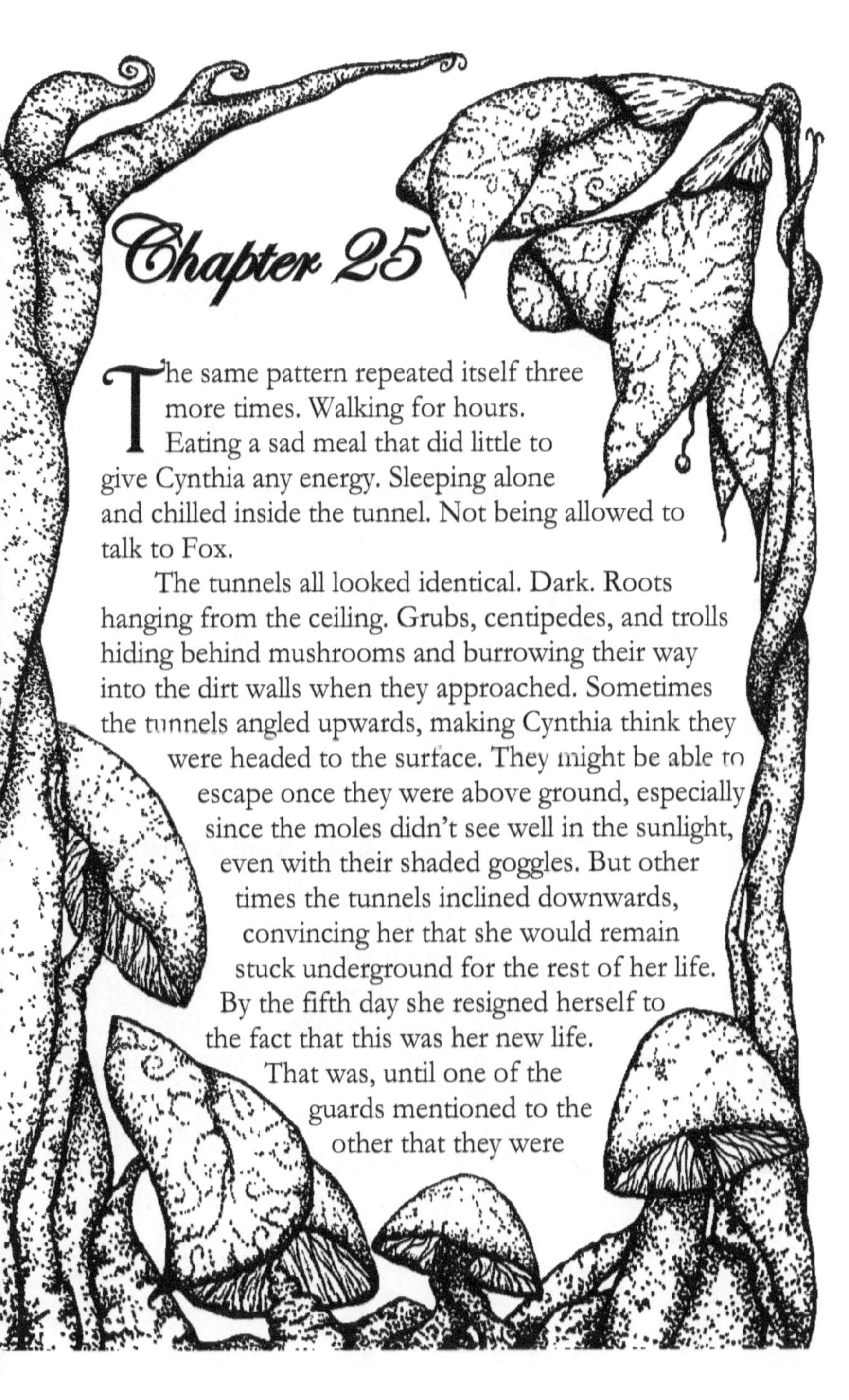

Chapter 25

The same pattern repeated itself three more times. Walking for hours. Eating a sad meal that did little to give Cynthia any energy. Sleeping alone and chilled inside the tunnel. Not being allowed to talk to Fox.

The tunnels all looked identical. Dark. Roots hanging from the ceiling. Grubs, centipedes, and trolls hiding behind mushrooms and burrowing their way into the dirt walls when they approached. Sometimes the tunnels angled upwards, making Cynthia think they were headed to the surface. They might be able to escape once they were above ground, especially since the moles didn't see well in the sunlight, even with their shaded goggles. But other times the tunnels inclined downwards, convincing her that she would remain stuck underground for the rest of her life. By the fifth day she resigned herself to the fact that this was her new life. That was, until one of the guards mentioned to the other that they were nearing their destination.

"We should be there soon. Keep a close eye on the prisoners, just in case." One of the guards motioned at Fox especially.

Cynthia hoped they would say something else, anything else, to give them a clue as to where their destination would be.

Were they to be transferred to someone else below ground? Then what was the point of binding their wings and hands? It's not like they could escape inside these narrow tunnels that crisscrossed in every direction and were patrolled by dozens of mole guards.

Not to mention the other creatures they had come across. Cynthia wouldn't want to face that army of ants or the line of centipedes without any weapons. And it would be impossible to take the weapons from their captors with their hands bound.

Perhaps the imminent "transfer" that they talked about would answer some of her questions.

She didn't have to wait long to find out. The tunnel they walked through sloped upwards all of a sudden. A dim light shone up ahead.

They were heading for the surface.

Cynthia gave Fox a hopeful look. He wore a determined expression on his face. Maybe they would be able to get themselves out of this disaster after all.

The sunlight blinded Cynthia when they reached the opening to the surface, but the fresh air and sunshine felt so good on her skin that she didn't care that she couldn't see a thing.

The moles hoisted her and Fox out of the hole and dumped them roughly on the ground above.

The ground didn't have snow, like when they went below, but it was hard and cold. Winter had definitely begun. The sudden humidity and chill made Cynthia shiver as she tried to right herself into a seated position on the ground. Her satchel hung around her neck, threatening to tangle with her legs as she repositioned herself.

Fox stood much more gracefully than her attempt and offered his bound hands to her to help her feet, too.

She accepted his offer, and he didn't release her hands when she joined him near the hole in the ground.

As her eyes adjusted, Cynthia got a good look at Fox. His face had sunken in from his lack of nourishment, leaving his eyes and cheeks hollow. Dirt caked in the fibers of his clothing, darkening the fabric by several shades. His wrists were in a worse state than Cynthia's from the ropes that bound them together. The moles must have sinched his bindings even tighter than her own. And beneath the awkward netting around his wings, she saw that they looked duller and more tattered than she had remembered.

A quick glance down her own front proved that she probably looked just as malnourished and disheveled. Her dress was wrinkled, dingy, and gray. Her own wings weren't as vibrant beneath the bindings as they would have been in daylight either. The way they pinched together left her concerned that she might suffer permanent damage to her wings, too.

That would make them quite a pair, wouldn't it? The two pixies with broken wings. Normally the thought might make her smile, but under the circumstances it only made the sick feeling in her stomach worse.

Cynthia studied their surroundings. They were no longer in the woods. The stench of rotten eggs assaulted her nostrils, and the thick, cold humidity spoke of water nearby. The sounds of winter crickets and flies buzzing filled her ears after the muffled silence of the underground tunnels. She flinched at the noises.

A group of four toothy-looking plants grew in a row between the hole they had emerged from and the edge of the pond in front of them. Their leaves came together like an eyeless face, and the pink in between gave the appearance of a mouth. They all turned in the direction of the pixies and the moles. They opened and closed their "mouths" as if hoping for a bite of one of them. It didn't seem to matter to them if it was a mole or a pixie that wandered too close. They would have been satisfied either way.

Maybe they could use that to their advantage. Cynthia hated to think like that, sacrificing one- or all- of the moles to the plants so that she and Fox could make their escape. But she didn't see what choice they had. Unless a different option presented itself, it just might be the only way.

Water surrounded the party. The tunnel they had emerged from was located in the middle of a mound of an island right in the center of a disgusting swamp. With their wings and hands bound, they couldn't swim, let alone fly. They were truly trapped.

A loud, ominous croak startled her from the direction of the pond. She nudged Fox to look toward the sound.

When Cynthia saw who the transfer had been arranged with, all hope of escape quickly evaporated.

The croak came from the biggest, ugliest toad Cynthia had ever seen. Its round belly hung in folds over its bumpy green legs. Its bulbous eyes stared at her with a hungry look. It wore a crown, of sorts, on top of its head, woven from reeds and dotted with flowers.

"Bring my prize forward." The voice of the toad didn't sound much different than the belch of a croaking angler-troll. The sound made Cynthia cringe.

The mole guards prodded Cynthia and Fox forward. He held her close with his hands clasped around hers. Walking with bound hands holding someone else's bound hands was awkward, but she didn't dare release him. They had to stay together, and she didn't think the intentions of the toad were good.

"What's with the other one?" The toad gave Fox a disgusted look and waited for the one of the moles to answer.

"They were captured together. A… bonus prize, if you will," one of the moles answered.

"I have no need for the second. I'll take the one with the butterfly wings. Do as you wish with the other."

"What? No!" Cynthia shrieked and gripped Fox's hands tighter.

Fox gave her an alarmed look. "What? What's wrong?"

"They want to separate us. The toad says she doesn't want you, only me. Fox, what will we do?" She didn't care that her voice sounded desperate and afraid. She felt desperate and afraid. She didn't want to be separated from Fox. She was afraid of what the toad wanted with her. She had heard tales of toads attempting to marry off their ugly sons to other species by capturing them.

"You must take us both. Or leave us both behind!" Cynthia shouted at the toad. She didn't care that she was putting her safety at risk by being so bold. She wouldn't allow them to separate her from Fox.

"Oh, it speaks. Well, isn't that just *fine*." The toad glared down at Cynthia as if she would make a tasty meal.

"I refuse to go with you if you leave him behind," Cynthia insisted.

The toad let out a laugh that sounded like a croak and shook her head. "I don't think you have much of a choice in the matter, now, do you?" She turned her round eyes onto the moles. "Put her on the lily pad to await our departure while I retrieve your payment."

"Fox!" Cynthia shrieked as the guards pulled her away from him. Emotions warred in her, threatening to overwhelm her. Fear, anger, despair, and… success?

He fought back, kicking one of the moles with his foot and attempting to steal their weapons from their hands. But they were outnumbered.

The mole guard hit him in the stomach with his hooked weapon again.

This time when Fox hit the ground, he didn't groan or writhe in pain. He lay still and silent.

"No!" Cynthia screamed.

She twisted and turned and attempted to free herself from the mole guard. But he was too big and strong. It was no use. He dragged her through the frozen grass to the edge of the swampy water.

"Careful or you'll end up in there instead of on top of it." The mole laughed in her ear.

She didn't care. She had to get away. She had to get to Fox. What would they do with him?

The mole pushed her onto the lily pad and shoved it away from the shore with his staff.

"No!" Cynthia stretched her bound hands forward toward Fox as she kneeled on the wobbly leaf floating on the surface of the smelly water.

How had it come to this? All she wanted to do was good. She had only ever thought about others instead of herself. And here she was.

Fox was right. She was too trusting. She should have listened to him.

Tears streamed down her cheeks as she gradually floated away from Fox. She watched as the moles pointed at him and tried to decide what they would do with him.

The toad retrieved a large sack that must have held the payment that the moles were expecting. She dropped it at their feet and then turned to face Cynthia.

She shot her long tongue out of her mouth and latched onto the lily pad. With a single tug, the lily pad lunged for the shore. Cynthia was knocked to her backside. Any hope of trying to subdue the toad and return to Fox's side vanished with her fall.

The toad took one enormous hop and landed with a thud on the lily pad. The water around the leaf vibrated and sent ripples out all around them.

The toad pushed the pad away from shore with a long mushroom she used as a paddle.

The island Fox lay on shrunk as Cynthia floated away. In the cold mist her vision became obscured.

The last thing she saw was one of the toads dragging Fox toward the shore. Then she couldn't see anything. She heard a loud splash as something heavy was tossed into the water.

"No!" She sobbed and curled in on herself.

If he was unconscious, he wouldn't be able to swim. And swimming with his hands bound would already be difficult. Had she really just lost him forever?

"You'll bring in a hefty price, won't you?" Cynthia had all but forgotten about the toad that floated on the pad with her.

"What?" she managed to squeeze out between sobs.

"The price on your head is high. I can't believe the moles let me have you for such a measly payment. Fools!" The toad croaked another wicked laugh. She paddled them across the pond and toward a fast-moving current from the attached stream.

The shore wasn't too far away.

Maybe Cynthia could jump overboard and swim to shore.

"I know what you're thinking. I can swim much faster than you. Don't even try. I'll have you back on the lily pad before you can even sink to the bottom." The toad had a haughty tone to her voice.

Cynthia caved. She didn't know what else to do. She curled into a ball on the lily pad and allowed the toad to carry her away.

The movement of the lily pad atop the water lulled Cynthia into a daze as she stared at the shoreline as it rushed by. The current became stronger. Maybe she would get tossed overboard like the last time she had traveled like this.

Her heart sank. Even if she did, the toad was right. She would be rescued and returned to captivity in the blink of an eye.

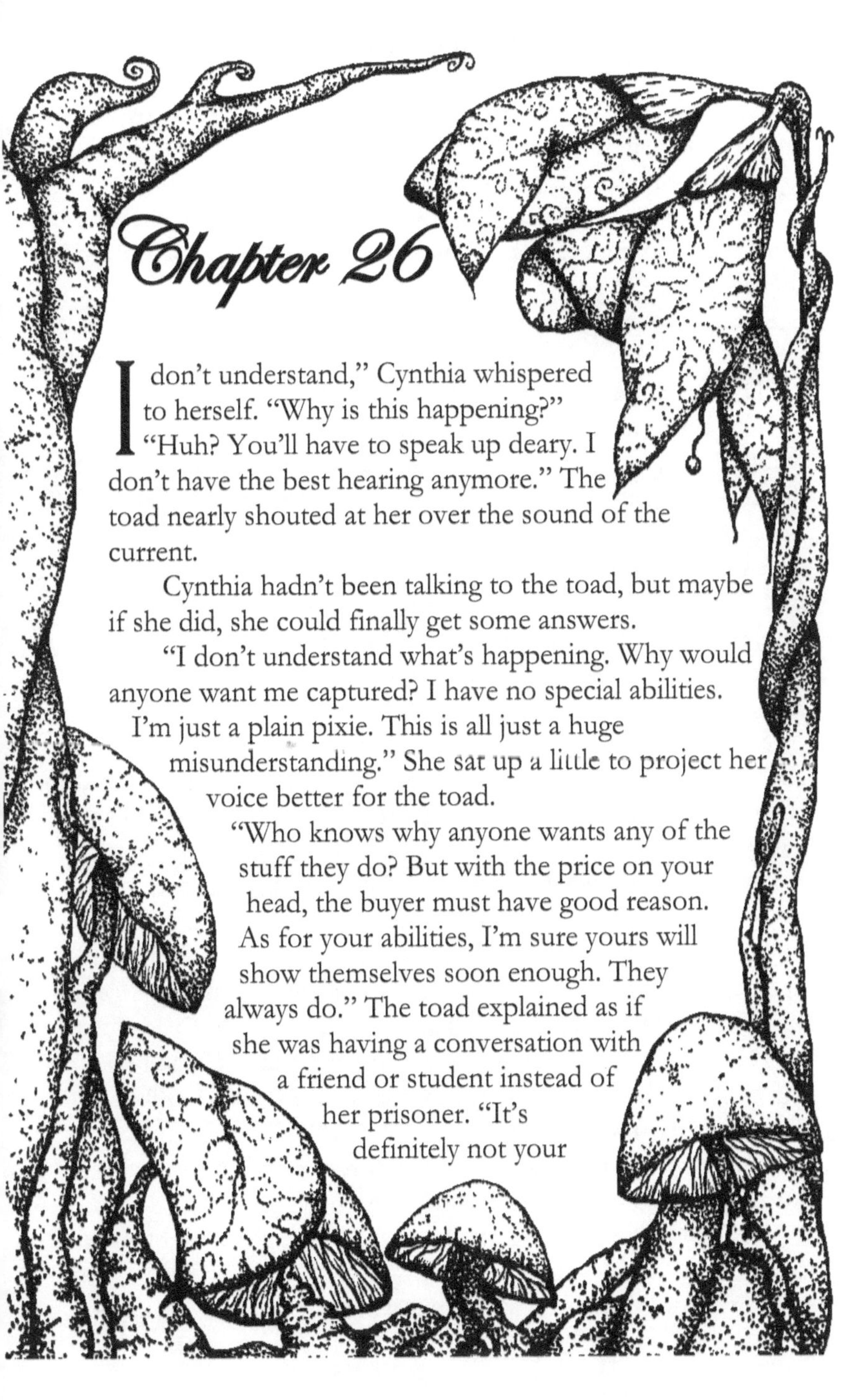

Chapter 26

I don't understand," Cynthia whispered to herself. "Why is this happening?"

"Huh? You'll have to speak up deary. I don't have the best hearing anymore." The toad nearly shouted at her over the sound of the current.

Cynthia hadn't been talking to the toad, but maybe if she did, she could finally get some answers.

"I don't understand what's happening. Why would anyone want me captured? I have no special abilities. I'm just a plain pixie. This is all just a huge misunderstanding." She sat up a little to project her voice better for the toad.

"Who knows why anyone wants any of the stuff they do? But with the price on your head, the buyer must have good reason. As for your abilities, I'm sure yours will show themselves soon enough. They always do." The toad explained as if she was having a conversation with a friend or student instead of her prisoner. "It's definitely not your looks anyone is after. I mean look at you. You're scrawny and ugly. If you weren't worth so much, I'd probably just eat you in one gulp." She let out a croaking laugh again.

Cynthia cringed. None of it made any sense. Would she ever learn why someone was hunting her down? Or if she was even the right prize at all?

The current carried them at a steady clip.

The toad put away her mushroom paddle and folded her webbed hands with bulbous fingertips over her chest. Her double-lidded eyes sunk closed. In moments, the toad snored in great croaks that drowned out the sound of the rushing water.

Cynthia looked around. There had to be a way to get the lily pad closer to the shore. If she could make landfall while the toad slept, perhaps she could slip away. She crawled around and searched frantically for anything that could help, but she found nothing.

She slapped the lily pad with her open hand. It made a loud sound that she was sure would wake up the toad, but the animal slept soundly still. The toad's hearing wasn't that great, as she had said.

There had to be a way! She just needed to find something…

Not two seconds later, a cattail stuck out into the water from the shore up ahead. It reminded her exactly of when she had been thrown overboard from the lily pad in the river before, and Fox had saved her from drowning.

Her eyes traced the stem of the plant from the water, past the bulbous brown fuzzy "tail," and toward the shoreline in search of her new rescuer.

"Grab hold!" Fox's voice rose over the sound of the rushing water. It was like music to Cynthia's ears.

His hands were still bound, but he held the cattail tightly and securely.

It wouldn't be easy without her wings or the free use of her hands, but the hope that swelled in her chest was enough to make her feel like she could fly even without wings.

She waited for just the right moment. When she was in the right position, she leapt from the lily pad and wrapped her entire body around the cattail.

The stem bent under her weight and lowered her close to the fast-moving water. Just when her toes touched the spray, Fox lunged backwards and yanked her to shore.

She fell in a heap on the ground when she landed, and he fell backwards from the sudden loss of resistance from the cattail.

They both leapt from the ground and rushed toward each other. They couldn't embrace, but they clasped their hands together and leaned against one another.

Fox shivered from his wet clothing and dripping hair. She rubbed her hands on his arms the best she could to try to give him some of her heat.

"What happened? I thought they threw you in the water? I thought you were…" She swallowed the last word instead of saying it out loud.

His teeth chattered and his voice wobbled from his shivering. "I woke up and knocked one of the mole guards into the water. I managed to swim to the opposite shore from where they stood. Then I followed you as fast as I could." His breath fogged the air.

A loud croak interrupted their conversation before Cynthia could respond.

"She's woken up. She knows I'm gone. We need to get out of here." Cynthia grabbed Fox's arm with both bound hands and ran into the brush beside the swift water.

Fox stumbled over his frozen feet but managed to right himself before he could accidentally pull Cynthia to the ground again.

Another croak came. Louder. Closer.

"She's on shore," Cynthia squeaked. She ducked behind a

round boulder and pulled Fox down beside her. "Shh." She pressed a finger against her mouth and pinched her lips closed.

He nodded and shivered beside her while they waited for the toad to give up searching for them.

For how much the toad bragged about being a good swimmer, she was very slow on land. Each of her hops took great effort, as Cynthia discovered when the toad hopped right beside the boulder.

Cynthia motioned for Fox to copy her movements, and she awkwardly crawled to the other side of the boulder, then froze in place again.

Fox's shivering got worse. His teeth chattered against one another. If they didn't warm him up soon, he would go into shock. But they had to avoid the toad.

"I can hear you!" The toad's croak came from the opposite side of the boulder.

Cynthia prepared to pull Fox to his feet so they could run again, but he shook his head.

He kept his voice as quiet as possible and barely whispered into her ear between his shaking. "I won't make it. My feet are numb, I can't feel my toes. You have to get out of here."

What? He wanted her to leave him behind?

"Please, Cynthia," he whispered, his eyes closed and his lips turning blue. "Run away. Cut the nets and ropes on a thorn or stone. Then fly as far away from here as you can."

"No. No! I'm not leaving you." Cynthia whispered in as harsh a tone as possible. "We just need to find a better place to hide." She searched all around from her crouched position, looking for any place that could hide the pair of them from the toad.

Another croak sounded closer. The toad had hopped further around the boulder.

Cynthia pulled Fox away from the noise, but he was right. He was losing control of his movements. There was no way he would be able to run away with her, let alone find a place to hide.

"Don't be foolish. Get to safety," Fox whispered.

Cynthia shook her head. Tears leaked from her eyes and steamed on her cold cheeks.

"I won't allow you to sacrifice your safety for me." He pleaded with her.

"I don't understand," she answered back close to his ear. "I'm only trying to take care of you. Trying to do what is right. Why does that upset you so much? Why do you insist that I only take care of myself?"

He sighed. Another puff of steam hung in the air between them. He awkwardly leaned his forehead against hers. She tried to hold his arm with her bound hands.

His words came out soft and warm. "I care for you. Your kindness. Your loyalty and protective instincts. The way the sunlight shines through your wings like stained glass. The way you always have a smile on your face. I've never met anyone like you before." His words became stuck in his throat, and he leaned slightly away from her so he could look into her eyes. "That is why I insist you find the Forest People on your own. You must go. Now."

Tears streamed down Cynthia's cheeks. She didn't want to leave him. Not like this.

But the toad continued to circle the boulder with her awkward hops. If they could run, they would easily escape. But that was out of the question for Fox. If the toad captured them, she would take Cynthia and leave Fox behind. Either way, he would be left behind.

Her heart broke inside her chest, like ice cracking. "How will I know where to find you?" She sobbed into his ear with her cheek pressed against his. "What if something terrible happens to you? What if... what if I never get to see you again? It would break my heart."

She cared for him, too. Even with his grumpy ways. His past

had made him unable to trust easily, but that didn't make him a bad person. It made him wary, but also wise.

Fox pushed her away from him with weak, shaking arms. "It's time to stop putting others before yourself and care about your own safety for once. The only thing that matters is that *you're* safe. Please, just go."

Cynthia backed away, not able to tear her eyes from his limp, shivering form against the boulder.

Just then, the toad rounded the boulder. "Ah, there you are. I knew you hadn't gone far." She took a large leap toward Cynthia.

"Cynthia! Run!" Fox shouted with the little breath he had left. The words came out in a wheeze.

It took everything she had to wrench her eyes from him, turn on her heels, and sprint away before the toad could land right on top of her and pin her to the ground.

Before she had taken a dozen steps, something grabbed the back of one of her legs and yanked. Her face smashed into the ground. She flailed her legs to free herself. A glance backwards revealed the trap. The toad had caught Cynthia with her sticky, barbed tongue.

The tiny barbs dug into the flesh on Cynthia's leg. She threw herself backwards and kicked at the tongue.

The toad slowly dragged her closer, even against all of Cynthia's attempts to free herself.

"No!" Fox's voice rang through

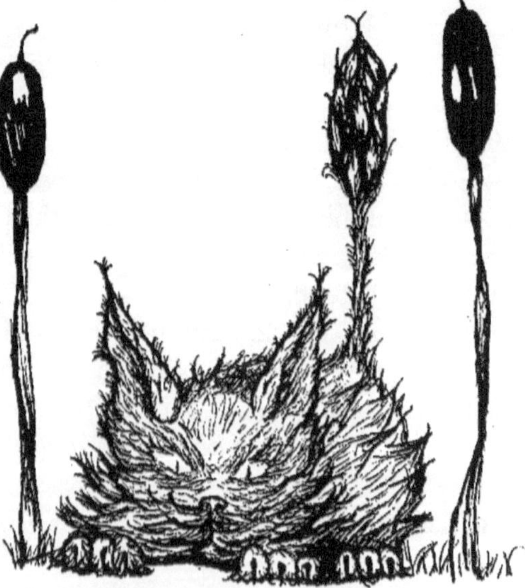

the air.

A large stone hit the toad on the head. It jostled. The barbs released from Cynthia's leg.

"Run!" Fox screamed at her.

Cynthia scrambled to her feet. Sobs shook her shoulders as she raced underneath the bulrushes, over the round river rocks, and through the cattails. Leaving Fox bound and alone with a very angry toad.

A yowl from among the cattails told her that there was a mire cat among the plants, but she didn't have time to worry about that. It prowled the area but not for pixies.

The toad's angry croaks followed behind her. It still pursued her! Slower on land than in the water, each of her hops still carried her surprisingly far.

Cynthia continued to run until the croaks died down. Either she had outrun her pursuer, or the toad had given up and returned to the water. Or worse. To Fox.

Cynthia collapsed on the ground beneath a mulberry bush and allowed her sobs to shake her body. A distant croak made her muffle her own cries and realize that she wasn't in the clear yet.

She stood and frantically searched the bush until she found a thorn to rub against the bonds on her hands. It scraped her wrists and arms. She cried in pain but kept the sobs silent. When the ropes had been cut enough, she tugged on them to break them and tossed them to the ground.

She turned to one side and awkwardly rubbed the netting against the thorn, careful not to get it too close to her wings or her body. The netting took longer, but after several agonizing minutes the netting fell away, too.

When she had finished, she collapsed to the ground. She wrapped her arms around her bent legs and buried her face in her knees. The stench from her own unwashed body and damp, dirty clothing assaulted her nose, but she didn't care. Her ankle throbbed where the toads barbed tongue had pierced it. Her wrists stung and her bones ached. She stretched her sore wings and took deep breaths to calm her crying.

How could she have abandoned Fox like that? She was so selfish. She shouldn't have left.

Another croak, a little closer this time, told Cynthia that the toad had not given up on her after all. The only way to find safety would be to fly away.

The Forest People would probably have answers for her. And if she looked in the right places, they shouldn't be too hard to find.

But could she really leave Fox behind to freeze to death? Was it worth the risk to attempt to go back for him? What would they even do if the toad caught up with them? They would be in the same dilemma they had been in before. Fox couldn't fly. He could barely walk at this point. And she was too small to carry him. How would she even be able to help him? The risk was too great.

She took a last, long look in the direction where

she had left Fox. Had the toad harmed him? Would he be able to loose his own bonds and find a way to escape? Or would he freeze to death before either of those things could even happen?

Without time to wonder, Cynthia's heart broke as she flapped her sore, stiff wings for the first time in a long time. Her movements left her unsteady, like a furry, long-nosed snoozlefly zig zagging through the sky, as she lifted herself off the ground.

Chapter 27

"Where do I even start looking?" Cynthia cried to herself as she hovered above the forest of conifers, mangroves, and hardwood trees. "I don't know where to find Forest People!"

She couldn't stop thinking about Fox. Trying to think of a way to save him, even though it was pointless.

She shoved away all of that and focused. If she didn't find the Forest People, there would be no hope of saving him, one way or another.

"I need to find an animal. Something that wouldn't be hibernating during winter." She ran through a list in her head.

Birds wouldn't be nesting right now. Small critters would be hiding or sleeping. Her best bet would be to start in a clearing. At least she'd have a good view to find something, anything, that might be able to carry a message, tell her where to go, or if she was lucky enough, come with her to rescue Fox.

She flew in spiraling circles away from Fox

and scanned the trees and forest for any signs of animal life. Many of the trees had lost most of their leaves, leaving a clear view of their aerial roots and flared trunks. The oaks that hadn't lost their leaves yet glowed red and orange in the bright daylight. Red burning bushes flickered on the forest floor, and shades of green from the ferns, moss, and other ground covers presented the perfect backdrop for the bright colors.

Cynthia lowered herself closer to the ground in order to locate an animal to ask for help. Close to the edge of the water, a dozen barbed butterflies perched on the cattails in the swamp while they looked for smaller insects to consume. Movement of one of the cattails caught her eye.

The mire cat lurked below. It wouldn't be wise to approach the fuzzy, brown, gilled cat that lived in the swamp and camouflaged with the cattail plants with its own uniquely tipped tail. They were known to be unpredictable, and it just might mistake her for its next meal.

Her breath hitched. What if it found Fox? He was down there.

Freezing to death.

Alone and vulnerable.

And the toad knew where he was. What would the toad do? Leave him there to die? Something worse?

The toad's words about eating Cynthia if she hadn't been so valuable returned to her mind.

Without another thought, she dived toward the ground. Back to Fox.

Shivers racked her body as the wind whipped against her face and wings. But she wouldn't leave Fox behind. No matter the cost.

She continued to scan the forest for any signs of something that would aid her in keeping Fox safe. And something to keep herself safe from the toad as well. It would do her no good to get captured again.

Movement further upstream from where she knew Fox

shivered caught her attention. She charged closer to investigate.

Her eyes landed on an unexpected scene. A black and white skunk with a wide, fluffy tail, black paws, and a white stripe all the way from nose to tail argued with a perfectly masked, gray and white raccoon. The argument looked pretty heated. The racoon attempted to hide something in a hole between the scales of an enormous white oak tree, while the skunk gestured with its hands and pointed at a hole in the sloppy ground. They looked like they were up to no good.

But… they were both natural predators of toads.

A pang of guilt stabbed her chest. She didn't want to harm the toad, necessarily, but she had to do something to take the toad's attention away from its search for Cynthia. It was the only way she'd be able to help Fox.

She landed on an enormous heart-shaped leaf of a wide philodendron bush near the unusual pair.

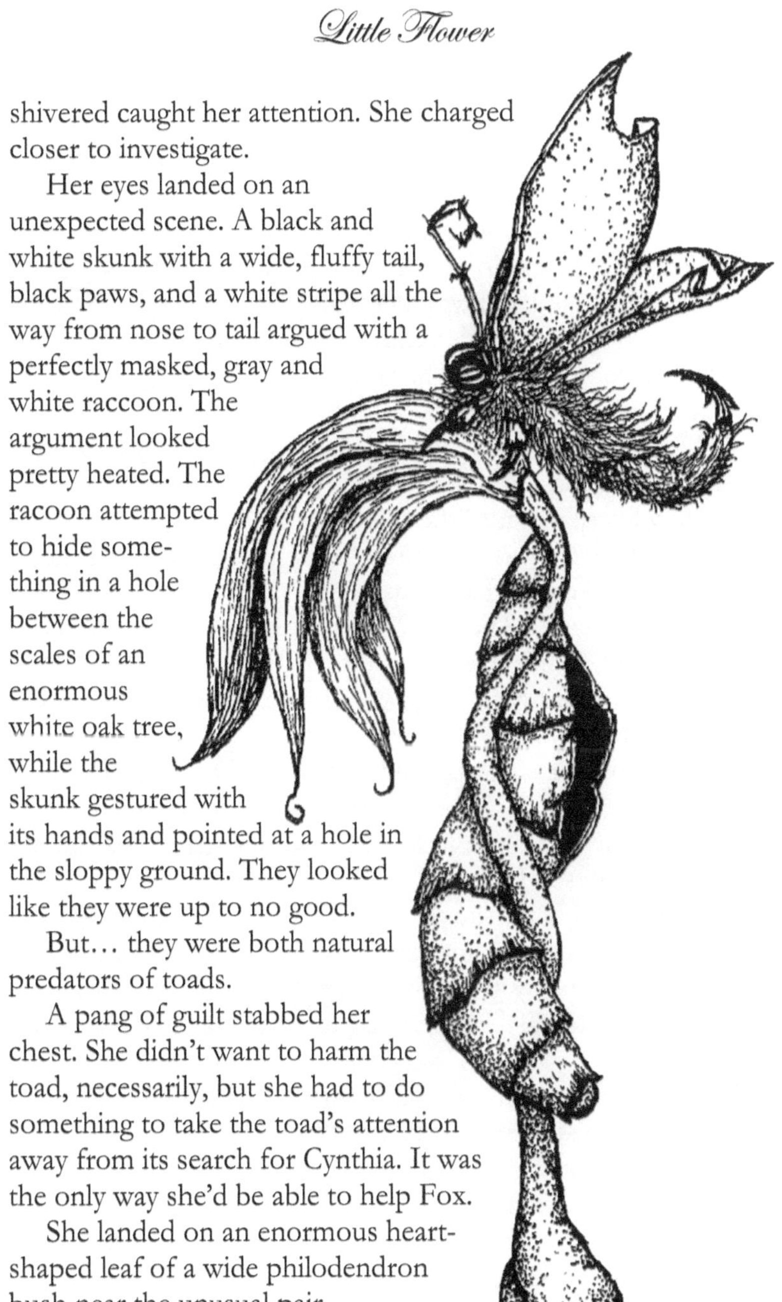

"Sorry to interrupt," she addressed the animals, out of breath from her hurried flight.

They both froze in place, as still as stones, as if maybe she wouldn't see them.

The skunk fluffed its tail and slowly lowered itself onto all four feet. In slow motion it turned its back end toward Cynthia.

"Wait!" she hollered with her hands outstretched. "Please. I need your help! I'm being hunted by this big toad and…"

The raccoon chittered. "Say no more." He rubbed his hands together and licked his black lips.

The skunk remained still; half-turned toward Cynthia with its tail in spraying position.

"How big of a toad?" the skunk asked in a suspicious tone.

Cynthia swallowed her guilt. "Big enough for the both of you." She choked on her words.

"Lead the way!" The racoon dropped the shiny silver coin that he held in his hands and prepared himself to follow Cynthia. "Put that stink away," he said to his companion. "We have a toad to catch!"

The skunk did as he was told and lowered his tail. He picked the coin off the ground, shoved it in the hole in the tree, rubbed his body against the bark to leave behind his stench, and joined his friend. "All set. Let's go."

Cynthia led the skunk and the raccoon through the underbrush, flying up and over low shrubs and grasses and underneath branches while they jogged on foot below her.

Would the toad still be looking for her? Maybe it had given up.

The toad's lily pad raft still rested on the bank of the wide stream. The toad probably still hunted for her. How much was the reward anyway?

"There's where the toad landed on shore. It should be around here somewhere." Cynthia pointed at the lily pad to show the racoon and skunk.

"We'll take it from here." The racoon scanned the tall

bulrushes and reed grass with its eyes, sniffed with his nose, and slunk along the ground.

Not entirely certain the pair would find the toad before the toad found her, Cynthia lifted herself higher and rushed to where she had left Fox against the boulder.

She landed harder than she intended and stumbled a little before dropping to her knees at his side.

He shivered uncontrollably. His eyes were closed and his face pale.

"Fox!" she breathed. She laid a hand on his cheek. It was like ice.

He moaned from the touch. "Cynthia? What are you doing here?" His words came out garbled as if he couldn't get his lips and tongue to work properly.

She rubbed his cheeks with her hands to try to warm him up.

His eyes fluttered open and his dark burgundy eyes stared at her with a confused expression. "The toad..." he groaned. "You're not safe here."

A thump came from behind Cynthia. "I knew you'd come back for him," the toad croaked.

Cynthia froze beside Fox but refused to move from his side. She frowned at the toad. "Leave us alone!" she shouted.

Anger and frustration rose to the surface of her emotions. It was all too much.

The toad let out a croak of laughter. "You have little say about what happens next, *fairy*." She hopped another length closer to Cynthia.

"Get out of here," Fox mumbled to Cynthia through his chattering teeth.

"No," she whispered to him.

"You're so stubborn," he complained.

"I won't leave you," she insisted.

The toad's raspy voice interrupted their stilted conversation.

"Very well, have it your way." She hopped another length closer to Cynthia and puffed her chin into a wide balloon.

Was she planning to rope Cynthia with her tongue again as if she was an insect? Cynthia braced herself for whatever happened next.

Just then, a faint smell of rotten cabbage reached her nose.

"Gotcha!" A person-like hand but with fur, pads, and claws wrapped around the toad and lifted it from the ground. The racoon wore a wide smile across his masked face.

The toad's long back legs stretched their full length as she was lifted off the ground.

"You'll do. Thanks for the tip." The racoon cupped both hands around the toad, ready to carry her off. He nodded in Cynthia's direction and smirked at the skunk beside him. "Ready for a delicious supper?"

The skunk nodded and scampered back through the underbrush, out of sight.

Besides his shivering, Fox's muscles relaxed with the removal of the toad. He allowed his eyes to sink closed again.

"Fox, stay with me. I'm going to find something to cut your bindings." Cynthia scoured the clearing for a thorn or sharp stone.

It only took a few seconds to find a shard of rock that she could use as a knife to cut the ropes that wrapped around Fox.

His head leaned back, and his breathing had become shallow.

"No! Don't sleep." Cynthia sawed at the ropes.

When the ropes split apart, Fox's arms fell limp at his sides. He slumped forward. The ropes had been holding him upright.

How could she have left him here in such a state? Her chest squeezed. Cynthia scooted beside him and wrapped her arms around him. She pulled him as close as she could and rested his head on her chest. She rubbed his arms and back to warm him.

"You are irrational, you know that?" he murmured, his eyes still closed and his body limp.

"I couldn't leave you," she answered.

He nodded twice.

"We need to get you warm." But she didn't want to let him go.

"Mm-hmm," he answered.

If she waited too long to find a warm place for Fox, she might still lose him.

"I'll be right back," she promised as she reluctantly let him go.

Another quick glance at her surroundings gave her the answer to her dilemma. There was a hollow in a black spruce tree nearby. She made quick work of stuffing it with moss and cattail fluff she collected from the area. Using moist sticks and lichen from the tree trunk she managed to build a fire near the opening of the tree hollow, so the smoke would not fill the hollow.

She didn't know if Fox would be able to walk the dozen steps to the shelter. She wrapped his arm around her shoulder and her arm around his waist and hoisted him from the ground. He leaned heavily on her, but managed to take weak steps with her support.

He collapsed inside the spruce hollow. Cynthia piled the moss and cattail fluff on top of him. He continued to shiver, curled up in a ball beside the fire which she stoked frequently to keep it hot.

She found an empty snail shell that she used to heat water, and made Fox drink hot tea to help warm him on the inside, too.

Minutes turned to half an hour, then an hour. His eyes remained closed. He still shivered. He barely remained conscious. Was she too late?

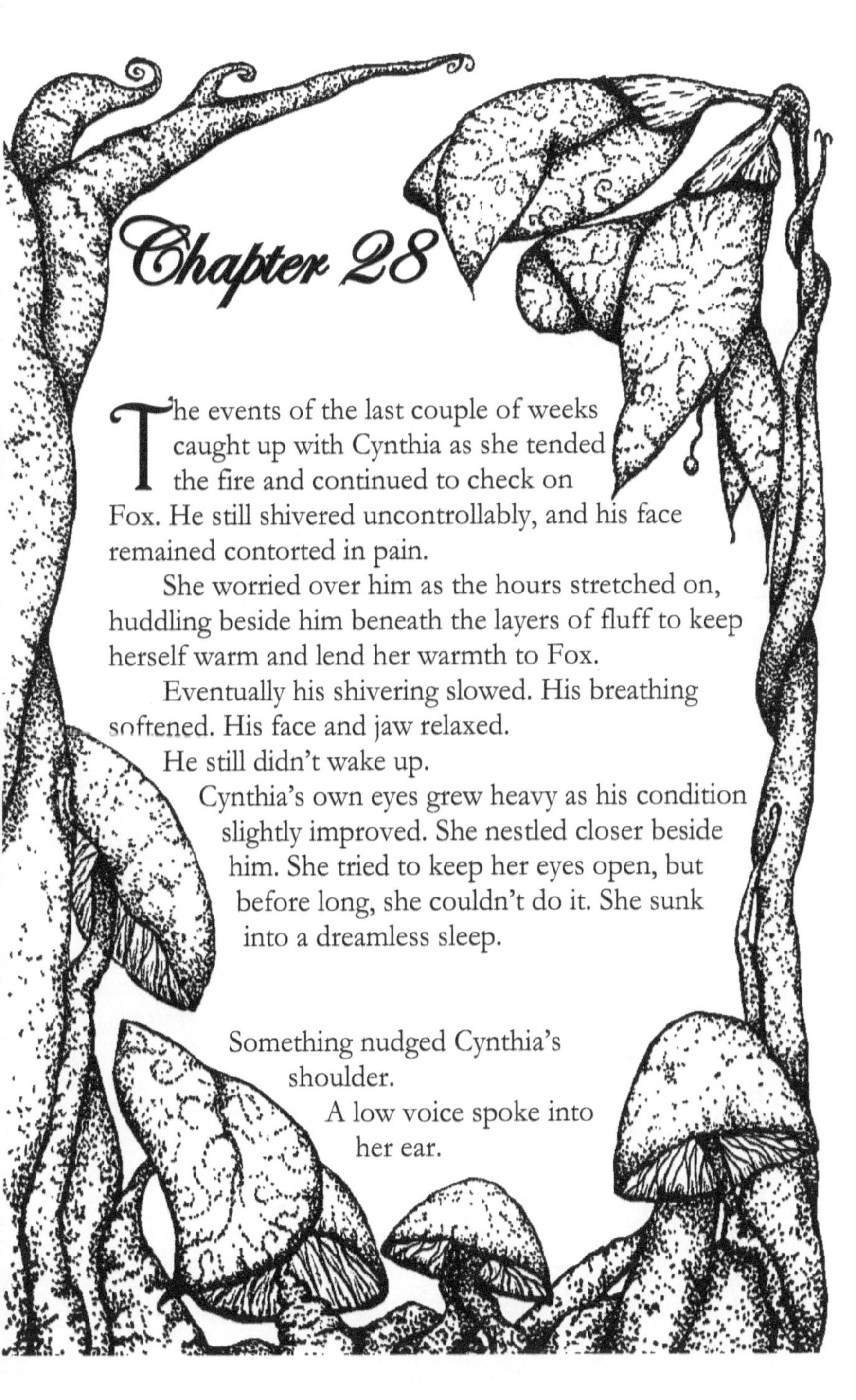# Chapter 28

The events of the last couple of weeks caught up with Cynthia as she tended the fire and continued to check on Fox. He still shivered uncontrollably, and his face remained contorted in pain.

She worried over him as the hours stretched on, huddling beside him beneath the layers of fluff to keep herself warm and lend her warmth to Fox.

Eventually his shivering slowed. His breathing softened. His face and jaw relaxed.

He still didn't wake up.

Cynthia's own eyes grew heavy as his condition slightly improved. She nestled closer beside him. She tried to keep her eyes open, but before long, she couldn't do it. She sunk into a dreamless sleep.

Something nudged Cynthia's shoulder.

A low voice spoke into her ear.

"Wake up, sleepyhead."

That voice.

Her heart sped up.

It was familiar.

She blinked her eyes to clear the sleep out of them.

It was Fox! He was awake! Sitting up. Stoking the fire. His lips didn't have a blue tinge to them anymore. His cheeks looked rosy and warm. And his eyes. They were bright and clear.

She jumped from beneath her pile of moss and threw her arms around him. Her tears flowed and her shoulders shook from her sobs.

He didn't move for a second, but then he wrapped his own arms around Cynthia and held her close.

"Thank you." His words were muffled by his face pressed against her hair. He stroked her back with one hand and held the other hand tight against her to keep her close.

He was alive! He was safe! And he was here, with her!

When her crying finally slowed, she pulled away and wiped the tears from her cheeks. "I can't believe I left you like that. I am so sorry." Her lip quivered and tears dripped down her cheeks.

He held both of her shoulders with his hands and bent forward to look her carefully in the eyes. "I can't believe you came back." He shook his head. "You should have stayed away."

"I couldn't leave you." She didn't take her eyes off his face. "I'll never leave you again." She whispered.

Her heart thudded against her ribs. In a non-direct way, she had just confessed her feelings for him. What if he didn't feel the same?

"You were right about one thing." He dropped his hands and rubbed his chin.

The mischievous look in his eye told her that he wasn't about to confess his feelings for her. Her heart sank but she made herself not react.

Instead, she gave him a soft smile. "What was I right about?" she asked quietly.

"Kindness has a way of finding you again, doesn't it? I mean, how lucky was it that racoon and skunk showed up?"

She blushed. "Actually… I kind of found them and brought them along."

He tipped his head back and laughed out loud. "You are an amazing person. Do you know that? It's what I love the most about you!"

Cynthia froze. It felt like her heart stopped beating at that moment. She held her breath.

"You look like you've just seen a ballybog. Are you alright?" He frowned, studied her face, and took her hand in his.

She didn't move. Had he just said what she thought he did? Was it a figure of speech? Or did he really mean it?

"Cynthia?" He waited for her to say something. His eyebrows pressed together, and his posture stiffened.

"I love you, Fox." There. She said it. No confusing teasing. No moment of danger. Just the two of them. Safe. Finally.

She waited with bated breath for his reaction.

He froze.

She slid her hand from his. This was what she got for wearing her heart on her sleeve. Rejection. Now she understood a little better why Fox didn't give himself so freely.

He grabbed her hand tighter, not letting her slip away.

"I love you, too." He leaned close and rested his other hand on the side of her face. He wrapped his fingers behind the back of her head.

Tears filled her eyes again, but not sorry, or guilty, or scared tears.

Before she could say anything else, he leaned his face closer and gently tugged her toward him.

She didn't hesitate, closing the gap between their lips.

His kiss tasted warm and sweet. She released his hand and wrapped both of hers around the sides of his face.

The kiss lasted just long enough to warm Cynthia more than any moss blanket or fire could.

They separated, just far enough to look into each other's eyes.

Then Cynthia's stomach growled. Loudly.

Fox laughed out loud again. It was the best sound Cynthia could think of besides the words that had spilled from his lips only moments ago.

"Let's get you something to eat." He slid his hand down her arm and wrapped it around her hand tightly. "Your fingers are still cold. Stay by the fire. I'll find us something."

She didn't love the idea of being separated from him, even if he was still within her line of sight, but he was right. She was still a little cold. And she was really tired. And really hungry.

She leaned against the inside of the tree and watched him move through the frozen marshy area to collect seeds and sun-dried berries for them to eat.

When had he gone from a total stranger to someone she never wanted to leave again? And how had she been so lucky to have stumbled into his life at just the right time?

A rustle in the leaves beside her startled her back to reality.

They may have gotten rid of the toad, but a mire cat still lurked in the area. And worse than that, there was still a bounty on her head.

Fox's head snapped in the direction of the sound. He hurried to join Cynthia inside their tree hollow. He dropped the seeds and nuts in a pile beside her and whispered, "Cover up with the moss."

He did the same, with only the tops of their heads and eyes peeking over the puffy green blanket. In the shadow of the hollow, they should be well hidden from anyone or anything passing through.

An enormous snail entered Cynthia's line of vision from

inside the tree hollow. Riding on its back sat something Cynthia had never seen before.

Cynthia's eyes widened. "What is it?"

She kept her eyes glued to the figure. A bit taller than Fox, the creature's sharp face and pointed ears scanned the small clearing as if looking for something.

Looking for us.

Its feathery beard hung the length of its body while it crouched atop the oversized snail that it rode like a pack animal. Its hairy hands, attached to disproportionately long arms, gripped a rope that wrapped around one of the snail's long eye-tentacles.

"A goblin," Fox whispered right into her ear.

Cynthia didn't know what that was.

Sensing her confusion, Fox whispered, "You know, remotely related to brownies?"

She nodded, though she still didn't fully understand. "Are they dangerous?"

Fox shook his head. "Usually harmless. But this one could be a bounty hunter, too. It's best if we stay out of sight."

Cynthia pinched her lips and waited. She didn't dare move a muscle. Not after the last time she had given her trust to a seemingly innocent creature. She wouldn't make that mistake again.

A pang of sorrow pierced her heart. When had she lost her open trust? Maybe Fox's distrust of everyone had rubbed off on her. But it was deeper than that. For the first time her desire to see the good in everyone around her had led to danger and disaster. It had nearly gotten them both killed. She had to protect herself from repeating her mistake.

"Are you alright?" Fox quietly wrapped an arm around her shoulders and pulled her close.

She met his gaze. Tears stung her eyes, but she held them back. She nodded and shrugged.

He kissed the top of her head and held her against him while they waited for the threat to leave.

The goblin dismounted from its snail-ride and hobbled around the clearing. When it lumbered near their burning fire, Fox and Cynthia ducked all the way beneath the moss blanket.

Cynthia couldn't see a thing. But the sounds coming from the other side of the blanket let her imagine the goblin poking at the fire while he murmured things under his breath in a language that, for once, she didn't understand.

It took a long time before the goblin returned to his snail and urged it away from their hiding place.

Cynthia peeked over the edge of the moss blanket again. The snail sped out of the clearing at a surprising rate and disappeared within moments.

Fox squeezed Cynthia's shoulders. "That was a good reminder that we need to stay alert and use an abundance of caution. We still have a way to go before we can consider ourselves safe. We may have escaped the toad, but the danger is not over. Not yet."

Cynthia nodded. Her heart sank. She desperately wanted their journey to be over. For them to be safe. But Fox was right.

They still needed to be really careful.

Fox handed Cynthia her meal of dried berries and seeds. "I'm sorry it's not more substantial."

Cynthia waved away his concern. "It's food. That's good enough for me."

Fox wrapped his arm around her shoulders again and ate with his other hand, while she snuggled up beside him beneath the moss blanket.

When they had finished eating, Fox turned toward Cynthia. "The sun's setting soon. We shouldn't travel at night. Let's hunker down here and we'll make our way in the morning."

His nearness, combined with the fire and mossy blankets, did their job of keeping her warm, but her nerves were still on edge. She didn't think she'd be able to get any sleep that night.

"Do you think we'll be able to find the Forest People?" Cynthia asked.

Fox stiffened.

"What's wrong?" Cynthia gazed at his handsome face. He wore a troubled expression.

"I know they'll be able to help you get home, but… I don't know if they'll be able… or willing, to fix my wings." Fox glanced away.

"What do you mean? Why wouldn't they want to fix your wings?" Cynthia frowned at the crease between his eyebrows.

Fox rubbed his messy blond hair. "The Forest People won't be inviting to someone like me. I'm a bounty hunter, remember?" He ducked his head like he was still embarrassed about his choice of jobs.

Cynthia rested her hand on his arm. She waited for him to make eye contact again. "But the reason you do what you do isn't bad. You are trying to make Tala a better place. Some might say you're more successful than someone like me who just helps everyone all the time!"

Fox chuckled. "No way, you have way more positive

influence on the world than me."

Cynthia smiled. "I know what you're saying but I don't know if that's true."

Fox started to argue, but Cynthia stopped him. "I'm not trying to be humble or anything. I'm just saying. Serving those who wish others harm isn't going to make them into better people overnight. But turning them in so they must answer for their crimes takes them away from those whom they might harm."

"Not everyone sees the world as brightly as you. They may not see it the way you do." Fox shook his head.

Cynthia squeezed his hand with hers. "I believe the Forest People will be able to tell that you are doing what you do for the right reasons. And they'll want to help you. We just have to find them first."

Fox leaned against the back of the tree hollow. He wrapped his arms around Cynthia and tugged her close. He rested his chin on her head, and she felt him nod. "We will, I'm sure. If we find the right animal to ask for help, we'll be able to send them a message, at least."

"I hope it doesn't take too long." Cynthia's confidence that the Forest People would help Fox hadn't diminished, but she worried that they wouldn't find them in time. "The nights are cold, and even during the day the air is staying chilled." She cringed.

It's not like he needed a reminder about how he almost froze to death earlier that day. Thanks to her.

She shoved those thoughts away. They were still in danger from the weather and potential bounty hunters. Speaking of which…

Cynthia hesitated before voicing her next thoughts. "Is it really a good idea for us to ask around for help finding the Forest People? What if we talk to the wrong animal?" It felt foreign to her to doubt the world and its inhabitants. Cynthia rubbed the hem of her dirty, tattered pale blue skirt between her thumb and forefinger. The thought of getting caught again scared her more than she realized until Fox had said that about asking an animal for help.

Chapter 29

I can sense whether someone is trust-worthy or not. I'm sure we'll be able to find the right animal to get help from."
Fox didn't seem concerned at all.

Maybe Cynthia shouldn't be either. He was right. He could sense dishonesty. She shouldn't worry about it.

"Then, how will we avoid being spotted by bounty hunters? Not to mention not freezing to death while we look for the right animal to talk to?"

She may have pushed aside her worries, but they were still there at the back of her mind. And in a pit in her stomach.

Fox answered right away. "We'll cover our wings, like we did before. It will keep us warm, in addition to hiding our identities."

"If we wear layers of leaves over our clothes, we might kind of look like brownies?" Cynthia pointed out.

He chuckled. "You're way too small to be a brownie!"

"Maybe…" She rested her head against his

chest.

Her mind raced with thoughts of the moles, the toad, even the mouse. Worries about Birdie. Wondering if they would get caught again before they could find help.

She didn't think she'd be able to relax enough to sleep again, but her eyes sunk closed.

When she opened them, it was morning.

Cynthia still had her head leaning on Fox's chest. His head was tipped back, leaning against the inside of the tree hollow. Warmth radiated from her heart.

She listened to his rhythmic breathing and his steady heartbeat. The steadiness of it calmed her. Being wrapped in his embrace filled her with joy even amidst their current situation. She couldn't help the smile that teased the corners of her mouth.

He had been such a distrustful grump when they first met. But he had opened himself to her, and she had seen the real person beneath the wall he had built around himself.

She let out a gentle sigh.

"So, you're not a dream," his raspy voice said as he squeezed her with his arm around her shoulders.

She blushed, but luckily, he couldn't see it.

He kissed the top of her head.

"I'm sure my hair is dirty and smelly." She winced when she suddenly realized how long it had been since she had been able to clean herself.

He kissed her hair again. "Worth it."

She tipped her face back so she could see his smile. She loved that smile.

He glanced at her lips.

She leaned forward and pressed her lips against his.

When their second kiss ended, she sighed again. "Definitely not a dream." She couldn't wait to share many more kisses with him.

"Unfortunately, neither is the fact that we can't just stay like this forever." Fox stretched his arms and back and gave Cynthia a sorry look.

Cynthia's own body ached with soreness. Bruises around her wrists and rib cage sent pain up and down her arms and torso. Even her wings hurt.

"Right." She nodded and stood.

He joined her and wrapped her in a warm hug. "But soon we will be able to relax together." He murmured in her ear.

"I can't wait." She nodded against his shoulder.

"Let's figure out what our next steps are."

She ticked off a list on her fingers. "Cover my wings…"

"*Our* wings. Brownies, remember?" He smiled.

"Right. Cover *our* wings. Disguise our clothes."

"Find the Forest People, or at least someone who can find them for us." Fox finished her list.

Her chest squeezed. "Should we really ask around for help? I still think it's dangerous…"

"We don't know where they are."

"But you know what direction they're in, right?"

Fox nodded. "In theory. But how are we going to find them when we don't even know where *we* are!"

"I can fly above the trees and get our bearings…" Cynthia started to walk toward the entrance to the hollow.

Fox held her hand and tugged. "What if someone sees you? It would defeat the purpose of the disguises. Of trying to stay hidden."

She frowned. "Maybe. But I'll go fast. We need to at least know which way to travel. Even if we do decide to ask around for help, it would be smart to be headed in the right direction."

He furrowed his brow and walked out with her.

They both took tentative steps, keeping their eyes and ears alert for any signs of trouble.

Before her wings could lift her from the ground, he squeezed her hand again. "The Forest People are about halfway between the mountains and the sea. Please be careful."

"I think it will be fine…" Cynthia peered up at him.

He nodded. "Go fast…"

Fox trudged through the woods beside Cynthia as the day stretched toward late afternoon. They wound between blades of tall triangular sedge grass; their feet bounced on the springy moss-covered ground.

They walked single file underneath droopy ferns, around mossy boulders and fallen logs, and between lemony-yellow witch-hazel blossoms. Unable to feel the ground through her makeshift shoes, Cynthia tripped over the flat, scaly liverwort leaves that covered the forest floor. She had been hesitant to wear anything resembling a shoe, but it added to their disguise as brownies, since many of the little men enjoyed shoes of all kinds.

Cynthia used both hands to collect a bright red berry from a burgundy wintergreen plant.

The fallen deciduous leaves released a sweet scent in the air with every step they took, while the clubmoss's needle-like leaves threatened to scrape Cynthia through her leaf-clothes.

The cold air stung Cynthia's cheeks and nose, and her breath created little clouds in front of her face, but the layers of leaves that covered her clothes and kept her identity hidden retained her body heat to keep her warm. She kept her arms and hands tucked beneath a mossy cape, close to her body, which helped her fingers stay warm. And the leaves they had wrapped their feet in kept her toes warm, too.

Fox kept a quick pace. Though they didn't know exactly how long it would take to get to the area they thought they would find the Forest People, they wanted to go as fast as they could. They had stuffed the satchels the moles had given them with plenty of mushrooms, berries, and seeds for easy eating while they walked.

Whenever they saw or heard another creature in the woods, they hunkered down beneath a wide leaf or dangling curtain of vines to wait out the potential threat. They couldn't be too careful, even if it slowed their progress.

They hid from a scruffy creature with droopy ears, oversized eyes, and a large nose. Twice the size of the trufflefox they had met before, it towered over the fern they hid beneath.

The animal snuffed its nostrils against the forest floor.

"It's tracking…" Fox explained to Cynthia.

"As long as it's not tracking *us*," she whispered back. She kept her wide eyes locked on the beast.

She only let out her breath when the creature had disappeared from sight.

"Let's keep going," she sighed to Fox.

By the time the sun began to sink, Cynthia huffed and puffed. "I thought I couldn't get any more sore and tired. But I was definitely wrong."

"I know what you mean," Fox agreed. "We're still recovering from our journey, being locked up in the prison for so long, and the escape from the toad."

"Ugh. Don't remind me!" she groaned.

He rubbed her back. "We'll rest for the night and set out again tomorrow."

"How long do think it will take?" She didn't want to sound whiney, since it was her fault the journey was taking so long. If they asked for help, they would be done with this journey much sooner.

But she still couldn't stomach the thought of potentially being tricked or captured again.

"I don't know. But we'll make it together, I promise."

"The clouds are coming in. It feels like it might snow again." Cynthia rubbed her hands together underneath her cloak. They couldn't risk having a fire, either, just in case.

They huddled close to one another for warmth and tried to rest as best they could.

The snow managed to stay in the clouds the following day, but the air felt heavy with the threat of it. They couldn't afford to get caught in another snowstorm.

"Do you think Birdie and the mouse made it out of the mole's prison?" Cynthia tried to keep her mind from her sore legs and aching feet. "Did the mouse make it home to her family?"

Fox didn't have answers of course. "That mouse tricked us. But you still want to make sure she's safe. You haven't changed too much."

She rubbed her hand against the side of her head. "This is all so confusing. I do want her to be safe. Even though she tricked us. I don't know."

"I'm sure she's fine." Fox tried to assure her.

They had no way of actually knowing, though. All they could do was hold on to their hope.

Before Cynthia could come up with a reply to Fox's comment, a sudden gust of wind tossed her silvery hair around her head.

A shadow passed overhead.

"Get down!" Fox pulled Cynthia to the ground beside him. "Quick, take cover!"

Cynthia hunched low to the ground and followed him. They scurried across the ground until they were underneath the canopy of a large honey colored mushroom attached to the side of a tree trunk.

"What is it?" She peeked from beneath the mushroom but could only make out a wide wingspan and long tail.

Was it a bird of some kind? The tail didn't match any description of a bird that she knew of.

"I don't know." Fox pulled her back underneath the mushroom cap. "Either a predator that thinks we're a snack, or something worse."

"Like someone looking for *me*, right?" Her stomach tightened and her heart sped up. If they got caught again, it would be because of her. Again.

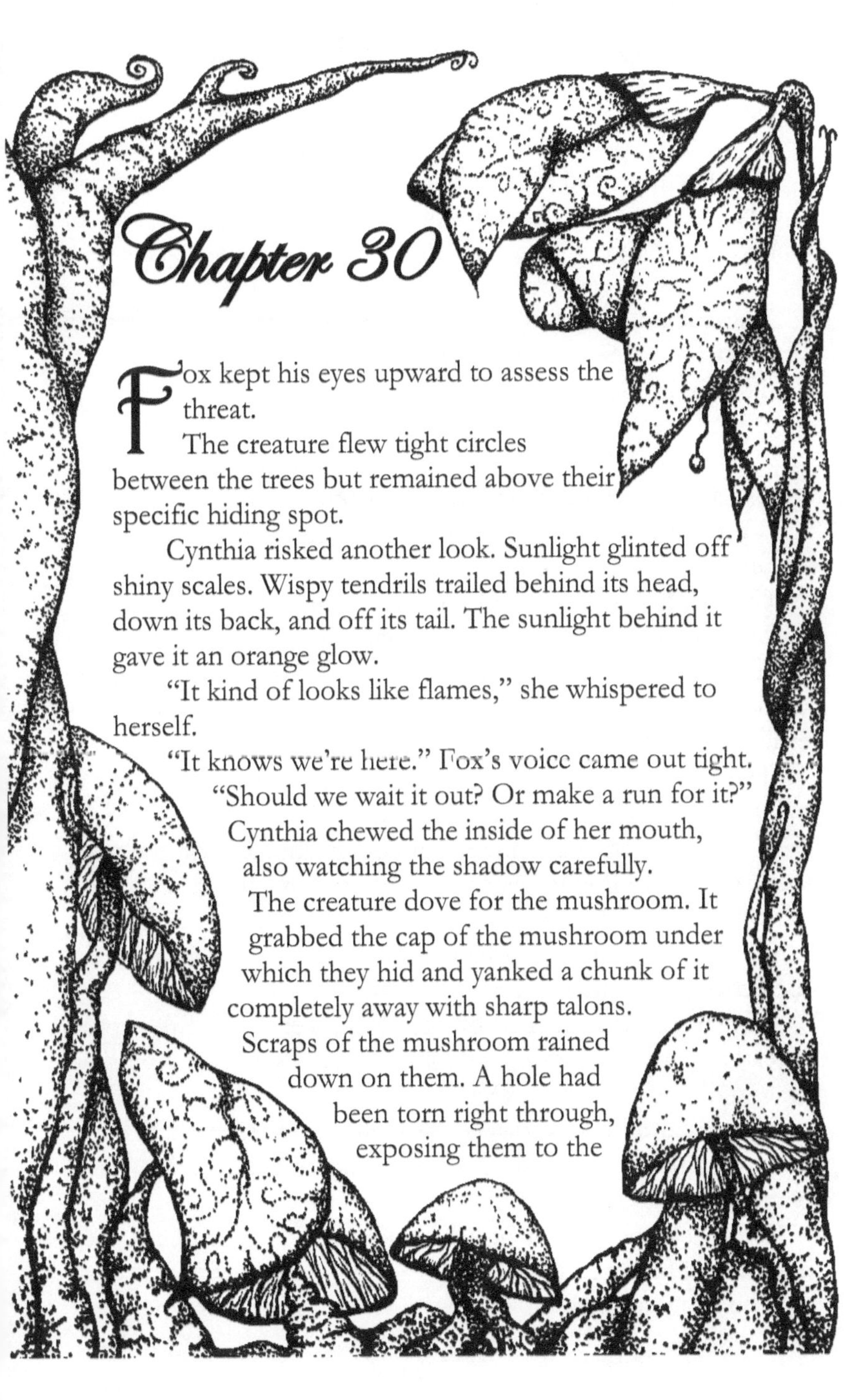

Chapter 30

Fox kept his eyes upward to assess the
threat.

The creature flew tight circles
between the trees but remained above their
specific hiding spot.

Cynthia risked another look. Sunlight glinted off
shiny scales. Wispy tendrils trailed behind its head,
down its back, and off its tail. The sunlight behind it
gave it an orange glow.

"It kind of looks like flames," she whispered to
herself.

"It knows we're here." Fox's voice came out tight.

"Should we wait it out? Or make a run for it?"
Cynthia chewed the inside of her mouth,
also watching the shadow carefully.

The creature dove for the mushroom. It
grabbed the cap of the mushroom under
which they hid and yanked a chunk of it
completely away with sharp talons.

Scraps of the mushroom rained
down on them. A hole had
been torn right through,
exposing them to the

flying assailant.

They didn't dare wait for it to attack again.

Cynthia motioned for Fox to follow her as she edged around the base of the tree, trying to stay hidden from above. A stairstep of the same honey mushrooms created a visual barrier between themselves and their attacker.

The animal swooped again. It ripped the remainder of the first mushroom from the tree completely.

The chunks landed on the forest floor in a series of thuds.

When it realized that they were no longer hiding in that spot, it let out an angry roar. Fire scorched part of the tree trunk. It ignited a trail of lichen that burned quickly.

"A pygmy dragon!" Fox hissed from their hiding place around the side of the tree.

Cynthia had met a couple of pygmy dragons before. They had never been threatening or dangerous. Why did this one hunt them? Did it mistake them for prey? Or did it recognize Cynthia and hunt them for a different reason? They couldn't exactly wait around or talk to it to find out.

They hurried away from the tree, using a nearby bushy oakleaf hydrangea as cover.

The dragon ripped at the remaining mushrooms on the tree trunk with all four of its clawed feet. It dove at a fern and ripped it from the ground, roots and all. When its search turned up nothing, another stream of flames shot from its mouth, lighting the lichen on another tree trunk on fire.

The moistness of the other plants kept the fire from spreading once the moss rapidly burned itself out, but the dragon did not slow its search.

Cynthia and Fox zig-zagged through the underbrush, turned sharp corners around slick stones, and ducked underneath plants that could offer cover.

Cynthia glanced over her shoulder, past Fox, to see if the dragon still followed them.

The dragon hovered overhead. With enormous, marbled

orange and red eyes, it scanned the forest floor for signs of its prey. Smoke continued to rise from its nose.

"Eek!" Cynthia forced her legs to move faster.

Parts of her disguise fell off her body. Her cape detached itself from around her neck. It tumbled to the ground, exposing her brightly colored wings against the monotone green backdrop of the forest.

"Oh, no!" she gasped.

The dragon instantly spotted her. It tucked its wings to dive right for her.

"Keep going." Fox urged her forward.

She skidded around a fallen log, hoping it was hollow inside so she could take cover.

Before she could find out if the log had a good hiding place for them, she smacked into an invisible barrier.

But instead of falling backwards, she bounced in place. Her wings and arms entangled in sticky ropes restricted her movements.

A second later, Fox skidded behind her and just managed to avoid running right into her, dodging at the last second. He, too, became stuck in the trap that Cynthia had found.

"What is this?" Fox cried as he struggled beside her.

With no time to assess the situation or try to find a way out of the tangled mess, Cynthia locked eyes with the dragon behind her.

The dragon saw its prey stuck. It released another stream of flames and spiraled in a dive right for her. It pulled up at the last second. It must have been worried about becoming caught in the trap, too.

Seeing a chance to escape before it made another attack, Cynthia yanked harder with her arms and legs to free herself. But it was no use. The more she struggled, the more the strands attached themselves to every part of her body.

The dragon hovered above, eyeing his prey with a hungry look.

A movement on the log above Cynthia caught her eye. Daring to take her eyes off the dragon, she pivoted her gaze.

The owner of the oversized web stared back at her.

Great. She was about to either be eaten by an enormous spider or burned alive by a miniature dragon.

"Cynthia!" Fox pulled her attention to him. "There's a sharp rock by your foot. Kick it over here and I'll try to cut us free!"

Cynthia found the rock and kicked it toward Fox. He lifted it with his feet and tried to reach it with his hands. But the web held him tight. His movement limited.

"It's no use," she cried. "I'm so sorry I got us into this mess. I love you."

Fox managed to find her hand with his and held it tight. Cynthia squeezed her eyes shut and prepared to meet her end. Whatever it may be.

The web held her in an awkward position, making it impossible to brace herself for either the blast of fire from the dragon or the inevitable bite from the spider.

The web vibrated with movement from above. The spider raced toward them.

The sound of the dragon rushing through the air sent chills down Cynthia's back.

This was not how Cynthia had expected her life to end!

Firey pain exploded across Cynthia's arm.

She screamed and her eyes flew open. The dragon had grazed her with its talons, but it had not ignited the web. Or those caught in it. Instead, it circled back around for another chance at capturing Cynthia in its feet.

"Not today, Firestarter!" a commanding voice shouted from above Cynthia.

She peeked overhead.

The spider turned herself upside down with the back of her body facing the dragon. Webbing burst from the spinnerets at the back of her abdomen.

The sticky white threads tangled around the dragon's wings. The dragon plummeted to the ground and landed in a heap of talons, scales, webs, and smoke.

The spider continued to bombard the dragon with more web.

The more the dragon struggled, the more tangled it became until it was a ball of white in a twitching mess on the ground.

The spider snipped the web connecting her with the dragon and, with an annoyed expression, watched it flop around on the ground. "Ugh. I hate those things. They don't belong here. They should live in the sky with the cloud dragons, or in a cave or something. But leave the flammable forest alone. Am I right?"

Cynthia hung limp on the web. Fox remained pinned beside her. Their hands still gripped each other tight. They were just as entangled as the dragon on the ground behind them.

Would the spider eat the dragon? Would it eat *them*? Cynthia gulped and tried to wriggle free again.

The spider turned her attention to the pair of pixies caught in her web.

"Oh, dear. You two are awfully stuck." Did her voice sound sweet as a trick? What game was she playing?

She climbed along her web closer to Cynthia.

Each of her steps jostled the web, sending vibrations along every strand.

Cynthia released Fox's hand and struggled more. Fox pulled on the web to try to free himself.

The spider clicked at Cynthia and Fox. "You have made a mess of things, haven't you?" In a flash, she snipped the web around Cynthia.

Cynthia collapsed onto the ground. Fox landed with a thud beside her. The pair quickly righted themselves. Cynthia prepared to sprint away.

Before she could take off, Fox wrapped a hand around her arm and cautiously pulled her away from the web.

Maybe running away wasn't a good idea. They should back away slowly.

"You needn't be afraid." The spider blinked at them

What kind of spider was she? She had a human-looking head and face, with two enormous shiny black eyes. Two horns jutted from the sides of her head, and her ears looked like an odd version of Cynthia's own. A braid of regular-looking hair hung down one side of her head. The remainder of her body looked like an enormous hairy spider, eight exoskeleton legs and all.

She gave the pixies a warm smile. "I don't eat pixies. Or *dragons*, for that matter." She tossed the disgusted words over her shoulder at the dragon who had given up his fight on the ground and tried to slink away. "Good luck with that!" She laughed as she watched him attempt his escape.

Cynthia glanced at the dragon, twitching on the ground.

With every convulsion he managed to move a little further from the spider and her now-destroyed web.

The web that had caught her and Fox. Had been their certain doom.

But had ended up saving them.

"Thank you…" Cynthia tipped her head to one side as she examined the spider.

Even with her enormous colorless eyes, she had a kind look about her. If one could get past her odd appearance.

"And I'm sorry about your web," Cynthia finished.

Fox made a disgruntled sound beside her.

She looked up at him. "We destroyed her web! It probably took a long time to make." Cynthia gave the spider a sorrowful look.

The spider tapped the ground with one of her legs. "It's fine. It's part of the job, you know? Always building, watching it get ruined, and building it again."

Cynthia smiled.

Then doubt creeped in. This was the kind of situation that had gotten her into trouble recently. Trusting the first person to give her a kind look or offer a good deed. Her smile faltered.

Fox glared. "Let's get out of here while we still can." He murmured right into her ear.

Did he sense something off about the spider woman? Or was he just worried about Cynthia? Was there something else going on that she couldn't know because of her lack of abilities?

Frustration welled. If she hadn't been so trusting, she wouldn't have met Fox or stayed with him for as long as she had. But she also wouldn't have ended up a prisoner below ground for days and days on end.

Before Cynthia could come to a conclusion about the spider, the strange creature spoke again.

"Your friend is right. That dragon will probably be back as soon as he figures out that he can just burn the webbing off of his body. His scales are fireproof, so it will only take him a minute…"

Cynthia nodded. "Thank you, again for your help." She hesitated. Normally she would offer some kind of gesture in return. Or well wishes, at least. But she didn't know what to say.

"Just pass it on!" The spider launched a web upward and then climbed it back to a perch on the decaying log. She waved goodbye with one of her pointed legs.

"She sounds like you," Fox commented. "But I do have to say, I didn't sense any dishonesty coming from her. She's right, though, we should get out of here before the dragon returns. And we need to find a way to cover your wings again."

Cynthia pondered his words. The way the spider had brushed off her gratitude and suggested she pass it on was something that Cynthia had said before. But would she be able to do it again so easily?

Besides the new, large philodendron leaf to cover her wings, the only thing keeping Cynthia warm was their quick pace through the underbrush again. They would make new disguises when they were far enough away from danger and had a chance to rest.

A branch or twig snapped nearby in the trees.

The pair froze. Something approached, on the ground this time. Slower. Perhaps more careful.

Probably not the dragon? But who or what might it be?

Fox pulled her to duck down beside a clump of brightly colored goldenrod flowers to hide while they waited in silence for whoever it was to show themselves.

Depending on the situation, they would either need to stay perfectly still or run as fast as they could. She didn't know if she had the energy in her to run anymore. She held her breath and hoped that they would be able to just hide this time.

Fox whispered into her ear to be ready, just in case.

Cynthia's heart pounded. Her breath came faster as the noises of someone approaching grew louder.

She was cold, tired, and scared. When would this all be over?

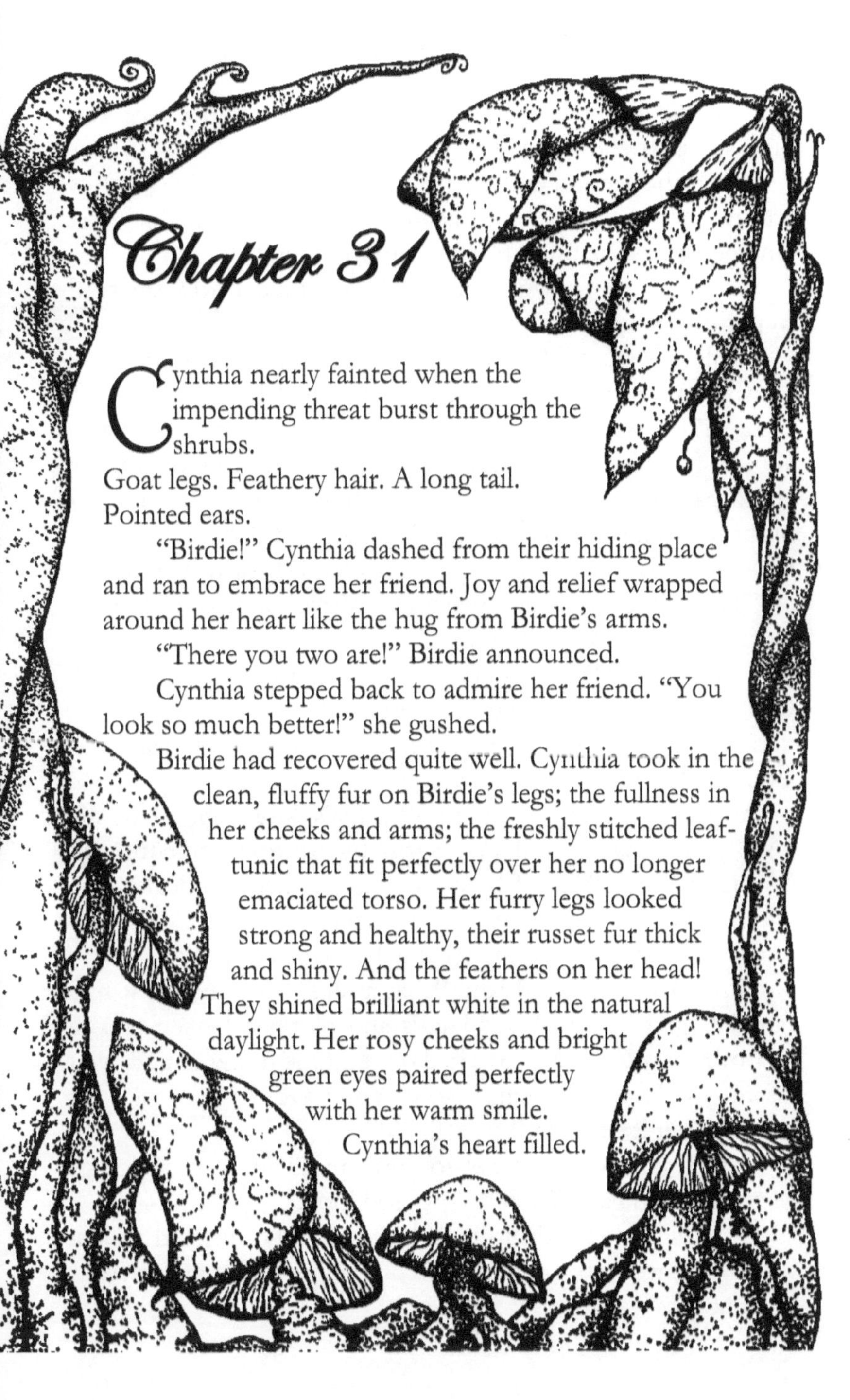

Chapter 31

Cynthia nearly fainted when the impending threat burst through the shrubs.

Goat legs. Feathery hair. A long tail. Pointed ears.

"Birdie!" Cynthia dashed from their hiding place and ran to embrace her friend. Joy and relief wrapped around her heart like the hug from Birdie's arms.

"There you two are!" Birdie announced.

Cynthia stepped back to admire her friend. "You look so much better!" she gushed.

Birdie had recovered quite well. Cynthia took in the clean, fluffy fur on Birdie's legs; the fullness in her cheeks and arms; the freshly stitched leaf-tunic that fit perfectly over her no longer emaciated torso. Her furry legs looked strong and healthy, their russet fur thick and shiny. And the feathers on her head! They shined brilliant white in the natural daylight. Her rosy cheeks and bright green eyes paired perfectly with her warm smile.

Cynthia's heart filled.

And so did her eyes. She swiped the tears off her face and hugged her friend again.

When the second embrace ended, Birdie cupped her hands around her mouth and hollered from where she had just emerged from the underbrush. "I found them!"

Another creature who looked a little bit like Birdie emerged to join the group.

"This is Marten." Birdie gestured at the satyr beside her.

Marten's furry legs and hooves matched Birdie, but that's where the similarities ended. Marten's arms boasted shaggy auburn fur, his flat nose reminded Cynthia of a rabbit's nose, and a pair of five pronged antlers extended from the sides of his head just above his long, deer-like ears and curly auburn hair. He wore a confused expression in his reddish-brown eyes.

"They don't look like pixies..." Marten announced as he squinted at Cynthia and Fox.

Fox looked Marten up and down with a wary eye. He took Cynthia's hand and tugged her closer to his side.

Did he think that Birdie was deceiving them? That she was a bounty hunter, too? Was he right?

A pit weighed heavily in Cynthia's stomach. Had she endangered herself and Fox again by trusting someone she shouldn't have? What if by nursing Birdie back to health, she had doomed herself to capture? To never seeing Fox again? Or worse... what if something terrible happened *to* Fox?

"I'm so glad I found you. What a relief!" Birdie thrust two familiar satchels into Fox's hands and plopped herself onto a nearby mossy log. "We have had quite a time trying to track you down, you know? I mean, I get it. You were trying to stay out of sight, but it sure made it difficult!"

Fox dug into his satchel to confirm all of his belongings remained, and gave Birdie a confused look.

Cynthia scrutinized Birdie and Marten- who reclined against a stiff mushroom stem and stretched his odd legs out in front of him.

Birdie's wide eyes gave her an air of innocence, while Marten's squinty eyes made him look suspicious. But the crinkles in the corners indicated he smiled a lot. Was that a good thing? Were they happy smiles or nefarious smiles?

Cynthia released Fox's hand and gripped the sides of her head. How did Fox do this all the time? The constant doubt, confusion, and anxiety must be overwhelming. Or maybe because of his ability he didn't suffer from trying to figure out everyone's intentions?

Either way, she didn't think she could take it much longer. Her heart and mind warred with one another. Her head told her to be wary, but her heart wanted to believe that Birdie and Marten could be trusted!

Which was it?

Birdie's lips turned down. "Are you alright Cynthia? You don't look very well." She furrowed her brow, and her tail drooped.

Cynthia opened her mouth but couldn't think of the words to say in response. No, she wasn't alright. But if she couldn't trust Birdie, then what was she supposed to say to that?

Before she could come up with a response one way or another, Fox asked Birdie a question of his own. "How did you escape?" The words dripped with suspicion.

"Fox," Cynthia hissed. Her trusting instinct kicked in without her permission.

Birdie might be a bounty hunter, or a spy or something, but Cynthia desperately wanted to trust the friend she had made underground.

"I have to be sure," Fox murmured while he waited for Birdie to answer his question.

How long would it take before he could tell their intentions? Did his gift allow him to instantly know if someone could be trusted? Or did it take time?

"Oh, boy, is that a long story!" Birdie grinned at Marten.

"Let's get you two warm and safe before I'll tell you the whole thing. Marten here is going to arrange a ride for us all. I'll tell you while we wait."

Fox stiffened. "A ride? To where?" His glare bounced back and forth between Birdie and Marten.

"Home, of course." Birdie looked at him like she didn't understand his questions.

Cynthia bit her lip. Should she trust them? How was she supposed to know? She shivered beside Fox.

Birdie frowned at Cynthia. "You look tired and hungry. And cold."

As if in response to the mere mention of food, Cynthia's stomach grumbled. She placed a hand over it and willed herself to remain calm. Even if Birdie's intentions were less than honorable, she was right. Cynthia was cold, tired, and hungry. And what did she have to lose from allowing them to help her fill her stomach and warm her body?

Marten and Birdie insisted that Fox and Cynthia rest underneath a wide mushroom while they gather the supplies to start a fire and forage food for the four of them to share.

It gave Cynthia the perfect opportunity to question Fox. "Well? Can we trust them?"

Fox frowned and watched them through the blades of grass and mushroom stems. He nodded reluctantly. "I think so."

Cynthia sighed. "You don't sound very confident."

He turned his gaze toward her. "For some reason, I *want* to not trust them. I *want* to send them away, or escape with you. But it's not because of my instincts. Or my ability to sense dishonesty." He hesitated.

"What do you mean?" She squeezed his hand to encourage him to keep talking.

"Deep down, I know they are safe. They only want to help. But with everything that's happened lately, my first instinct now is to protect you. It's making everything confusing. I am looking for reasons to *not* trust them. Frankly, it's exhausting."

Cynthia chuckled. "I know what you mean! Normally, I instantly trust everyone. But lately that hasn't worked out so well." She looked away and blushed. "And now, I don't think I can trust *anyone*, even though I desperately want to. My mind is spinning and my stomach hurts. I don't know how you do it."

He squeezed her hand back. She met his gaze again.

"I can usually tell right away. And if I'm being honest, I could with them, too." He pointed at Marten through the grass. "But I think… I'm worried now, too. What if I'm wrong? What if something happens?"

"Has your instinct ever been wrong before?" she asked.

He laughed with a frown. "I haven't given anyone a chance to prove me wrong in so long, I wouldn't know. It's depressing, really."

She placed a hand on the side of his face. "You gave me a chance…"

"Barely," he whispered.

"So, if you think they can be trusted, then… let's trust them." Cynthia's heart instantly felt lighter.

Fox nodded. His shoulders relaxed. "I love you."

Cynthia's cheeks warmed again. She smiled wide at him and glanced at his lips. "I love you."

They leaned toward one another to share a kiss.

"Oh! Sorry! I didn't mean to interrupt!" Birdie dropped the armful of twigs she carried. They clattered to the ground.

Cynthia and Fox jumped apart, though she kept his hand squeezed tight in her own.

The three of them laughed out loud at the awkward moment.

Fox stood and tugged Cynthia to follow. They helped Birdie pick up the fallen sticks. Marten returned with a pair of plump blackberries, a few ripe walnuts, and a flat, tan mushroom as big as Cynthia's arms could stretch. Together, Marten and Fox prepared the fire.

"Tell them how you managed to escape," Marten prodded

Birdie while he poked the fire with a stick.

Cynthia sat beside Birdie, who held one of the enormous blackberries in her lap. Cynthia removed a druplet from the berry and placed it in her mouth. The juice burst from inside and filled her mouth with a sweetness that ran down the back of her throat. She closed her eyes and savored the flavor.

Birdie broke a single ball-shaped druplet off one of the blackberries and popped it into her mouth. She swallowed, then began speaking. "You won't believe what happened! That mouse that was in the cell across from us? You know how she didn't move a muscle the whole time you were there? Well, a few days after they took you away, the guards came through like usual to drop food inside the cell. Except, I don't think you can call what they fed us 'food.' It was barely edible!"

"Focus, Birdie," Marten reminded his friend while he settled beside her. He took a couple of blackberry druplets for himself and smiled at her.

"Right, sorry. I do have a tendency to let my words run away with me! Anyway!" She ducked her head and looked around at the others.

Fox snuggled beside Cynthia, and she leaned against his shoulder, allowing the growing fire to warm her on the outside and her skipping heart from Fox's nearness to warm her on the inside.

Focus, Cynthia, she told herself, chuckling inwardly.

"Right. So, the moles dropped off the food, and one of them pointed at the mouse.

"'You think it's still alive?' he asked the other mole.

"'Only one way to find out,' the second mole said.

"They pushed the door open and crept closer to the mouse. When they got close enough, one of them poked her with the handle end of his staff. She didn't move. She didn't flinch. Nothing."

Cynthia gasped and sat up. "What? She died in there? Oh! I knew I should have done more to try to rescue her! She didn't deserve that... what about her family?" Cynthia covered her face with her hands and forced her breathing to remain calm. She swallowed the tightness in her throat.

Birdie looked at Cynthia with wide eyes. "Wait! No! She didn't die. That's what I'm trying to tell you! She tricked the moles! When they bent over to pick her up and carry her away, she bit one of them on the arm!"

Cynthia sucked in another breath. "She did what?"

Birdie nodded. "Yeah! He dropped her and screeched with pain. It was the worst sound I've ever heard. It pierced right through my ears and into my head!" She cringed as if she could still hear the sound the mole made.

"And?" Fox encouraged her to keep talking.

"It confused the moles so much they didn't know what to do! She slipped past them, swiped the keys from their belts, scurried across the floor, and slammed the door shut behind her!" Birdie sat with her mouth agape. Even she seemed to have a hard time believing what she had experienced firsthand.

"Wow!" Cynthia breathed. The mouse had done all that? Was she planning it the whole time? Or did she just see a chance and take it?

"Tell them the next part." Marten nudged Birdie's shoulder.

"Right! So! I expected her to just scurry down the tunnel never to be seen again. But that's not what she did at all! She used the keys to open my cell and the other one holding a prisoner."

"That goblin thing with the ladybug wings?" Fox asked with raised eyebrows.

"That's the one! He beat a hasty retreat down the tunnel with wings abuzz before either of us could even find out anything about him. But I was still not very strong. My legs had only just healed, and I was stiff and sore. The mouse helped me stand, let me lean on her, and walked with me down the tunnel and away from the prison.

"The guards shouted for help, but their cries fell on empty tunnels. No other guards were expected to come for hours for the shift change.

"Once we had gone a fair distance, the mouse released me and leaned me against a wall. She promptly started digging at a furious speed. I couldn't believe my eyes!" Birdie reenacted the mouse's digging motions with her hands. "I hadn't seen her move once the whole time she was there, and she hadn't eaten anything in so long, I don't know where the energy came from! But she dug into the wall, then straight up until she breached the surface."

The mouse had surprised Cynthia once, when she had betrayed the pixies.

But, it seemed she had a few other tricks up her sleeve, too.

"Go on," Marten urged Birdie to finish the story.

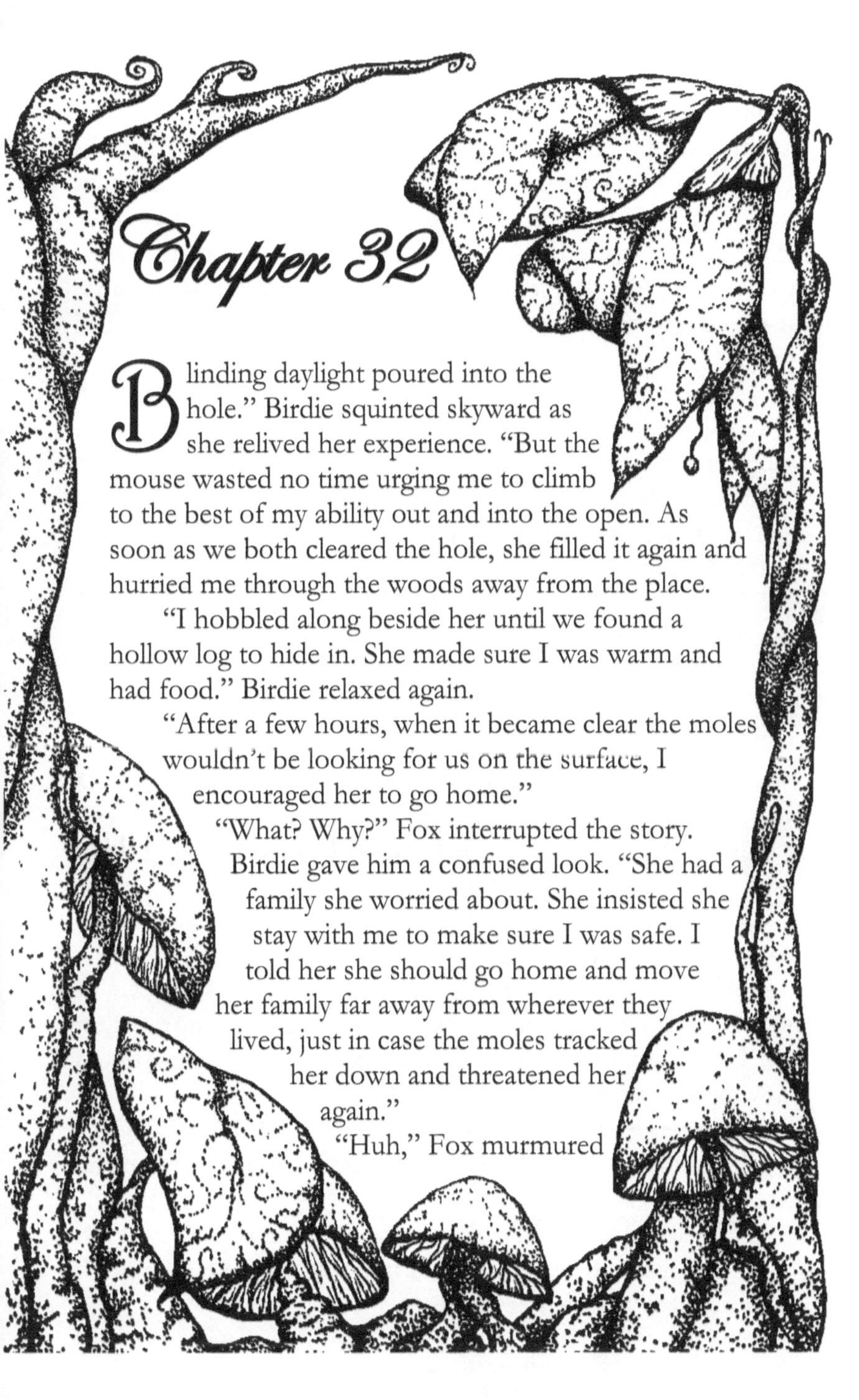

Chapter 32

Blinding daylight poured into the
hole." Birdie squinted skyward as
she relived her experience. "But the
mouse wasted no time urging me to climb
to the best of my ability out and into the open. As
soon as we both cleared the hole, she filled it again and
hurried me through the woods away from the place.

"I hobbled along beside her until we found a
hollow log to hide in. She made sure I was warm and
had food." Birdie relaxed again.

"After a few hours, when it became clear the moles
wouldn't be looking for us on the surface, I
encouraged her to go home."

"What? Why?" Fox interrupted the story.
Birdie gave him a confused look. "She had a
family she worried about. She insisted she
stay with me to make sure I was safe. I
told her she should go home and move
her family far away from wherever they
lived, just in case the moles tracked
her down and threatened her
again."

"Huh," Fox murmured

to himself.

But Cynthia's focus was on the mouse. She couldn't believe the mouse had saved Birdie! Perhaps she wanted to redeem herself for what she had done to Cynthia. Or perhaps her desperation to see her family again gave her the drive she needed to mount an escape. But she didn't *have* to rescue Birdie or the other prisoner in the process. The faun only slowed her down.

As if she could read Cynthia's thoughts, Birdie said quietly, "I know she didn't do right by you, but she turned out to be a good little mouse after all."

"I couldn't agree more!" Cynthia nodded.

"But that still leaves you stranded in a hollow log with weak legs and no food…" Fox puzzled through the situation.

"Right. Well, a tree frog hopped by a little bit later, and I asked him to send a message to find Marten here. I knew if the frog told the right people, Marten would be able to find me." Birdie smiled at her friend.

"And that's exactly what happened," Marten interjected his part of the story. "A swallow found me and told me that a dragon fly had told her that a chipmunk had told her that a frog had told him that there was a weird deer-brownie-girl-thing stuck in a tree, and she needed help."

"*What?*" Fox laughed at the strange message. "How did you know it was Birdie?"

Birdie and Marten shared a smug look. "Let's just say, we've both been in strange situations before. It didn't surprise him that I had somehow managed to disappear for weeks and then show up in a tree!"

Marten agreed. "Except the swallow and I searched *up* in trees! It took us a bit to realize she was in a hollow log on the forest floor."

Birdie laughed at their error, and Marten rolled his eyes. "Once we found her, I helped her finish regaining her strength and was ready to take her home."

He gave Birdie a serious, disapproving look as he said the next part. "But *she* insisted we find the *'pixie with the butterfly wings.'* I thought she was still brain-rattled from her ordeal. Pixies don't *have* butterfly wings, you see." He wiggled his eyebrows at Cynthia and gave her a funny smile. "At least, not that I've ever heard. But she kept on insisting. She said you and your friend might need our help making your way home. That you were still in danger. And no matter how much I insisted that SHE needed to go home, she wouldn't listen. As usual." He folded his arms and glared at Birdie.

She gave him a sheepish grin. "But I was right, wasn't I? About the whole thing!"

He dropped his arms and sighed. "Yeah, you were right. Of course. Like usual. So, here we are. Ready to help the pixie with the butterfly wings and her friend go home."

Marten popped the last of the blackberry druplets into his mouth and wiped his hands on his furry legs. "I think the fire's ready to roast the walnuts and mushroom." He stood and prepared the food for heating.

Birdie helped Marten roast the walnuts and the mushroom, leaving Cynthia and Fox reclining against the tree trunk.

"Is it really almost over?" Cynthia gave Fox a hopeful look. "If they can get us to the Forest People, then we can get your wings fixed…" She hesitated. Her shoulders dropped. "It seems too good to be true."

Fox rested a warm hand on her shoulder. "It is lucky that they found us, but it's not too good to be true. You always said your good deeds had a way of being repaid. This," he gestured at Marten and Birdie huddled together over the fire, arguing about the best method for roasting mushrooms, "is because of you."

Cynthia watched them bicker. In a good-natured way, but still. She shook her head.

Fox poked her arm. "It's because *you* took the time to help

Birdie in the prison, and because *you* trusted the mouse in the woods. We are going to find the Forest People and go home, but it's not because of Birdie or the mouse, or Marten, or anyone else. It's because of *you*."

Home. That wasn't something Cynthia really wanted to think about. Would she return to live in Magnolia's garden? Would she live wherever Fox lived? Would he come stay with her? What did their future hold? Was there even a "they" to have a future together, or was that also just wishful thinking?

She shoved those worries aside and focused on the present. "You're right. Thank you, Fox. And I'm glad we'll be able to find the Forest People really soon. Just think, your wings will be fixed in no time!"

A cloud of doubt passed behind his eyes, but just as quickly it disappeared. "Speaking of getting my wings fixed…"

Birdie handed each of them a warmly grilled chunk of the mushroom topped with crumbled toasted walnuts. "Enjoy!"

"Thank you, Birdie. And Marten," Fox spoke to their rescuers. "Now, what about this ride you mentioned earlier?"

Marten gave Fox and Cynthia a nervous look. "Yes. About that…"

Dread filled Cynthia's stomach again. She thought they could trust Marten and Birdie! Fox had felt their sincerity. Why would Marten hesitate to tell them about the ride?

"It's a little… unconventional." He glanced around the clearing as if the right words might be hanging in the air. Then he shrugged and gave them an apologetic grin. "The ride will be here in the morning. I guess you'll just have to see for yourselves."

"Well, that doesn't sound foreboding or anything!" Birdie chimed in. She shoved Marten playfully on his shoulder, then turned to look at Fox and Cynthia. "Don't worry, he wouldn't arrange anything dangerous. By the end of the day tomorrow, you'll be home. Or, at least, safe. I promise."

Cynthia chose to push any concerns with Marten's plan out

of her head for now and just enjoy the fact that she was warm, fed, and relatively safe. Fox remained by her side. Birdie had recovered and come to save them. Whatever Marten had in store for them the next day, she'd deal with it when the time came.

Marten leaned against the mushroom stem near the fire made of nothing but embers now. He pulled out a flute made from gradually longer bamboo pipes bound together in a line with cords. He gently blew across the flat holes, producing a tranquil melody that helped chase away Cynthia's fears and allowed her mind to rest.

Marten left before dawn to fetch the ride that he had promised. Not long after she awoke, Cynthia heard a rustle from the underbrush.

A moment later, two massive grass-hoppers hopped out of the shadows. Their leaps didn't take them as high as Cynthia would have expected though. A quick survey revealed the reason. Each had a string tied around their neck. The two strings joined together in the hands of another new creature that Cynthia had never seen before. A goblin or troll of some kind with long arms, hooved legs, a round nose, and ears that looked like hairy bat wings. He wore a grimace that seemed permanent, and eyed Cynthia and her friends with suspicion.

Marten stepped into the opening with a wide smile. "Here we are!" He gestured at the grasshoppers, as if presenting them to the group.

Cynthia and Fox exchanged surprised looks. Were they going to ride… grasshoppers?

Before she could form her confused thoughts into any sort of question, the grasshopper handler spoke in a gravelly voice. His large, watery eyes pinned Marten in place. "Make sure you return them as arranged. And do *not* let them out of your sight." He patted one of the grasshoppers on the head.

The grasshopper's black, beady eye didn't hold any emotion, but the little man brushed a stray tear from his own cheek. "I'll see you again soon, buddy."

Marten handed Cynthia the rope tied loosely around one of the grasshopper's neck. "We'll ride two per grasshopper. Fox and Cynthia, you take this one. We'll take the other one." He motioned at himself and Birdie.

Cynthia nodded. She allowed Fox to assist her mounting the grasshopper, then scooted forward to allow Fox to join her.

A soft voice whispered in her ear. "It's a pleasure to serve you." A strong feeling of admiration entered Cynthia's chest.

She didn't have a chance to think about what it meant before Fox wrapped his arms around her waist and pressed his chest against her back. His nearness kept her warm and calmed her nerves about this new, and hopefully last, adventure. Not that she *never* wanted to go on another adventure, but she needed some time to reflect and recover before she decided to set out on anything new and different for a while.

Marten, a head shorter that Birdie, rode in front on the other grasshopper, with Birdie holding onto his shoulders from behind. "Thank you again," he said to the man who twisted his hands together.

"Bring them back whole!" the man grumbled at Marten.

Marten gave him an easy smile. "Of course! See you soon."

Marten demonstrated how to handle the grasshopper. "Tap its sides with your feet. Hold on tight to the rope, but don't pull on it. Squeeze with your legs. And try not to be too stiff. Go with the flow. Feel the movements. Anticipate the landings and takeoffs. You'll do great."

He did as he said, and his grasshopper bounded off the ground and took a great leap in the direction they needed to travel toward the Forest People.

"Here goes nothing," Cynthia murmured under her breath.

"It's going to be great, you'll see," Fox said in her ear. His breath tickled her and sent a warm shiver down her spine.

He was right. Before all of the disastrous events of the last few weeks, she would have been thrilled at the chance to experience something like this. She should let go of her worries and enjoy the moment. Especially since Fox had his arms snug around her waist.

She released a deep breath and tapped the sides of the grasshopper. It leapt from the ground in a fluid movement. The leap took a long, high arc, then they landed softly on the ground. Before she could even blink, it took off again.

The ride was surprisingly smooth. Cynthia allowed her body to relax into the movements. The cold air stung her cheeks, but the rest of her stayed warm against Fox.

The view from the peak of the hops wasn't quite as good as if Cynthia could just fly upward and hover to look around. And the blur of the trees as they sped past them made her stomach turn a little. She kept her eyes focused forward.

A high-pitched screech filled the air.

Cynthia's heart skipped a beat. "What was that?"

Fox stiffened behind her. She tensed, too.

"It sounded like a hawk," Fox announced. From the shifting of his body behind her, she could tell he searched their surroundings for the source.

"I see it. How do we steer these things? How do we tell Marten and Birdie to stop?" Cynthia started to panic.

They were on their way to safety. They were so close! And now they were going to get eaten by a hawk!

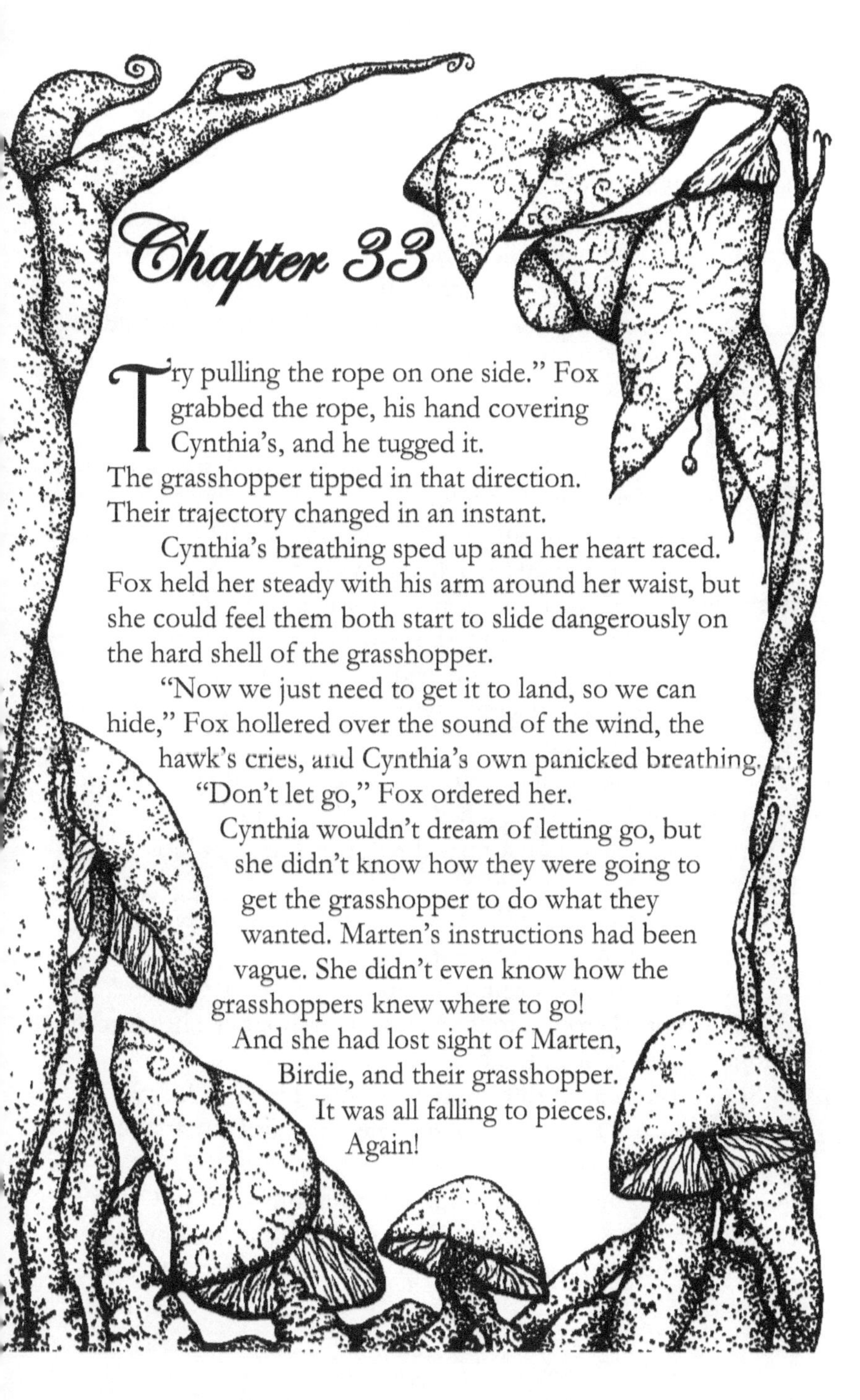

Chapter 33

Try pulling the rope on one side." Fox grabbed the rope, his hand covering Cynthia's, and he tugged it.

The grasshopper tipped in that direction. Their trajectory changed in an instant.

Cynthia's breathing sped up and her heart raced. Fox held her steady with his arm around her waist, but she could feel them both start to slide dangerously on the hard shell of the grasshopper.

"Now we just need to get it to land, so we can hide," Fox hollered over the sound of the wind, the hawk's cries, and Cynthia's own panicked breathing. "Don't let go," Fox ordered her.

Cynthia wouldn't dream of letting go, but she didn't know how they were going to get the grasshopper to do what they wanted. Marten's instructions had been vague. She didn't even know how the grasshoppers knew where to go! And she had lost sight of Marten, Birdie, and their grasshopper. It was all falling to pieces. Again!

The shadow of the hawk passed above, while the grasshopper descended toward the ground. At any moment now, they were about to be eaten.

The grasshopper landed. Fox tugged hard on the rope. The grasshopper stumbled a little, but didn't take off again.

"Tell it to go under that bush," Fox told Cynthia.

Right! She could talk to animals! And though she hadn't sensed any communication between the grasshoppers, she had to believe it would be able to understand her.

"Over there!" she commanded.

The grasshopper took wobbly steps and hid beneath the wide leaves of a magnolia sapling.

Cynthia held her breath. Would the hawk come after them? Why hadn't she understood the hawk's cries? Was she too distracted by her fear to be able to understand it? That had never happened before, but she had never had such distrust toward another creature as she had been having lately, either.

The seconds passed slowly while they held perfectly still on top of the grasshopper.

When the hawk didn't dive for them and they could no longer hear its cries, Fox sighed. "I think it's safe."

"Now what?" Cynthia turned to get a sideways look at his face.

He squeezed her hand. "It will be fine. I'm pretty sure the grasshopper knows where we're headed."

A whisper entered Cynthia's mind. "I do know the way."

She whipped around to look at the grasshopper's head from behind. It had spoken to her.

She forced herself to calm down. "Alright. Then let's go."

Fox held her tight again as she encouraged the grasshopper to finish their journey.

As soon as they started leaping through the forest, Cynthia confirmed that there were no signs of a hawk or any other predator. But there were also no signs of Marten or Birdie, either.

"We'll find them again, I'm sure," Fox reassured Cynthia while they urged their grasshopper to keep going.

They had only been traveling for a few minutes when the grasshopper that Fox and Cynthia rode jolted beneath them. Fox's arms tightened around Cynthia's waist. She clung to the rope as tight as she could and squeezed her legs against the grasshopper's exoskeleton to maintain her position.

A dread filled Cynthia's chest. A feeling that they had been caught.

With the grasshopper's momentum interrupted, it did its best to land without losing its passengers.

Cynthia's eyes darted around to find the source of the terrible feeling that had come over her. Fox ground his teeth in her ear, his own body shifting as he looked for something wrong, too.

In a smooth movement, their grasshopper took off again. Before it could reach the apex of its hop, though, something tugged it backwards. Hard.

Cynthia and Fox jerked forward as the grasshopper moved backwards. The rope attached to the grasshopper jerked in Cynthia's hands and left burns across her palms before she could think to release it.

They plummeted toward the ground. Cynthia's wings instantly tried to open, but Fox still hugged her tight from behind. His wings attempted to flap, but their damaged state didn't allow any useful movements.

Fox must have realized their predicament at the same moment as Cynthia. As if in slow motion, he released his arms from her waist and slipped down her back.

As soon as her wings were free, they held her aloft. She lunged forward and grabbed Fox's wrist just before he fell out of her reach. His weight yanked her down, but her wings attempted to counter the force that pulled them toward the forest floor.

Just as she had suspected weeks ago, her wings were not strong enough to carry herself and Fox.

"Let go!" he hollered at her.

"No!" She struggled against his added weight. She grabbed his wrist with her other hand and pulled with all her strength to keep him from slipping from her.

They both fell toward the ground faster than was safe. Cynthia's wings flapped as hard as they could. The ground sped toward them. Cynthia gritted her teeth and screamed from the effort of keeping Fox from plummeting to his death.

Her wings slowed their descent, but they still hit the ground hard enough to push all the air from Cynthia's lungs. Every muscle in her body seized upon impact. She wheezed to catch her breath from her crumpled position on the ground.

Fox did the same beside her. Only seconds later, he managed to crawl closer and rested his hands on her sides. "Are you alright?" he gasped.

She could only nod in response.

"Say something," he begged.

"Yes." Her words came out strained. "I'm fine."

Instantly her heart twinged. She wasn't fine. It wasn't the truth. She corrected herself. "I'll be fine as soon as I catch my breath," she managed to squeeze out.

"What happened up there?" Fox pulled himself into a seated position and rubbed his side with a grimace on his face. His breathing normalized and he kept his eyes on Cynthia.

Cynthia shook her head. "No idea." She slowly sat up and looked around for their ride.

Back in the direction they had come, she spotted movement. She turned her head to get a better look.

An enormous spider had their grasshopper between its front legs. It spun it over and over and wrapped it in its webbing.

"Oh no, Fox. Look!" Cynthia whispered without taking her eyes off the spider and the unfortunate end of the grasshopper. "Is there anything we can do?"

"Yes. Hide." He scurried to his feet and pulled Cynthia to stand beside him.

Her muscles no longer protested as a burst of energy coursed through her. Her fight or flight instinct kicked in, but her body wouldn't pick one. Instead, she froze.

Their sudden movement must have caught one of the spider's eyes. It paused its work and pinned its gaze on them.

In one quick motion, the spider flung the back half of its body sideways. White, stringy webbing pulsed from its backside toward Fox and Cynthia.

Fox lunged to one side. He pulled Cynthia with him, but managed to stabilize her so she didn't topple over again.

Without speaking, Cynthia followed Fox as they raced through the undergrowth of the forest. A quick glance over her shoulder confirmed that the spider had chosen to pursue them. It's eight many-jointed legs carried it swiftly along the ground.

"Fox!" she squeaked. "It's chasing us!"

As they ran, Fox pulled his bow and arrows from his bag. He paused and urged Cynthia to keep going while he let off a shot toward the spider. "Look for a place we can take cover!"

Cynthia spotted a crack in the droopy, tan cap of a weeping widow mushroom and lunged for the opening. She turned on her heels and yanked Fox in after her.

Completely out of breath, with hearts racing, the pair huddled on either side of the crack in the soft cap of the mushroom that drooped all the way to the ground. Hopefully the spider hadn't seen them dart inside to hide.

Cynthia locked eyes with Fox. His chest heaved and his wide eyes looked more frightened than she'd seen before. That only made her own heart keep beating too fast.

After several long moments of staying perfectly still, Fox whispered to Cynthia. "I think it's clear."

"Let's wait a couple minutes longer, just in case," Cynthia whispered back, trying to keep the panic that squeezed her throat out of her voice.

Fox nodded.

At last, Cynthia agreed with Fox that the spider was no longer a threat. She sunk against the white gills of the inside wall of the mushroom cap and collapsed onto the ground.

Fox rushed to her side and held her hands with his. "It's alright, we made it."

"Barely," she complained. "And to what end? There's just going to be more dangers for us out there. Between normal threats to pixies walking along the forest floor, and the potential bounty on my wings, we'll never make it. And where did Birdie and Marten end up? We'll probably never see them again." Her voice wobbled.

Fox squeezed her hands. He rubbed his thumbs over her knuckles. "You're panicking. Just breathe. It's going to be fine, as long as we're together."

Cynthia looked into Fox's dark burgundy eyes that matched his freckles and the spots on his damaged wings. She saw only determination in them. His strength and sureness calmed her. She forced herself to calm down. Forced her mind to stop racing. And focused on the fact that they were safe, for the moment.

She let out a slow breath. "Thank you." She threw her arms around his neck.

He wrapped his arms around her waist and pulled her close. They held each other, calming one another with their steady breaths for what felt like a long time.

Finally, Cynthia pulled away. "Now what?" She searched his eyes and face for that certainty that had grounded her.

"We keep going. Keep looking for help. We'll make it." Fox glanced at Cynthia's wings. "But we should cover your wings again. I'll be right back."

Fox left the protection of the weeping widow mushroom for a few long seconds, and then returned with pumpkin colored maple leaves big enough to cover her wings from anyone who might still be looking for her.

Once both of their wings had been sufficiently hidden, Cynthia took a deep breath. "I'm ready."

They cautiously walked along the forest floor together, keeping their eyes, ears, and other senses attuned to their surroundings.

Before they had taken a hundred steps, another creature approached. Cynthia heard footsteps before she saw who the long, narrow feet belonged to.

A vaguely familiar figure emerged from behind a clump of crimson mums. His furry body, boulder-shaped head, and long nose reminded her of someone. The hard-shelled, red with black polka dot wings resting on his back jogged Cynthia's memory. The creature spoke in a raspy voice that grated against Cynthia's ears. "You're the ones from the mole prison, aren't you?" A wide, toothy grin stretched across his bearded face and recognition flashed in his eyes.

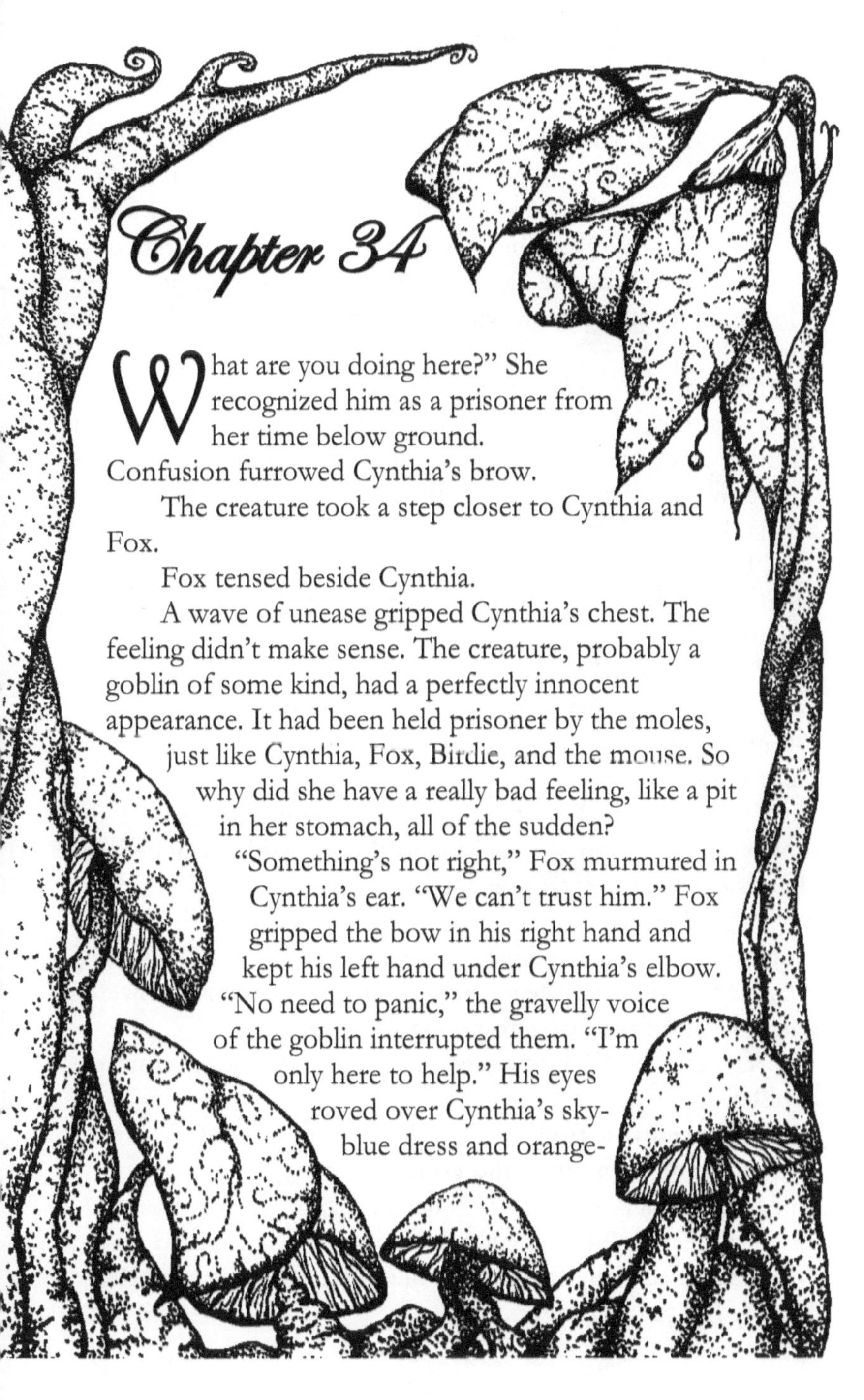

Chapter 34

W hat are you doing here?" She recognized him as a prisoner from her time below ground. Confusion furrowed Cynthia's brow.

The creature took a step closer to Cynthia and Fox.

Fox tensed beside Cynthia.

A wave of unease gripped Cynthia's chest. The feeling didn't make sense. The creature, probably a goblin of some kind, had a perfectly innocent appearance. It had been held prisoner by the moles, just like Cynthia, Fox, Birdie, and the mouse. So why did she have a really bad feeling, like a pit in her stomach, all of the sudden?

"Something's not right," Fox murmured in Cynthia's ear. "We can't trust him." Fox gripped the bow in his right hand and kept his left hand under Cynthia's elbow. "No need to panic," the gravelly voice of the goblin interrupted them. "I'm only here to help." His eyes roved over Cynthia's sky-blue dress and orange-leaf-covered back.

More dread washed over Cynthia. He had seen her wings in the prison. He had probably heard all the conversations Fox and Cynthia had there, too. Even if he wasn't a bounty hunter, he knew she, or at least her wings, were valuable. To someone.

Fox growled beside Cynthia. "You aren't here to help." He slowly retrieved an arrow with his left hand and loaded it in the bow.

The goblin held his three-fingered hands out toward them in a placating gesture. "I promise, I have no intentions of hurting you." He took another sidling step closer.

"Stay back." Fox raised the bow and aimed it at the goblin's chest. He, and Cynthia, both backed away from the goblin.

"I just want a peek at the pretty wings in the daylight, that's all." The goblin's eyes widened, and he blinked innocently at Cynthia.

When the goblin took another step closer, Fox released the arrow loaded in his bow. It tore through the air toward the strange creature. He tried to dodge out of the way, but the arrow nicked his arm.

The shrill shriek that escaped his mouth bounced off the rocks, flowers, and shrubs around them. Cynthia clapped her hands over her ears and flinched.

When her eyes returned to the goblin, she gasped. His eyes squinted into slants and his lips pulled back in a snarl, revealing rows of needle-sharp teeth. He hunched his back and lowered his body, as if preparing to pounce or strike.

"Cynthia! Run!" Fox pushed her backwards, away from the goblin.

Another arrow from Fox's bow shot through the air toward the creature. This time, the goblin blocked the attack with a quick movement of one of his hard wings.

Cynthia didn't hesitate a moment longer. She turned on her heels and fled away from the goblin. Fox ran right behind her, urging her to run faster.

They dodged evergreen saplings and weaved between the tall stems of globe shaped purple blossoms. Cynthia's heart pounded and her lungs burned. She glanced over her shoulder. The goblin wasn't as fast on his feet as Cynthia and Fox. And his wings appeared to be useless for flying.

Cynthia dodged behind a fallen log covered in moss and stairstep mushrooms and ducked beneath a green leafy dwarf dogwood shrub no longer in bloom. Fox skidded to a stop beside her. They both panted as quietly as they could and watched the goblin hobble past the log without pausing.

"We need to get out of here," Fox whispered.

"Maybe I can help." A trill came from a branch just above Cynthia and Fox.

A blue and white bird flitted to the ground and stood in front of them. The sunlight shone iridescent off the blue feathers on top of her head and down her back, where they darkened to almost black at the tips of her tail. The bird's tiny black beak in the middle of her face separated the azure feathers on the top of her head with the white feathers on the bottom half. White feathers covered the lower half of the bird's body, with downy edges near her feet. Dark ovals around the bird's black eyes gave them an almond-shaped appearance.

The bird tipped her head sideways and fluffed her sapphire feathers. "We don't have time to spare. Hurry." She turned sideways to invite Fox and Cynthia to climb on her back.

Before Cynthia could translate for him, Fox addressed the bird. "But I'm afraid you won't be able to carry both of us. Cynthia," he extended his hand toward her, offering to help Cynthia climb on the bird's back, "you go."

Cynthia startled. "What? No. I don't want to leave you."

"Please." The bird's head jerked in every direction as she observed their surroundings for potential threats. "We must hurry."

"The bird is right." Fox held Cynthia's arms with his hands.

"We don't have time to argue about this."

The fact that Fox understood what the bird had said wasn't lost on Cynthia in the moment, but she had more important things to think about.

"I'll fly. You ride the bird. We'll go there swiftly. Together." She slid her hands from beneath his and finished untying the maple leaf.

The broad, orange leaf floated to the ground and Cynthia stretched her rainbow butterfly wings wide.

The bird whistled sharply. "You've been spotted!"

Fox didn't hesitate. He bounded the two steps to the bird and threw his leg over her back to settle himself behind her now-outstretched wings. "Like I said, no time to argue. Let's go!"

At the same moment, Cynthia and the swallow flapped their wings and lifted themselves off the ground. Fox hung on to the bird's feathers with a tight grip with one hand and clung to his bow with his other hand.

"Which way?" the bird trilled.

Fox pointed with his bow the direction they needed to travel.

As they pulled themselves higher off the ground, a loud croak came from below. "I see them! They're over there!"

Cynthia searched for the source of the voice. Her eyes landed on a small frog perched on top of an enormous sunflower. She did a double take when she realized that two of the "flower petals" weren't petals at all, but wings protruding from the frog's back. They blended perfectly with the bright golden petals of the sunflower, except for intricate thin black lines like veins on a leaf all over each wing.

"Watch out!" She caught Fox's attention and pointed at the frog.

Just as she did, it leapt to another sunflower. Its wings flapped, carrying it higher than a normal frog could hop, but it didn't fly like a bird or butterfly or other flying creature.

Distracted by watching the frog, Cynthia didn't notice the

new threat that dashed out between two stubby bushes laden with crimson berries. She caught movement in the corner of her eye and turned just in time to see a bright rust colored fox-like creature with a half dozen fluffy, white-tipped tails leap onto a log and propel itself through the air toward the swallow carrying Fox just ahead of Cynthia.

Cynthia screamed and flailed in the air.

The strange fox- a kitsune, she remembered- snagged the swallow's two-tipped black tail with one of its paws. The bird wobbled mid-flight and let out a shriek of her own. Cynthia zig-zagged through the air to avoid being the kitsune's next target. She watched in horror as Fox nearly slid off the bird's back.

She prepared herself to lunge forward and grab Fox again in a controlled fall so that he wouldn't fall to his death, but the bird righted herself and Fox returned to his position on her back.

"We must go higher!" Fox yelled at both the bird and Cynthia.

They each flapped their wings as fast as they could and carried themselves even higher through the fall foliage of the forest and above the trees.

Without even a moment to catch their breath or gain their bearings, a pair of enormous black wasps with blue wings darted up out of the canopy and zoomed straight for Cynthia and her friends.

Cynthia flung herself to one side to avoid the sharp stinger at the end of the one of the wasps' teardrop shaped abdomens. The stinger was as long as her own forearm! The other wasp darted for Fox and the swallow.

Cynthia dodged the wasp. Its long, skinny legs flexed as its wings beat so fast, they were a blur of blue above its narrow, segmented body as long as her own.

If it got its legs, or stinger, on her, she'd be captured with no way to escape.

She darted through the air, finding herself being steered further from Fox by the wasp's quick movements.

Before Cynthia could find a way to do more than just dodge its attacks, a voice came from just below her feet. "It's no use. You might as well give up."

She peered past her feet to catch a glimpse of the new bounty hunter. A tiny person, smaller than even Cynthia, with only a few wispy hairs growing between its oversized pointed ears, and wearing a dingy tunic, clung to a clump of fluffy tipped windborne seeds of some kind. With one hand around the base of the clump of seeds, he used his other hand to point at Cynthia while wearing a wicked grin on his face and an evil gleam in his eye.

"You're trapped." He taunted from below.

The tiny man was not wrong. A glance behind her showed her that Fox and the swallow had been driven far away from her. The swallow, bigger than the wasp, *could* fly away, but she was certain Fox was demanding they stay close enough to try to help Cynthia.

Before she could even try to decide what to do next, a large black beetle jetted out from the foliage below the bird. Cynthia kept one eye on her own attackers. She dodged their advances and tried to move closer to Fox, but with little success. At the same time, she observed liquid gush from the back end of the beetle and squirt toward the bird and Fox.

The bird flailed in the air the instant the liquid landed on its body. Fox let out a scream of pain. The bird barely held herself aloft. Cynthia couldn't see Fox's face from her own movements avoiding the wasp and the miniature goblin. But from the arrows flying from his bow and his precarious position on top of the bird, she knew he was in grave danger of falling from the sky.

Because of her focus on Fox and the swallow, Cynthia didn't notice the arrival of the second wasp. It stabbed her with its stinger in the back of her leg.

She let out her own cry of pain and her wings stopped flapping from the shock.

The world spun around her as she fell out of the sky like a whirligig maple seed falling to the ground.

"Fly, Cynthia!" Fox's pained voice reached her ears from far away.

Cynthia forced her wings to work even as her leg throbbed from the sting.

The buzz of the wasps and the triumphant hollers from the tiny man followed her from overhead.

She managed to slow her descent just enough that when she hit the first circular leaves of the grove of quaking aspens in the forest below, she didn't get knocked unconscious from the impact.

She bounced off the leaves, crashed through the canopy, between the branches, and landed with a hard thud on the mossy forest floor between two chokeberry bushes.

The two wasps, beetle, little man, and kitsune quickly surrounded her on the ground.

She wheezed from the impact for the second time that day. Every bone in her body ached. She didn't have the strength to flee or defend herself.

"We've got you now." The kitsune taunted in his strangely human-sounding voice. A wicked gleam in his eye sent a shiver down Cynthia's back.

The swallow crash-landed not far from Cynthia, interrupting the kitsune's announcement of her capture.

Fox tumbled from the bird's back. He jumped to his feet and aimed his arrow at the kitsune while he edged closer to Cynthia. He kneeled beside her and glanced at her, then returned his gaze to the animals.

The kitsune let out a guffaw that sounded like the awful human man who had captured her so long ago. It locked its beady eyes on Fox. "We're only after the one with the wings." It licked its lips and stretched its mouth into a toothy, hungry grin. "You'll make for a nice treat, though."

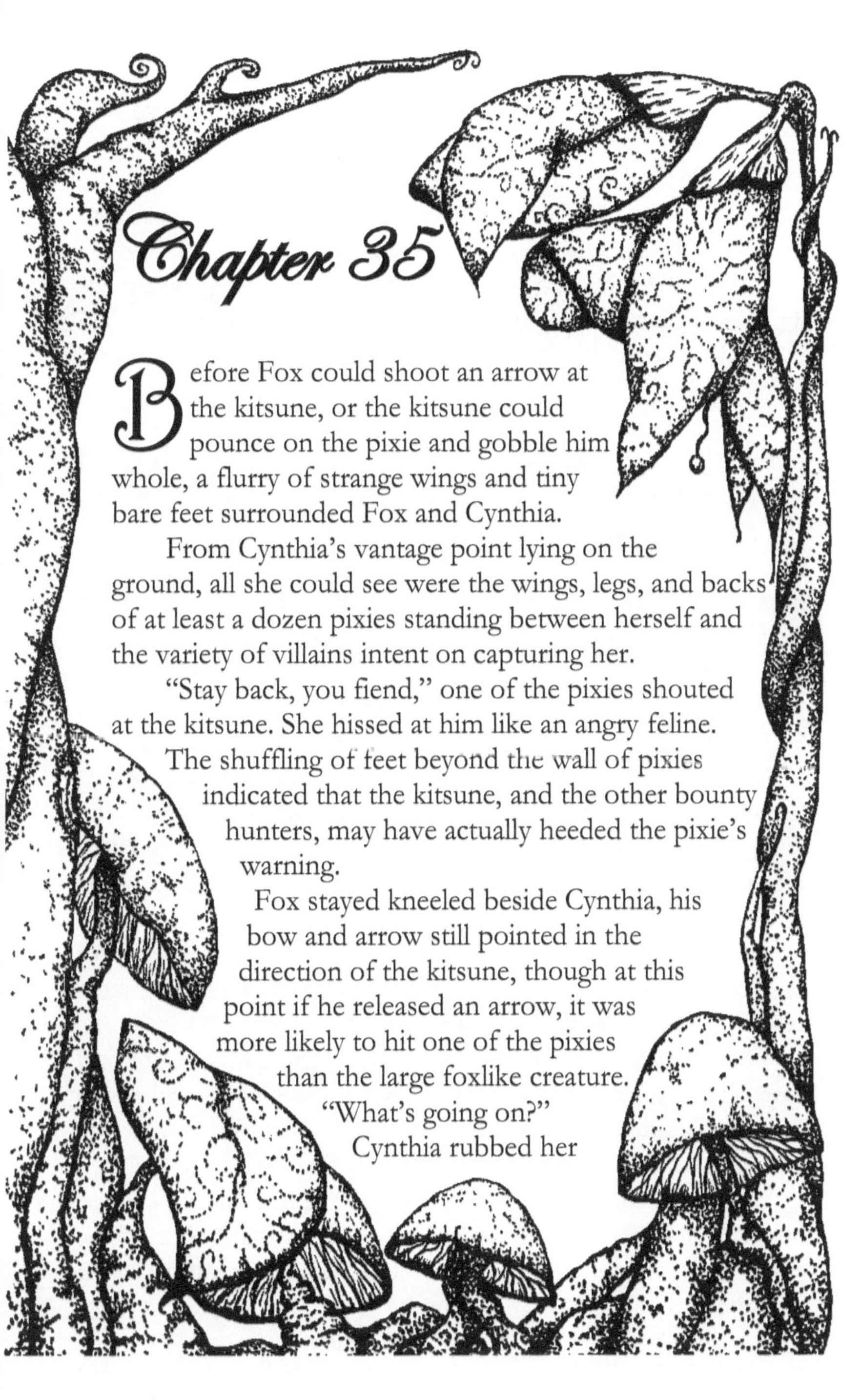

Chapter 35

Before Fox could shoot an arrow at the kitsune, or the kitsune could pounce on the pixie and gobble him whole, a flurry of strange wings and tiny bare feet surrounded Fox and Cynthia.

From Cynthia's vantage point lying on the ground, all she could see were the wings, legs, and backs of at least a dozen pixies standing between herself and the variety of villains intent on capturing her.

"Stay back, you fiend," one of the pixies shouted at the kitsune. She hissed at him like an angry feline.

The shuffling of feet beyond the wall of pixies indicated that the kitsune, and the other bounty hunters, may have actually heeded the pixie's warning.

Fox stayed kneeled beside Cynthia, his bow and arrow still pointed in the direction of the kitsune, though at this point if he released an arrow, it was more likely to hit one of the pixies than the large foxlike creature.

"What's going on?"

Cynthia rubbed her

head and attempted to sit up. Her fatigued muscles gave out, and she fell back to the ground.

Fox pinched his lips. He looked at the threat beyond the pixies, then back at Cynthia. After a long, thoughtful pause, he rested his bow on the ground and reached for Cynthia.

With an arm behind her shoulders and a hand gripping her wrist, he pulled Cynthia to a seated position. "They are guardian pixies. I've heard of them, but have never seen one, let alone so many, before."

The "guardian pixies" stood in a half circle around Fox and Cynthia. Their wings were unlike anything she had seen on an animal, or like Fox had described for a pixie before. Instead of leaf-shaped, or wings that resembled flowers, they looked like the wings of a bat or a mountain dragon- leathery skin stretched between long bony digits with a talon on each joint. They each wore clothes of some kind of fur, giving them the appearance of a satyr, like Marten, but their human-looking feet proved they were not winged satyrs. A pair of gnarled horns protruded from each of their heads among hair of various lengths and colors.

One of the pixies left the lineup and approached Fox and Cynthia. Her short horns curved inward between her brown wavy hair that cascaded down her back and ended with red tips. Her loose, red tunic matched both the ends of her hair and the red string tied in a loose knot around one ankle.

"Do not fear," she said to Cynthia and Fox in a kind but confident voice. "We're here to protect you until the Princess arrives. She should be here momentarily."

Before Cynthia could ask the pixie to explain, a great wind tossed the wings and hair of all the pixies, the flowers and plants that surrounded them, and the branches on the trees. Any stronger, and the force of it might blow them all away.

Fox pulled Cynthia to stand beside him, and she peered between the formidable wings of the guardian pixies. The alarmed expressions on the faces of the bounty hunters caught her by surprise.

"The Princess? Coming here?" The kitsune backed away from the pixies. "Gotta go!" He turned around and bounded away with one fluid movement.

The two wasps, hovering just above where the kitsune had stood only seconds before, exchanged confused looks. The beetle and the menacing miniature man appeared unphased by the announcement of the imminent arrival of a princess.

Two large, white wings with long, tear-drop shaped appendages, flapped overhead, blocking the direct sunlight and casting the whole scene in shadow. An impossibly large pixie landed to the right of the strange collection of pixies and insects facing off with one another. Dozens of smaller butterflies of every shape and color fluttered around her like a cloud.

The human-sized pixie wore a satiny lavender dress and had long, flowing blond curls that reached her waist. The serene look on her face gave her a friendly countenance, and Cynthia instantly felt safe in her presence.

"Oh… *that* princess…" one of the wasps murmured to his companion. The pair beat their wings faster and zipped away.

"I would leave, too, if I were you," one of the guardian pixies spoke in a harsh tone to the remaining two bounty hunters.

The beetle and tiny man didn't hesitate. The little person hopped on the beetle's back, just behind its head. The beetle stretched its hard wings wide to reveal a pair of thin translucent wings that blurred and buzzed. It lifted both itself and the little person just off the ground and flew through the underbrush, away from the pixies, both large and small.

"Now, let's get you somewhere safe." The same guardian pixie motioned for Fox and Cynthia to follow her toward the… princess.

Cynthia limped forward, the sting on her leg throbbing with every step. She wanted to lean heavily on Fox, but he had burns up his arms and the short brown sleeves of his tunic had a splatter of holes in them from the beetle's blistering toxin it sprayed on him.

Cynthia's own wings tried to lift her from the ground, but each movement sent a shock of pain down her back.

Two of the guardian pixies hurried to Cynthia and Fox to assist them in making their way toward the larger pixie.

"Don't forget the swallow." Cynthia winced from the pain in her leg. She pointed back toward the blue and white bird huddled on the ground behind them.

The human-sized pixie squatted low and rested her hands on the ground in front of her. Her soft voice and warm smile put Cynthia more at ease. "Welcome, little friends. We will take you away from here and make sure you are safe."

Cynthia collapsed onto her knees on the woman's hands. Fox sunk down beside her, his face contorted with pain.

The woman flapped her enormous luna-moth wings and lifted them from the ground. The cloud of multi-colored butterflies flanked her on all sides, while the crew of guardian pixies took wider defensive positions.

Cynthia had so many questions. But for once, she couldn't seem to put her questions into words. Her whole body felt like it would break if she moved. Her emotions felt like they would shatter if she spoke. Her mind wanted to race, but it only felt numb.

She wanted to believe that she was safe, finally, but it seemed too good to be true.

Cynthia tried to keep her eyes open as they flew high above the trees. The slow flapping of the pixie princess's wings lulled Cynthia with their steady rhythm until she felt herself sinking toward sleep.

"Rest. Heal. We will be there soon," the woman spoke softly to Cynthia and Fox.

As if it was a command instead of a suggestion, sleep overtook Cynthia like a warm blanket.

"We have arrived." The simple, gentle words pulled Cynthia

from her restful sleep.

Night had fallen. Cynthia's wings no longer looked like rainbow painted-lady butterfly wings but instead had turned pale in the moonlight. They must have been traveling for several hours.

Cynthia sat up and looked over the edge of the giant pixie's hands as they descended lower over the treetops, until the woman alighted on tiptoes in a serene moonlit meadow.

Cynthia gazed all around. Tall grass that had gone to seed, along with the surrounding aspen trees with their quaking orange leaves, gave the entire meadow a golden glow even in the moonlight. Small burning bush plants scattered in clumps gave the meadow bursts of bright red. A blanket of fallen oak and maple leaves decorated areas of the meadow where the breeze had swept the leaves into piles.

Fluffy, long eared bunnyflies, and elebats with their wing-ears and long trunks, flitted from flower to flower under the starry sky. Cynthia made a mental note to remember this tidbit for Magnolia's journal back home. She had no idea they were nocturnal!

The trembling of the aspen leaves in the wind sounded a lot like the river they had traveled beside weeks ago. Cynthia closed her eyes and breathed in the sweet scent of decaying leaves and listened to the sounds of the dry grass and blowing leaves rustle all around her.

"You will both be safe here," the pixie princess announced.

Cynthia opened her eyes and turned to look up at the enormous pixie. Several small nocturnal creatures including a hedgehog, badger, and a few rats crowded around the woman's feet. A swarm of fireflies hovered over one of her winged shoulders, their fires glowing low but warm in the moonlight.

Cynthia observed the giant pixie as she nodded her greeting at the various animals as they joined her in the meadow.

Suddenly, the luna moth wings separated from the pixie's body and flew away, entirely separate from the person who remained.

She wasn't a pixie at all! She was a…

"Forest Person!" Cynthia whispered. She didn't know how she hadn't realized it sooner. It made sense. The way she had been able to understand the animals. The way the pixies listened to her and respected her.

The woman released a soft sweet laugh. "Yes. I am a Forest Person. My name is Juliette."

Fox released a slight groan behind Cynthia. She remembered that he thought the Forest People didn't like him, or might even loathe him, because of his choice of how he spent his time as a bounty hunter. Cynthia had assured him it wouldn't be true, but how could she be so sure?

Cynthia had a completely different reaction than Fox. "You're Princess Juliette?" Cynthia stared up at the sky-blue eyes of the woman in who's hand she rested. "I've… heard about you…"

Magnolia had mentioned the princess before. She spoke of her as someone she knew well and admired greatly. But she had never talked about trying to visit her or about Cynthia ever meeting her.

"And I have heard about you." Princess Juliette smiled at

Cynthia. "I am here to help you. To answer your questions about anything you wish to know."

Anything?

Cynthia would finally get her questions answered? She would finally learn why her wings were different. Why she was being hunted. Why she didn't have any powers or abilities like the other pixies all had.

Fox gripped Cynthia's hand tight.

She squeezed back.

This was it. She didn't want to wait to get cleaned up or rest or anything. She wanted to know everything right then.

One of the guardian pixies, this one adorned with eggplant-colored accents in her hair and clothing, arrived suddenly and flew close to Juliette's face. She spoke quietly right into the princess's ear, so that only the woman would be able to hear her.

Juliette squinted her eyes a little, then nodded her agreement. "Yes, at once," she murmured to the pixie.

The guardian pixie folded her hands in front of her and hovered beside the princess to wait for her to finish speaking with Cynthia and Fox.

Juliette addressed Cynthia and Fox again. "Before we talk, you two should get cleaned up, eat, and rest."

What? The princess was going to leave them? What about Cynthia's questions?

As if the princess could understand Cynthia's thoughts, she closed her eyes and nodded. "You will not have to wait long. I just have a few things to attend to first." She bent toward the ground and extended her hands flat among the grass so Fox and Cynthia could dismount.

She set the injured sparrow beside them in the soft grass. Several of the guardian pixies hovered overhead, as if still on guard for potential threats.

Before rising to her feet again, Juliette said softly, "I will see you both soon."

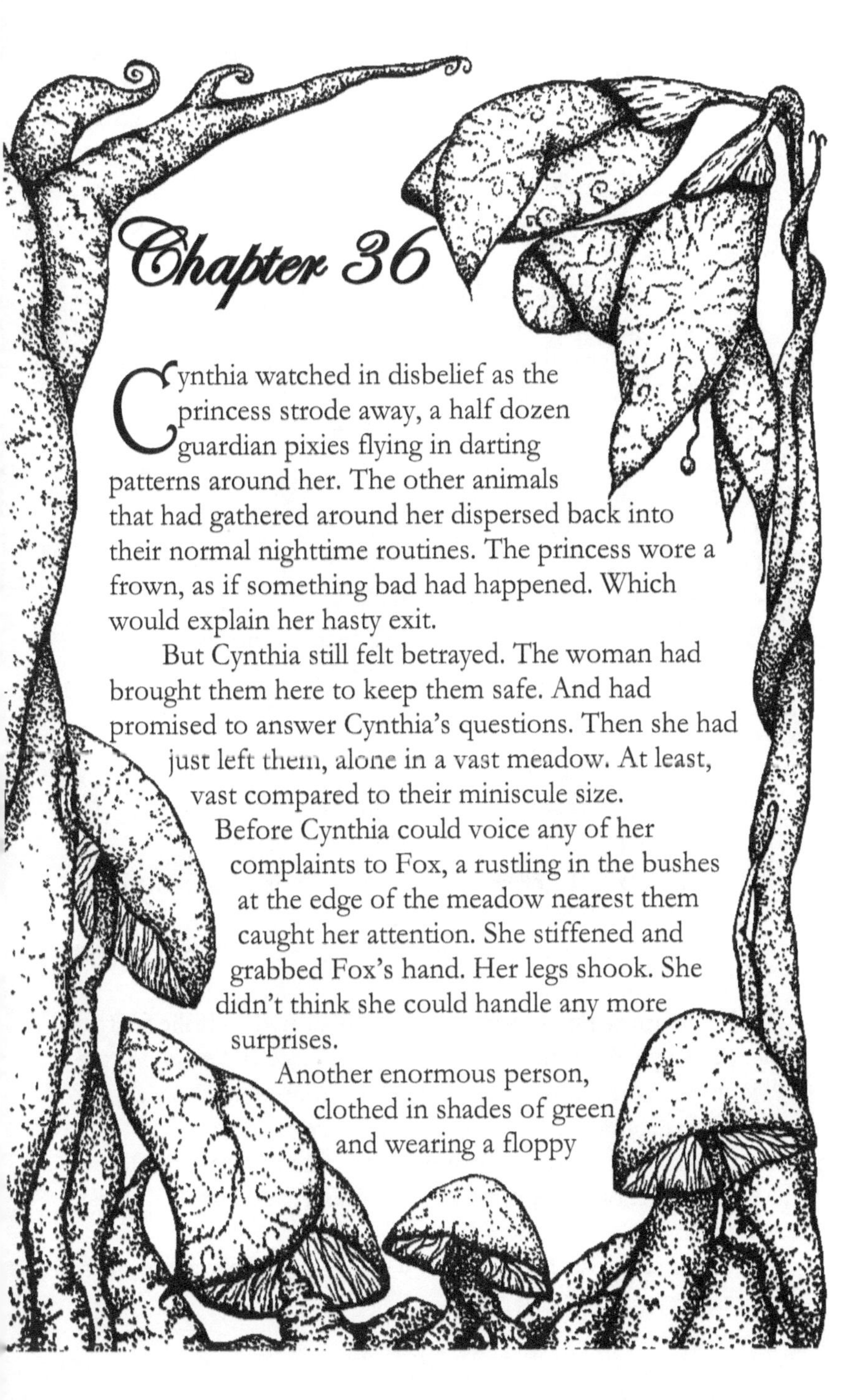

Chapter 36

Cynthia watched in disbelief as the princess strode away, a half dozen guardian pixies flying in darting patterns around her. The other animals that had gathered around her dispersed back into their normal nighttime routines. The princess wore a frown, as if something bad had happened. Which would explain her hasty exit.

But Cynthia still felt betrayed. The woman had brought them here to keep them safe. And had promised to answer Cynthia's questions. Then she had just left them, alone in a vast meadow. At least, vast compared to their miniscule size.

Before Cynthia could voice any of her complaints to Fox, a rustling in the bushes at the edge of the meadow nearest them caught her attention. She stiffened and grabbed Fox's hand. Her legs shook. She didn't think she could handle any more surprises.

Another enormous person, clothed in shades of green and wearing a floppy straw hat, stepped from the shadows of the woods. She wore a pleasant smile and sent them a friendly wave.

"Welcome friends!" the woman called. "I'm Hazel." Tipping her head upward she said, "I'll take it from here. Thank you for your help!"

Cynthia looked toward the sky to see who Hazel spoke to. A few more guardian pixies hovered overhead. The dark sky had obscured them from her peripheral vision. So, the princess hadn't left them alone, after all.

The guardian pixies bowed slightly at Hazel in the air, and then the three of them zipped away into the darkness. Would Cynthia ever see guardian pixies again?

Hazel crouched down so she could better see Cynthia, Fox, and the injured sparrow. She reminded Cynthia of Magnolia, in a way. This Forest Person, Hazel, seemed so comfortable in her environment. A quick glance at her feet confirmed that, like Magnolia, this woman also didn't wear shoes. And the softness around her eyes made Cynthia instantly want to trust her.

"Let's get you something warm to eat and someplace comfortable to sleep." Hazel waved them forward with an arm.

"What about the swallow?" Cynthia stroked the bird on the top of her head.

"I'll take care of her and make sure she is returned to her home in no time." Hazel pointed ahead of her at a waist-high-to-a-Forest-Person sized funny-looking person. "Pip here will show you the way."

"Follow me." Pip said in a deep, almost melancholic sort of voice. His eyelids hung halfway over his large brown eyes, the same color as the gown-like sleeveless tunic that hung all the way to the ground.

One look at his folded, pointy ears, long arms that reached his ankles, and bulbous nose told Cynthia exactly what she was looking at.

She leaned close to Fox and whispered, "He's a hobman. Distantly related to brownies."

Fox gave her a surprised look. "You didn't know about goblins, but you knew *that? How* do you know?"

She understood his reaction. So far, he had been way more aware of who and what lived in Tala than she had on their journey. "I recognize him from one of the books Magnolia has."

The tattered hem of Pip's gown exposed his big toes with each step he took. He leaned heavily on a gnarled branch he used as a walking stick and walked with a noticeable limp. Cynthia didn't mind the slow pace. Her own leg still throbbed with pain from the wasp sting and had swollen to nearly twice its normal size.

But it was the thing on his back that surprised Cynthia the most. A canvas tarp wrapped tightly around something lumpy and strapped to Pip's back with a woven belt. Cynthia studied the makeshift knapsack. What did he carry in there? A scaly tail slipped out of a hole at the bottom of the bag, and two large, black eyes peered out of the top and met Cynthia's stare.

"A dragon!" Cynthia stiffened.

"Nothin' to be concerned about," Pip said in his monotone way. "He's been separated from his nest and I'm takin' care of him until he can live on his own."

Cynthia and Fox exchanged shocked looks but didn't say anything as they continued to follow Pip around the edge of the meadow.

Pip stopped outside a wide-trunked pine tree with reddish bark and pointed at it with his cane. "Here ya' go." Before Fox or Cynthia could say anything to him, ask him any questions, or even thank him for his help, he hobbled away from them without another word.

"What…?" Fox started to ask.

A chunk of the tree bark flew outward, and a mob of feathers and fur surrounded Cynthia and Fox.

"You're alive!" Birdie's wobbly voice yelled right into Cynthia's ear.

Cynthia flinched at the loud volume, but she couldn't be annoyed. She was so relieved to see her friend that she didn't care if her ear rang for a whole week!

Over Birdie's shoulder, Cynthia watched Marten slap Fox on the shoulder in a friendly gesture of greeting. Fox stood with his mouth hanging open, not sure what to do in the situation. Cynthia couldn't help but laugh through her relieved tears. This whole situation was like something out of a dream.

Was it all a dream? She focused on the feeling of Birdie's feathery hair against her cheek, and the ringing in her ear from Birdie's still shrill voice as she gushed over how worried she had been and how she thought she'd never see Cynthia again.

A peaceful calm came over Cynthia. She relaxed as she pulled away from Birdie. She was truly safe, at last.

The four friends stood outside the now closed door of the tree house.

"What *is* this place?" Fox held Cynthia's hand again, even

though he still had painful looking burns on his arms.

Her own leg still throbbed, and she wondered when they'd all feel better again, even though they were now safe.

"Come see!" Birdie brushed past them. She glanced at them with a wide, mischievous smile and pressed against the trunk with the palm of her hand.

A section of the trunk swung inward to reveal what looked like the inside of house. A house just the right size for Cynthia and her friends.

"As far as hollow trees go, this is the nicest one I've stayed in." Fox gave Cynthia an impressed look.

She laughed at his comment. Compared to the other places they had stayed together the last several weeks, this was, by far, the best.

Embroidered pillows and thick, soft quilts filled the edges of the hollow. Instead of the sweet aroma of decaying wood and leaves, lavender scented steam filled the air with softness. A stone fireplace took up one corner of the room, with a blazing fire dancing inside.

A teapot full of lavender tea sat in the middle of a low table, and beside the tea rested a tray of warm rolls filled with nuts and honey.

The smell, the softness, the warmth all combined to make this the perfect place for Cynthia to nibble on a honey roll, take a few sips of lavender tea, and then snuggle into the warm blankets and cozy pillows beside Fox while they waited for the princess to return.

The relief from no longer being on her feet or putting weight on her injured leg left her feeling suddenly exhausted. Again.

Birdie and Marten whispered together in the opposite corner of the room. When this was all over, she wanted to know more about her new friends, too.

After sitting in comfortable silence beside Fox for a little while, Cynthia finally spoke in a soft voice just for Fox to hear. "Do you think the Princess will be able to answer all my questions? What if she doesn't know any more about me than you do? You know a lot about Tala and pixies. What if I don't find out anything?" Cynthia rubbed the tattered hem of her dress between her fingers.

Fox stilled her anxious movement by lacing her fingers between his. "If she doesn't know, then she'll be able to tell you who does. It's going to be fine, you'll see."

Cynthia studied Fox. For once he didn't have any doubts but trusted the princess completely. She needed to follow his lead and do the same. "I really hope they can heal your wings, too." She whispered.

He nodded but didn't say anything. Did he believe they could?

Not much later, a knock sounded on the door of the house. Cynthia took a deep breath. "This is it," she breathed.

Fox squeezed her in a tight hug. "This is it," he agreed.

Birdie and Marten followed Fox and Cynthia out the door of the hollow tree.

The sun had started to brighten the sky to the east and the birds in the forest sang their songs to greet the new day. If Cynthia listened carefully, she could probably understand what their songs meant, but her mind was too distracted to be able to do it then.

The moist morning air felt warmer than Cynthia would have expected for the season. Perhaps that's why the Forest People had chosen that place to settle. Something about it did feel warm and inviting.

Princess Juliette sat with her legs tucked beneath her on the ground just outside the tree. She invited the four of them toward her and lifted them onto a fallen log that would bring them closer to her height so they could talk more easily.

A handful of floppy-eared bunnies cuddled together on the lavender dress of the princess's lap. A long-legged squirrel scratched at the ground beside Juliette's feet, bending to collect seeds from the ground with its mouth. A pair of fuzzy striped caterpillars inched their way up Juliette's arm. And a scarlet cardinal perched on the princess's opposite shoulder.

Just hidden in the shadows, Cynthia spotted several of the guardian pixies again, scanning their surroundings with serious expressions on their faces.

A group of white button mushrooms grew in a half circle in the moss on top of the fallen log. Birdie settled herself on one of the mushrooms and crossed her hooved legs beneath the low cap. Marten lowered himself to sit directly on the moss. He leaned his arm on Birdie's knee in a relaxed position and gave Juliette an expectant look.

Fox led Cynthia to an extra wide mushroom, just big enough for the two of them to sit upon together.

"Thank you," she whispered to him. She didn't want to be separated from him when she found out the truth about herself. Nerves made her stomach feel strange, but Fox's hand in hers countered it just enough that she thought she could do this. A shiver ran down her spine.

"Are you cold?" Fox looked at her with concern.

She shook her head. "Just nervous."

Princess Juliette looked at each of the small people gathered in front of her. Her eyes settled on Cynthia. "I have heard about your adventures. For one so small you have made quite an impact on those around you." Her warm smile made her face glow.

Cynthia opened her mouth. "Really? You heard? But… how?"

She was a talentless pixie from nowhere speaking with the princess of the Forest People. And this woman said she had heard of Cynthia? It didn't make any sense.

The princess covered her mouth with one of her dainty hands and released a soft giggle. "I have my sources. I am aware of much of what happens in the land around me. I attempted to rescue you sooner, but you evaded the friends I sent to find you."

"What do you mean?" Fox questioned the princess this time, though not in a distrustful way as he would have anyone else.

"I sent a friend to help. I believe he rides a snail as his mode of transportation?" The princess looked back and forth between Fox and Cynthia.

"The goblin on the snail?" Fox exchanged surprised looks with Cynthia.

Princess Juliette nodded. "And a mire cat. We had heard that the wanted pixie with butterfly wings was in the Little Browning Bog, but my friends couldn't find you. It would seem you are better at hiding than I would have imagined with beautiful wings like yours." She pointed at Cynthia's wings.

As if on their own, her wings stretched a bit wider, like they wanted to show off their beauty to the others around her.

"So, they *were* looking for you!" Fox faced Cynthia with wide eyes.

"Just not for the reasons we thought!" Cynthia nodded her reply.

"Word reached me about your kindness to Birdie in the mole prison. The way you helped the mouse, even when you had learned of her betrayal. And of course, how you wanted to or did help numerous people and creatures while you traveled. You are as selfless as they come. When you evaded our friends, I thought I might never get to meet you. And yet, here you are!

"I am so glad the guardian pixies received intelligence as to your whereabouts and arrived in time to protect you from the bounty hunters. They sent a dragonfly with the message as to your location and I arrived as quickly as I could.

"I am impressed with how far you managed to come on your

own though. I am not sure there are many others, besides the guardian pixies, of course, who would have been able to do the same."

Cynthia waved away Princess Juliette's praises. "Marten was the one who found us some grasshoppers to ride, and Fox saved me on more than one occasion." She squeezed his hand in her lap.

Marten poked at the moss of the log with a stick he had found and bent his antlered head down. "It was nothing. I'd do anything to help my friend." He gestured at Birdie. "And the friend of my friend is also my friend! Wait... no. I mean... never mind."

Birdie gave him a confused look and shook her head.

He shrugged with a sheepish grin.

Cynthia ignored Birdie's reaction and interrupted Marten's rambling. She placed a hand on her forehead. "I have so many questions."

Princess Juliette smiled and nodded. "What would you like to know?"

Fox blurted his question before anyone else could say anything. "Why is Cynthia being hunted?"

It was the question that burned within her, too. Along with what made her so different among the pixies. She held her breath and squeezed his hand even tighter to keep her hand from trembling while she waited for the princess to answer.

"It is because of her gifts." Princess Juliette's countenance clouded. A sad expression filled her eyes. "There is someone who wants *all* power for themselves. They will stop at nothing to get it. There are others being hunted for their abilities, too." A faraway look crossed her face.

Off to the side, Cynthia caught a glimpse of movement from Birdie and Marten. They shared a knowing look, but they didn't say anything to interrupt the conversation.

Cynthia returned her attention to Juliette and shook her

head. "But I don't *have* any abilities. Not like the other pixies. Not like Fox."

She squeezed his hand again. He squeezed back.

"You may be a late bloomer," the princess said, "but your ability to see the good in everyone is nothing to be ignored."

"That's not a *special power*, though," Cynthia argued.

"Perhaps." Princess Juliette allowed a small smile to grace her lips. "But what you can *do* with it certainly is."

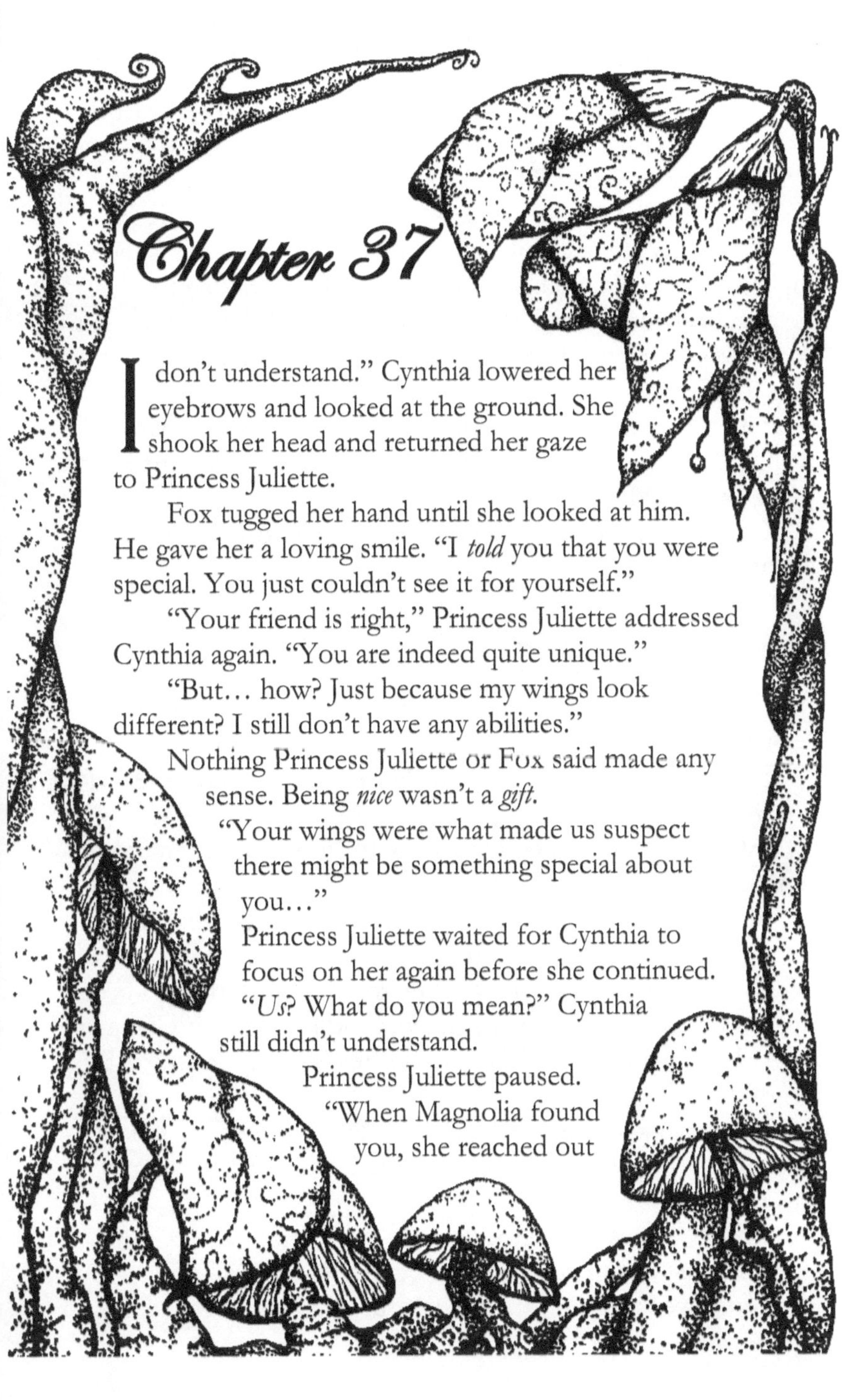

Chapter 37

I don't understand." Cynthia lowered her eyebrows and looked at the ground. She shook her head and returned her gaze to Princess Juliette.

Fox tugged her hand until she looked at him. He gave her a loving smile. "I *told* you that you were special. You just couldn't see it for yourself."

"Your friend is right," Princess Juliette addressed Cynthia again. "You are indeed quite unique."

"But… how? Just because my wings look different? I still don't have any abilities."

Nothing Princess Juliette or Fox said made any sense. Being *nice* wasn't a *gift*.

"Your wings were what made us suspect there might be something special about you…"

Princess Juliette waited for Cynthia to focus on her again before she continued.

"*Us?* What do you mean?" Cynthia still didn't understand.

Princess Juliette paused.

"When Magnolia found you, she reached out

to me. Your unique wings made us suspect that there might be something special about you."

"But you're wrong. There isn't anything special about me…" Cynthia interrupted the princess.

"You have unique abilities that no other pixie has. Magnolia figured it out quite quickly. We have just been waiting for them to manifest more fully. When I heard the news that you had been captured, and then the reports about you being hunted, I knew that your abilities were about to blossom. It would seem that the word has spread about the powerful pixie with butterfly wings. Rumors can be dangerous, but there is always some truth lying beneath the surface."

Cynthia interrupted again. "But I don't *have* any abilities. Other than talking to animals."

"Hmm." Princess Juliette touched her finger to her pinched lips. Then her eyes lit up. "Let me show you."

Cynthia gave Fox a nervous look.

He looked excited for her to finally find out what her abilities would be.

But the feeling in her stomach like exploding bunnyflies left her feeling nauseous.

"Wait." She motioned for Juliette to stop. "Just… give me a minute."

She took several deep breaths and pressed her hand against her stomach to still the fluttering. This is what she had wanted. This is what she had been searching for ever since she had been forced to leave home. Ever since she had met Fox and learned that she was different. But was she really ready to know the truth?

Juliette tipped her head to one side and motioned toward Cynthia. "It is alright. We can take our time. But first, may I heal you?"

Cynthia's eyes darted to Juliette's face. "You can *heal* me?"

Princess Juliette nodded with a confident smile.

"Fox needs healing more than me. Please, fix his wings."

Cynthia tugged Fox's arm, urging him to stand and approach the princess.

Princess Juliette shook her head. "I would like to heal you first. Your leg looks awfully painful, and your wings look a little worse for the wear. May I?"

"Go ahead." Fox gently pressed his hand against Cynthia's back. He wore a relieved smile. "I would have insisted you go first, anyway," he promised.

"Alright." Cynthia stood from her place on the mushroom and stepped forward on the log, closer to Princess Juliette. Two of the guardian pixies approached, revealing themselves from their camouflaged hiding places. They stared at the princess with great interest. The bunnies in Juliette's lap shifted their position as she leaned forward, and the cardinal hopped from the princess's shoulder and landed on the log a little bit away from Birdie and Marten to watch with a keen eye. "Place your hand against mine." Juliette rested her hand, palm up, on the log.

Cynthia crouched and placed her hand on Juliette's, just like the princess wanted.

Princess Juliette closed her eyes, breathed deep, and released her breath. A tingling sensation, barely noticeable, spread up Cynthia's arm and across her shoulders. She felt her wings strengthen.

"This is something I learned to do a very long time ago," the princess explained in a near whisper with her eyes still closed. "Not many Forest People know about this, and even fewer can actually do what I am doing. By pulling the pain and injuries from your body, I absorb them into my own. I imagine you healthy and whole."

The strange feeling spread down Cynthia's legs. Instantly the swelling in her injured leg vanished. The bruising disappeared.

Behind Cynthia and to her right, she heard Birdie and Marten whisper words of amazement to one another.

"Look at that!" Birdie exclaimed in a hushed tone.

"Wow," Marten breathed.

Cynthia noticed Fox sit up straighter and lean forward from his position to her left.

More animals approached from among the tall grass, behind the log, and amidst the trees. They had acquired quite an audience.

"With this ability I can heal any ailment and cure any disease," the princess continued. "It is a gift bestowed on one Forest Person in a generation. And our kind live a very long time!"

As the feeling spread, every aching bone and sore muscle in Cynthia's body returned to their healthiest state in an instant.

"This is not a gift that can be taught or learned by anyone else besides me for hundreds of years, at the soonest." Juliette opened her eyes and smiled, removing her hand to her lap again. "How do you feel?"

Cynthia took a moment to think about all of her aches and pains and injuries she had acquired over the last several weeks. Everything had vanished. "I feel… better than I have in a really long time. Thank you!"

Marten burst into applause, and Birdie almost knocked him over when she stood in a hurry from her mushroom stool. She rushed to Cynthia's side and squeezed her in a tight hug. Her smile was bigger than Cynthia had seen yet.

The birds in the tree branches around them chirped their amazement to one another, and the two guardian pixies leaned toward one another to point and whisper at Cynthia and the princess.

Cynthia turned toward Fox. She beamed at him. But then her smile fell when she saw his broken wings again.

"Now it's your turn." Cynthia extended a hand to Fox and invited him to stand beside her. To the princess she said, "Please, can you heal his wings? We weren't sure you if you could or not…"

The princess's mouth turned down. "I can… but I will not."

Birdie, who had returned to her place beside Marten, gasped. The bunnies wiggled their noses at one another in surprise, and the caterpillars scrunched themselves into little fuzzy balls on the princess's shoulder.

Cynthia's eyebrows arched. "What? Why not?" she cried. Anger erupted inside of her. Why would the princess withhold this… magic from Fox?

"All right, everyone." Juliette swiveled her head and torso to address everyone around her. "That will do. Please. We require privacy now."

The guardian pixies instantly darted away from them, while some of the other animals took their time to reluctantly leave the area.

When they had all cleared, Princess Juliette returned her attention to Cynthia and Fox.

"I will not heal him." She stared hard at Cynthia with a determined expression. "But *you* can."

Cynthia blustered and stuttered. The angry words she had been about to unleash on the princess fell flat in her mouth and incoherent sounds replaced them. Finally, she managed to stammer, "What?"

"Just as I said. You can heal him." The princess remained serene while Cynthia's mind raced.

Fox gave the princess a confused look. The woman nodded at him and tipped her head toward Cynthia.

Cynthia let go of Fox's hand and paced the length of the log where the mushroom stools grew.

Birdie and Marten looked at one another, but didn't say anything. Fox followed Cynthia with his eyes, his head turning from one side to the other with every pass she took in front of him.

She shook her head, and her hands flew while she talked. "I can't heal him. I don't have your magical Forest Person, once-in-a-generation healing abilities! You said it yourself! No one does! Why would you put that kind of responsibility on me when it's clearly impossible." She stopped in front of the princess again. Her eyes filled with tears. "Are you trying to make me feel even more disappointed in my lack of abilities than I already do? Because I assure you, as much as you, and Fox, and Birdie, and the others insist I'm special, there is no way I can do what you are saying I can do. It's impossible!"

Princess Juliette leaned forward. Her large, cornflower blue eyes stayed on Cynthia's tiny face. "You *can* heal him. You now have the exact same ability to heal as I do."

This woman spoke in riddles! It was the only explanation. How else would Cynthia be able to heal Fox?

Cynthia folded her arms across her torso. "Explain," she demanded.

"You have an incredibly rare ability, incredibly *valuable* in the wrong hands, that allows you to absorb the abilities of others. When you are with others who have abilities, especially if you come into physical contact with them repeatedly, you adopt their abilities as your own."

Cynthia's mouth fell open. "That's not true! I would never take someone's ability from them!" Her heart stung at the accusation.

"It is not something you choose to do." Juliette shook her head. "And it does not take their ability from them. It adds it to you. That is why you can talk to animals. The gift of being able to speak with them is not because you are a pixie who talks to animals. It is because you absorbed the ability from your time with Magnolia. Who is a Forest Person who speaks with animals. Do you understand?"

She locked eyes with Fox. He looked just as shocked as she felt.

Princess Juliette continued. "As you mature, you will be able to transfer your power to someone else if you wish. It may have already begun…"

"That's how I understood those bounty hunters yesterday!" Fox's eyes widened even more. He looked at Cynthia like she was a treasure of infinite worth. "It's because you gave me that ability!"

Princess Juliette smiled and nodded. "Indeed."

Fox continued. "And I've felt like I can trust easier than I used to be able to. I just thought it was your positive attitude rubbing off on me! But you must have shared that part of you with me…"

"I don't believe it." Cynthia interrupted everyone's awe-filled exclamations about her oh so amazing magical powers. But there were other explanations for everything that had happened. It couldn't be true.

"You can put it to the test, Cynthia." Juliette spoke softly to her. "You can heal Fox's injuries. You can heal his wings. You have absorbed the ability to do so from me when I healed you. Focus on what you want. Picture his wings whole and healed. You can do it." Princess Juliette sat back and waited with a patient look on her face.

Fox grabbed both of Cynthia's hands and pulled her to face him. He had a look of expectant joy. "You can do it, Cynthia. I know you can," he whispered to her.

Chapter 38

ook!" Birdie sucked in a sharp breath.
Cynthia's wings prickled, like they
were being rained on, even though
the sky was clear. She pulled back from
Fox and turned her head to get a better look at them.
The rainbow of colors against their dark background
glowed brighter, as if a light shone through them. But
the intensity of the daylight hadn't changed.

"What's going on?" Cynthia marveled.

Fox continued to grip both of her hands tight in
his own, staring at her wings with a stunned expression,
just like Birdie and Marten.

Princess Juliette hummed as if she wasn't
surprised by the turn of events.

"What's happening?" Cynthia tried to pull
away from Fox. The last thing she wanted
was to hurt him even more.

"Wait…" He urged her to stay.
Her hands tingled more. The glow
from her wings grew brighter.
The light spread from
Cynthia's wings down
her arms and into her

hands.

She gasped but didn't let go.

The light continued to spread up Fox's arms. The burns from the beetle poison on his arms and shoulders smoothed over. The angry red skin returned to its usual beige dotted with tiny black-cherry dots.

The glow spread over Fox's shoulders beneath his tunic and around his back. His wilted, crumpled, broken wings glowed, just like Cynthia's. Their creamy color enhanced. The burgundy spots stood out against the brightness.

Fox's wings trembled. He flinched.

"I'm hurting you," she whispered.

"No," he insisted.

The glow spread down both of their torsos, down their legs, and to the tips of their now bare toes.

They kept their eyes locked on one another. Marten stood with mouth agape on one side, while Birdie squealed and clapped her hands on their other side.

Fox's wings unfolded. Every crease smooth. Every tear restored.

Cynthia gasped, but didn't dare let go of him.

Stretched to their full size, Fox's wings extended above his head and wider than Cynthia's own wings. Their flower-petal texture, soft edges, range of spots from large to small, and glowing buttery color gave Cynthia so much to look at.

Her eyes watered. She met his gaze. She hadn't seen him smile that big before, not even after they had survived all their adventures. Not even after they had shared their first kiss.

"They... they're not broken anymore!" Birdie cried and covered her mouth with her hands.

The glow faded from top to bottom on both Fox and Cynthia, until neither of them shone brightly anymore.

"What just happened?" Cynthia whispered.

Fox scooped Cynthia with both of his arms into a tight embrace. He flapped his own wings and lifted them both off the ground.

"You healed my wings!" He let out a hearty laugh, followed by a loud whoop of joy. "Now *those* are some pretty amazing *magical powers!*"

Fox and Cynthia landed on the ground again, but they kept their arms wrapped around each other.

Cynthia turned to face Princess Juliette, still snuggled underneath Fox's arm.

The sad look on the princess's face instantly made Cynthia's smile disappear. "What's wrong?"

"This is why you have been kept hidden away with Magnolia. This is why you have not been introduced to other pixies or magical beings before. This is why you are being hunted.

"The more time you spend with others, the more abilities you will absorb. The more abilities you will be able to share."

A pit in Cynthia's stomach replaced her bliss at Fox's newly restored wings. That's right. She was still being hunted. She held Fox even tighter.

"The woman who seeks Cynthia's power is named Jessamine." Juliette sat inside the opening of the hollow pine tree. She leaned her back against the door frame and crossed her legs in front of her.

Birdie, Marten, Fox, and Cynthia lowered themselves into a semicircle on the log beside Juliette. Cynthia leaned forward to hear what Princess Juliette would say next.

The celebratory atmosphere had vanished, and a somber mood had come over the group.

"Jessamine has been searching out abilities and powers of all kinds for a very long time. It is safe to say she will not stop anytime soon." The princess bit her bottom lip and squeezed her eyes shut. She rubbed the bridge of her nose with her thumb and pointer finger, then dropped her hand in her lap.

She let out a heavy sigh. "We must spread word that the pixie with the butterfly wings is not gifted, as we thought. That should protect you, at least to some degree."

Fox shook his head. "Then what? What if this Jessamine woman doesn't give up? How will we protect Cynthia?" He squeezed her hand tight.

"This is why we need to hide you, Little Flower." Juliette gave Cynthia an apologetic look.

"Hide her? Hide her where?" Fox stiffened beside Cynthia. He held her hand tight, like he was afraid that if he let go, she would be taken from him.

If she was being honest with herself, she squeezed his hand for the very same reason.

How was Cynthia supposed to hide? She wanted to be with Fox. To return to Magnolia's garden and her dust bunny friends at the bookshop. She didn't want to live her life always looking over her shoulder, wondering if someone recognized her for her wings.

Birdie's voice interrupted Cynthia's thoughts. "The pixie haven! It would be the perfect place!"

Marten nodded. "It would."

"What's a *pixie haven*?" Cynthia looked back and forth between her hooved friends.

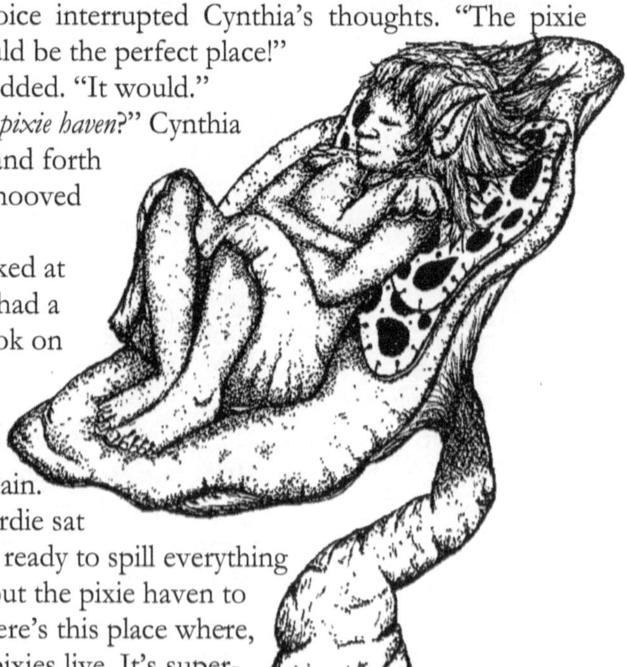

Birdie looked at Juliette, who had a concerned look on her face. The woman nodded for Birdie to explain.

"Well." Birdie sat up straighter, ready to spill everything she knew about the pixie haven to Cynthia. "There's this place where, like, a lot of pixies live. It's super-secret, so no one really knows where it is, and there are pixies of all kinds there. I've heard it's inside a massive hole in the ground, or maybe a big hollow tree or something? But most pixies don't live there because, well… I don't really know why. But if they need a safe place to stay, then it's open to them all…" She looked at Marten. "I'm not really making any sense, am I?"

Marten gave her a kind smile and shook his head. "Not at all."

Birdie huffed out a breath and tossed her feathered hair with a jerk of her head. Her shoulders slumped. "It's a safe place for pixies. I guess that's the best way to describe it."

Marten chuckled and squeezed Birdie's knee with his hand. "That's a good summary."

"So, if we go there, Cynthia would be safe from Jessamine?" Fox asked Princess Juliette.

"No." Juliette shook her head. "I am sorry, but she cannot be around that many pixies. They would figure out that her abilities, and theirs, were changing. They would know that she is gifted. Word would get out…"

Birdie frowned. "Couldn't you send the guardian pixies to, I don't know, erase any knowledge of the pixie haven from existence or something?"

Juliette let out a sad laugh. "If it were only that easy…"

"Where, then?" Fox asked. "Where can we take her to keep her safe?" Fox's voice sounded formal again, like he was on a job.

Is that what she would become to him? A job? She wanted him to be with her because he *wanted* to, not because he felt like he had to.

Her heart sank.

The conversation continued in spite of her somber silence.

"We will return to Magnolia's house. She will help us hide Cynthia." Juliette planned Cynthia's future for her.

Cynthia's heart wilted a little more. Because of her super special, super unique "magical powers," she would never be able to live a normal life again.

She had imagined a future where Fox and Cynthia would return to Magnolia's garden, but not like this. Or where they would travel to the places he had seen, but not to hide from the world. Right then, she would have given up her special abilities if it meant she would get to be with Fox for the rest of her life. But together because they were in love. Not because he could keep her safe.

A few more silent tears slipped down her cheeks. But everyone was too busy trying to figure out what to do with her or where to send her that no one noticed.

"I'll be able to keep her safe." Fox's firm voice broke through Cynthia's own woeful thoughts.

Princess Juliette gave him a funny look. She tipped her head to one side, and then a look of understanding came over her face. "You have a unique gift too, do you not?"

Fox clenched his jaw and didn't answer.

"It's alright, Fox," Cynthia whispered. "You should tell her. Tell her what you told me. Then she'll understand."

Fox hesitated but then surrendered. "I can tell when people are lying. To be honest, Cynthia is the only trustworthy person

I think I've ever met." His frown deepened.

"Fox!" Birdie cried. "How could you say that? We're sitting *right here!*"

He shrugged. "Not sorry."

Marten rolled his eyes. "He's being dramatic."

Cynthia laughed despite her melancholy. "Of course he is, it's kind of his specialty."

Juliette ignored the others. "Having someone with your experiences and your gift would be useful to keep her safe. That is all Magnolia has ever tried to do. With your help, Cynthia would be safer than with just Magnolia alone. Are you willing?"

Fox nodded. "Of course!"

"It will come at a cost…"

"Whatever the cost, it will be worth it."

"But Fox," Cynthia started to protest. She didn't like feeling like a project. Or a treasure that needed to be protected.

"I won't leave you." Fox met Cynthia's eyes. He looked surprised that she had started crying again. He tenderly wiped the tears from her cheeks. "No matter what happens or where you have to go, I'll stay with you from now on."

Cynthia believed him. She could tell that he was telling the truth, thanks to her newfound abilities to sense dishonesty in people. But she still didn't know if he said it out of love, or a sense of duty.

Only time would tell, she supposed.

They spent the remainder of the morning and into the afternoon busy with preparations for their hasty departure. Juliette met with several other Forest People, dressed much the same as Hazel had been. She requested one find a ride for them that would take them swiftly and secretly to Magnolia. She tasked others with assignments to accomplish while she was gone, something that seemed important but confidential. Her people wore serious expressions, nodded with understanding, and hurried away to whatever it was that the princess had asked them to do.

Hazel returned to help Cynthia and Fox prepare. She outfitted them with new clothing, since the clothes they had been wearing for nearly a month were dirty and tattered. Cynthia hadn't ever been so excited to receive new clothes before! She received a pair of snug, knee length pants and a long fitted tunic, both shades of green like the Forest People wore. She preferred blue because it went well with her silvery blue hair, but the green stood out nicely against her rainbow wings. Fox's new clothes looked similar to what he had worn before: calf-length dark pants and a loose, short-sleeved tan tunic.

When they had finished changing and packing fresh bags with food and canteens for a swift overnight journey, they talked with Marten and Birdie about the future.

"We'll probably arrive in less than a day. I'm excited to be reunited with Magnolia." Cynthia rubbed her hands together. "But after we get there, I have no idea what's going to happen."

Birdie and Marten came up with wild ideas about Magnolia faking Cynthia's death, or making a super-secret home for her to live in. Fox suggested that the woman would know of a place for Cynthia to travel to in order to hide, away from everyone.

"But where would that be? In the clouds? The northlands? Cynthia would freeze!" Birdie disagreed. "Maybe she'll send you to a tropical island to live with the white tortoise that can see the future!" Excitement gleamed in her eyes.

Cynthia tuned out her friends' speculations as her mind filled with her own questions. Would Cynthia have to leave Magnolia's garden again? Would the woman come with her, or would Cynthia never see her again either? Would Cynthia be able to see the dust bunnies before she had to hide? And once Cynthia got to… wherever she ended up… would she be able to make new friends or would she have to live all alone? What did Cynthia's future hold?

She wanted to talk to Fox about her feelings, but didn't want him to feel pressured to do more for her than what he wanted, so she kept her thoughts to herself.

"It is time." Princess Juliette motioned Fox and Cynthia to say goodbye to their friends when she had finished her own preparations.

Birdie and Marten were to stay behind, with the Forest People.

Chapter 39

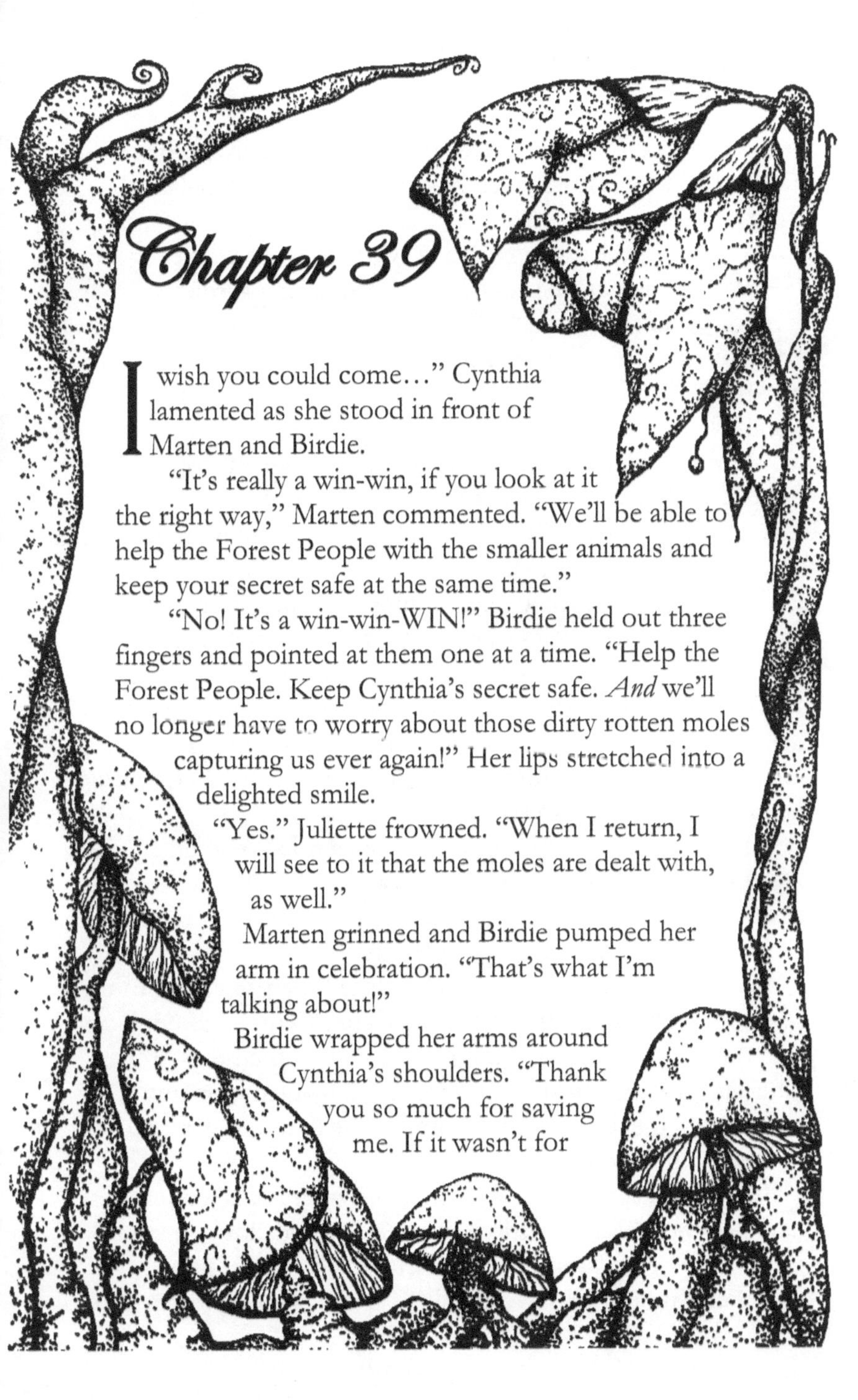

I wish you could come…" Cynthia lamented as she stood in front of Marten and Birdie.

"It's really a win-win, if you look at it the right way," Marten commented. "We'll be able to help the Forest People with the smaller animals and keep your secret safe at the same time."

"No! It's a win-win-WIN!" Birdie held out three fingers and pointed at them one at a time. "Help the Forest People. Keep Cynthia's secret safe. *And* we'll no longer have to worry about those dirty rotten moles capturing us ever again!" Her lips stretched into a delighted smile.

"Yes." Juliette frowned. "When I return, I will see to it that the moles are dealt with, as well."

Marten grinned and Birdie pumped her arm in celebration. "That's what I'm talking about!"

Birdie wrapped her arms around Cynthia's shoulders. "Thank you so much for saving me. If it wasn't for you, I'm afraid I wouldn't have made it. You really are one of a kind." She wiped tears from her cheeks when she pulled away from Cynthia.

"You saved me too, you know." Cynthia smiled at her friend. Her heart ached at the thought of never seeing Birdie again. If Cynthia didn't have to hide, they could have had so many adventures together, made so many memories together. But the way things had turned out, she would probably never see Birdie again. Her smile faltered at the thought.

Marten and Fox shook hands and spoke quietly to one another. Birdie gave Fox a tight squeeze, too. He gave Cynthia a surprised look over Birdie's shoulder, but he didn't hold back when he hugged her back.

Marten gave Cynthia a gentle hug, and then he returned to Birdie's side. Tears still leaked from Birdie's emerald eyes, and Cynthia had a hard time controlling hers from spilling over, too.

Birdie wiped her face with one hand. "Travel safely. And stay away from mice. And moles. And insects, too, I guess... Actually, never mind. Just... keep an eye on each other." Birdie laughed at her own rambling.

Marten wrapped his arm around Birdie's shoulders and squeezed. She leaned against his shoulder. "They'll be fine," he assured Birdie. Then to the pixies, "Goodbye, Fox. Goodbye, Cynthia. Thank you for helping Birdie..."

Cynthia held Fox's hand as they lifted themselves from the ground and flew upward toward Juliette. Cynthia couldn't get over how beautiful Fox's wings were every time he used them. The way the sunlight shone on them and made the creamy color richer and the burgundy shimmer. She'd never get tired of seeing them in action.

The princess wore a soft white cloak over her lavender dress and her long blonde curls had been braided down her back, while a few loose strands framed either side of her face.

Juliette motioned for the pair of pixies to settle themselves in a pouch on the front of the cloak. "We will be traveling far and flying at high altitude. You will be safe and warm in my cloak."

The princess turned and addressed the handful of Forest People and animals that stood around them. "I will be back as soon as I can."

She strode out of the woods and across the meadow to where their ride waited for them.

"What is it?" Cynthia asked the princess as they approached the unusual creature.

The animal's body looked like a horse- tawny fur, pointed ears, elongated nose, and a fluffy mane that grew from the crown of his head all the way along the center of his back where it met the tail- but nothing else about him looked horse-like. He had a pair of enormous bat wings growing from his shoulders, and a long harry beard sprouted from his chin. A tall, spiraled horn grew from the center of his forehead and pointed at the sky. Instead of hooves on his front feet, a pair of three-taloned feet peeked from beneath the long hair around his ankles.

"A dragoncorn," Juliette answered.

"I can see why it's called that, but I've never heard of it before," Fox studied the creature the same as Cynthia.

"They are extremely rare on the ground. This one only came because of who I am. No one else will get a glimpse of him, and he will probably never return." Juliette approached the magnificent creature.

The dragoncorn scraped at the ground with his talons, leaving gashes in the soft soil. Steam poured from his nostrils. His ears flicked back and forth. He turned his head to get a good look at the princess and the pixies.

When he recognized the princess, he bowed his horned head and closed his eyes. The princess returned the gesture. She rested one of her delicate hands on the side of the dragoncorn's face and stroked the fur with her thumb. She whispered words under her breath to the animal quiet enough that Cynthia couldn't hear even at their close proximity.

The dragoncorn nodded. He bent his legs and lowered himself to the ground so that the princess could sit on his back, just behind his wings.

Seconds later, the dragoncorn carried them high above the meadow and the surrounding forest. The ground below turned miniature, until they ascended so high the clouds obscured it from their sight.

Juliette had been right. The air temperature this high would have been fatal to Fox and Cynthia, especially in their lightweight short sleeved shirts and knee-length pants. They huddled close to one another inside the pouch of Juliette's cloak, close to her body, which kept them warm enough.

Because they were near Juliette's shoulder, they weren't affected by the wind too much, either. Cynthia's silver waves bounced a little, and Fox's golden locks swayed gently on his head. Conversing at a normal volume, even with Juliette, proved to be comfortable.

Juliette offered to tell Fox and Cynthia the history of pixies, and how she and Magnolia had known that Cynthia would be special.

"But you must share this information with no one. It is sacred and meant only for your ears. Do you understand?" Her serious voice seemed at odds with her pleasant expression.

Cynthia and Fox both agreed, and the princess began her tale.

"All pixies are descended from a single Mother Pixie from long ago. Created from an angelica blossom, her wings glowed day and night. Those who knew her developed a sense of wonder about the world around them. Some called her an angel because of the peaceful feeling she brought wherever she went.

"The more she shared her gift with others, the brighter her glow became, until finally, her light exploded with the force of a shooting star. The light beams settled on plants far and wide, and the next generation of pixies was born not long after.

"It is said that the Forest People created the Mother Pixie with their own magic. And that her light was too good for this world. That it is because of her that each pixie has their own abilities unique to themselves, just like she had."

Cynthia absorbed the story that had clearly been passed down through the generations of Forest People.

"Why do pixies not know this story?" Fox quizzed.

Cynthia raised her eyebrows at him. Now who was the one asking questions, she thought. But she didn't want to interrupt this moment with the words, so she kept them to herself.

"Some do. Some do not. I only learned it from my grandmother. Many know versions of the story. And some do not agree with the part about Forest People creating new creatures. It can be a difficult subject, and it is mostly advised to not discuss it with those you do not trust."

"What other kinds of pixies are there?" Cynthia asked her own question while Fox pondered the princess's answer to his.

"You have seen the guardian pixies. There are pixies born from blossoms of every flower imaginable.

"There are others, still, that are less well-known. Fungus pixies that can mimic other pixies by changing their appearances. Sunflower pixies that can sing songs to comfort a troubled mind. And even some that call themselves pixies but are not born from flowers and must fashion their own wings in order to fly.

"There have been pixies like the Mother Pixie over the generations, though their appearances have been few and far between. They always have abilities far beyond what most pixies carry. They always have wings that glow. And they are always hunted for their uniqueness.

"It is one reason why I believe the Mother Pixie chose to leave this world, but leave parts of her behind. To spread her power so that no one pixie would have to carry the burden of being so powerful. The Forest People always suspected another would come along eventually. When Magnolia found you, we wondered if you might be the one. It looks like we were right."

Juliette stopped talking and let her words sink in for a few minutes.

Cynthia ran them over in her mind. Her wings glowed. She had unique abilities. Was Juliette trying to tell her that she was special like the Mother Pixie had been?

If so, what did that really mean for her future? Would her

life come to an end in an explosion of light, like the angelica pixie? Or would she end up captured and have her powers stolen from her?

If she was supposed to be so special and important, then why would Juliette want her to just hide? Wouldn't that lead to a life just as useless as not living at all?

Fox studied her face. He knew she was thinking hard about all these things, but she didn't think she could express herself clearly enough, nor was she sure she wanted to in front of Juliette. The woman had high expectations from her, or so it would seem. What if Cynthia's doubts left the princess disappointed?

As night darkened the sky, Fox and Cynthia both relaxed in one another's arms and drifted to sleep.

When Cynthia opened her eyes, the sun had started to rise in front of them. The sky turned various pastel shades of the rainbow across the horizon. No clouds blocked their view of the miniature world far beneath them.

The landscape below the dragoncorn confused Cynthia. It didn't look anything like the landscape near where Magnolia lived. She nudged Fox awake.

"Where are we?" she whispered to him and pointed below.

White sand dunes stretched across a great swath of the landscape below, surrounded by rolling hills of various shades of green. An oasis of some kind took up the very middle of the sandy desert. A great lake far to the north glinted in the sunlight. To the south, Cynthia could just make out the beaches of the southern shores of Tala, something she never thought she'd see in her lifetime. And some man-made shiny golden structure far in the distance stood out of place against the natural landscape.

This was definitely not the way home.

"We have had a change of plans," Juliette answered

Cynthia's question in a quiet voice. "We arc no longer going to take you to Magnolia's home."

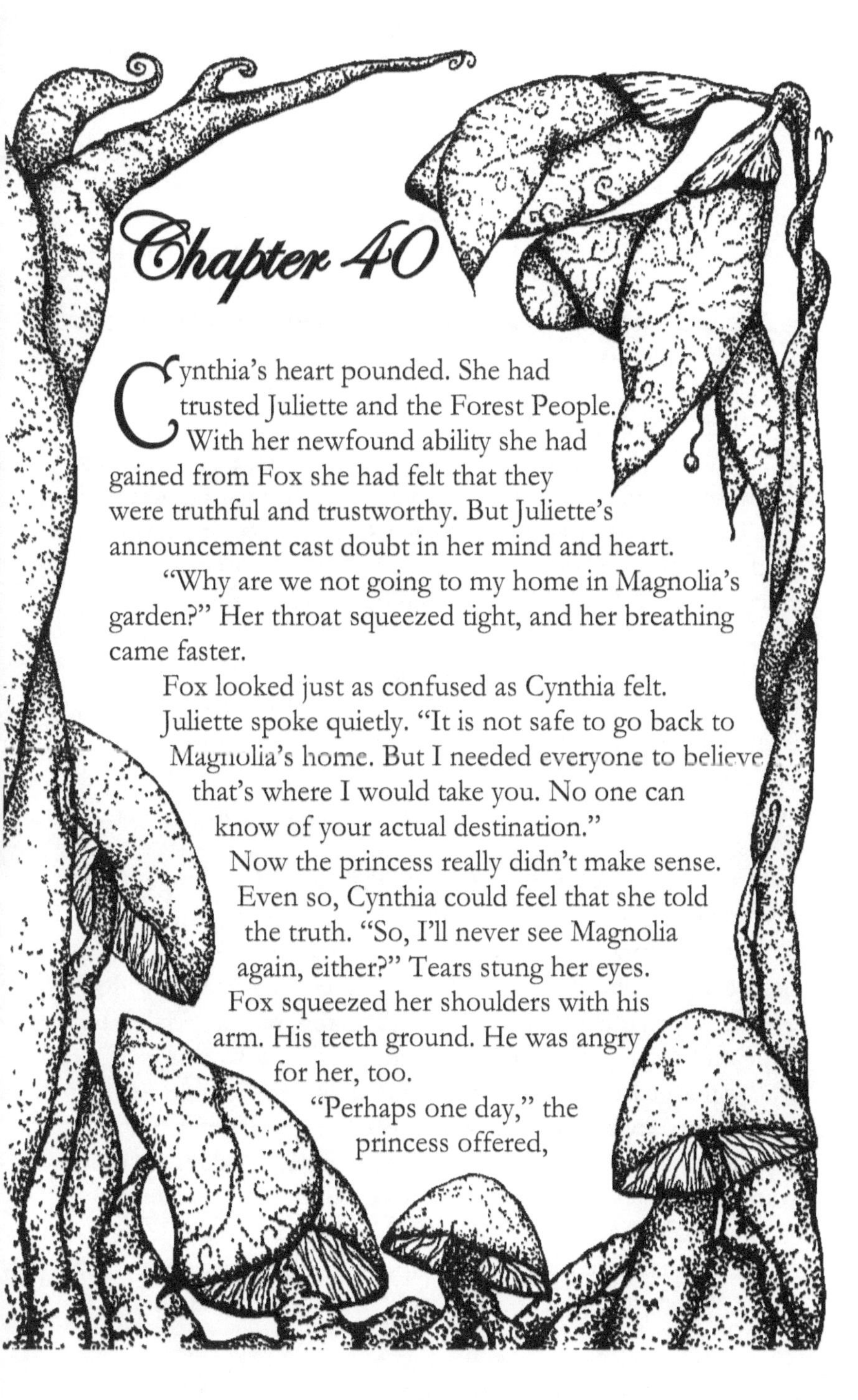

Chapter 40

Cynthia's heart pounded. She had trusted Juliette and the Forest People. With her newfound ability she had gained from Fox she had felt that they were truthful and trustworthy. But Juliette's announcement cast doubt in her mind and heart.

"Why are we not going to my home in Magnolia's garden?" Her throat squeezed tight, and her breathing came faster.

Fox looked just as confused as Cynthia felt. Juliette spoke quietly. "It is not safe to go back to Magnolia's home. But I needed everyone to believe that's where I would take you. No one can know of your actual destination."

Now the princess really didn't make sense. Even so, Cynthia could feel that she told the truth. "So, I'll never see Magnolia again, either?" Tears stung her eyes. Fox squeezed her shoulders with his arm. His teeth ground. He was angry for her, too.

"Perhaps one day," the princess offered,

"when the world becomes safe again, you will be able to reunite with Magnolia. This has always been our plan for when your abilities began to manifest. Magnolia has always known. I will pass a message along to her that you are well and that you miss her."

It wasn't good enough! Cynthia wanted to go home! She wanted Magnolia and Fox to meet one another. She wanted *Magnolia* to help her hide. Why was Juliette doing this to her?

Once again, as if the princess could understand the way Cynthia felt, she responded to Cynthia's unspoken complaints. "I am truly sorry, Cynthia. I know this is not what you wanted. But I assure you, it is for your own safety. Jessamine has ways of discovering information besides hearing rumors or sending spies. You and Fox will go into hiding so secret, that even *I* will not know of your destination."

"*What?*" It was Fox's turn to question the princess. "You're just going to drop us off somewhere to fend for ourselves? How is that keeping Cynthia safe?" He squeezed his fist in his lap.

Cynthia placed her hand over his and rubbed her thumb across his knuckles. They shared confused and concerned looks.

As if the dragoncorn knew that they would no longer need his services soon, he began to descend, pulling the ground closer to them at a fast pace. The feeling left Cynthia dizzy and her stomach churned. She closed her eyes and took a deep breath. When she opened her eyes, she focused on Fox's hand beneath hers and kept her eyes from peering downward.

"Some guardian pixies have the ability to be able to hide people or things from the world. It is a rare gift, but one that you now have as well," Juliette explained, as if telling Cynthia something she should already know.

Cynthia's head spun. Again. "What do you mean?"

"The guardian pixie who helped you before is one such pixie. When you touched her, you absorbed this ability. You now will have the power to hide yourself- and whoever you choose to be with you- from the world. I do not understand how it works," she quickly added, knowing that Cynthia would probably start asking questions, "but she assured me you would be able to figure it out on your own."

Juliette paused her words and sighed. Her next sentence came out in an even softer voice. "I really am sorry about the way this is turning out."

The dragoncorn continued his rapid descent toward an environment completely foreign to Cynthia. He weaved through a grove of oversized succulent trees with cylindrical trunks covered in smooth reddish-gray bark and flat webs of horizontal branches like hats on top. Shorter leafy shrubs grew around the bases of the trees, and tall narrow grass swayed in the breeze created from his wings.

The dragoncorn landed on the soft ground. He stomped his hooves and pawed at the red muddy soil with his talons. The moist air filled with the scent of broken grass and turned soil. It reminded Cynthia of the garden back home. The dragoncorn shook his head, tossing this thick mane side to side, and swished his tail a few times before he stood perfectly still.

Juliette slid from the dragoncorn's back and planted her feet, the bent grass acting like a mat to keep her feet from sinking into the rusty mud and the hem of her lavender dress from getting dirty. She rubbed the dragoncorn's face again with her hand and leaned her forehead against his cheek. "Thank you."

He breathed clouds of smoke from his nose, flapped his wings, and departed.

Cynthia and Fox flapped their own wings to lift themselves out of the pocket of Juliette's cloak. They hovered side by side in front of her.

Cynthia stared at Juliette with wide eyes. "How will you get home now? I though you said you weren't coming with us?"

The princess gave them a kind smile, but her eyes looked red and puffy, as if she had been crying. "I have other methods of returning home. They will take longer and be much more conspicuous. I needed *our* journey to be swift and for no one to know where we were headed.

"Now." She looked back and forth between the pixies. "I need you to find a place for yourselves to hide. Use your abilities to protect yourselves from the outside world. And stay safe."

"For how long?" Fox frowned and rubbed his chin.

"Perhaps for the rest of your lives." Juliette bowed her head and blinked away fresh tears. "No more traveling. No more adventures."

Fox nodded.

"No." Cynthia blurted.

The princess and Fox both turned their eyes onto her.

She clenched her jaw and her fists. "You can't, Fox. It's not fair to you."

He held out his hands, palms facing her, to tell her to stop. "Cynthia. I *want* to do this. I love you. I want to protect you."

She shook her head. "I can sense dishonesty now, too. I'll be fine on my own."

"Cynthia!" He closed the gap between them and rested his palm on her face.

She leaned into his hand. She committed his dark burgundy eyes, matching freckles, and creamy skin, along with the feeling of his touch, to memory.

"I won't leave you." He tucked a strand of her "frozen moonlight" hair behind her ear but didn't move his eyes from hers.

Tears leaked from her eyes. "But what if you get tired of me? What if you decide you don't want to stay with me anymore, that life is dull in hiding?"

"That could never happen. I love you!"

She sniffled from the tears dripping past her nose. Her chin quivered and she swallowed the lump in her throat. "You shouldn't have to give up your life for me. Give up seeing the world… for me."

"You don't understand." He gazed deep into her eyes. "You *are* my whole world. You're all I want. All I've ever wanted. You make me a better person. You saved me, healed me. How can you not see how special you are? I would give up my *life* for you. There's nothing you can ever do to make me change my mind. I love you."

Before she could argue, he rushed his lips towards hers and kissed her deeply. His kiss expressed all the words he had just said, and so much more.

She slid her hand around his neck, sunk her fingers into his golden hair, and cradled the back of his head. She leaned into him and allowed the kiss to settle her fears, dry her tears, and fill her heart.

When they finally broke apart, they stared into one another's eyes.

"I love you, Cynthia." Fox's voice was husky.

She could sense the complete honesty about everything he had just said to her both with his words and with his kiss.

"I love you, too, Fox." She smiled at him through her own tears.

Princess Juliette shifted her feet on the ground, reminding Cynthia and Fox that she was still there. She had slipped her white fluffy cloak from around her shoulders, and held it draped over one arm.

Cynthia held Fox's hand tight in her own and turned to face the princess. She wished things had turned out differently for herself. She wished she'd be able to go home and be with Magnolia and her friends again. But she also realized that if all of this had never happened, she wouldn't have met Fox. If she hadn't been wanted for her wings and powers, he might never had stayed with her to protect her. Everything she had been through during the past several weeks had changed the course of her life forever. Some for the better- like Fox. Some for the worse- like having to go into hiding. In the end, she was the only one who could decide how she would allow the rest of her life to play out. Whether to view her circumstances as a blessing or a curse.

Her innate positivity rose to the surface and her mind and heart settled. "Thank you, Princess Juliette. For everything."

Princess Juliette leaned forward and a warm smile spread across her face. "Oh, Little Flower. You have done all this for yourself. Your friends are right. You have made Tala a better place."

"I don't know about that…" Cynthia mumbled quietly.

Fox squeezed her hand.

The princess continued. "And someday, when the threat is gone, you will be able to do so much good for so many more friends." She looked back and forth between Fox and Cynthia. "Until then, stay together, stay safe. I will send word when the threat is gone."

"But, how? If you don't know where we are…?" Fox asked Juliette.

"Just like there are ways to stay hidden, there are hidden ways to be found." A light glinted in the princess's eyes.

Before Cynthia could make sense of the phrase Juliette had just spoken, the princess continued. "Now, for goodbyes. I am so honored to have been able to meet you. Both of you. I am sure we will meet again."

Fox tugged Cynthia's hand so they could fly away from the princess, but Cynthia hadn't finished talking to Juliette yet. "I just need to ask her something. Do you mind?"

Fox nodded and flew far enough away so that Cynthia could talk with the princess. Though he didn't take his eyes off her for a second.

"What would you like to know, Little Flower?" The princess kept her hands folded serenely in front of her.

"I just… how will my life have any meaning if I'm stuck hiding from… everything? I mean, I'll be happy with Fox and everything, but…" Guilt stung in her chest. She didn't want Fox to think she wanted something other than being with him. But she didn't see how hiding for who knows how long would help anyone, let alone herself.

"I think I understand your question. And I am glad you asked." The princess paused to think. "You should spend your time growing your abilities."

"How would I do that if I'm not supposed to be around others?" Cynthia scrunched her eyebrows together.

"What makes you stand out?" Juliette asked another question instead of answering Cynthia's.

"My wings." Cynthia glanced at them over her shoulder. The sunlight made the colors glow against their black background.

"Yes. But only *during the day*. At night, your wings look different. Use that to your advantage. Seek out others that need your help. Absorb abilities as they present themselves to you. Learn how to be powerful. Perhaps you can even help those that Jessamine and others like her are trying to capture or use. There is much good you can do even while in hiding."

Cynthia could imagine herself becoming nocturnal and helping all kinds of people and animals during the night when her wings were much less conspicuous. She beamed at the princess.

Princess Juliette lowered her voice. "There may come a time when you may be called upon to use your abilities for a greater good. When that time comes, I will send word. Be ready."

Cynthia swiped a tear from her eye and released a little laugh. "Thank you. Again! If I could hug you, I would."

Princess Juliette smiled at her and nodded. "Be safe, Little Flower."

She turned to walk away from the pixies for the last time.

One more question popped into Cynthia's head. "Wait!"

The princess paused and turned halfway around again. She brushed her blonde curls from her face and tucked them behind her ear.

Cynthia fluttered toward her. "I just have one more question. Why do you call me 'Little Flower'? I don't understand. I don't look like a flower at all."

Princess Juliette gave Cynthia a sweet, but knowing look. "It's a metaphor. You feel small and insignificant, like a tiny wildflower in this big world. Unnoticed, unimportant. But your faith in those around you, in the goodness of the world, and your ability to spread that goodness to those who need it most…" She glanced past Cynthia at Fox. "Are bigger and more important than you can imagine. Even the littlest flower in a field of blossoms plays an important role, just like you.

"Never doubt yourself, Cynthia. You may be small, but you are anything but insignificant." She gave Cynthia one last kind, warm smile, then turned again to disappear among the trees.

Cynthia hovered there and stared.

Fox flew over to join her. "What was that all about?" he wanted to know.

"Something incredible." Cynthia gave him a big smile. "I guess I have something to tell you while we find a place to hide." She grabbed Fox's hand. "Let's go home."

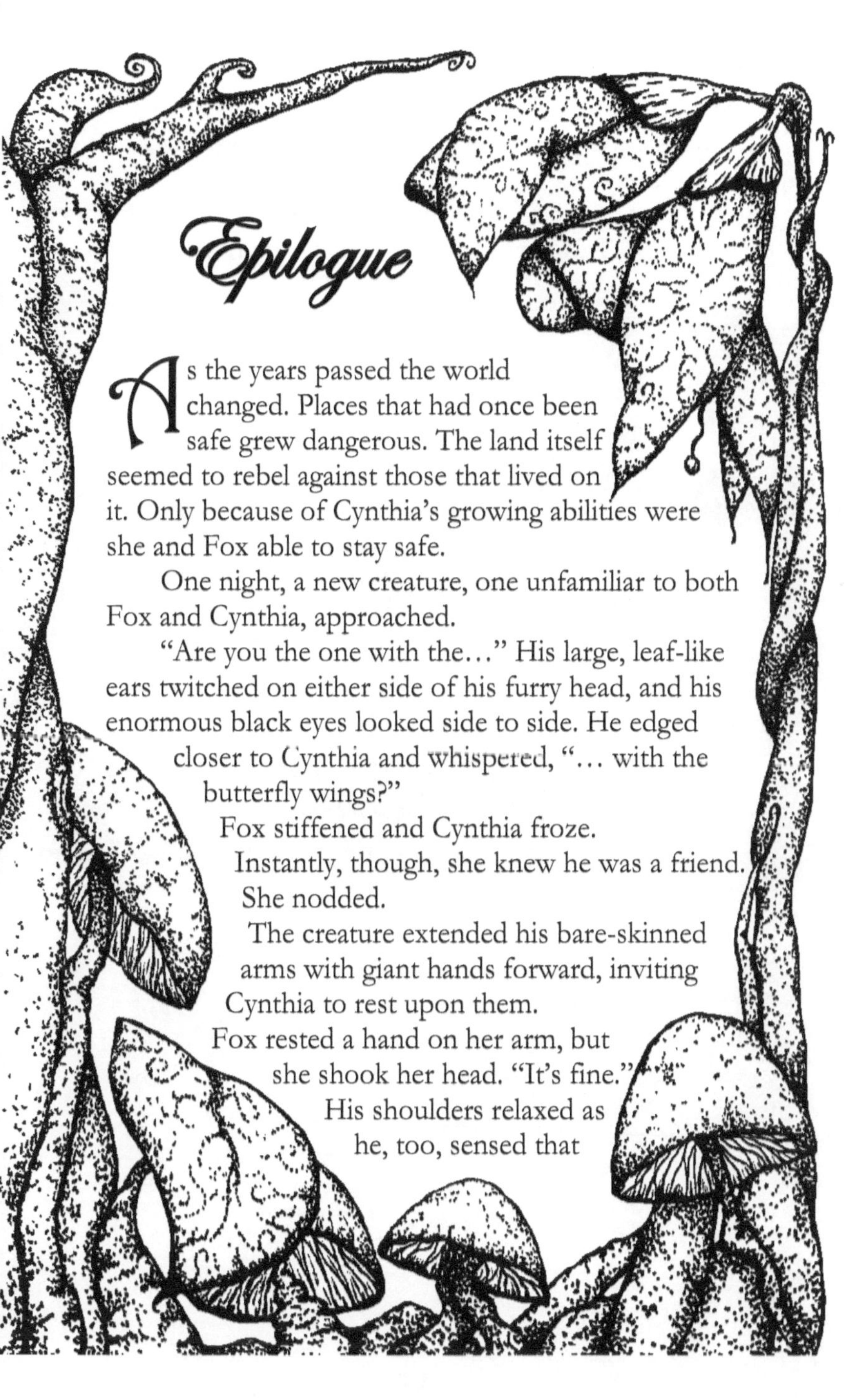

Epilogue

As the years passed the world changed. Places that had once been safe grew dangerous. The land itself seemed to rebel against those that lived on it. Only because of Cynthia's growing abilities were she and Fox able to stay safe.

One night, a new creature, one unfamiliar to both Fox and Cynthia, approached.

"Are you the one with the…" His large, leaf-like ears twitched on either side of his furry head, and his enormous black eyes looked side to side. He edged closer to Cynthia and whispered, "… with the butterfly wings?"

Fox stiffened and Cynthia froze.

Instantly, though, she knew he was a friend. She nodded.

The creature extended his bare-skinned arms with giant hands forward, inviting Cynthia to rest upon them.

Fox rested a hand on her arm, but she shook her head. "It's fine."

His shoulders relaxed as he, too, sensed that

they were safe.

Cynthia stepped onto the palms of the creature and looked up into his face.

He spoke in a hushed tone again. "The princess has sent me with a message. Tala needs you. It's time to return home."

Thanks for Reading!

I hope you enjoyed this book!
Please leave a review on **Amazon** and **Goodreads**. For indie authors like me, reviews are our lifeblood. Help a girl out, it'll only take a few minutes!

Little Flower: A Retelling by Christine Marshall | Goodreads

www.goodreads.com

Amazon.com: Little Flower: A Retelling (Charlie and the Giants) eBook : Marshall, Christine: Kindle Store

www.amazon.com

Check me out on social media!

Facebook: Christine K. Marshall-author
www.facebook.com/christinemarshallauthor

Instagram: @the_christine_marshall_24
www.instagram.com/the_christine_marshall_24

TikTok: www.tiktok.com/@christinemarshallfantasy

Email: christinemarshall24@gmail.com

Welcome to Tala!

All of Christine's fantasy books take place in one fantasy world called Tala.

Each series or standalone book can be read in any order in relation to the other series or books.

You'll see character crossovers, hidden secrets, and clues to the other stories, characters, and settings as you read the collection. The more you read, the deeper you'll understand Tala and all the characters that live there.

Here's a chronological diagram if you prefer reading in chronological order. Otherwise, pick a book or series that sounds good to you and start there!

Enjoy exploring Tala!

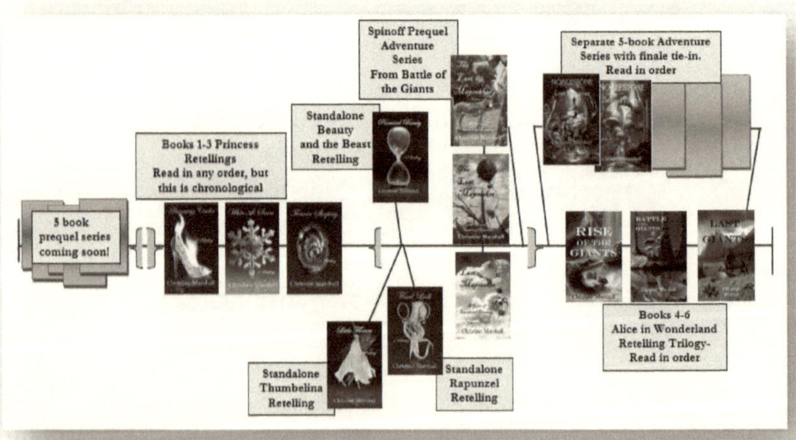

Keep turning pages to learn about each book in the collection (so far!) and don't forget to sign up for Christine's e-newsletter for all the latest news and updates for future books.

Find all Christine's books at CMarshallFantasy Etsy shop and Amazon today.

Buy direct!
CMarshallFantasy
Etsy

Order from
Amazon here

Here's why you'll love these books:

~Mythical creatures like centaurs, griffins, pixies, brownies, elves, golems, giants (of course!), and so many more

~Magic that prolongs life and heals, and attracts the wrong kind of attention

~People who can talk to animals and make flowers blossom just by touch

~Stories of friendship, romance, family connections, and epic journeys that will keep you reading for hours

Princess Retellings

When Cinderella becomes the villain of her story...
and all the other stories, too.
A villain origin story for the biggest villain in all of Tala.

Amazon.com: Becoming Cinder: A
Retelling #1 (Char...
www.amazon.com

BOOK 1 Paperback + Swag - Etsy
www.etsy.com

What if Cinderella was already a princess?
What if her step-sisters weren't mean?
What if her family, her crown... and her love were ripped
away from her?
What if in her grief she made a terrible mistake?
Maybe not all fairy-tales end with happily ever after...

Read *Becoming Cinder* today!
Available in print, ebook, and audiobook.

What happens to Jessamine next?
Why does Juliette ask Jessamine to come home?
What happened to Peter?
Read the next book in the series from Juliette's perspective.

Amazon.com: White as Snow: A
Retelling #2 (Charli...
www.amazon.com

BOOK 2 Paperback + Swag! - Etsy
www.etsy.com

A princess in hiding.
A huntsman as her protector.
Seven unlikely companions by her side.
Can she stop the growing evil threatening her world?

Add *White As Snow* to your bookshelf now!

Available in print, ebook, and audiobook.

The *Charlie and the Giants* Trilogy

Fifteen-year-old Charlie leaves home and ventures into the unknown to battle monsters, befriend fairies and giants, and discover who she really is. Oh, and try to save the world. *Alice In Wonderland* vibes in a brand-new setting.

What happens when the land of wonder is broken upon Charlie's return?

Who will she find this time to help her put an end once and for all to the evil that has spread?

How can a girl full of dreams face the reality of what must be done?

A tale of strange creatures, twists and turns, and ever-growing darkness.

The final chapter in an epic saga of fairy tales, princesses, and a world of dreams.
From the Queen of Cinders to the Queen of All.
From a powerless princess to a Princess of power.
From a girl with dreams to a Dreamer destined to save the world.

Christine's ***Charlie and the Giants*** books are filled with magic, mythical creatures, and an *awesome* female protagonist that has to figure out who she wants to become.

If you love books that will help you forget the real world for a little while, are full of surprising characters, and will keep you guessing, then these are the perfect books for you!

Available in print, ebook, and audiobook.

Get ready for another exciting fantasy adventure!

Steampunk? *Check!*
Pirates? *Check!*
Dwarves? *Check!*
Peter Pan vibes? *Check!*

These books are perfect for readers young and old who love friendship, family, and adventure!

Amazon.com: Noblestone and the Lost Dwarves: 9798...

www.amazon.com

Noblestone and the Lost Dwarves Paperback - Etsy

www.etsy.com

Join brownie brothers Max and Eliot as they go on
another wild adventure, this time into the clouds. Tag
along as they encounter cloud dragons, giants, mermaids,
and leave a trail of mayhem in their path.
You'll laugh til you cry and then laugh some more.

Available in print and ebook.

Fantasy world? Check!
Playful antics? Check!
Fun for the whole family? Check!
Positive sibling relationships? Check!

Let Max and Eliot take you on another exciting
adventure!

CMarshallFantasy Etsy

Also see what kind of trouble these two cause in
the **Charlie and the Giants** series where they make their
appearance in ***Battle of the Giants.***

Available in print and ebook.

Read our Illustrated Guides of Tala!

Insects & Mechanical Things

Dragons & Flying Creatures

Unexpected Creatures

Folk Creatures

Order Here!

Coming Summer 2025

Book 3 in the
NOBLESTONE
and the Lost Dwarves
series

Coming Fall 2025

A Little Mermaid Retelling

Sign up for Christine's e-newsletter!

Check out Christine's website!

www.ChristineMarshallAuthor.com

E&O Creative's Etsy shop
Featuring art by Steve, signed books by Christine,
and other awesome swag!

Coloring books featuring illustrations from Steve including
chapter heading art from Christine's books!

Acknowledgements

No book is written alone! ***Little Flower*** would not have been possible without a lot of amazing people.

Beta readers: Steve, Belle, Sophie, and Pepper. Y'all rock!

Moral support: My IRL friends, new book club, and all the amazing readers we've met at events this past year. Thank you for your support!!

Original cover art & chapter heading art: my amazing husband, **Steve.** ♥ And thank you for the collaboration on the story and the art. I love you too much.

About the Author

When Christine isn't spinning tales on her laptop, she probably has a book and a chocolate chip cookie in hand. She loves all kinds of books: fantasy, sci-fi, historical fiction, non-fiction, and even textbooks.

She also loves to play her ukulele, stand in the rain, stay up late, and try new foods... but not all at the same time! Christine has moved over 20 times in the past 20 years, and firmly believes that people are more important than things.

Photo Credit: Amber Richards